Hawaiian Retreat

By

Debbie Flint

Published by Flintproductions

www.debbieflint.com   @debbieflint

eBook   - ISBN 978-1-909785-21-2

Paperback - ISBN 978-1-909785-22-9

Amazing front cover illustration by Angela Oltmann
www.angieocreations.com

Published by Flintproductions
www.debbieflint.com   @debbieflint

Dedication and Acknowledgements

Without beta readers, where would we be…? and friends, including Litty and Sharon, and the girls in *Debbie's Readers* Facebook group - my angels, who have helped so much as usual, especially the people that read early versions and said 'eh?'. Plus Caz Jones, the most amazing proof-reader. And Jill Dowding-Walker and Elizabeth Gray for thoughts on the back cover blurb on the paperback (see I told you I would!)

Acknowledgements Chris Stringer from the Natural History Museum, London, for the kind email confirming the facts about Neanderthals - we really are 2% caveman! The internet, for the wealth of info about tantric massage and Tibet and Thailand. The mountain shrine is based on those in Mustang. There really are spas that luxurious and they really do have oxygen in the rooms. No Alessandro though, sadly… Finally, Rebecca Kempton and Brad Carter for the elephant ride, LJ Rich for the parachute jump and Mark Fairhead for the military bits (kind of. If I told you the truth he'd have to kill me.) And my lovely mentor Julie Cohen, genius author and queen of *show don't tell*, I salute you.

Thanks to you all.

And to all my new readers, and those who have been regulars on my @qvcuk blog on www.qvcuk.com, I thank you all for taking the plunge and ordering this book. I await your feedback with anticipation!

I'D LOVE YOUR THOUGHTS

I'd really appreciate a review on Amazon or Goodreads! Or just email me on debbie@debbieflint.com. Enjoy!

Keeping in touch -

Go to www.debbieflint.com where you can -

- Sign up for updates and get my regular newsletter
- Plus news of free downloads and short stories
- A full list of my novels
- Follow my weekly QVC UK blog
- Find *RiWiSi* – Read It Write It Sell It – my weekly look at all things book.

Or keep in touch via Twitter @debbieflint

Or Facebook - search DebbieFlintQVC

Or Goodreads.

Hawaiian Retreat

Book 3

Hawaiian Prize Trilogy

(Steamy Version*)

By

Debbie Flint

*PG   Version also available

Chapter One.

The coals weren't just fiery, they were throbbing. Or perhaps Helen was. The fire-walk was getting closer - just a few rows of chanting people in front of her. It gave her palpitations. Smoking, glowing, smouldering - and very, very daunting. Oh and rather hot.

So much for this Try it For the First Time lark.

She could feel the vibration throughout her body - the rhythmic drum, beating in time with the chanting crowd - urging them on, nearer and nearer, to the point of no return. Every now and then the embers flared, accompanied by a scream, and the tell-tale 'tssssst!' sound.

How the hell did I get myself into this? thought Helen, as she broke out in a sweat. She could feel the heat, smell the smouldering coals and the perspiring bodies either side of her. Pretty soon they would block her escape. It was now or never.

Focus, she said to herself, *cool moss, cool moss, cool moss...*

Only twenty four hours before, she'd been throwing herself off a cliff and tomorrow would be the biggest challenge of all.

If her sister Sadie could see her, she'd be proud. If her mother Grace could see her, she'd freak. She'd roll her eyes, and tut, as usual. Not that it mattered - Helen and her mum were currently just healing after a rift - giving each other space was part of their thing. And spurring each other on was part of her and Sadie's thing. *Thank god for sisters*, thought Helen.

And thank god for… the guy on the stage… What was he to her, now, anyway, after everything that had happened in the last six months? And now he was standing there, banging a drum.

Cool moss, cool moss! Chanted the crowd at the front.

Shit, shit, she told herself frantically, realising that she was now just two rows away. She tried to hold back but an over-excited woman behind her pushed forwards a little too hard, and Helen ricocheted into the tall guy in front. She flung her hands into the middle of his back. He turned, eyes blazing, and Helen gasped. He was young, and very handsome… and she knew that face from somewhere.

'Sorry!' Helen shouted, above the pounding drums, jabbing a thumb over her shoulder. 'Eager crowd!'

'I can't hear you,' said the entrancing face, 'but next time, give it a little rub whilst you're there!'

'I'm sorry?' she cried.

He smiled and pointed over his shoulder at his back. 'Joking,' he added, 'I meant give my shoulders a rub - they ache from karate chopping all those planks earlier on! What else are you doing, whilst you're here?' he said.

If it hadn't been a complete impossibility to back out now, Helen would have made herself scarce as fast as she could. 'Cos that's what she always did - well, nearly always - when a gorgeous stranger made a pass at her. That's what he was doing, wasn't it? After all, she didn't trust handsome men - not any more. Not after all the recent experiences on her friend's dating experiment. Heck, Helen had even talked about them on TV, so it wasn't a matter of being brave. But still he smiled, and still she was wary.

'Run, run a mile, don't get involved,' the little voice inside her head usually said. But maybe he wasn't making a pass - this request for a back rub was not unusual in this new community of happy-clappy people - with their frequent massages, hugs and instant familiarity amongst strangers. So Helen just smiled and played along - she'd come too far to back out now - so she reached up and rubbed his shoulders a little.

They were rock solid. And not in a good way.

'Jesus, what are you so tense about? They're hard as granite,' she shouted, leaning into his ear from behind as she pushed into knots the size of golf balls. She felt him laugh. Smelt his fresh male body scent. She rubbed harder and felt him relax into it - rolling his shoulders against her touch, almost in time to the all-engulfing pounding of the drums. And then she remembered where she knew him from. *Oh god.* She stepped away and looked round her, frantically.

And then it was his turn at the front.

And then she caught the scowl on the face of the man banging the drum.

And then she realised with a jolt that the outstretched arms of the Fire Crew and the maniacally grinning faces lining the fire-walk were all beckoning *her, come on Helen* - she was next. And he'd distracted her and her trance was broken, and every bone in her body began rebelling, screaming *'run'* instead of *'cool moss...'*

Her knees went weak and the air went thin. This was going to be interesting. Very interesting indeed...

Chapter Two

Six months earlier...

'Well you'll do it if you want to keep your job!'

The boss wasn't happy - not happy at all. In fact, he was pacing. At least he wasn't drumming his fingers, or that would have meant real trouble. And then he drummed his fingers. *Uh oh...*

'But I've never even been *up* in a dodgy old bi-plane, let alone wing-walked,' protested Helen again, looking over at her friend Kate on the other side of the spacious executive office - but Kate just shrugged. 'What if I die?' Helen said.

'If you die, the other girl will take your place - what's her name?' Mr Anthony Adams clicked his fingers in Kate's general direction. Helen's friend - immediately straightened and replied in her light New York accent.

'Cheryl?' she said, 'I take it you're talking about Cheryl Goodman? The one who sends you chocolates twice a week begging for a job?' He nodded, and she rolled her eyes. 'Mr Adams, are you serious? She's just out of college isn't she?'

'Yes that's the one. So she's young, so what? So were you two, once. See what some people are willing to do to get on in life?' He opened a drawer, pulled out a box of expensive chocolates, and brandished one in the air, pointing it at Helen. 'See? She even found out my favourite brand.' He chomped into it then grimaced, and threw the other half back in the box. He chose another candy then bit it. 'The wrong kind of centre, but the right brand. That's a girl full of ambition,' he continued, with his mouth full. Helen raised an eyebrow. 'I bet she'd wing-walk,' he said. 'I bet *she'd* wing-walk withOUT the safety harness!' And he threw the remaining half of the chocolate into a wire rubbish bin along with the rest of the half-eaten box, and all its fancy ribbons and bows. 'Maybe it's her I should give the column to - would *she* argue with me? Would she?' Then he picked up an E-cigarette and fiddled with it.

Helen scowled unhappily over at Kate, who reciprocated with a 'not now' face.

Their boss thrust the fake cigarette into his mouth, then stared at Helen. He was a balding, red-faced man and in the year or so she'd been working at TransGlobe Inc she'd never seen him laugh. Her contract wasn't permanent, and most weeks he made her terrified - like most of his freelancers - terrified he'd hate her very next pitch and she'd be out on her ear immediately. He terminated contracts at his world famous online magazine as easily as he discarded his nicotine cartridges. Helen looked at the rubbish bin - sorry - the *trash can* full of them. She was always getting pulled up for using '*English* English' instead of Americanisms. The discarded plastic shapes were all mixed in with the remains of the half eaten chocolates and screwed up sheets of paper, all just tossed aside, unwanted. Helen wondered if she'd be in there herself one day - if she wasn't dead first.

The phone rang and he rolled his slightly protruding eyeballs skywards and took the call, then started muttering into the handset about clashing diary dates. Helen looked over at Kate who indicated to her watch. Then instead of finishing, the phone conversation turned to a youngest grandson's baseball match, so Kate began checking her smartphone. Helen just stared out of the massive window, deflated.

No sooner had she got back to New York than her precious job had been whipped away from under her nose and suddenly her whole future was up in the air again. The lifeline job that had got her back into the land of the living last year after a disastrous relationship - the job she'd grafted to make her own - was about to be handed over unceremoniously to some grasping celebrity. And she knew that if she didn't take this alternative offer, the boss would wash his hands of her. Mr Anthony Adams didn't suffer fools gladly, but then neither did Helen.

His voice droned on into the phone, getting more and more heated, and she exhaled, shoulders slumping - there'd be no talking to him after this call. This was his kingdom and she was a mere courtier - a serf, not even a lady in waiting.

This new role was daunting. Inheriting the famous TiFFT column felt like taking charge of a juggernaut - one which was heading over a cliff unless its new columnist could pick up where the last one left off, making it even bigger, even better, even more exciting. It was a big step for Adams to give it to feisty Helen, and it was well known that he didn't like being challenged. How far could she push him? She'd probably reached her limit. From the look on his face as he finished the call, now wasn't the time to find out.

'Fine!' he shouted, 'you go this time - but if he gets through to the final, I'm the one taking him there!' He slammed the phone down then drew heavily on his E-cigarette. 'Damned ex-wives. All four of them.'

He stood up again and leaned his fingertips against the huge floor-to-ceiling window behind his desk, gazing outwards on the 26th floor view, hazy in the mid-summer afternoon heat. The women looked at each other as he cursed under his breath, then he inhaled deeply. The vapour trail drifted away from his head making it look like he was smouldering. Which he probably was. And not in a good way.

'So - here's the thing. *Use* your fear. It's not a bad thing to be scared, it might make you a better writer - more raw,' he declared in his strong New York drawl, without looking round. 'BE terrified up there - be REAL.' He was gesticulating wildly, as he always did when one of his famous lectures was about to begin. 'Reality is everywhere. We've been the market leaders, but with this new channel launching online soon, the, the...' he clicked his fingers, expecting an answer.

'The ParlourGames Channel,' Kate supplied, paying attention suddenly.

'The Parlour-freakin'-Games-freakin'-Channel - what kind of name is that? How that woman could leave us for some European conglomerate, God only knows. I made her a household name, I practically created her... what was her name again?'

Helen opened her mouth to reply but Kate got there first. 'Martha Crowne,' she said, then poked her tongue out at Helen when the boss turned back to the window.

'Martha *goddam* Crowne. Plain Margo Crump she was, when she came to me. Then *I. Made. Her.* Now she's been stolen away and they thought they could swipe our *Try it For the First Time* concept too. Well, no-one makes a monkey out of Anthony Adams - no *sir-ee*. I got the lawyers in - I fought tooth and nail to hold on to *my* intellectual property, *and* the sponsorship deals she'd already booked - they're mine. Ours. Yours,' he half-turned and gesticulated sideways at Helen. 'I'm giving it all to you. It's your turn, Parker, to step up next to me and show them we don't need Martha-freakin'-Crowne to stay number one - we can do it without her.' He scratched his crotch absent-mindedly, still facing the window and Helen rolled her eyes at Kate, who made a face like she was being sick. 'Everyone's competing for the next big reality thing,' he went on, oblivious, turning to face them once again, waving the E-cigarette around. 'I want *your* reality to be even *more* real than *their* reality... Keep that massive online following she built - *we* built. Show the board that I'm right to follow my hunch and give it to a Brit. Prove me right to the big, fat, cigar-smoking investors who wanted to dictate to me - *me!* - how to salvage the situation,' he gnashed his teeth and snarled a little, and if smoke could have come out of his ears, it would have done. Then he rounded on the two girls. 'So - *give* them the nuts and bolts, give them the warts and all. Our online community out there,' he said, turning back to the window and spreading his arms wide, gesturing across the city scape like it was his kingdom, 'our Precious Readers, they just love...' he began, and Helen and Kate looked at each other and mouthed the rest of the sentence in time with him, '*...the Nitty Gritty.*'

The girls suppressed a smile, narrowly avoiding being caught imitating him. He squinted his eyes at one then the other as they tried to keep a straight face. Then he strutted over to stand in front of Helen, who was seated against the wall in one of the visitors' chairs. It was chosen specially for its height - deliberately low - Mr Adams wasn't very tall, and his own office chair was always pumped up higher. He bent down, inches from her face and she could smell his slightly stale breath and the weird vapour mixed with the usual faint spicy aftershave.

'Give. Them. *Blood.*' His arms prodded the air either side of her head as he spoke faster, rising to his theme. 'Give them *emotion* - give them the ride of their boring, fat-ass, internet-dependent couch-potato lives. They hang on every word - make every word a meal. Make them feel like they are right there with you, Parker. Up there in the clouds. Make it nitty, make it gritty, make it *gutsy*.' He bent a little closer with every word. 'Make. It. Good. Make it *real* good.' He stayed there, panting slightly, and waited for a reply. 'I *need* you to do this for me. You're my man for the job. Deal? Say "I will."'

Helen's nostrils flared a little as she backed up as close to the wall as she could get. 'I will.'

'Say it louder,' he said, standing upright again and raising his arms in the air. 'None of your British reserve! Say "I will Boss!"'

'*I will! Boss.*' Helen said.

His arms were still waving as he waddled back towards his desk. A quick flick of his wrists higher in the air indicated *louder still.*

'I WILL, BOSS!' cried Helen, so loudly that the secretaries outside the closed glass office door turned round in surprise at the outburst. Kate looked down, avoiding eye contact with Helen - but her shoulders were shaking.

'Fantastic!' he said, as he plonked himself down in his office chair and started stabbing at the keyboard. 'Now get *outta here!* You've got a head start. Don't show your face again until you bring me a new list to-die-for... figuratively speaking. Add yours to Martha's outstanding events. I want to see you beat her hollow - bring me some of the most exciting 'TiFFT's' we've ever seen! Oh, and Parker - you've got till tomorrow lunchtime. Time is of the essence - the next six months are crucial - I'll tell you why, tomorrow. Now go.' Kate got up to leave, but Helen didn't. Instead, she raised her hand in the air, to speak. Kate glared at her and shook her head vehemently, jerking a glance towards the door. Helen got the message and took her hand back down again.

'I will, Mr Adams,' she said, as she exited the room. 'I will.'

'I CAN'T,' Helen wailed later that evening in the local bar. 'I can't!'

Brad the bartender put a shot down in front of her and she knocked it straight back. Kate indicated for another and nursed her own, instead of drinking it. 'I can't - *can't* - *CAN'T* do a wing-walk - I will literally piss myself,' moaned Helen, her outburst in a middle-England accent drew glances from a suited couple sipping cocktails nearby. 'It'll be a first, all right - the first *wing-walk wee-wee!*'

Kate splurted some of her drink out, laughing. Brad smiled.

'More nuts, girls?' He spoke in a slightly husky voice with a tiny lisp, as he put more bar snacks down in little dishes all along the relatively empty counter. It was still quite early to have retired to their usual haunt, but Helen had dragged Kate along as soon as she clocked off.

Helen carried on ranting. 'That damned column used to be all about simple things like eating snails and getting kicks on Route 66 when Martha Crowne was doing it. Why, now, does it have to get lethal? *She* never had to bungee jump off the Macau Tower in China, or go tandem parachuting over the Nevada desert, or - or wrestle alligators or...'

'Sweetie, you made the last one up,' said Kate.

'OK, but you've seen his memo! The Macau Tower! Do you know how high that is? Do *you*, Brad?' Helen said, as the handsome bartender pushed another shot her way. He shook his head. She took the glass and raised it to him, 'Fucking high!' she exclaimed, and downed the drink in one.

'Look, what choice do you have?' Kate continued. 'Don't you think it's great that he's giving you another column? So soon after taking away the last one?'

Helen shrugged. 'But it's who he gave it to! Whom. Whatever. Makes my blood boil. Now he's added this danger element - bloody wing-walking,' said Helen, with a shudder. 'You know I don't...' she lowered her voice to a husky whisper, '... it's just... well, you know about my... thing,' she looked around furtively.

'Of course. I'm not likely to forget - remember when Damian took us to the Grand Canyon? The helicopter pilot couldn't hear for a week!'

'I'll cock it all up. I can't risk it. In fact, I think I've lost my mojo to perform well under pressure. I can't feel it - it's gone. It's over. *No-no mo-jo*. So there.'

'Well, you'll just have to find it again,' Kate cajoled her friend, with a *'heard it all before'* look on her face. 'You heard the boss - literally dozens of wannabes want to take your place. They'd give their right arm, remember?'

'Huh!' Helen snorted. 'It wouldn't surprise me if he made that one of the tasks - *give your right arm for the very first time* - to someone who needs it more than you do. You've got two, what do you need both for? Try doing up your bra with one hand for the first time...! *God*,' Helen said, slamming her empty glass back down on the bar, making Brad jump, 'I swear that man will be the death of me...'

'Well this new TiFFT column could also be the *making* of you,' Kate said, leaning across and patting her friend's hand. 'Just like it was for Margo Crump. She got head hunted to go to Parlour

Games Channel for six figures, they say. Six figures! Imagine getting six figures.'

'Doesn't matter - if you're dead,' grumbled Helen.

'And anyway, so what if something goes wrong whilst you're up there - it'd probably go viral! It'll work out - it always does.'

Helen raised her eyebrows - *I don't know.*

Kate nudged her friend's elbow off the counter. 'Ok, enough with the pity party - what did that film say? The one you made me watch, set in India with all those ancient British actors in? *It'll be all right in the end...*' Kate gestured for Helen to join in with the rest of the sentence.

'*... And if it's not all right, it's not the end.*' They both said together. 'See? Marigold Hotel logic. It works.' Kate beamed.

Helen looked up at her old college pal - the same eager blue eyes, olive skin and long blonde hair. Except Kate's was never sleek without hours of straightening - so different from Helen's which took ages to make it curl. Even at college in London when Kate's dad had worked in the UK, they'd wanted each other's attributes - Kate's curves, Helen's better legs, but at least they could share clothes, both being the same height, and when they scrubbed up they could have been straight off the catwalk. Height that gave them gravitas to succeed in a man's world, together with an element of kickass which usually scared men half to death. Or attracted the ones like their college pal Damian. And barman Brad.

Kate continued. 'In any case, you can't change your mind and run away again - you've only just begun talking about getting your stuff out of Milton's storage unit. Right?'

Helen nodded. 'But perhaps it's a sign. Perhaps I should just jack it all in now, like Sadie said - sod off in search of adventure.'

'And that's just what this new column will be - an adventure. So suck it up. Like your sis. Sadie's off to Hawaii soon, right?'

'Yes, the little academic, my geeky sister.'

'With your shoes,' Kate teased.

'Don't remind me about the shoes.' Helen made a mock *hit in the heart* motion. 'Or the sister,' she pouted. 'Or the column. My smooth as clockwork, no-heights-involved, celebrity-shmoozing old column ...' She drooped her head.

'Yes, well, maybe it was more complicated than that.' Kate said.

Helen carried on regardless. 'It's not fair. She just wants everything I have.'

'Who - your sister?'

'No - Kim Kardigan,' said Helen. '*She* got my column. I got Martha Crowne's cast-offs.'

Kate flared her nostrils and narrowed her eyes, then put down her drink, took Helen's and placed it by her own, then turned Helen round to face her. '*Come onnnn*! Yes, Ki-Ka's getting more and more in demand - even if it *is* by proxy because of having gotten some A-Lister's embryo inside her.'

'*Pah*, IF it's even his,' said Helen, scowling. 'In fact, she's such an attention seeker it might not even be *hers*!'

Kate ignored her. 'And you may be hurt that the Boss gave in to Ki-Ka's demands. But right now, everyone does. Half of the guys at work have. She was already pinching most of the guests you found for her TV show. But...'

'Yes, see? Not content with being the host of her own online chat show, her own fashion range on TransGlobeShopping and her own monthly magazine, she works her evil spell and gets my column too.'

'And my staff,' said Brad as he walked past, pouting. 'She stole my hunky Johnny Two Shoes.' Both Kate and Helen looked blank, and sat blinking at him until he explained. 'The latest young accounts clerk at your place - he was *my* discovery. I blame Miss Ki-Ka myself - taking my cute numbers-guy over to the dark side. I tell you, I'll give that girlfriend a piece of my mind when she comes in here next with her *entourage.* A big piece. Right after she's settled her account.' He gave a defiant wave of his hand in the air and turned tail.

Helen and Kate laughed at his diva gestures, then sipped their drinks in silence for a moment.

'Helen - think about it - if the Boss sees you as part of the souped-up revamp, you must have done something *right* - not wrong - with that last column. You didn't lose it, he gave in to Ki-Ka's demands because he knew he needed you for Something. Far. Better...' Kate was emulating the Boss's hand movements again. She paused and Helen furrowed her brows. 'Anyway, that's what Kieran thinks.'

Helen mimicked her. *'That's what Kieran thinks, meh.* Whatever way you look at it, it stinks - now *she* sits in the cosy studio and I have to go *wee-walk*.'

Kate chewed on the side of her mouth and squinted at Helen. 'What's wrong with you? You've gone all morose on me this evening. Come on, is it the man? Or the sister? Was it that goddam phone call earlier? Ahh I'm right - it was the phone call, wasn't it. Wasn't it!?'

'She's still not answering.' Helen was staring straight ahead.

'Maybe Sadie's just busy,' Kate replied, 'she's off to Hawaii, remember? Partly because of you.'

'She still says she hates the way I made it happen.'

'She always comes round in the end.'

'Well roll on the end,' Helen said, 'for more reasons than one.'

'Stop being so down on yourself. You're no fun when you're miserable. Are you due on?'

Helen whacked her arm, looking around her to see if anyone had heard. Then Kate whispered. 'Kieran knows something - seriously. The Boss is doing it for a reason, you and I just don't know what it is. But maybe… maybe his *insider* does.'

'His what?'

'Oh nothing. Just something Kieran showed me.'

'Finally,' said Helen, raising her eyebrows suggestively.

'No, not *that*! He wouldn't have one left anyway, if his wife ever caught him.'

Helen shrugged at Brad, as if to say 'what am I going to do with her' - and he smiled back as he held out a refill for the bar snacks and Helen pushed the empty bowl closer. 'Kieran been brown-nosing the Boss again?' she asked Kate, flicking a peanut at her friend's mouth. Brad caught it and wagged a finger at the girls.

'Don't know. Maybe. I'll ask him for you tomorrow. All I know is there's something going on...'

'Doesn't surprise me. I've heard the Boss has got spies everywhere,' Helen said, taking an olive from the new dish the barman was placing just in front of her. She grabbed his hand. 'Everywhere. Are *you* a spy, Brad?' she teased.

He shook his mop of blonde hair, and smiled, picking up a few glasses from the counter top. 'No sadly, unless it means being interrogated by that dishy friend of yours - Damian something? He's a bit James Bond. I could be the baddie. He could tie me up and ... ooo... interrogate me! Is he coming in again tonight?' His face had lit up - it wasn't the first time the girls had seen this reaction to their pal. Damian Grant was a handsome hot shot business man who garnered admiration amongst guys like Brad right across New York. And San Francisco. And Miami. And Sydney, Paris and London and...

'No, our Damian has just gone AWOL - he's disappeared off the radar again, off on another of his long trips. Singapore I think he said, didn't he Kate?'

'Then China,' Kate replied.

'Backpacking?' Brad asked, wiping down the area where Helen had made a mess with pistachio nuts earlier.

'Backpacking? Good God, no! Our Damian? Not in his Italian pointy shoes and two thousand dollar suits!' Helen exclaimed.

'He's always been a high flyer - it'll be first class all the way for him I expect,' laughed Kate. 'Business trip.'

'He was telling me and Miss Cheryl last time that he made a fortune in marketing,' Brad said. Helen and Kate looked at each other at the mention of Cheryl Goodman's name.

'Yes but now he's expanding. Might be getting into publishing with our Helen here,' Kate said, patting her friend on the back.

'*Maybe*,' added Helen.

'All work, huh? Might make Jack a dull boy,' said Brad.

'Na-hah - he'll be sampling his fair share of Eastern Delights, if I know Damian,' Kate said.

'Well if they're my kind of delights, you just tell him if he ever needs a chaperone, Brad's here waiting, sweetie.' He winked and went to serve another customer. O'Reilly's was getting busier and the amiable barman eagerly greeted every new arrival with the same puppy-like enthusiasm.

'Brad's funny. I miss Damian.' said Helen, protruding her bottom lip in a petulant pout. 'He was so sweet after the showdown in Tuscany despite his brother turning up at the conference causing trouble.' She shuddered at the memory. '

'Water off a duck's back - you know Brad loves you to pieces.'

'I'm beginning to wish I'd accepted his offer to do a book.'

'Too easy - you prefer to make life difficult for yourself. Besides,' Kate said, doing a complete turn on the revolving bar stool, 'You can't resist the whiff of a new challenge. I know you - even though you're miffed at Ki-Ka getting your column, in truth, you can't wait to show Mr Adams that you can do far better TiFFTs than Martha Crowne. Plus, you don't want anyone to think you run away from a challenge, right? Even if you do? Run away? Frequently? But usually from commitment.'

Helen paused, opened her mouth, closed it again, shrugged, and reluctantly nodded.

'Well, Missus "I work for all I've got." Maybe one day you'll meet your match,' Kate said, an eyebrow raised, 'a man who makes you feel able to let go and just be a goddam woman.' Kate swigged back her shot. 'If such a guy exists.'

'He does,' said Helen, staring at her drink. 'He's in Tuscany - like I told you, I buggered up any chance I ever had with him. You should have seen his face when I turned him down.'

'Ahh,' Kate's eyes opened wider. 'Still the smitten kitten? Don't be depressed about a guy you had a one night stand with, at a boring marketing conference with your sister in tow, for God's sake! It's not exactly Harlequin Channel.' Kate paused and looked at her friend's dreamy face, then leaned in confidentially. 'Was he *really* that good?'

Helen just raised one eyebrow, smirking.

'Well maybe you should go back there. After all, you told me...' Kate paused and looked towards the bartender. 'Close your ears, Brad.' Brad looked up. 'You don't want to be listening to forty year olds talking about their sex lives,' she told him.

'Is this where I say "you? Forty? Never!"' he replied.

'No, this is where you walk away with your fingers in your ears going *la-la*.' Kate said. Comically, swaying his bottom, Brad did just that. Kate continued, quieter. 'You told me he rocked your world - well, your bed anyway, this Mr Italy...'

Helen felt a pang in her stomach.

Alessandro.

'He did. *Does*. Did.'

'... But you also said he was very domineering.'

Helen sighed, 'Yesss, very, very domineering.' She smiled, knowingly.

'Pervert.'

'Mmmm,' Helen smirked.

'You seemed really keen at first - how long after your steamy session did you Skype me?'

'Whilst he was in the bathroom.'

'See? Couldn't wait to gloat. Then you get back here and you clam up about him. So will you tell me now, what changed?'

'Everything,' Helen said, looking down dolefully and taking a deep breath. 'Everything's changed. He changed it.'

'Did he dump you?'

'No, he asked me to travel the world with him.'

'And that's a problem how?'

'As his companion. Round the world as someone's companion. Paying for me.'

'So? You're the one who's spent most of her adult life going from place to place, job to job, man to man.' Kate continued. Helen's eyebrow raised and she shrugged in acknowledgement.

Kate went on. 'Now you find a hot Latino stud who thinks the world of you, is great in bed, and has asked you to go on a fabulous trip with him, and you're in hiding. You can't keep running away forever when someone gets close to you. You've been doing it since Jason, for God's sake. Nearly twenty years, woman! You don't have to act like a little wifey, but isn't it time to stop with the crusade? To prove yourself to the world?'

'You can talk.' Helen snipped.

'Look, leave me outta this - we're talking about you. You're the Queen of running away.'

'Well *you've* got the gold medal,' Helen countered, then poked out her tongue.

'Then you've got the world record,' Kate replied, and made a '*ner ner*' face.

'The internet even ran out of men for you to date,' Helen laughed, '... you used them all up - all gone! All the - what did you call them? Losers and Harbourers of Baggage? So let's just be single together, for the rest of time. Save the hassle and the heartbreak. Men. In the end they all lie to you or leave you, right?'

'Right,' agreed Brad, reappearing with some glasses. Helen laughed. 'Apart from Damian Grant of course,' he said, hopefully.

'Of course,' both girls answered together. Brad beamed.

'Anyway, my internet thing was so *last* year, Helen,' Kate said, miffed. 'New project now, remember. I'll tell you soon but not right now.' Helen went to ask, but Kate flicked her eyes towards the people who were crowding in around them and made a 'zip it' motion across her own mouth.

Helen rolled her eyes and changed the subject. 'Tell me - did the Boss pick me because I'm expendable? So it won't matter one bit if I become the first wing-walker to die on camera? Being, like, just a Brit?' Helen sighed and popped another olive into her mouth.

'Don't be silly.' Kate bit her lip and paused. Then she said, mysteriously, 'But Kieran was with the Boss at the golf course for a lot longer than usual. He knows stuff.' Kate lowered her voice even further. 'I saw some Powerpoint slides - Kieran showed me in the editing suite.'

'Oh yeah? You absolutely sure that's the only thing he showed you? I wondered what you were doing in there with the door closed and the lights off.'

'That's how you edit, numbnuts,' Kate laughed, 'anyway, how many more times? Stop saying that; you know Kieran's happily married.'

'I know he's *married*,' said Helen, provocatively, but Kate just carried straight on.

'Seriously - Kieran wouldn't show me all of it. But the Boss is planning something. What if...' She paused.

'What?'

'In confidence?'

'Boy scout's honour.' Said Helen, holding up a few fingers in a mock salute.

'OK - it seems as though - well I mean, there's some evidence that... that the competition were looking at poaching you too - like they poached Martha Crowne.' She paused for effect. It worked -

Helen's eyes opened wider. 'So his revamped TiFFT column - with you at the helm - is part of an attempt to "spearhead a pre-emptory strike."' Kate said the last bit in broader New York, as if she was in voice-over mode, and waved her hand in the air to indicate headlines.

'Pre-emptive. Pre-emptive strike. Pre-emptory's not a word.'

'You tell the Boss that. Listen, I shouldn't really be telling you this, so act impressed and kinda surprised if he lets you in on the secret at your meeting tomorrow morning, OK?'

'OK - but are you sure the Boss thinks that?'

'Maybe you'll be even bigger than Ki-Ka - now make the most of it.'

'Hmmm,' pondered Helen under her breath. A light bulb seemed to come on. 'I wonder what TiFFT's I could do in Tibet...'

'That's it! Get started on that list - think big. Go do what your kid sister keeps telling you - go live a little? Go live a lot! After all, Sadie's going off on her *own* - all the way to Hawaii.'

'I wonder what TiFFT's I could do in Hawaii.'

'Hey! That's *her* adventure - she'll be pissed even more if you elbow in on this too, after the devious way you got her there.'

'...She'd never have gone otherwise! I needed to lie about it, or the set-up wouldn't have worked, and she...'

'Nah-huh! Don't change the subject.' Kate sighed and got serious. 'HellsBells, take this chance. Isn't it about time you had an adventure of your own? A proper one? Stop trying to fix-up other people's lives? Seriously? Maybe it's time.'

Helen just made a face and turned towards Brad. He shrugged and nodded as if to say 'why not' then gestured to her empty glass - she shook her head and indicated the iced water in the pitcher next to her.

'Take a chance? That's rich coming from you!' Helen said to Kate. 'What are *you* doing to mix things up in *your* life, huh?'

'Well... Actually, now you mention it...' Kate replied, looking a little sheepish, and sitting back on the bar stool, picking up her handbag. She stared at it for a moment, avoiding Helen's gaze. 'I wanted to tell you sooner, but I wasn't sure if it was working out - all going in the right direction. But...'

'But? But what?'

'Nothing,' said Kate.

Helen hesitated, then waved at Brad as she left some money on the counter. He waved back and the two girls stood up to go.

'Nothing, my ass,' Helen demanded, taking her friend's arm and whisking her towards the exit. 'Spill.'

That night, Helen sat up in bed in the spare room at Kate's apartment, thinking about what Kate had told her. She was totally blown away by what Kate had finally shared. Sworn to secrecy, about her new dating method and the most recent turn of events, the more she thought about it, the more she believed it could work. When they'd discussed it briefly last year, Helen thought it would be another one of Kate's five minute wonders, but no, it really seemed there was something special about this new system. Good for Kate.

But it only made Helen even more depressed.

Helen had just kissed off the most gorgeous Italian hunk, to come back to a friend she thought was a kindred spirit, only to find that friend had just made the most incredible discovery that had changed everything.*

Plus, Helen was about to commit to a make or break international internet fiasco if her 'thing with heights' resurfaced and ruined everything. She'd managed to keep it a secret for so long, from so many. Too bad it wasn't ordinary vertigo. No, Helen had to have the weird version. And whom did she turn to at times like this? Her sister Sadie. But she was still mad.

Helen toyed with the keypad on her cell phone. They had things to discuss and maybe she'd have calmed down a bit since the Tuscany incident. But after a bit more cheek-chewing, Helen put the phone back down. Nope, in two days it was her sister's birthday - she'd call then - there would be more chance of an answer.

In six months' time, she figured, everything would be a bit more settled. Sorted. It had to be - anything was better than this. Who knows what changes were ahead - for her, for Sadie, and for Kate by the sound of it. For everyone - maybe even Alessandro, wherever he was, and whomever he was with. Who was he with? Maybe... *Was there still time?* Helen googled Tibet for a short while and then sent one more email before turning out the light. She dreamt of falling. In more ways than one.

*(Kate's story – 'The How to Find a Husband Manual' due 2015)

Chapter Three

Back in the offices of TransGlobe Inc the next morning, Helen was hot-desking. She'd spent the night tossing and turning and had woken up with a fire in her belly and a dream in her heart. She was first in the office, surprising Janice, the Boss's PA who was always the earliest - usually. Janice had given Helen a cursory five minute chat as she had 'so much to do before the fire breathing dragon got in,' then left Helen to spend the next two hours pounding the keyboard and scribbling furious notes, ignoring the rest of the office as it slowly filled up. Tired-eyed, yawning people trooped in and the quiet hum gradually became a hub-bub. Suddenly a steaming cup of hot chocolate was placed down next to her and she looked up gratefully.

'Here, I saw your note on my kitchen counter this morning. I'm glad you understand. Thought you deserved this.' It was Kate. 'Hey, look,' she said and jerked her head towards the closed glass door. Helen followed her gaze. At the receptionist's desk directly outside Mr Adams' office was a hunky young delivery boy in shorts, and Janice was signing for a big gift-wrapped box, covered with ribbons showing the Godiva chocolates logo. She looked over at Helen, rolled her eyes and shook her head as if to say *'again.'* Helen smiled back and nodded. Kate quipped, 'Must be costing that Goodman girl a fortune. Wonder which executive assistant he'll give *that* little stash to - hey maybe that's how he gets his info - expensive chocolate in return for spilling the beans on what the other board members are getting up to.'

'Your guess,' Helen replied, sipping at the take-out cup and making a face as the scalding liquid touched her lips. 'It won't be me getting his hard centres, that's for sure.'

'Eouwww. Your time will come,' Kate said, and gestured to take the hot chocolate back if Helen didn't like it. But Helen wouldn't let go of the cup, resisting her friend's attempts to reclaim it.

'Heard anything from Kieran yet?'

'Nope,' Kate said, 'I'll catch him later.' And she leaned in to try to reach the hot chocolate again but sneakily began to read the computer screen. 'So what have we here?' she asked.

'Oi, no peeking,' Helen said.

'Tibet? Really? A TiFFT in Tibet?'

'Yes,' Helen replied, indignantly, switching the screen to email.

'And what exactly would your exciting "try it for the first time" experience be there? Milk a yak? Weird place to start.'

'Why not? It's got one of the highest spas in the world - luxurious, decadent, seven star - imagine the photos I could post - just the sort of thing he'd want in his new look, no-expense spared, aspirational online column - isn't it.' She gave in and flicked the screen back, showing images of a beautiful mountainside retreat.

'Mmmm. Twelve hand massage? Ice cold skinny dipping?'

'Actually, there is a Tibetan *Tantric* experience,' Helen responded, with a smile. 'If he wants risqué, he's going to get it.' Then she tapped some buttons and a nearby printer began whirring.

Kate smirked. 'Oo I like how you're thinking! Hit the Huffington Post headlines *and* get some hot sexy-time all on the company's ticket!'

Helen made a smug face and reached over to pick up her documents from the printer. As she did so, Kate flicked the screen back to email.

'And who, might I ask, is going to be the lucky person to accompany you on this trip? Might it be a certain Italian paleo-wotjamacallit turned new-age adventurer?'

'Paleo-astronomer. It might.'

'Really?!'

'If he still wants me to go,' Helen gestured towards her screen. 'He might have asked someone else by now.' Helen sat back and stared into the middle-distance. 'To think, I so nearly said yes - it was all heading that way. I don't think he's used to being told *no.*'

'Sweetie, if he knows what's good for him, he'll jump at the chance to have you...' Kate said. The delivery boy walked by in shorts and they both watched his backside disappear towards the elevators. '...to have you come along. You told him you'd only changed your mind because of your column though? That might not be so good for his Latin pride.' Kate was blatantly reading the email.

Helen paused as if she was going to speak, then shrugged, and flicked through her papers, looking thoughtful. 'Don't forget to let me know what Kieran says,' she whispered to Kate, who nodded. 'See, there's something I don't understand,' said Helen, flicking at the papers. 'Where's this extra budget coming from so suddenly for this revamp? I mean, who invests like that? Janice let me in on the big names they've just signed up for our *Late Night Late* Live Podcast. Big names. It's all going to cost a fortune. It's not just Try it For the First Time club they're investing in.'

Kate thought for a moment. 'I'll have to grill my "source" for more dirt.' She looked over both shoulders furtively then winked at Helen.

'You never know what goes on in the editing suite,' Helen joked.

'Or on the golf course. Perhaps I should learn properly. Remember when we tried doing it once for my Real Grown Ups Guide?'

'You found the only thing you're really crap at - a golf swing?'

'It was so funny - Kieran faked the shoot in the end, by putting the camera on the ground for the close up, then he put on my trousers and golf shoes and filmed himself doing it. No-one knew it wasn't me. Had offers to join the local ladies clubs for months afterwards!'

'You always were crap with balls... Ball sports,' Helen added quickly. 'Anyway, you have your assignment for today - find out what Kieran knows,' she whispered. 'I'd love to know who they are?'

Janice breezed by at that moment. 'Who are who?'

Kate sat up straighter, Helen retrieved the hot chocolate and sat back in her chair, nodding towards Kate as if to say *'ask her.'* Kate explained - they trusted Janice, she'd started at TransGlobe Inc at the same time as Kate and was a kindred spirit in the post-40 club, amongst the many young nubile females sashaying around the office. 'So come on, Janice. Give your pals a clue,' Kate asked.

'All I know is that it's some rich hot-shot - some sort of media investment guy - with an unusual agenda. The Boss closes the office door whenever the guy calls.'

'Unusual? Like what?' asked Helen.

'Can't say,' said Janice.

'Word at the water cooler is…' Kate began.

'*Kieran's* water cooler?' asked Janice, smiling knowingly.

'Yeah, that one - Kate *drinks* from there as often as she can…' winked Helen.

'I would have thought his wife would have had it re-plumbed after the last time,' Janice laughed, joining in the teasing.

Kate ignored it with a roll of her eyes. '…Word is, that they want to stop anyone else from being poached.'

'Maybe,' said Janice. 'If some new investor felt protective enough about a big local success story like TransGlobe…'

'Someone rich from New York?' asked Kate.

'Someone like the Godiva-briber's moneybags father you mean? I couldn't possibly comment,' said Janice. Kate hesitated then went 'ohhhh!' as if the penny had just dropped.

'Godiva Briber - sounds like that internet sensation the Boss discovered a few years back,' asked Helen. 'So who's Cheryl Goodman's father, then?'

Kate said, 'He's stupid-rich, isn't he, Jan?'

'Oh yes,' added Janice. 'Haven't you heard of Geoffrey Goodman?' she said to Helen. 'Dot coms, pre bubble-burst?

'No! That's Cheryl's dad? *Those* Goodmans?' Helen's face was a picture. 'The "tawk of New Yawk" a few years back. Seriously minted?'

'Seriously minted!' said Kate in a mock English accent.

'So *that's* why she's bribing Willy Wonka over there with his favourite chocolates,' Helen replied. 'Rich father eh. Probably another one who always gets her own way. Spoilt rotten her whole life with daddy doting on her every whim. That explains it all - she's loaded.'

'Honey don't be jealous. You didn't need a father to help you, you made your own way in life,' Janice laughed. 'And by the way, I know you've been away from New York for a year or so now, but to say she's loaded means she's had one too many Jacks, you know what I mean?'

Helen just winked in reply. 'I know what I mean. I'm not that out of touch. I saw her down the bar while I was waiting for Kate to tear herself away from Kieran - she was with that good looking sports commentator from CNN.' Then Helen sighed and stretched, reaching out her arms above her head. 'Babies, both of them. I'll have to ask Brad for the goss next time we're in O'Reilly's.'

'That'll be tonight then.' Janice left them with a wink, and a small dark chocolate each. 'Don't be late for the big announcement this afternoon,' she called back over her shoulder 'Don't forget - board room, 4pm.' And her slightly plus-sized posterior sashayed away, reminding Helen fleetingly of sister Sadie's rear-view.

'More upheaval. Things *have* really changed since I've been away, Kate,' Helen said, turning back to her keyboard and jabbing a few buttons then resting her chin on her fist. 'I thought I'd just pick up where I left off but I'm not sure I fit in any more. The whole city's moved on since last year. Since all that nonsense with... you know who... it's kind of lost its lustre for me here, you know?'

'I *do* know, because I know *you*,' Kate said, leaning over and examining the new document on the screen. 'I know you, like the back of my hand sometimes - I can read you like a book. I can predict you like a horoscope. And that,' she said as she reached for the keyboard, '...is precisely why you should grasp this opportunity,' and with a flourish she pressed 'send' on the email Helen had been dithering over. 'Grasp it with both feet.' Kate paused, waiting as usual for Helen to correct her turn of phrase, but this time Helen was transfixed to the screen.

'Message sent,' Helen said in a small voice, 'it says *message sent*. Shit.'

'OK, so your email was a little bit needy, but it said everything. I speed-read it. The little bit in Italian didn't look quite right, but the rest? *Perfecto.*' Kate made like a top chef, kissing her fingers and thumb in a *mwah* gesture, and then stood up just as the door opened and the Boss stepped out and bellowed Helen's name. 'Ooo Mr Adams looks horny. He looks all hot and raring to go. Looks like you might be getting that chocolate from him after all.'

'Shut up, idiot,' Helen said smiling.

'Go, play your trump cards and I'll see you later,' Kate said, and picked up the take-out cup as soon as Helen turned her back.

'Hey, you can buy me another one at lunchtime,' Helen warned, without looking round.

'Sorry honey, no can do. At lunchtime I'm meeting a guy about his sister's flatmate's brother for my new dating thing, remember?

When your world stops spinning, maybe you can try it too. I'm thinking of patenting it. If you're not fired I'll see you at four o'clock in the brainstorming meeting on the 28th floor.' And Kate left, taking Helen's hot drink with her.

'Are you resigning Parker? Is that what you're doing, by keeping me waiting?' came the bellowing voice across the room once more. Mr Adams turned around in a cloud of vapour and stomped back into his office. Helen picked up a wad of papers containing her hastily researched presentation and trotted across the office to the open door, slipping inside just before it slammed shut.

'Wish me luck,' she'd said to Janice as she passed her desk on the way into his office. 'I may be gone some time...'

Behind her, on the computer screen, a little message popped up. It said, 'You have 1 new message: Alessandro...' and then it flicked into screensaver.

'Tonight? You're flying out tonight? Jeez, The Boss doesn't waste any time does he?' It was 3.50pm and Kate was twirling herself round on an executive leather office chair next to the massive oak table in the biggest, plushest conference room the company owned. Staff filed in slowly, collecting coffee and cookies from one corner then taking their places at the table. A couple of pristine cover-girls sitting opposite were staring at Kate. She stopped herself mid-spin, and stuck out her tongue at them. They just looked down their noses and turned away. Kate had been filming, dressed in her standard issue denim dungarees, and still had paint around her nails. A little had also got in her hair, which she'd twisted into a sexy up-do on top of her head. She might be over forty but she always looked fabulous, even when she'd just been filming her Real Grown Up's Guide *Fix-It* programmes. 'Helen!' she hissed. 'Earth to Helen.'

'What?'

'I said you're flying out tonight? Good God, the mind's left the building already,' Kate said. 'A certain Italian stud's reply got you in a spin?' Kate jibed, twirling Helen's chair. Helen stopped it spinning and glared at her friend. Kate was unabated. 'Well, you just keep going all... dreamy. The last time I saw you with a look *that* far-away, was when Jason bought you that green sports car.'

'It was because he'd proposed, not just bought me a car.'

'Whatever. And no, my Lucy's still not restored it. She's just too busy at the shop selling her vintage knick knacks. Unless maybe she knows what you used to do on the back seat... Helen!'

'I can hear you, I'm just ignoring ancient history.'

'Do you want it back?'

'What the ancient history? No. That's why it's ancient. And you know *exactly* why it'll stay that way,' said Helen, picking a piece of paint from her friend's tendril. 'You're one of the few that does.' Then she span Kate round.

Kate slapped her arm on the table to stop, making several of the office girlies jump. She leaned in. 'I'm not talking about Jason Todd, I'm talking about the car. I keep telling Lucy I need my garage space. If you had it back, I could finally set up my...' she trailed off, Helen was staring out the window. 'Oh never mind. Your head's already on the plane back to Italy, right?'

'Yes - I go tonight on the red-eye. First assignment by next weekend.'

'Whoa! Seriously? That's fast. Boss is serious about keeping Martha Crowne's momentum going on the TiFFT column then.'

'And then some. Plus he liked the tantric theme for Tibet. Signed off on it straight away. Despite the price ticket.'

'Oh yeah?' Kate said knowingly. 'I bet he did - dirty old bugger. I'm looking forward to seeing how you write that one up!'

'I just write it and email it - he can do the rest. I'll put the *nitty gritty* as he's so fond of saying, and if it's too much he can just edit it down.'

'Tantric Tibet - 50 shades of Orange.'

'Yes, apparently it's like with all those steamy novels at the moment - the more risqué, the more popular it is. Boss said if we spice it up we can attract more viewers and more importantly, bigger sponsorship deals. Hopefully some more interesting assignments than what Martha Crowne left behind.'

'Yeah? Oh yeah! What was that one? Like finding out which caveman you're related to? How does that fit into *risqué*?'

'Exactly my thoughts! He said I had to find a way - the deal's already set up and if I don't have it, Martha will get it and he doesn't want her to have anything. He doesn't like her, does he?'

'Did once,' said Kate, and then she winked. Helen shuddered.

'It's going to be a hectic time that's for sure,' Helen said. 'So many TiFFTs to do - and all in the next six months - if I'm to get my...' then she mouthed the word 'bonus'.

'Your what?'

'That's what Mr Adams said. Six months - building to some sort of grand finale I have to come up with. Then - you'll never guess - he actually smiled. I was gobsmacked.'

'Don't tell me he was actually pleased about something?'

'Well, he did the usual,' Helen replied, then mimicked him - sat hunched over, 'smoking' a pretend E-cigarette, alternately shaking her head then nodding, as she drew her finger down a make-believe list, whilst taking a mock phone call and waving her fists in the air.

'Uncanny,' said Kate, laughing, and patted her friend on the back. 'You're a wasted talent, Cousteau.'

'Marceau, you mean Marcel Marceau, the famous mime artist. Cousteau was the...' Helen stopped, seeing her friend making a 'you think?!' face. 'Anyway I threw in a few ridiculously expensive adventures too - I was amazed at what he said yes to.'

'Really? The ones in Damian's email this morning?'

'Yes - but in return, he threw in several others from his list - the ones with the highest chance of me meeting a sticky end.'

'Even so, your ideas must have blown him away if he gave you the go-ahead that fast! Well done, HellsBells! He's clearly keen to send ParlourGames Channel on their way before they've even launched.'

'He's clearly keen to send me to my death before I've even lived. But at least I get to kick it off in Tibet.'

'With Alessannnnndrrrro?' Kate asked, in a mock Italian accent.

'I didn't think Alessandro would even reply. But... yes. He said yes. I'm going to Tibet with Alessandro.' Helen paused. 'I couldn't believe it - he wants me to fly out to his villa in Tuscany then set off together for Tibet!'

Kate pulled her fists down hard through the air in a 'yesss!' motion. 'Honey he wants a repeat performance of what happened last time you were there.'

'I hope so.' Helen said. 'But...' She paused for a moment and felt Kate's eyes examining her face. 'He sounded a bit weird on the phone. More... distant. Funny how things work out, isn't it. If they hadn't given my column to Ki-Ka, I'd never have even considered going back to him. And if there hadn't been a tantric TiFFT in Tibet, Mr Adams wouldn't have approved this extortionate trip. I hope I'm not making a mistake.'

'Did Mr Italy sound pleased?'

Helen thought about it. 'I nearly left it too late.' She spoke quietly. 'He said if I didn't come straight away, he'd be leaving without me.'

'You? Taking orders?' Kate asked. Helen just half nodded and flicked her eyebrows upwards in reply. 'Seriously - a Bossy man? Doesn't he know that you not only expect to *wear* the trousers, you have them hand-made to your exact specifications - with a bigger pouch under the crotch to house your enormous balls?' Kate used her hands to illustrate the point. Again a few glances from the executive assistants.

Helen laughed. 'Shh...' She sipped her tea. 'Such a shame I just couldn't let him sweep me off my feet - in many ways Alessandro felt like such a perfect fit...' Helen looked over at her friend and Kate's eyebrows were raised, her mouth open about to make the predictable quip. 'Don't say it,' said Helen. And Kate closed her mouth again like a fish. 'He *was* amazing - in that department too, but...'

'But? But what?'

'Maybe too perfect. There's always something, isn't there. With men? In the end? Sooner or later?' Helen said, looking wistful.

'If you *think* there will be, then there will be.' Kate replied, popping a mint into her mouth and offering Helen one.

Helen shook her head. 'Now you sound like Sadie. But you're probably right.'

'Perhaps it's time to let go - let go of the spectres of the past!' said Kate, making a dramatic arc in the air with one hand then the other, standing up as she said it. Those taking their places nearby glanced over and smiled, apart from the man next to her who ducked. 'Rewrite your destiny and forge a new future - a whole new future!' She smiled as the production team from her show made mock gestures of adulation. Kate did a little bow and sat back down again. '*Maybe* a happy future is possible with a man - stranger things have happened. I certainly still live in hope. And you never know - for you, maybe it's a guy with bigger balls than you. Maybe it's this Italian god.'

Helen snorted. 'We'll see what happens when I touch down tomorrow. And how we get on in Tibet. But it won't be long term - it can't be. I'll be jetting all round the world after that, on my new assignments... My scary new assignments.'

Kate narrowed her eyes, examining Helen's worried look and offered her a mint again, not taking no for an answer, thrusting it nearer and nearer her nose until Helen eventually took one. 'Maybe soon it'll be both of us getting laid,' Kate said, and winked.

Just at that moment, an athletic looking late thirty-something came and sat in between them, huffing a little and finishing an email on his phone. He glanced up as he took his seat.

'Hi girls. Kate, you've still got spackle in your hair. Helen, why's your mouth open like that? What's Kate being saying? You look like an idiot. Are you stressed? Do you want me to rub your shoulders?'

'Hi Kieran,' they both chimed.

Kate started picking at the paint in her hair and pouted, 'It's not spackle, it's paint.'

Helen closed her mouth and sat up straighter, observing the two together, as they bickered over the white blobs in Kate's hair.

Kieran was Kate's Boss, the producer of her weekly online video 'how to' series, The Real Grown Up's Guide. Her short *Fix It* clips showed how to do the most common jobs around the house and garden - from basic to slightly more adventurous - all with a quirky girl-next-door style which was neither too patronising nor too highbrow. It had built a big following on YouTube, and the local TV channel had also picked it up with a 'must-see' sponsored co-production every Friday. Kate was now recognised in the street - one of the many reasons why her dating quest was such a challenging one.

'Eurgh. Watching you two together is like watching an old married couple,' Helen teased, and in unison they both stopped bickering and folded their arms and tilted their heads slightly - at the exact same angle. 'OK, more like Statler and Waldorf,' she corrected, 'from the Muppets?' They just glared at her then carried on.

Helen decided she'd add 'Any developments with Kieran?' to her next 'Truth or Dare Q & A' on Skype with Kate. Maybe as soon as she was on Tuscan soil. Well, maybe with a bit of luck it'd be the *second* thing Helen did after she arrived - Alessandro was, after all, picking her up from the airport and taking her 'straight back to his place.' Apparently.

Helen watched, amused, as Kieran reached over and removed a bit of paint which Kate had missed on the top of her head, and Kate smiled sheepishly at Helen from below Kieran's arm then shrugged. He was a typical bossy producer, complete with a 'scruffy jeans and un-ironed shirt' approach. His wife didn't like irons, apparently. She also didn't like Kate.

'Anyway, 'Plastering 101 is in the can,' he said, flicking the bit of spackle and paint onto the floor, and brushing Kate's hair back over her shoulder. 'With a special section on spackle. What do we need to call it for the UK?'

'Polyfilla,' replied Helen.

'Ok. Weird. Oh and Kate, I thought you'd be pleased to know that your guest, what did you call him... Stephen the Sophomore... wanted your number. I told him you're not a cougar but if his dad was free, to get back in touch.' Kate bashed his arm but sat herself up straighter and didn't protest - as a muted hush had swept the room. A couple of top management had entered and were clearing an invisible force-field of space ahead of them as they swept over to the coffee area and helped themselves, making polite conversation with the serving staff.

'So,' said Kieran, in a more hushed tone, turning to Helen, 'you're off on some exotic adventures I hear. Excited?'

'About some. Not so keen on the sudden-death ones, plus a couple of boring Martha ones already on the schedule. Boss said in our pow-wow this morning that I gotta get them done before she does. With a grand finale in six months' time. And a massive bonus at the...'

'... end of it. So you know now. Yes, he mentioned this time limit thing the other day at the 18th hole,' said Kieran, fiddling with his phone. 'Good old Legal department - made Martha Crowne leave behind all the sponsorship deals. Not sure that was half the reason why ParlourGames Channel poached her. By the way, did he find out who the ten thousand dollar deal was set up by?'

Helen splurted out her tea. 'What? Didn't mention it. What was that for?'

'Just for a banner - that's a mention on the top of the online TiFFT column.'

'Kieran,' said Helen, smacking her cup back down in the saucer with a clunk. 'I know what a bloody banner is,' she hissed.

'Yes but Kate doesn't,' he mock whispered. 'She's not too au fait with the hi-tech. Give the girl a Leatherman belt full of tools and she's right at home, but technology? Nah.'

Kate shrugged in acceptance and offered him the packet of mints.

He took them. 'It's her age, you know,' he teased. And she promptly snatched the candies back, but not before he'd taken three or four.

'I have an I.T. bitch for that,' she said, jerking her head towards Kieran, who gave her a playful punch on the arm. 'Ten thou' tho'?'

'Yes, that's gotta soften the blow for the Boss' he whispered, conspiratorially, '… of being told how to run his own show.' Both girls stopped and looked up at this news. He beckoned them closer. 'Kate says you want to know what I know,' he breathed. They nodded, Helen vigorously. 'But if I told you all my secrets, they wouldn't be secret any more, would they?' He made a face and looked at Kate. 'Do you think she's a trustworthy citizen?' Kate suppressed a smile and nodded again. Helen sat wide-eyed. 'OK. Anthony Adams has boasted to the board that within six months, the new Try it For the First Time Club column will become THE international go-to resource for "adventure seeking females with disposable income," with a hundred per cent increase in the number of unique hits. Double the viewing figures. That's what he's expecting of you, Ms Parker-Todd.'

Helen's jaw gaped open. 'So that's why they gave him the go ahead to expand the budget?' she said, suddenly very focussed. 'Double viewing figures would mean premium advertising revenue…'

'Exactly. And he told you about the bonus? If you achieve his targets?' Kieran asked. Helen responded with a nod of the head. 'Well it seems there's one for him, and one for you. And it's not just big, Helen - it's huge. It could be everything you need for your new start.'

'To finally shake free of what happened in New York a year ago,' Kate said. Helen's mind was working overtime. Kate hissed, 'Think, woman! This TiFFT column could be your salvation,' she said, dramatically.

'And you, my dear,' Kieran added, 'will be pivotal to the re-launch.'

'Wow,' Helen said, taking it all in. 'Well I better start thinking of how to sexy up the "Tracing your DNA" assignment,' she caught their looks. 'Don't ask.'

'Perhaps you can play on the personal angle - people love a confessional on the internet nowadays, don't they?' Kieran said. Kate looked at him strangely.

'Even so, it'll be a challenge to make a nerdy DNA thing sound exciting!' Kate said, screwing up her face.

'Oh I don't know - maybe they'll find me a dad,' Helen said flatly.

'Well if they don't, you can always adopt Kieran, he'll be 50 next year. He's got the middle-aged shirt already - and a new knitted vest hiding away in the icy editing room. He'll soon look old enough to be the Father You Never Knew.'

'Ha-ha funny.' Helen replied deadpan, half-heartedly smiling at this old territory, the usual look of pensiveness on her face.

Kieran was straightening up his scruffy shirt, mock-offended. 'Well if I'm not wanted, I'll go get some coffee. Anyone? They both shook their heads but watched him go. Helen watched Kate's face for clues but she was good at hiding her thoughts. They sat in silence for a little while. Helen had learned that this was the best way to get Kate to talk. Being on TV, she didn't like silences.

'Anthony Adams nearly didn't accept it, you know, the deal,' Kate said, eventually. Her voice dropped to a whisper. 'Kieran told me in the hope that I'd fill him in about my date-lunch.' She caught Helen's face. 'No, I didn't tell him or you. Anyway, the Boss was livid 'cos the new investor came in flashing his cash and demanding results within the deadline. He ranted for ten minutes to one of the board on the phone - whilst I was talking to Janice. But they pulled rank. And that's when they offered him the bonus. And a huge injection of cash.'

Kieran rejoined them, rubbed his chin and sipped a black coffee. 'You telling company secrets to the minions again? Tut tut.'

Kate just shrugged. 'Course. She wants to know who gets a bite of the funding cake.'

'Well,' he said to Helen, 'let's put it this way. You get exotic trips around the world. *Late Night Late* get top A-list celebs, with a kick-over to Ki-Ka's show. The *What'sHot* trending team get several more staff. And Bob the Builder here,' he said, prodding Kate, 'gets a modest spending spree at Home Depot - maybe a couple of brand new sharpened switch blades and a trowel - they won't know what's hit them.' Kate visibly brightened. 'Easily pleased, aren't you?' He ruffled Kate's unruly blonde hair, which made parts of it flop down over her eyes again, and she smacked his hand as he tried to put it back up in her up do. He smacked hers back and they did play-fisticuffs, much to the chagrin of the two management, who were now seating themselves at the head of the table, coffees in hand. Helen elbowed the other two.

The room fell silent.

'Good afternoon, dear friends,' said one of the suited executives, standing at the top of the room. 'Exciting times ahead - changing times. As you may have heard, we have new investors on board and we have agreed a programme of changes ...'

Helen looked across to Kate and they exchanged knowing glances. Kieran did a double take at them both, smiling. By the look on his face, he knew even more than he was letting on.

With the meeting over, people piled out of the room. Kieran marched off at double speed as usual. Helen caught him up and grabbed his arm. 'Kieran, I need to ask you something.'

'I can't Helen. Not if it's the storage. The last time I came to help supervise taking all your stuff back out of storage again, I was sneezing for a week...'

'Oh God,' said Kate, passing them by, 'spare me domestic stuff. I'm off to scrape my fingernails - another date tonight. Excuse me whilst I go clean up,' and she walked away up the corridor.

'Didn't you already have a date today?' Kieran called after her, watching her bottom in the tight dungarees. She just made a gesture at him behind her back. 'Classy chick,' he said, smiling.

'She wouldn't tell *you* what happened at lunchtime either, huh?' Helen asked him.

He ignored her. '...As I was saying, if you're thinking of moving your crap again. I...'

'No, it's not that, my stuff's going to be staying in storage for a long while yet, if I'm off travelling. No... it's...' Helen looked awkward. 'Remember that debacle last year?'

'When it all went down with Victor? How could we all forget?'

'I didn't mean that. But, yes, that was also a debacle.'

'Which Kate told you it would be, if I remember rightly? I still haven't gotten over what went down myself, I'm not a fan of the old *stealing someone else's guy* thing, as well you know...' he said, then dropped his voice slightly, and leaned in a little, '... as well you know better than anybody, Helen.'

'Well anyway,' said Helen, brushing aside his comment. 'Remember when Kate helped me get my first job here? After the previous incumbent was suddenly incapacitated...'

'When the first reporter dropped dead, yes, tragic and sad. Shit happens. You got the column. What about it?'

'Well - why? Why me? It's happening again now - he could have chosen any of the other high flyers - why me?' She batted her huge blue eyes at him. 'I thought if anyone can find out, you can. Only...' She squinted her eyes at Kieran as if deciding whether to tell him the next bit. 'Ok, well - Mr Adams got a phone call as I left the room earlier today, and I caught the start of it, before he walked across and closed the door behind me. I held back outside for a while and...'

'And?'

'And I could have sworn I heard him saying my name.'

'So? Perhaps he was reporting back to the board on a successful meeting with you.'

'He didn't sound happy.'

'Anthony Adams never sounds happy. I thought you'd know that by now.'

'Yes but, I'm still wary of this whole new column. Surely things don't happen this easily? Call me suspicious but - do you have any idea if there is a catch?'

'Look, Helen, as far as I know, you got this on your own merits. Get used to it. I know your confidence had a few knocks last spring but the fuss has died down now and the world doesn't care. Maybe it's simply that you're way better than a grumpy Boss makes you *think* you are.' Kieran looked at Helen then put his hands on her shoulders. 'If I find anything out I'll let it slip to Kate and she can let it slip to you. OK?'

'OK,' said Helen, and Kieran bid her goodbye. She watched him disappear up the corridor in search of Kate.

But it wasn't OK, not really. Helen had accepted a job knowing at some point she may have to abandon it. She wanted the job and now she wanted the bonus - *oh God*, did she want the bonus. She'd missed being well off, and her designer shoe collection was fast going downhill. But had she bitten off more than she could chew?

Was she flying out to be with Alessandro because deep down she really wanted someone else to be in charge for once?

Or was it that she was simply terrified that her secret thing with heights would be exposed. How long could she could carry it off before the truth came out? She only knew with these stakes, this once in a lifetime stakes, she had to try.

Chapter four

All the way over to Italy on the plane, Helen sat safely away from a window in an aisle seat. But even so, she still kept having visions of herself strapped to the wing every time she looked outside. *Forget about spectacular stunts from high places*, she told herself, *think about Alessandro*. Alessandro - the man who not that long ago, had given her one spectacular-stunt-filled night.

She tried - and failed - to work out what she would feel when she laid eyes on him again. Especially after that last phone call. She hated not knowing. She hated not being in total control. Their encounter at the marketing conference last month - when her sister Sadie's whole life had changed - was also a major watershed in her own.

She thought back on the horrendous time last year where not only had she lost her man - well, someone else's man to be fair - but also her entire career, which had gone up in stupendous flames that lit up the whole advertising industry in New York then crashed into charred cinders. She'd had to flee yet again back to her sister's, to the temporary sanctity of the family enclave. A longer-than-normal bout of recovery, peppered as usual with the familiarity of bickering nieces, home-made flapjacks and feeling like Goldilocks in a house that was too small.

Then Helen pondered her part in 'helping' Sadie change her life - for which there was no thanks, just mountainous angst - but she couldn't really blame her in the circumstances, thought Helen.

Not working. Think of something happier.

Thank god for Kate - without Kate, sounding-board and kooky best pal, this new chapter would not have begun. Sticking her neck out further than anyone else would have done, to push for Helen to get that pivotal first job last year at TransGlobe Inc. Typical Kate. She'd been there through most of Helen's adult life, and they'd shared it all - well, almost all. College, marriage, divorce - and endless nights-in together as Kate's daughter Lucy slept upstairs, having heart-to-hearts about how to find the perfect man. Kate moaning about being a single mum and Helen moaning about being single for the millionth time.

Nope. Think of something a bit more happy than that?

Without Kate, Helen would not have been able to afford the towering designer shoes that were safely tucked in the overhead.

That's better.

Helen always travelled in her flat pumps with her one of her few remaining pristine pairs of heels ready to step into at the destination - five inches taller and suddenly a magic transformation took place within her. Whatever her mood, she could walk tall, strut proudly and be head and shoulders above most others whilst arriving in an unfamiliar place. She looked impressive, even if her insides were churning.

Only a month before, she and Sadie has been preparing for a trip to exactly the same airport she was flying into now. The shoes had definitely helped them both back then. Helen puffed up with pride. Events at the conference itself had been the icing on the cake.** It was only afterwards that the bitterness set in.

(**see Hawaiian Escape, book 1 in the trilogy).

Nonetheless, little sister Sadie's business now truly had a rescue in sight, her future certainly on an upward trajectory. Helen couldn't wait to hear about Sadie's imminent trip to Hawaii** - despite the current lack of response coming out of quaint old leafy Surrey.

Now everything on the surface seemed so promising for Helen too but she felt uneasy - she couldn't help but be suspicious. She'd never had it this easy in her life.

Sadie had been the academic. Helen had struggled at school, and then at college. Attracting boyfriends was the only thing that had always come easy to Helen - well, lovers, to be more precise - and they didn't seem to stick around very long. She furrowed her brow at the image that kept cropping up, of the latest bounty being handed to her on some enormous silver-gilded platter. *Things just don't happen this easily.* She pondered - she usually fought for everything, always had.

Helen wished she could be a bit more like her optimistic sister - go with the flow and expect the best from the universe. Instead, this recent good news had had the opposite effect - she now found herself worrying, stressing and focussing on the down-side once more, always anticipating a backfire.

Bad habit - glass half empty - really should give it up.

Talking of which, she accepted her airplane refreshments, a cool glass of white wine and a tray of airplane food she merely picked at. It didn't help being at thirty thousand feet.

Her stomach was churning now, for a multitude of reasons. The more she pondered, the more she focussed on the negative.

** *(see Hawaiian Affair, Book 2 in the trilogy)*

For a start, her column being commandeered by a simpering, fame-hungry, reality show celeb still stung - just as Helen had built up a good following and was starting to make her name.

In its place she'd accepted the glare of a pressurized spotlight, with tough shoes to fill, a deadline to meet and a domineering Boss intent on sending her on kamikaze missions around the world. And as for the massive pay-off after six months if she hit her targets - well, what if she failed? What if she didn't make them? What then? Then the plane hit some turbulence and so did Helen as her mood went from bad to worse, slowly developing a feeling of foreboding about the whole Tuscany trip - she was committed to going to Tibet now - but what if it all went wrong?

By the time the plane touched down she'd churned herself right up. At least she could begin with changing her shoes, ready for her attempt to rekindle things with the hunkiest Italian she'd ever slept with... er – met. AND slept with.

She collected her matching designer luggage from the carousel - one of the remnants of a life spent in the fast lane - and trotted out to the arrivals entrance, heart pitter-pattering in time with her heels on the concourse. Heads turned as she walked by. She concentrated hard but by now she couldn't even really remember what Alessandro looked like. Tall, dark, thick hair, gorgeous deep brown eyes, tanned skin, great cheekbones - but what else? *Weird how that happens.* But then she'd only known him fleetingly, in the grand scheme of things, and here she was expecting them to pick up where they left off. Well what if *he* wasn't? What if they couldn't? What if he didn't turn up, what if...? And suddenly there he was before her.

Standing towards the back of the crowd of sweaty taxi drivers and anxious relatives, was a tall, sophisticated Adonis, with not a hair out of place, dressed in a lilac polo shirt and smart jeans, bronzed biceps bulging below the short sleeves, holding a card in his hand which said two words - and they weren't 'Helen Parker'.

There it was on the name card – 'Tesoro mio,' – his pet name for her, the first night they'd stayed together. Well, the only night they'd stayed together - so far.

The rush of recognition spilled through her body making her heart pound faster, and she picked up the pace towards him. So far so good.

Crunch time. She knew that everything rested on the next step - the way he greeted her - it would indicate how things stood between them now. After their initial powerful explosion of passion, her surprising refusal to accept his invitation had cooled his fiery enthusiasm and things had nose-dived. Was it too late?

She was filled with anticipation as she approached him. There it was - that same chemistry, that magnetic attraction, that sparkle of recognition in his eyes.

As she reached him, she held her breath. He lowered the name card, bent down towards her and... took her cases.

Then he kissed her - on both cheeks.

Okaaayyy...

'Amore mio, so good to see you again,' he said, 'come quickly - we must walk fast, I am in short stay parking.'

'You too Alessandro, I ...'

'...Give me the other cases,' he demanded. 'Both of them.'

'Oh, it's ok, I can take this one, it's...' but he'd lifted her carry-on from her hand too, and then turned around and swept away in front of her - she had to trot to keep up in her hastily donned high heels, with the flat pumps she'd worn on the plane safely tucked out of sight.

'Come, my darling,' he called over his shoulder, 'I have a surprise for you...'

Helen jogged slightly to get level with him. 'Really? What is it?'

'*La pazienza è una virtù*' he said in Italian, 'if I tell you now, it will not be a surprise, will it? *Dai tempo al tempo, cara.*'

They reached a little crossing outside the main airport entrance, and he halted as several cabs and an airport bus breezed by. He bent his head down towards her. She lifted her lips as if to be kissed, and he just pecked her on the nose. Then he was off again and she followed in hot pursuit. *This was getting a bit awkward.* Helen wondered what on earth was going on. She'd just go with the flow - she was his guest, this was his town, and this meeting was on his terms. She made herself accept that it may be a while before she found out.

The drive back to Alessandro's home town was pleasant enough - polite even, and filled with a catch up of epic proportions - they'd not really spoken in the 2 weeks since she'd departed Tuscany in dramatic fashion - leaving behind his offer, his hurt pride and him. It had been a whirlwind in her own life since then - no sooner had she got back to New York than everything turned upside down, and off she went again. But if no-one else in the office had been surprised at the Boss's speedy turn of events, why the hell should she be. Alessandro nodded his head in agreement as she talked, giving nothing away.

Helen realised that the conference in Tuscany and that incredible one night stand might as well have been two years ago not a few weeks. Their banter was tinged with a feeling of distance - the familiarity they'd enjoyed before had drifted away, and it now felt like day-one again - a little formal, a little distant, a little cool.

He was well, thank you, his college had agreed his request for the six month sabbatical to be extended to a year, starting this term, and his plans to visit the retreat in Tibet were almost complete.

It was the trip he'd originally invited Helen on, the one which he'd gushed about when showing her the brochure on the day he'd asked her to go with him - and which she'd declined. As they pulled onto a wide road, she started to explain why she'd changed her mind, but he dismissed it. He didn't want to know, he said.

What mattered now was that she was there. Her heart leapt.

And that he had a companion for his travels, he said. Her heart fell.

There was something else, too, she knew there was, but when she enquired, he waved it away with a sideways glance and a flick of his hand. Manly, masterful... bossy. *Hmmm.*

So conversation turned to the surrounding colours, fragrances, birds and buildings, as towns gave way to villages and the land turned ever greener.

She could have told him she'd missed him and needed to see him again. But after this initial stand-offishness, she didn't. She just couldn't. Especially not since the bossiness.

'So does it feel good to be coming back out here again?' he asked, just after she took a deep breath of clean Italian air blowing on her face through the car window.

'After the urban jungle - and a long plane ride - it's wonderful.'

'It is good that you could come. And to accompany me to Tibet after all, especially considering...' he paused. 'It's good that you came.'

Then, instead of a thousand other things she could have said, she dressed-up her about-turn as having merely been the perfect opportunity to impress her Boss. *Ouch.* Damn my stupid pride, Helen thought, as the words came tumbling out before she could stop them.

'Mr Adams was thrilled with such an unusual topic for my first self-generated column,' Helen continued, feeling like she was in an interview. 'So, thank you so much for allowing me to come with you. It's quite a find, the luxury spa in deepest Tibet - with classes like that. It's a difficult place to get into isn't it - huge waiting list.'

'It is.' He seemed somewhat taken aback at her bluntness. Then almost immediately recomposed himself. 'I am glad The Try it For the First Time Club will benefit - it sounds like a brilliant concept for your women readers,' Alessandro said, coolly, his face unperturbed. Helen hated how he did that. 'I am only glad I could help. In fact...'

And then he dropped the bombshell.

'... I am only too pleased your email came when it did, as my intended companion had just informed me she could not come. So having you tag along will be a perfect substitute. And at the same time, you are able to get some work done. So everything turns out right in the end, as you say?' There was an edge to his voice she'd never heard before.

Touché.

'Alessandro - I'm so sorry I initially turned you down,' she blurted. 'It's just that I wasn't in a place I could just up-sticks and leave everything behind. And now - you see - now I don't have to. My new work can come with me.'

He listened intently and just nodded. He seemed to be mulling over what to say next. After a pause, he spoke. 'As I said, your work comes first. No further explanations are needed.' He pushed his hair back off his face and turned away from her again. He continued, an enforced lightness back in his voice. 'And what of the sister who relied upon you so heavily at the conference? What of Sadie? Is her visit to Hawaii underway?'

A pang of remembrance and nerves about making the Skype call punched Helen in the chest. 'Soon,' she said.

Alessandro knew all about Helen's meddling in Sadie's prize win - from beginning to end. He said he hoped the rift between the sisters would be short-lived.

'Will you be in contact soon?'

'Yes - I'm due to call her later. It's her birthday and - well, after what happened I'm... giving her space. You know, to get on with things under her own steam - no more interfering from big sister.' *For now anyway,* Helen couldn't help but think.

'And tell me, *cara*, how does *big sister* feel about this... enforced space?' he asked, perceptive as ever, as he took his eyes off the road for a second to look at Helen's face. She felt like he was boring into her soul - *he hasn't lost his touch*, she thought.

'You have always been so close. It must feel strange to be apart in this way.'

'It was... time. That's the only thing I can say. It was about time.' There was a sadness in her voice she could not hide, and she glanced up at him to see him nodding, but she didn't elaborate. He lapsed into thought.

She'd told him much of her background. But some parts had to remain hidden - some parts only Helen knew and not even her sister would ever find out.

Ever.

They climbed up a particularly spectacular hillside in silence. The view into the fields and glades below was breath-taking and the early summer air seemed filled with promise - and with fragrant aromas of blossom and fresh greenery.

Helen sighed. She looked sideways at the handsome profile, the slightly wavy hair - which touched his collar now. A gust of wind through the open window blew his hair back slightly and he raised his chin and took a deep breath. He was as magnificent as ever. Right on cue, he turned to smile at her, a beaming smile which lit up his whole face, before he put his foot down. They roared off into the open roads ahead, through the luscious Tuscan countryside and over the verdant hills. His smart red vintage sports car wasn't the most comfortable of rides, but perfectly fit the part for this journey back to his kingdom.

Her heart skipped a beat - and not in a good way - when she realised that after what had just happened, she had even less idea about where things stood.

Helen decided to wait until later to tackle him about it. She knew he'd been miffed and she wasn't at all surprised that in the time she'd been gone he'd found someone else to take her place - he was, after all, very eligible and deliciously charming. But the air in between them in the car still crackled with a tangible tension.

And then it hit her. Maybe he was just being kind - allowing her to come.

Maybe she *was* just filling a space.

Perhaps that's all she'd done, even on that special night with him. Helen's mind started working overtime, trying to recall what had been said when she was last with this man. She felt a little sick, not in the least because she suddenly felt terribly small - overwhelmed by memories of the past. Her last train wreck of a relationship had finally, she realised, sealed her mistrust of men in general. And Alessandro had suffered from the fall out.

Now he had changed towards her - was it really just because of turning him down? She had to find out what.

The silence between them in the car was broken by a phone call which Alessandro asked if he could take. Helen said yes, glad of some thinking time. As he spoke in the language she didn't understand but which sounded utterly magnificent to her ears, she looked at his hands on the wheel and wondered if they'd ever touch her again.

Her mind began scouring through each of her past loves wondering which moment had been the point of no return. Some of it she'd told Alessandro during their recent weekend together. He had known that her history with the opposite sex was chequered. He'd comforted her and made her feel safe. Something she'd really never felt, growing up as a maverick. It took her unawares - he'd taken her unawares, and then he'd taken her by surprise with his skills in the bedroom. Imagine being married to that.

She smiled to herself, but it didn't last long. What had she expected her chances at marriage to be, she thought? On the back of a fatherless childhood - she hadn't had the best start, thanks to her mother Grace and her hippy ways.

Helen thought about her nieces, the light of her life. Their dad had just recently cleared off too. Poor Sadie. Just as well Helen had never had kids to worry about - she'd have probably ended up a single mum like mother Grace had mostly been - like pal Kate had become - and like sister Sadie was now.

Mind you, Sadie was on a roll - perhaps destiny would bring her a tall, dark, handsome - and rich - stranger to complete her own family. And for once it would be nothing to do with Helen's machinations. It would be all Sadie's own work.

Helen was glad. It was, after all, time.

For now, Helen must focus on this next stage in her own life - and make it the best it could be. She was glad of the challenge. She felt a little sigh of tension leave her body as she thought of how being a TiFFT columnist suited her. Travel, change, variety. And how the thrilling time ahead made her feel alive.

Write the most exciting, compelling, innovative columns possible, make her tricky Boss proud of her, smash the targets and win the bonus. And not worry about men. *Simple.*

She smiled again - and this time it did last.

The breeze flowing through the car's tiny interior must have been clearing the cobwebs because another realisation hit home as she reached her conclusion.

Yes, Helen had to face facts. Although the man sitting next to her had seemed so promising, now it turns out he'd had someone else on standby! Was he just another bloody typical man? Maybe he'd rushed this woman to his bed straight after Helen had turned him down. Considering how distant he was acting now, that seemed very likely. So there it was - he was no different from the rest.

So this could be fun, or not. But it too, would pass.

Although he *was* exceptionally good looking. And fun, and good in bed.

And rich, too - it transpired - as they finally arrived at his family home. It was sprawling, a beautiful white stucco palace set in acres of multi-coloured lush gardens, high up on a hill near Siena, outside Florence, with distant views which reached for miles.

Introductions over - mostly to staff - he showed her upstairs and her heart began to pound as she realised that this was the moment of decision - which room would she sleep in. His? Another? The bedroom she slept in would indicate his intentions - wouldn't it? She soon found out. Her heart sank.

'And this is the room I asked to be specially prepared for your stay here,' he said, opening an old wooden door onto a spacious, bright room with rough plastered walls, colour-washed in terracottas and rich ochre, and a big comfortable looking four poster bed amply covered with white cushions and pillows and the most gorgeous view of the distant hills and the beautiful gardens. 'Is it not delightful?'

This was her surprise, this was it, then. She smiled at him, knowingly, but the look was lost on him, as he immediately placed her luggage on the bed and started to open it.

'Oh it's ok, I can do that, don't you worry yourself, you've done enough,' she said, pushing his hands aside and opening the locks herself and not taking no for an answer this time. 'I'll do it when you've gone back to your own room. So,' she said breezily, adopting a carefree tone, 'what's the plan for later?'

Alessandro stood back a little, a questioning flicker on his eyebrow. 'Later? Well, first, lunch - when you are ready - then later I will take you on a tour of the grounds if you would like to join me? We have a pool and you are welcome to use it.'

'I suppose you've got a gym and a cinema too?' she teased.

'The gym is on the ground floor in the annexe by the pool, yes,' he said, without blinking, 'and the home cinema is currently being replaced whilst my parents are away visiting my brother in South America. You may recall I told you he is working for a charity there?' Helen nodded, vaguely remembering something he'd talked about when they first met. He continued. 'So we have the whole of *Colline Verde* to ourselves for two nights, before we leave for Tibet. Make yourself at home. *Mi casa es su casa,*' he said, waiting for her reaction. She raised an eyebrow and then laughed.

'Mi casa es su... isn't that Spanish?'

'Yes, it is not so different from Italian, but I'm glad you noticed,' he said, a glint in the corner of his eyes. 'I will see you later, *amore mio.*' And then he hesitated, and gazed at her with brown eyes so piercing they were almost black. *Oh oh, that look again.* She felt her knees wobble. 'We have some important things to discuss after dinner tonight, Helen.'

'Yes, we probably do,' she agreed.

'Till then I will continue with my work, but I will be around if you need me - just get one of the staff to call for me - mobile phones do not work so well up here.'

'Or maybe I could Skype you using the Wi-Fi?' she joked.

He smiled, almost reluctantly - was the cool façade beginning to break down? 'Maybe,' he said, then leaned forward and almost kissed her on the mouth, but then diverted to her nose once again, before leaving the room.

Lunch was taken on the delightful sunny veranda - covered in vines and blooms, a gently breeze keeping temperatures comfortable. Helen had dressed up for it, showing off her slim legs and toned thighs in a short sun dress and strappy sandals. Not quite the designer price levels she used to buy but still elegant and attractive. At least the young waiters seemed impressed. She posed then rearranged herself, several times, for best effect should Alessandro join her on the veranda, to the amusement of the older waiter standing by the food, who stifled a grin as she crossed her legs a different way for the seventh time.

Helen waited and waited but eventually got a shrug and a nod from the waiter standing nearby which she took to mean 'begin.' It was a delicious buffet lunch with endless salads and healthy dishes, cold meats, cheeses and ciabatta bread dipped in flavoured oil and balsamic vinegar, and pretty soon Helen sat back, and pushed her plate away. She picked up her glass of chilled Chianti and admired the amazing view. A gentle breeze was blowing little wisps of her sleek blonde hair around her face, and somewhere, a piano was playing. She looked around once more, but seeing no sign of either the source of the music nor any evidence that Alessandro would be making an appearance any time soon, she took out her iPad and logged into the Wi-Fi. What she discovered soon took her mind off whether a handsome Italian was likely to be sneaking into her room anytime tonight.

It was an email from Kate, entitled 'interesting discovery.'

She sat up, looked around slightly - although quite why, she wasn't sure, as no-one would have any idea what this email would mean even if they could see it. Then she opened it up.

'Helen, ciao Bella - is that right? Anyway hope the Italian stallion is keeping you amused. Ref your chat with Kieran yesterday (beeyatch wife Claire is still monitoring his emails so as usual I'm the raspberry in the middle)' Helen smiled - she meant gooseberry of course, but she also knew that Kate did it deliberately nowadays to make Helen smile. *'I did discover something interesting about what else our Mr Anthony Adams has been up to, so I thought I'd get in touch with all this straight away. First things first - considering your state of mind at the moment, I got our lovely Damian Grant to give you a big dose of whoopass reassurance - he's actually emailed a contract for you with that amazing proposition - not the one in Brad's bar last month about hooking you up with those cowboys, but the one we discussed in the coffee shop just after you arrived back in New York. Well, he's come good. I know you'll probably say 'I won't need it', but it's there, just in case, when the six months is up. Just in case Adams does the dirty on you. Can't wait to talk to you about it.'*

That's good, thought Helen, it's always a good plan to *have back up*. And though she'd never accept a mate trying to bail her out like a charity case, it means a lot that he'd offered. And maybe even if Mr Adams doesn't 'do the dirty on me' in six months time, she thought, perhaps I can still write the book as well...

Helen decided to keep the contract to write the book in a very safe place. She then carried on reading.

'Secondly - Helen - I found out it's vital that you get that list of Martha Crowne's assignments done as soon as poss - apparently ParlourGames Channel are planning to go do them anyway and litigate later. So much for her non-compete clause.

The Boss is drafting an email which you'll get tomorrow - well his new assistant is drafting it whilst he struts about in his office being a dictator.

As opposed to just being a dick.

But basically, expect your six months to get even more hectic.

Oh and you're never going to believe who's rumoured to have been on the golf course with Mr A....... (Is that enough dots?)... The mystery investor! Still a mystery, but his identity is getting closer, as is the reason he's so interested in your column ...'

Helen took out the clasp holding her hair in a messy but sexy up-do, poured herself some more wine, sat back on the comfortable chair and began to read.

Chapter five

Later on - after cogitating for a while on the contents of Kate's email - and the urgent one 'from the office of Anthony Adams' - Helen decided the net effect was that it was mainly good news, and she'd finally relaxed. Especially now that she had the luxury of a plan B - back-up - courtesy of Damian Grant. She'd spent a productive afternoon in the sunshine, on the internet researching all kinds of extra info for her upcoming TiFFTs and was now sitting at the little desk just inside her bedroom suite, feeling the warm breeze on her skin and sipping ice-cold, home-made, 'proper' lemonade.

Diversity was the aim, according to the *official* brief, which naturally had no reference to 'sexing up,' just in case it got in the wrong hands. And Helen now had bookings for all sorts of fascinating experiences - and not just ones in which she might die. From an elephant ride to driving a classic car, from tracing your ancestral roots to wake-boarding, the assignments were stacking up before her. Let alone all the events that involved being up high somewhere - which she didn't want to think about just yet as it gave her palpitations. And finally, right at the back of the list, for fun she added the best TiFFT of all - 'find a good man.'

Huh. Maybe not in this life - not the way Alessandro was acting. Not after the news about Stand-By Woman. Still it would be a nice trip to Tibet - Helen was determined that she'd keep it simple and if no ties were what he wanted, it would be indeed be no-strings attached. She'd stopped being anybody's puppet a long time ago - so that worked just fine for her. She was still in the high heeled shoes and she felt her old confidence filling her veins.

Now that's what you call a pep talk, Helen.

After bringing forward as many of the original assignments as she could - to thwart Martha Crowne's attempts to upstage Helen's column - the months ahead were gradually being packed out on a very tight schedule - and it was looking increasingly Alessandro–free. He'd invited her to Tibet. Only Tibet. Nothing after that had been discussed again since the last time she was here. So she'd be off again afterwards as usual - unless… unless… *Don't be silly Helen,* she told herself. He hadn't even come to say hi since they arrived.

Having realised that, Helen sipped her drink. Surely he can't be that busy? The straw made a gurgling noise as she got to the bottom of the crystal glass and she stopped gazing out the window at the beautiful gardens and got back to business. Next item on her agenda? Sister's birthday call.

Yes, more important, more pressing, even more so than finding out where Alessandro was, was planning tonight's Skype call to her sister. She moved back out onto the terrace to tan her legs some more whilst she mulled it all over.

Despite the heat of the sun, Helen felt a shiver go down her spine when she thought back to that showdown after Tuscany, and Sadie's ultimatum.

Perhaps it was for the best - Sadie's new found thirst for independence was spurring her on like never before. *Maybe my work is done,* thought Helen. Her sister had never been so driven. Not just shaking loose from Helen's 'older sister guidance' but also repelling any kind of claim that she wasn't capable of running her own life - let alone her health food business.

Helen found herself welling up with pride. The fact that Sadie was due to go to Hawaii on her own - imminently - was testament to the fact that Helen's plan had worked - for all its clumsiness. For Sadie at least, the new era was so far a good one. So, hopefully she'd be in a good mood tonight, no doubt out celebrating her birthday at her favourite restaurant with the girls - and their mother. Helen frowned a little. She was keen to see and talk to Sadie, but she hoped she wouldn't have to play nicey-nicey with their mum for a little while yet. Grace had given Helen a massive dressing down on the morning she'd flown back to New York, and it was still ringing in her ears. So - find a good spot to make the call, and... make the call. Actually *make* the call. Ok. Good plan.

Then, feeling the stirrings of hunger - and not just for food *dammit* - she couldn't put it off any longer - time for an Alessandro-hunt.

Helen came off the sun-kissed terrace with its cool jasmine and honeysuckle-tinged breeze and went inside the ancient stone building, immediately feeling a drop of some ten degrees compared to the outside heat. The further she went inside the house, the cooler it felt, and she was glad she'd brought her little cotton cardigan with her. As she pulled it over her shoulders, she heard once again the vague sound of piano music - a sonata she recognised but couldn't name - and followed the gentle, enchanting tune down the old stone corridors to the other side of the house. There, in a huge open lounge, stood a grand piano and the source of the sonata - Alessandro himself.

Helen just stood there for a short while, utterly enthralled.

Eventually he became aware of her gaze and looked up, coming out of a classical music trance. After a fleeting moment where he seemed to forget who she was, his face broadened into a beam and he stood up and came over to greet her.

'Tesoro mio,' he said, the term of endearment somehow seeming far less meaningful than when he had first used it, 'you like the music - my little *concerto*?' The crinkles were back in his eyes.

'Yes, Alessandro, I had no idea you played that well. Are there no end to your talents?'

'It is nothing. Our whole family are very musical. My brother the saxophone, my mother the flute. My father - he likes his percussion, he is not quite so - how you say - skilled. Skilful. We perform at family functions. Do you play?'

'Oh well, actually, I'm very good,' said Helen, sitting herself down at the piano and taking a stance like the ones she'd seen impresarios do just before a major performance. Then she attacked the keys and the sound of the beginners' 'chopsticks' theme filled the air. He laughed, she laughed, and finally the tension was broken. *Thank god.*

The tour of the grounds soon afterwards was peppered with stories of his happy childhood there, annual garden parties, a sense of belonging within the local community, a sense of significance. The familial solidarity was totally alien and the overall effect on Helen was to remind her that she was, quite simply, a nomad. It must have shown on her face, because when they reached the shade of a huge rhododendron bush with overhanging branches bursting with fuchsia coloured blossoms, he turned to face her and crooked his little finger underneath her chin, raising her face to his.

'What is it, Helen. Are you too hot? Have we been too long outside in the sunshine?'

She twisted away slightly as she replied. 'No, it's not that, not at all. I'm completely covered in factor 30. Even my white bits. And especially my white bits.' She smiled up at him and there was a twinkle of amusement in his eyes. 'No it's just - I'm very happy you had such a wonderful childhood - it's lovely to hear.'

'It's just that it's so very far removed from your own experience, yes?' he asked. Helen nodded, and looked away, his sudden tenderness bringing a tear prickling to the corner of her eye. 'I remember what you said to me, that night at the conference. Well, most of it,' he said, his voice becoming lower and more breathy. 'The rest was, how you say, lost in the moment.'

'Or lost in translation,' said Helen, smiling, and blinking the tear away. 'Anyway,' she breezed, 'tonight I must Skype with Sadie, and wish her a happy birthday. She doesn't know I'm here - it will be a surprise to her.' *So will my Skype call*, thought Helen. *If I get through.*

'Well then, my sweet, let us go get ready to dine. Our chefs are preparing a feast for your first night here. I will be dressing for dinner - I would be happy if you wanted to, too?' he said, eyebrows raised, glancing at her sundress, indicating with a little trepidation that he wasn't sure if she'd brought the right outfits. But there was one thing Helen was good at - it was dressing to impress. All her years in corporate entertainment had got that down to a fine art - and her black number would be a knockout tonight.

Then after dinner she could Skype her sister. Hopefully she'd accept the call. If ever she was going to, it would be on her birthday, surely? Helen thought. Then she realised she was actually nervous. Nervous about a dinner date with him? Or nervous about contacting her own sister. What was the world of Helen Parker-Todd coming to…?

'You look stunning,' Alessandro said later, as Helen entered the main drawing-room of the 16th century home they called *Colline Verde* - green fields. She was wearing her Moschino gown set to 'stun.' It was the only one not in storage that travelled well enough to take half way round the world - and onwards - it could turn out to be essentially 'a back-packing holiday.' She would be going back to New York every so often, but for now, she'd packed what she could. So there she stood in a simple black shift dress, which dipped at the back and followed her every curve, displaying the *magic confidence of the* shoes - from her single pair of elegant black kitten heels. Those as well as the towering pink heels she'd changed into on the plane, had just had to come with her.

Helen had good genes - according to Sadie who had almost always complained about being heavier and curvier. Plus - one upside at least of not having seen childbirth - Helen's body retained a youthful shape and an air of vitality brought about through careful eating and decades of stressful jobs, living on nerves. Those nerves were jangling now as she approached the hunky Italian who was once again taking Helen's breath away, dressed in a light cotton designer jacket, dark stylish jeans, plus shiny black Italian shoes. Damian Grant would have loved those, Helen thought. He'd have loved Alessandro too - he'd have fought Helen for a stud like this, given half the chance. The year round

Italian tan made Alessandro's handsome face even more striking, and it contrasted starkly with the crisp white shirt.

'And you look very handsome,' she said, reaching him, as he took her hand and kissed it gracefully. Her heart skipped a beat at the physical contact. Especially with those lips. It was still a long way from the unreserved passion from the night of the conference, though - a lot can change in two weeks.

'I have something,' he said, and Helen waited, her heart skittered, instantly thinking back to the bedroom Olympics, as he reached inside his pocket. But he produced a small, square, solid looking box. If she wasn't mistaken, it was a...

'It is not a ring,' he said bluntly. And in an instant the skittering stopped. *Well what is it then?*

He opened the box, and without first showing her, he took out a small brooch in the shape of what looked like two little cymbals attached by a tiny cord - made entirely of burnished brass with the remnants of red enamelling still showing on the 'cord.'

He reached down and pinned it to her dress, gently, his fingers fluttering over her skin. 'It's a Tibetan charm,' he said, 'an image representing the famous singing bowls.'

'Thank you, if I don't say so later, I had a really nice time today,' she said, as he took her hand and kissed it, then held it against his chest and looked into her eyes, searching.

'You can wear it for our whole trip but if you don't mind please return it to me when we return home. Please look after it, it is very precious to me.'

Oh right.

For a moment he hesitated, as if he was going to share something important but then he dropped her hand and gestured towards the drinks on a table.

'May I get you a pre-dinner aperitif?' he asked, opening a Martini and making a cocktail, whilst listing the choices available. She chose the same as his, and they took their drinks out onto the terrace. In the distance, the sun was moving towards the top of the highest hills far away, and there on the hillside was the silhouette of the ruins she and sister Sadie had seen whilst at the conference - they really *hadn't* been that far away from Alessandro's home.

'Tell me again about the ruins?' Helen said, and Alessandro regaled her with the story of the San Galgano roofless Gothic Abbey and how a mysterious sword in the stone - preserved there since the 12th century - is believed to have been the original source of the legend of King Arthur. It was very romantic, as his voice took on a mellifluous timbre, hypnotic, melodic and soothing.

'The ruins would make a lovely backdrop for my call to Sadie later,' Helen said.

'*Bella*, then do it now, before the sunlight dips too low - it will be too dark after dinner. Come walk with me to the arbour on the other side of the garden - you can see it even more clearly, the signal just about works there. It will be worth it to see your sister's face. If...' he paused, '... assuming I am permitted to accompany you for the call?' He shifted a little awkwardly.

Now it was Helen's turn to hesitate. This was a big deal, and he seemed to know it. He'd been there when Sadie had hit the roof over Helen's decision to be economical with the truth - ok, to lie - to her sister in order to manipulate events her way. Now, he could probably see the concern in Helen's eyes. He took her hand again.

'Or I can just lead you to the location and then give you privacy, if you prefer...'

Helen didn't know what she preferred. She'd prefer to rip his clothes off there and then, if she had her way to find out if the rest of his body was as warm as his hand. But that wasn't currently an option - and might never be again, considering how aloof he'd been acting. It was a shame, since he seemed to have changed overnight from the passionate person she'd almost fallen for, into a slightly stand-offish stranger once again. Only his warm touch on her bare shoulder hinted at the connection they'd once shared.

It made Helen sad, but she'd brought this on herself and now she had to suffer the consequences. Anything she could do to help ease the situation wouldn't go amiss, she thought. 'No it's ok, you know most of what's happened. I just have to warn you, though, what I say to Sadie will be for her own good, and mine, and for the sake of an easy life considering my mother will be sitting nearby.'

'And you're still not talking to her, either?' he asked.

Helen just shrugged. 'It's complicated,' she said.

'Families always are, my darling, families always are. But they are one of life's most precious things - which could be snatched away in an instant.' Helen swung round to see a vague look of nostalgia skitter across his face then disappear. He went on, 'Now send a text to say you will connect in fifteen minutes, by which time we will be at the highest point in the garden with the perfect view beyond. Then you can talk for ten minutes and we will be back down in time for chef to serve.'

'Um. ...OK.' Helen fleetingly pondered a witty comeback warning him against bossing her around, with his 'to-the-minute' command, then decided it was easier just to do it anyway. Besides, if Sadie knew she was going to call and still didn't answer, at least she'd tried.

Fifteen minutes later, the face of her sister came into view and Helen's heart leapt - she'd answered.

'Sadie!' she began, then sang a very bad version of '*hippo birdie two ewes*'. Sadie pointed the screen at her girls Abi and Georgia, and mother Grace who frowned then smiled, told them to say *hi* briefly, and then said she was taking her laptop out to the foyer of the restaurant, to get a clearer picture on Skype. Helen began to tell Sadie what had happened in New York, and what her old pal Kate and Damian Grant had done for her.

'A book? Not a column?' Sadie asked.

'I, er... can't rely on the signal being good enough in the places I'll be going, to meet regular column deadlines,' Helen explained, the signal flickering a little, 'But you never know. I'm going to give it a go - plus the Boss in New York has changed me onto a new blog I can do at the same time. Are you there Sadie?' The picture juddered briefly before it became clear again. 'And some of the challenges will take weeks on end.'

Helen knew she wasn't giving Sadie the full run down, but Sadie had enough on her plate right now. This simpler version was fine - it would mean Sadie wouldn't worry about her older sister's life.

'What did you say it's called again?' Sadie asked.

'Try it For the First Time club!' Helen said, and laughed. 'TiFFT for short! Damian Grant's got such faith in me, it's amazing. He heard what happened with his brother and me in Tuscany - said he wanted to make amends.'

That was a simpler explanation than having to waste a Skype call going through Mr Adams' devotion to bullet-breasted, column-stealing celebrities, six-month deadlines and theoretical bonuses that may never happen - let alone all the shenanigans to do with the previous columnist, Margo. Nor sharing the anxiety Helen was feeling about assignments involving heights. '...So I'm off, sis. I'm doing what *you* told *me* to do for a change!'

There, simple.

That would do fine, Helen told herself, considering the 'big chat' they'd had on the plane home from Tuscany about Sadie being left alone to do her own thing, without Helen interfering.

Helen had thought it all through. If she could pull off the Boss's challenge in six months, she'd get the bonus, then write the book too. Cake - eat it. Plus it was reassuring knowing she had the back-up offer from Damian in black and white, to fall back on.

More importantly - Sadie would never need to know that Helen had lost yet another job - this time to a celebrity who'd made her name on the size of her bottom. Alessandro, however, seemed to be curious. She saw him out of the corner of her eye, raising his eyebrows.

The chat with Sadie was warm and friendly but there was just a tinge of tension between them. Helen knew it, and Sadie clearly knew it too. Maybe that's what Mr Super-sensitive here, was picking up.

'I'm so pleased! Really. This is just the break you need,' Sadie replied. *And just the space we need, by the look on her face,* thought Helen. Sadie continued, 'So when do you go?'

'Well that's what I wanted to talk to you about,' Helen said.

'Oh, oh, I know that look,' Sadie grinned.

'You see, I've already gone. I'm here. It's begun,' Helen said, and she swung the iPad round so Sadie could see what was behind her. Slowly, the distant ruins on the hillside came into view - the ruins Sadie and Helen had seen during the conference, and then a little more turning and there beside her, in the shot, was Alessandro.

'Happy birthday, *Bella*,' he said, and blew a kiss to Sadie. Exactly as predicted, Sadie's face was a picture - her jaw dropped and her eyebrows shot up. If Helen heard right, she even gasped too. *Bingo!* Helen swung the camera back round again and made a cheeky face and gave a big thumbs up to Sadie.

'Oh Hells, I'm so pleased for you - you go for it girl!' Sadie said. The signal started to break up again. Helen jiggled the screen a bit but it didn't seem to make any difference. She looked at Alessandro and he shrugged. Then Helen heard Sadie's voice, even though she couldn't see her very well. 'Did you want to speak to mum?' Sadie asked. The picture came back suddenly.

Helen hesitated and then shook her head, knowing neither she nor Grace would have much to say, not yet. 'I'm losing you. Next time, maybe. Oh, and Sadie, just to let you know, I've rented out my flat again and Crystal's putting some of my remaining stuff in storage for me. But she'll be bringing you a couple of things I can't risk getting damp in my lock up. Is that ok?'

'What are they?' asked Sadie.

'My best designer suits and the rest of my most precious shoes. Keep them under lock and key, ok? Apart from those ones I said you can use.'

'Oooo - well maybe as a penance, now I know where the expensive stuff is, I'll have to borrow them - once I lose a bit of weight.'

'Yeah, I won't be too worried about that then,' said Helen, laughing. Sisterly teasing - that was a good thing. Then the sound went all metallic and they said their goodbyes.

'Good luck, sis, on your escape to Hawaii,' Helen said. 'You might not hear from me for a while - after Tuscany we're off to Alessandro's retreat in Tibet, but I'll check in every so often. And remember - no news means I'm having fun! I've got a year to come up with as many TiFFT's as I can!'

And the first one, thought Helen, *is getting a grip on this bending the truth thing.*

'Safe travels,' Sadie said, just before the signal froze and Helen was gone.

A new era indeed. For both of them.

Alessandro was sensitive enough to leave Helen to her thoughts on the slow walk back to the house afterwards. Helen felt a dull ache from being left out of an important family occasion - like she always did - with all the family there at the restaurant together and Helen thousands of miles away like the prodigal daughter.

Eventually Alessandro spoke, his tone gentle and warm. 'Things will all work out, will they not? Family blood is thick, and there was genuine affection in your sister's eyes. Every family has their little problems.' He placed his warm hand in the small of Helen's back. She leaned into him and shivered a little as they walked, and just nodded, staring straight ahead as she negotiated the stone pathway back to the terrace where they were to dine. 'So a book deal - as well as the online column you told me about?'

'It's... complicated,' Helen replied. 'But yes, I have got the chance of a book deal too. I... it was simpler to explain it that way - I just didn't want my sister to worry. She needs a clear head to salvage her own business, free from worry - including about her errant big sis possibly not having a job in six months' time.'

'I understand. And she will not mind if it is in order to spare her from worrying.'

'Exactly. You have understood the situation perfectly, Alessandro.'

'That is because I understand *you*, *Mio cara*,' he replied, holding out his elbow for her to tuck her hand under, as they walked along the final section of pathway with overhanging greenery and birdsong filling the air, as the sun finally set behind the distant hills.

Dinner was delicious - Papardelle pasta with wild boar sauce, and Florentine steak - and Helen learned all about the history of the place, from the time of his great, great, great, grand-parents right through to the present day. How they were all intrinsically involved employing the local community in the vineyards, up until the legacy Alessandro's father wanted his sons to leave behind. The wine served at dinner was vintage *Brunello di Montalcino*, and Helen appreciated hearing about *this dense, robust red - one of the most sought after wines in the world.* It seemed like at least the wine recognised it was a special occasion even if Alessandro's coolness didn't. He then told her more about his family.

'I wish I'd known my paternal heritage,' she said in the end. 'I never even knew who my father was - mum told me she had *several choices*,' she said with an apologetic shrug. When she saw the look on his face she was persuaded to tell him the full tale.

Helen's father was known only to the gods, not even Grace knew which one of the transient lovers he'd been, and none of them could *stay on the scene, man.* Eventually, it was little sister Sadie's dad, George, who'd finally come back permanently - shaven, short-haired and in a comfortable family hatchback, promising stability with his new job. Within weeks he'd convinced Grace to marry him. He'd tolerated bolshy Helen but idolised Sadie, a bewitching seven year old. Suddenly her mum had a husband and her lucky sis had her father figure - a real one, instead of a nearly-teenage Helen doing the job - and they all moved into their new home. For Helen, this unwelcome competition disrupted the tightly-knit little nucleus forever and she shunned her new step-father, much to Grace's disgust. Things came to a head on a trip to Paris, which George had saved up for, for months - when Helen had inexplicably threatened to throw herself off the Eiffel Tower - even beginning to climb to prove she was serious. Things had been tricky at home after that. Alienated, and refusing George's suggestion of therapy, Helen had thrown herself into her college studies - and her college sweetheart.

She'd not gone into too much detail with Alessandro previously about her first short-lived marriage, and she didn't add much now - apart from the length of it and how old she and Jason were. She couldn't blame it all completely on him - they were 'simply too young, *cara*,' Alessandro observed, and he was probably right. That had certainly been a contributing factor.

'But when your first love is ending it always hits hard, doesn't it,' she asked, and he nodded vigorously.

At one point she hadn't thought she'd ever recover. But then tragedy struck, and ten years stability of life back at home had been turned upside down once more, leaving Sadie once more without a role model. Her father George had died, leaving Grace alone once again, naturally. Sadie was bereft, went wild at college, and Helen tried once more to fill the gap. But it didn't last long - a few years later Sadie had been married herself, her own family on the way and Auntie Helen, not wanting to be around smelly nappies all the time, had begun regularly escaping to build her international marketing career.

'And you pretty much know the rest,' she said. 'The tail end of a glittering career, anyway.'

'And now the launch of a new one,' Alessandro said, raising his glass in a toast. Helen smiled, and joined him. 'To new beginnings,' he said. Helen finished the delicious wine and put down her crystal goblet carefully on the table. She could feel Alessandro's eyes on her. She was wide-eyed, but not yet legless.

'Come walk with me, *carissima*,' he said, holding out his hand to her. She slipped hers into his and felt the heat of his palm. A little sizzle coursed through her veins but she tried not to show it, merely followed him out to the terrace, and down a little pathway to the arbour with its small stone wall and colourful trailing plants cascading out from the gaps in the ancient mortar. Helen felt a little frisson of nerves run up her spine then down her arms, and the hairs on her skin stood on end. *What was it with this man?*

'You are cold, Helen? Shall we return for your jacket?' he asked.

'No,' she said, *although you could have given me yours,* she thought to herself. 'I'll be ok for now - you can always warm me up if you want to.'

'So tell me about this running away,' he replied, either ignoring it or not hearing it. Helen swallowed. 'It seems you and I have quite opposite paths in our lives, leading us to where we are today. I want to know more about you - what made you who you are?'

They discussed Helen's many jobs and the reasons why she'd moved on each time - something better, more exciting, more money. Or a bad relationship which had taken her back to Sadie's -

where the spare room always had some of Helen's clothes and shoes. Until the girls were bigger and demanded their own room each. Then Helen had had to decamp to their mother's - *eurgh* - but the shoes stayed at Sadie's. If their mother had a man in tow, it was back to sharing a room with one of her nieces, much to their father Stuart's distaste. But once he'd left home for good, it was a given that Helen could return on a regular basis.

'It's kind of symbolic, I guess, wherever I lay my shoes, that's my home,' she said. He nodded, then took a deep breath and turned to face her. *Oh–oh.*

'When I first met you, Helen, I thought that maybe our encounter would be the pivotal moment - just as with the stars - there is a moment of explosion and then nothing is ever the same again, as a new super-nova is created, burning brightly on all around it.' *Gotta love a paleo-astronome like Alessandro.* He went on, his voice dripping with carefully chosen tones. 'But when you returned to New York and I did not hear from you... well, maybe it was not meant to be.'

'You seemed to take the being turned down thing pretty badly,' said Helen bluntly. *Gotta love a straight-talking high-achiever like Helen.* 'I can't be the first woman to have refused your wishes? Surely it's happened before?'

'Yes, once,' he said, beginning to slowly walk on once more. 'But I swore if someone did not want to be with me, I would walk away immediately - even if it meant I never saw them again.'

'But what exactly happened to you, Alessandro? What happened to make you feel that way?' Helen asked him, and she heard him take a slightly longer breath. His face was, as usual, unreadable. They stopped walking and he turned to lean his elbows on the ancient stone wall, gesturing for her to join him.

The distant hills were bathed in moonlight, faint aromas of jasmine and night time dampness tickling the air, and Helen could feel the warmth of his shoulder against hers.

'It's a long story,' he said. 'Maybe for another day. Suffice it to say that as I told you - on our night together - that I was married once, and had a family once, well, as you can see, I do not now. I am a single man - again. And the pain of it was very strong. I buried myself in my studies, in business affairs, and until that moment with you - until that night - I had not wanted to risk heartache again because of what had happened to me the last time...' he trailed off and pushed away from the wall, indicating that it was time to walk on, then marched a few paces without waiting for Helen. She jogged a little to catch him up. She was starting to shiver a little bit now, so was glad of the movement.

'Did you... was she...'

'Helen - would you like to take a nightcap and I will play another sonata for you? It helps me relax - it helps me forget,' he said, whirling around to face her and taking both her hands in his.

'Yes,' she said, resigned that she wouldn't find out any more tonight. 'Race you!' And she gathered up her skirts and even in her precious kitten heels he let her beat him back up the path to the terrace once more. She was beginning to warm up now, thank goodness. She kicked off her heels and they stood laughing together, catching their breath, as the clouds parted in the sky and the moon shone brightly on their two glowing faces.

'Hug?' she said, swinging her shoes from her fingertips.

And with that Alessandro embraced her - a big warming hug, followed by the tiniest, briefest kiss on the lips. 'Come,' he said, 'Bach awaits.'

Just before bedtime, after a pleasant evening listening to concertos and being serenaded with some fifties big band sounds, Alessandro pecked Helen on the lips lightly, and said good night, so she wandered down to his office where she had permission to use the phone to call New York.

'Parker!' came the booming voice on the other end of the phone. 'I got news for you! I felt bad for having to tell you to speed up the assignments so I got you an assistant - now don't get excited, she's only an intern on a free test run, I mean on a trial period of employment. But she's your point of contact here now, to help get this thing done.' Anthony Adams spoke without stopping for breath until finally she heard an inhalation - Helen could imagine the vapours being breathed into the handset as he sat in his huge office on the 26th floor. 'Her name is Cheryl,' he began, and Helen's heart sank.

'Good God, no,' said Kate a short while afterwards. 'Cheryl Goodman's finally wormed her way into the office on an *official* basis?'

'Yes,' said Helen dolefully into the webcam. 'Recruitment by chocolate. And the worst thing is, she sounded really helpful when he put her on the phone. She's going to take my schedule and help book the assignments, handle the expenses, all my confirmations, and generally be the conduit between me and the Boss - I won't even have to deal with him until the final edit's sent back to me for approval and each TiFFT gets posted online. She'll even resize the photos I take, to help the web team. AND she's not even getting paid. It's quite a turn up for the books, if I'm honest.'

'Well don't you go wetting your pants too much, because let me tell you something - Miss Fancy-knickers is already going round telling everyone she's his new executive assistant. Not *yours*, his. The water-cooler drums are hot with the gossip. You've only got to drop one of the balls you're juggling and he'll be putting her on stand-by to replace you. Don't show any weaknesses. Just watch yourself with that one, OK?'

'OK I will,' said Helen, swallowing hard. Whatever Kate's talents, she was pretty accurate about people. Now, what about that question Helen had been meaning to ask... 'So when do you and Kieran set off on this latest jaunt? Separate bedrooms?'

'Of course! You don't think wife-zilla will let him come anywhere near me in his little white sleep-vest do you?' Helen laughed and Kate then proceeded to tell Helen all about the plans for her next shoot for the Real Grown Ups' Guide. But before Helen could ask more about Kieran, she changed the subject swiftly. Instead, she took great joy in informing Helen about the latest gossip from TransGlobe towers - apparently, Ki-Ka had finished recording a show and invited the guest - a young, drop-dead gorgeous, B-list actor - for a lunchtime drink but the actor had paid more attention to Brad the barman than to Ki-Ka, much to Brad's amusement. She'd left in a huff, apparently.

'Is it bad of me to feel glad about that?' asked Helen.

'Course not - it's why I told you!' They laughed and Helen felt the tension in her stomach ease - she hadn't realised how wound up she'd been all evening. They'd already discussed Alessandro, not that there was much to tell - yet. And now Helen asked Kate how her dating thing was going, and it was Kate's turn to be tight-lipped once more. They finished with Helen reminding Kate what to say to Sadie if she called - about the book deal, not just the column.

'Not that Sadie will ask - she'll be far too busy for a while. When I get my bonus, though, she'll be the first person I treat.'

'How do you know she'll *want* you to treat her? And how do you know she won't be the one treating *you* in six months' time?' Kate said, raising one eyebrow at her old friend. 'Teasing!' she quipped, then she bid Helen goodbye and quipped about going off to record a feature about changing a ball-cock.

Helen was still smiling at the image that created when she finally got in bed after a long, long day. But as soon as she turned out the light, it was a different vision that flooded into her mind.

Alessandro.

His touch, his voice, his smell - even the male toiletries he'd left in this room. And his fingers - ohhh, his fingers, as they danced over the piano keys.

She remembered the last time they were in bed together - when he had played her body in a similar way. He'd given her a challenge, that night - to be subservient to his needs - '*amore mio*, tonight you are to give yourself over to destiny, to my command, to do what I wish without question...' Helen had been more turned on than she could remember in a long, long while.

She replayed the scene in her mind, and as the gentle breeze blew through the open window, she felt herself stirring - stirring to the memory of Alessandro's body next to hers. Helen bared her breasts to the breeze, as she lay in the bed, caressing herself gently, making her nipples harden, as he had done. She felt tortured - he was so near and yet so very, very far. And not just physically. So unlike the last time... *'And, tonight, Tesoro mio, tonight I want you to act as though you are an innocent. Sure, you are a woman of the world, you will have made love, but act as though you have never - never - done the things I am to do with you this evening. Can you play along with my wishes, my darling?'* Ohhhh yessss, she'd played along all right.

Outside her door, Alessandro stood with his hand on the door handle, but stopped when he heard a faint moan from inside. He took his hand off, holding it in the air as if to say to himself 'stop'. Then he took another big breath, shook his head slightly, and walked back to his own room once more.

Over in New York, Mr Adams was no longer sitting in his high chair at his big desk - he was on the other side, seated in the guest chair. Someone was in his place - raised above him, as usual. Adams had to look up somewhat, to the person in his chair. He looked red faced as ever.

'Well,' he was saying, 'satisfied now?'

The person said nothing. And Anthony Adams went ever so slightly more red.

Chapter six.

Tibet was nothing like the old YouTube clips Helen had seen - nor the Brad Pitt film. They journeyed an hour and a half from the airport to Lhasa, with its ever growing concrete jungle and neon signs, men in smart suits and ties, and kids in logoed baseball caps and football shirts playing soccer in the street; which contrasted starkly with the other side of the city - tiny cobbled lanes lined with street vendors selling locally made Tibetan foods beside traditionally dressed locals doing their praying thing in the shadow of the remaining monasteries and temples that weren't destroyed in the 1950's, and women carrying bags on their backs full of cut firewood that were nearly as big as they were.

'The praying regime looks more like a keep fit session,' quipped Helen, as she watched a group of people all in rows, crouching and scooping the floor then laying prostrate then standing to reach for the sky then repeating it again.

'Many people still traditional here - and yes, it keeps you fit!' shouted back their guide and driver, over the hubbub of the nearby market stalls.

Then they were up and out towards the luxury hillside spa, and en route they passed traditional Tibetans in their colourful ponchos and several groups of farmers with their animals, plus the occasional Monk in their dark reddish robes. Helen nudged Alessandro when she saw two of them walking along ignoring each other, both on mobile phones. Ancient cliff side buildings cropped up with no visible means of reaching them and lots and lots of colourful signs and banners, some painted on slabs of rock in the hills, had both foreigners snapping away with their cameras at the signs of old Tibet. But the road was new, and the van was air-conditioned.

'Good job my assignment wasn't to live like a local,' Helen called to Alessandro, who was entranced, drinking in the views, eager not to miss a moment. They were both obviously feeling exhilarated, pointing things out all the way from the airport, from the suburban influence of the West, with familiar advertising icons on display, to the solitude of the high farms and temples.

Helen was well aware of the history of the country - there was so much of it online and she liked to do thorough research. Also annoyingly she'd been sent some very useful links by Cheryl and had begrudgingly had to favourably fill in the feedback form she was sent by the Boss. They included finding out how many languages and dialects were spoken in Tibet, how many hundreds of thousands were living in exile since the uprising in 1959 - including over a hundred thousand in Dharamsala in India along with the Dalai Lama; and how to make Himalayan Brown Barley Curry. Vegetarian Sadie would have been very impressed.

In a quiet part of the journey with nothing but endless fields and the occasional dwelling, Helen turned to Alessandro, who had been unusually quiet for most of the journey. 'I meant to say thanks - for getting my visa sorted out - Cheryl the intern said that it usually takes at least ten days.'

He didn't look at her, just kept staring out of the window. 'It pays to have friends in high places,' he said, then turned and smiled, and immediately turned away again.

'Are - are you ok?' she asked, feeling the slight awkwardness that had reared its head again once they'd touched down at Lhasa airport. 'Are you sure you won't tell me about the text you got earlier?' She was sure it was after that that his mood changed.

'I'm fine - I am just... overwhelmed at the sadness of the true Tibetans. I will be fine when I reach the spa. At least the spa works hard to support local people. You will see. Anyway, *mio caro*, I have booked us some interesting sessions already - you will enjoy them very much,' he said, pasting on a beaming smile as he squeezed her hand.

Oh will I? She thought - nice to have the choice - not. As her irritation bubbled under, she thought back to the conversation at their final dinner last night. Or was it the night before? She'd been travelling for so many hours she'd lost all track of time. But she hadn't forgotten the subjects he'd wanted to discuss.

Alessandro had issued another challenge to Helen - one she had agreed to, since she really had no choice.

'Can you put yourself in my hands this trip?' he'd asked, and sadly for Helen, it wasn't what she initially hoped he meant. 'With the itinerary? To save me having to go over obvious information in absolute detail?' He'd been super-organised since she'd said yes to coming back to Tuscany and made all the travel plans. He'd emailed her the summary and sorted the documents and settled the payment for Helen's half with Cheryl Goodman at the office - who had apparently been 'very efficient with the transfer and very pleasant on the phone' - *damn her*. He wasn't intending to accept Helen's offer to reimburse him, but she'd insisted, especially since it was going on company expenses. And why should he even expect to pay for her anyway - it's not like she was skint, or like they were partners...

Not partners.

Helen had swallowed down her immediate panic at the thought of someone else holding the passports, and said, yes, *of course* she would trust him entirely to handle all the finer points.

If only he knew how monumentally difficult that was for Missus Independent here - Missus Need to Be In Charge. She felt the questions rising up in her throat and quashed them, over and over again. All the 'hows' and 'whens' and 'wheres' that she would ordinarily know like the back of her hand on a journey like this. It took a big leap of faith for someone like Helen to do that but done it she had, and to be honest, she was so far pretty proud of herself. Especially with something as important as the visa, but yes, he'd sorted it as promised and they'd sailed through the airport arrivals.

However.

She was really, really, *really* finding it hard right now to button her lip over his choosing *all* of their activities for this journey - and worse - liaising with bloody Cheryl bloody Goodman over which ones were right for Helen's column! With her blood just slightly boiling whenever she thought of the control being taken away from her and making a mental note to give *The Intern* a huge piece of her mind once she found a Wi-Fi signal for her laptop or a computer she could Skype on, or even - old school - a *telephone* she could use, Helen swallowed down her bad feeling - Kate would have called it 'disgruntled-ment' - and looked back out of the window.

Let's just hope he'd chosen some fabulous activities - if he had, she could rest easy. But until she found out, she was jittery for the rest of the journey. And he remained as pensive as he ever was.

Great start she thought to herself, as the driver, sensing the air of tension, turned on some sort of Tibetan singing bowls music on his car CD player and began to hum. Then he changed it to Frank Sinatra. Helen just smiled.

'So,' said a lithe young yoga instructor-come-spa-guide once they'd arrived at the swish luxurious reception and had their luggage whisked away, 'what do you hope to achieve this visit?' He was very zen, and had an immediate calming effect on Helen, who once she'd been to the loo and was given some coffee (the last one, she promised Alessandro) began to relax a bit more. *If anyone could make sure she had what she needed, this guide could,* she thought to herself as Alessandro listed his own needs. Then it was Helen's turn. She opted to be harmonious and listed similar ones to him, apart from the last one.

'To relax and connect with the unified field, meditate, get in touch with my inner Buddha,' she began, batting her eyelashes at the instructor, who smiled sweetly at her as she continued listing her aims. 'Oh,' she finished, 'and to find some Wi-Fi.' Alessandro looked daggers at her and she mouthed 'what?'

'To be honest with you, Miss Parker, we have a no-gadget policy here, did you not find out when you booked? You would have had to tick a box.'

'Oh.' She said, feeling her hackles rise and a feeling of tightness clamp in her chest. 'Oh, I didn't... I guess...' she shot a look at Alessandro, who chose that moment to look the other way. 'OK,' she said in a small voice, mainly because she had absolutely no alternative but to do so. She was here now, she would write her article, and then get a taxi out in search of a signal at some point later in the week. Suddenly the five days ahead of them seemed an awful lot longer. 'Well can I just...'

'I think what Helen means is that we will be fine,' Alessandro chipped in. It was all she could do not to douse him with her glass of water. She forced an incredibly difficult smile on her face, and shut up. She didn't really listen to the rest of the chat and could feel a mood coming over her which she hadn't had for thirty years - the feeling that it didn't make a blind bit of difference what she said, or how she felt, no-one would take any notice of her. The 'George Effect' she used to call it, after Sadie's dad.

Helen made a face as it suddenly dawned on her that she may have had her first enlightened realisation already - based on the sudden arrival into her young life of a new step-father who insisted on organising everything, she'd become who she'd become. Should she be grateful? Or get more therapy...

She mulled it over and whilst Alessandro discussed the various things like spa protocol, attire, meal times, silent times and other stuff, Helen drowned out the sounds of being manipulated - with the shouts of her 13 year old self, echoing protests that had gone unheard for the next five years. Uncomfortable tandem.

Finally they were alone, as they walked to their rooms with their card keys, information folder, and hand luggage.

'Helen, I...'

'Alessandro, I...'

They both spoke at once, then smiled, the tension broken a tiny bit. But still she had so much to say to him, and most of it critical, that she couldn't trust herself to speak. 'You go first,' she said.

'Helen, *cara,* I am sorry I have not been too good company for you on this last journey. I will promise to you, that the rest of this stay I will be making the ultimate efforts to rise to your level.'

'What?'

'I know how much you rely on your Wi-Fi and tablet and mobile and laptop and... I omitted to tell you there is none here. I planned on doing it near Lhasa so we could stop if you insisted on finding an alternative method we could buy and bring here, if such a thing were even possible, but - I had, ahh, other things on my mind.' He looked slightly pained and she could tell it had taken him a lot to say all that. She thrust her chin out and stood a little taller.

'Right.'

'Also, *amore mio*,' he said, sheepishly, 'I have one more thing to tell you which I also omitted to deal with prior to our arrival.' They'd reached the first door, and he used his key card to open it. As he pushed open the door, he said, 'I forgot to change our accommodation.'

As the door went back, Helen saw a massive double bed over by a huge window, which looked out onto the distant snow-capped mountains. She walked in and looked around, there were two robes on the bed, two glasses on the tray set out with water and wine on the little side table, and his and hers sinks peeping out from behind the bathroom door.

'We're sharing,' she said, her eyes wider than she intended them to be but unable to help it.

'We are sharing,' he replied. 'Perhaps I should see if there's another place to sleep in this giant suite,' he said, doing his best to smile. Then he turned to face her and put his hands on her shoulders. She was still wearing her comfy shoes as she hadn't bothered to become 'power woman' with a change of heels, and he stood a full head above her. 'Tell me, *Tesoro mio*,' his voice was soft and tender and her body reacted immediately to a memory of that very tone in a completely different setting not so long ago. 'Tell me, can you bear to share with me?'

'Of course I can, Alessandro,' she said. 'I'll just pretend you're gay.'

Helen had showered, changed into loose linen shorts and a cool white shirt, plus a big sun hat - it was only May and rainy season was about to start, but the weather in this part of Tibet was very mild and extremely pleasant. Apparently in some parts of the country it was so high up that the average temperature was below zero all year round, or so the instructor had said when she'd gone marching straight back down to him to book a couple of extra classes that *she* wanted to do. Including a psychic discovery class and one of those twelve hand massages Kate had joked about. She also mischievously changed one of his classes so that both Alessandro *and* she would be attending Tantric Sensuality class the very next day. Hah. That'd serve him right for putting her in this position. Making her sleep in the same bed as him and... and... what? She didn't know what - yet. And the not knowing was driving her crazy.

For now, it felt very good to have left him humming Vivaldi to himself in the shower, and to be sitting in peace in the quiet courtyard, after their long journey. She sat rubbing on some sun cream as she listened to the sounds of a gentle fountain trickling away and a distant hum of singing bowls. It was incredibly calming. Helen stayed there under the dappled shade of a buddleja tree with her eyes closed, doing deep breathing exercises that Sadie had taught her, until she was well and truly back to neutral and ready to go back and face him.

'Ahh, Miss Parker,' said the instructor as he emerged into the evening sunshine with his bag over his arm. 'Are you settling in well?'

'Yes, sure am,' she said, her usual level tones having returned.

'I'm so sorry we cannot help you with your column, my brother lives in New York and he follows TransGlobe Inc podcasts on many topics - and his girlfriend likes the woman who shows females how to fix things.'

'Kate - yes, she's my best pal.'

'Oh how fabulous - it's like I know a celebrity by proxy,' he said, beaming. 'So yes, I know of your website and I am sorry we could not be providing you with a better service at this time.'

'Oh that's ok... what's your name again?'

'Just call me Paul,' he said, 'many visitors prefer it - it's easier than Lobsang.'

'That's for sure,' said Helen, laughing as he did. 'But I like Lobsang - can I call you that instead?'

'You can, but if I don't realise you're talking to me, just say Paul,' he laughed. 'Listen, I tell you what,' he said, stopping to rest his foot on the edge of her bench, and lowering his voice, 'if you have any emails that are urgent, for your column, just come and ask me out of hours - I will see what I can do to enable the Wi-Fi within the office to remain on whilst no-one is there. As long as you don't tell anyone else that I have allowed it - otherwise there will be no end of favours being asked by our very rich and very - ahh, opinionated - residents, if you get my meaning?'

'I get it... Lobsang - Paul... don't worry. And thank you.'

'And you are able to use the telephone too - the public one or come through to the office and they will log your call. I do hope you have a wonderful stay.' And with a squeeze of her shoulder as he passed her, he was gone.

When Helen clicked open the door of their suite, she half expected to see Alessandro standing in his towel, dripping wet, dominating the doorway. Then she realised how ridiculous that was and that she should have stopped reading her steamy novel *before* it got to the raunchy bit, to help preserve her sanity.

To her surprise, Alessandro wasn't there.

Helen changed, had a quick wash and brush up, did her make-up and made her way down towards the dining hall, since it was nearly time for dinner. She'd had some of the fruit basket in the room, but her belly was very definitely telling her it was meal time. However, Alessandro was nowhere to be seen.

Helen completed her circuit of the luxurious, pristine complex, and some of the extensive, manicured grounds, and ended up back at the restaurant, where a certain freshly showered, clean smelling, well dressed room-mate was standing looking at the menu board just outside the entrance door.

'Helen,' he said, acting like he was amazed to see her, and embracing her warmly, 'here you are at last. Come, we must eat,' and he turned tail, her hand in his, and wound through the fairly packed dining hall to a table with 'Reserved - Alessandro and Helen' on a card in the middle.

The restaurant was filled with a scattering of international visitors - just walking in between the two dozen or so tables on their way to their window seat revealed many accents amongst the divers guests. About half were dressed up smartly, about half were in casual t-shirts and dressing gowns, but they all had the air of money about them. The restaurant, whilst simple, was immaculate, no peeling paintwork, not a single crumb out of place, with appropriately subtle - flattering - lighting on the walls and set back into arched alcoves bedecked with elaborate greenery or an ancient symbol or two. Music played at a low level, with vaguely Tibetan sounds, and the staff were smartly turned out. The restaurant was a reflection of the whole of the rest of the spa - as far as Helen had seen it, and was obviously a place for the well-heeled.

So how come Alessandro was able to offer to pay for Helen to go with him in the first place then? Perhaps he knew someone? He'd said he had contacts when he talked about the visa. But she'd seen the tariff when they'd booked in, and it wasn't cheap, so she was glad he'd agreed to accept her half of the payment. Otherwise who knew what he might expect in return. Even though Helen might quite like giving it to him...

He ordered wine without asking her what she wanted, water for the table which he chose to be sparkling when she would have liked still, and proceeded to ignore the sensitive topic of sharing the same bed tonight - in fact he hardly spoke at all, throughout the meal until after the main course. Helen then saw him fidget with the remaining cutlery on the table, putting the fork and spoon at perfect right angles to each other, then placing them tip to tail, then back again. His wine glass was empty and Helen was a little surprised to hear him ordering more.

'In fact,' he was saying to the impeccably turned out Tibetan waiter, 'we can take the rest back to the room. Can't we?' He'd said the last bit to no-one in particular. 'Can't we?' he said again - to Helen this time, and he held her glance. A flicker of longing coursed through her body as she held his gaze and for a moment, she was back in that hotel room on the night of the conference. Somewhere it felt like a halo of light had just burst and the fall out parachuted down onto Helen's mood. She brightened immediately.

'Yes. Yes, that'd be nice,' she replied. But she still didn't get to choose which wine.

After a very enjoyable meal of Ma Po Tofu and A Yii Abalone, both local dishes, and both very satisfying, Helen and Alessandro walked knowingly back up to their suite, their arms brushing every so often as they walked closely along. The small talk had turned to banter which had turned to a more intimate level of sharing, and Alessandro began to open up more about his own past.

'You really don't have to tell me,' Helen said, and she genuinely meant it, not least because of its ardour-dampening effect. There had been a sexual energy since they'd left the restaurant, and she was damn sure she wanted to use it, not waste it. But it seemed Alessandro had other ideas.

And after all, he's the Boss, Helen sighed.

Later, after much sharing about his childhood fear of loneliness, but none of it really explaining what she needed to know, she slid into the bed next to a sleeping Alessandro. He had almost nothing on, and Helen looked at his body, prone beside her, dead to the world.

'God, you're beautiful,' she said to him, laying as near as she dare and looking down on his sculpted features - god-like and angelic - and moving her hand across to touch his chest. But before she could, he suddenly stirred slightly. She flinched away from him as he moved a little way towards her, but his hand had come to rest casually touching high up on her thigh. Her heart beat extraordinarily fast, stupidly, given that the hand was attached to a sleeping man and he clearly didn't know what he was doing. But then his hand moved against her skin - just a little. And still he 'slept' on. Helen was lying as motionless as she was able, and she could almost see the pulse in her leg. He moved again, this time the hand went a little higher.

'Alessandro, are you awake?' she whispered, her voice quavering slightly with the motion of her heartbeat. Nothing. *He's really asleep,* she thought to herself - *he's 'sleep-groping.'*

'Well if you can do it, so can I,' she said quietly, and reached down further below the cover. Slowly she pushed the cover off his hot body until she reached the most enormous sign that he was completely turned on. It was huge and so, so hard. She didn't 'grope,' but delicately laid a feather light touch on the very tip of it, the heat coming through the boxers that he'd chosen to wear in bed. He didn't move, but it did, pulsing slightly against her touch. She felt a warmth spreading through her stomach and she wriggled a little, enjoying the sensation.

But still he didn't move.

'God I'd love to carry on, but that would be weird,' she said, and reached over and kissed him lightly on the nose, turned out the light and went to sleep.

As soon as the tell-tale signs of Helen sleeping could be heard, Alessandro opened his eyes and peered sideways towards her. He let out a deep sigh, tension draining from his shoulders, then lifted the covers to look at himself, shaking his head at it in dismay. Then he adjusted his boxers, sat up carefully, silently left the bed and went to the bathroom.

Helen opened her eyes. She blinked a few times, flicked her eyes towards the bathroom, then closed them again, and went to sleep.

Chapter seven

'Well I'm doing a psychic class whether you do it or not,' she said to him at breakfast. She'd woken irritable, and was trying hard to cover it up - not very successfully. He'd woken almost as testy, and had gone straight out for a run, then showered, leaving her to stew.

'Suit yourself, *mio caro*,' he said as he stirred his traditional Tibetan butter tea, 'but remember we are booked on the mountain trek later this afternoon. It will be a first for you, yes?'

Helen looked up from her grapefruit and locally made yogurt. 'Yes! A TiFFT. Super. Er... This mountain trek - is it high?'

'Well, we are already nearly at 9,000 feet above sea level, but it will be higher than that - do you want to request they bring along the oxygen bottles?'

There was one in every room anyway, as a precaution - many of the luxury hotels in Tibet now catered for Westerners who with their bad diets and excess weight suddenly found they needed a little extra help in the breathing department.

'Lobsang - Paul, the instructor, told me just now that they will probably bring one anyway,' she said, and Alessandro raised an eyebrow briefly then recomposed himself at the mention of Paul. 'He said it's quite a long walk but there's a temple at the top of it which has a beautiful mural inside - one of the ones that's remained untouched by the troubles here - you have to climb a bit to reach it, but it's supposed to be worth it.'

'Good for another assignment then - excellent? Is your Mr Adams still pushing you harder and harder?'

'Yes, he's told me via... Cheryl...' Helen was going to say 'via The Intern' again but thought she'd better not in front of gracious Alessandro. '...that he wants me to pack in as many as possible to get them in the bag, then they'll choose the best ones and build a little mini-series about it. He emailed this...' and then she stopped. She gulped, about to say 'this morning' then realised it would give the game away big time, that she'd sneaked back to the office whilst he was out jogging. '...this information... the other day, but I only just opened it - amongst the junk - in my inbox.' She finished with a sudden full-beam-headlights grin.

Alessandro's face looked shrewdly at her. 'Now Helen,' he said, 'I thought we agreed you were going to be *In The Now*? Leave aside everything but the laptop to write your articles? No checking anything else, we had a deal. There's no Wi-Fi here for a reason.'

'No, yes, I know, I...'

'Surely, *carina,* you want to fulfil the purpose of this magical place? This opportunity to switch off the modern world and allow your inner peace to come through?'

'Yyyyes. Of course, yes.' She sat fiddling with her spoon and the rounded bowl-cup in front of her and its green tea concoction, and pursed her lips to one side. 'Inner peace - that's exactly what I want.' *Even though my 'inner' is very unpeaceful - every time I'm near you, can't you tell?*

'So, I will make a deal with you - you obviously want to go very much to the psychic class this morning. I will go to the yoga meditation alone then, if you promise you will make up for it this evening - perhaps you can come with me when I do my private meditation session in the temple? You seem very unsettled today *mio caro*, it sounds as though you need it.'

'Sure,' Helen replied, 'I will.' She sat looking at his defined cheek bones and jawline and shoulders and mouth for a few minutes longer, as he deftly devoured his breakfast and kept her amused with a commentary of what he'd seen on his run. *Yes,* she thought, *inner peace is definitely what I need - and I know exactly how to achieve it. Too bad you're out of reach.*

The class for the psychic event was packed, but intimate. Not too many 'weird westerners' as she'd heard one of the waiters call them, and she hoped they didn't include her in that. Or maybe she did hope.

Helen took a place near the back, still feeling a little bit disgruntled and feeling once more that fear of the unknown as it crept back into her body.

It was a very unusual assignment - one she'd volunteered, but chosen from similar themes on a short-list Martha Crowne had compiled. Mr Adams had commandeered the list when Martha had 'gone over to the dark side' as some of the office were calling the competition. He'd then ceremoniously handed it over to Helen like the Holy Grail, to use as a basis for her own schedule. Probably Cheryl friggin' Goodman had now been given that list too, and was probably going through it like Teacher's Pet, judging by the list of suggestions Helen had received in her inbox from The Intern this morning. Including yet another batch of 'things to do that are high up, dramatic or could kill you.' OK, so it hadn't said that, not exactly, but it seemed that way to Helen. She breathed deeply. *Let me just focus on the Now.*

The little chat that there was, quietened down to a hush as a lithe silver haired lady with a streak of black in it took the stand at the front of the air conditioned room. Large windows overlooked the fields and hills beyond, and the vague sound of Tibetan singing bowls could be heard - if you listened carefully, it could always be heard around this place. It was oddly comforting, like the notes were resonating with parts of your body and Helen liked it. She'd sat for another short while out in the courtyard earlier being calmed by it, after receiving yet another peck on the nose from Alessandro. The echoing long notes and little tinkling bell sounds had managed to reduce the gnawing feeling inside her. Helen made a mental note to find some tracks online once they got back to humanity. Well, back to Wi-Fi.

The tutor was small, older than most of the other instructors at the spa, and had an unsettling aura about her and a piercing gaze. As she scanned the crowd, frowning at the empty seats in the front rows, she made eye contact with Helen. Or maybe it was the person behind her. She then beckoned for the attendees to move nearer the front, and soon Helen was the only one still on the back row. Again her eyes locked with Helens, and without words, Helen found herself rising and moving forward a few rows. Still safely at the back, mind you.

'Morning everyone. My name is Serena. I am a professor of meditation study, and if you have not read my blurb on the company brochure, I established my name internationally with a research project in India with Tibetan meditation practitioners. We were looking at the relationship between meditation attainment and psychic awareness. Now there is not much in the way of literature about Tibet's psychic practices, but some of you may have come across anecdotal accounts of unexplained activities - for instance, the many works of T. Lobsang Rampa, and his astral projection, crystal gazing, and aura deciphering. Anyone?'

Several hands went up around the room. Helen's stayed down. She was glad she was at the back.

'Or maybe Roney-Dougal's work on beliefs. He studied Tibetan oracles, Mo divination, and warnings about psi - the fear of sorcery, and its detrimental effects on one's spiritual development. Anyone?'

Oh.

Good.

God.

Surely it's not a lecture? Helen thought, appalled that she'd given up an hour of laying on her back listening to singing bowls for some academic talk. Helen wanted to find out if there was a knack to being psychic herself, not the history of Tibet's ancient traditions. But Serena continued unabated.

'Tibetan traditions are a unique mixture of original shamanic Bon practices, Buddhism, which came to Tibet about 1,300 years ago, and Indian Buddhist tantric traditions...'

Ahh, tantric! Helen pricked up her ears.

'...which came to Tibet about 1,000 years ago. The psychic aspects of Tibetan tradition primarily date from the pre-Buddhist shamanic period, though they are not inimical to Buddhism per se and so have been extensively incorporated by the monks into their practices.'

Her disappointed sigh must have been audible, because a couple of heads in front of Helen twitched. She coughed, pretending it was part of a throat clearing exercise. She looked at her watch then remembered she'd agreed not to wear one this week.

What the hell am I doing here...?

If she was psychic she would have known.

But she found out soon enough.

'So, that's the background. If you'd like to come spend some time with me talking about those fascinating subjects, do see me afterwards. First, then, we are going to dive straight into an exercise.'

This is more like it, thought Helen, and sat up straighter in her chair.

Serena proceeded to take the group of about thirty women and a few men, mostly with beards, through a brief meditation, in which she gave them images to conjure up. She ended with a silence and a space clearing bell, which jingled nicely creating a dissonance in Helen's body that made her tingle. It also made her think of the brooch Alessandro had given her, tucked into her luggage. A good feeling resonated through her. So far so good.

'Now I need you all to partner up.'

Oh damn.

Everyone swiftly turned to the person next to them and happily exchanged names and hugs as instructed. The only person left out, sitting at the back like Billy No Mates, was Helen. She just knew what was coming next.

'We have an odd one out at the back,' Serena trilled. *Ain't that the truth,* thought Helen. And two minutes later Helen was no longer in the sanctity of the back row of the class, she was slap bang at the front, on a chair by herself, next to Serena, facing everyone.

'Now you need to give an object to the person next to you. We are going to do a simple psychic vibrations exercise.'

Helen took off the ring she always wore on her right hand. *If she can guess the story behind that one, I'm a convert,* she thought. She handed it over to Serena. Serena herself took off her friendship bracelet - a purple beaded one with a Chinese knot fastening - and closed Helen's palm around it.

'Now I'm going to play some music. I want you to close your eyes and focus your intention on the object.' A couple of people put their hands up, worried looks on their faces.

'I don't have an object,' said a glamorous blonde in a German accent.

'This is quite common in a place like this - do not worry. If you don't have an object, that's ok, just hold the person's hand.' Everyone adjusted themselves and the music began. 'Eyes closed, everyone.'

Naturally, Helen peeked.

Serena, whilst holding Helen's ring, gave short group instructions on the type of thing to focus on - locations, moods, smells, feelings - and soon the time was up. Helen was the first to describe what she'd 'seen,' whilst holding Serena's bracelet, although Helen suspected she'd made the whole lot up.

She told her about seeing open grassy fields with long grasses blowing in the wind, some sort of shore line in the distance. A massive cruise ship - and ice. A key, an old brass key about two inches long. And a seven year old in a headmistress's office.

Serena smiled, and Helen thought she could see a look of pity in her eyes. *Silly Helen,* bet not one was right.

But what Serena described was a childhood growing up near a port where large ships would come in, an issue with being dyslexic at around 7 or 8 where she was given lines for spelling 'you' 'y-u-o', and an issue with a cottage which Serena and her first husband had once rented in Scotland - where there only existed one key and it was small, traditional looking - just as Helen had described.

The class applauded. Helen didn't know whether to be proud or to ask Serena if she'd just made it all up.

'Now tell your partners what you saw, and we will discuss the ones you want to share after,' Serena said to the class, squeezing Helen's hand as she took back the bracelet and replaced it on her own wrist.

As a hum of excited conversation began in the room, Serena turned to Helen and just smiled. She took her hand and held it, and just smiled. 'It is ok to be sceptical, Helen,' she said, and Helen could feel herself start to blush slightly. 'But as you just heard, sometimes even the most hardened cynics can surprise themselves. Now. You are here with a man, a man who does not love you, is that correct?'

'Yes,' said Helen, quite amazed. 'How did you know?'

'I saw you both at breakfast.' Serena laughed, then Helen laughed, and the ice was broken. 'The tension was palpable - I could feel it a few tables away.'

'He's not a boyfriend, we're here as... companions,' Helen replied, shuffling a bit in her seat.

'That may change - and only you have the power to change it, but it will not be without effort.' Suddenly, Helen was wide-eyed, listening in rapt attention. 'Listen, not everyone *gets* what I do -

what we are all capable of - but if you open your mind, you will be amazed at what may be unleashed.' Helen opened her mouth to speak, but Serena continued. 'Your ring has much sadness. And loss. You were young when you got it?' Helen nodded. 'I see a man, a handsome man with dark hair and darker skin. A green car...'

Helen sat bolt upright, motionless.

'... and a hospital. A mother very sad for her child. I see an aeroplane with red windows - it is symbolic - some sort of tension or anger inside it - and a laptop, causing arguments. Not the laptop itself but the lies surrounding it... And the gorgeous man you were with earlier - his heart has been broken, but not by you. And I see a passion in the past, that is no longer there - but it will return - you must trust your instincts, it will return.' The smile was back, along with the piercing green-eyed gaze into Helen's very mind. 'Is any of that accurate?'

'More than you know,' said Helen and explained why. Then Serena finished her session with one last vision.

'Helen, I don't normally connect with spirit in these sessions, but one has arrived and is coming through quite strong,' she whispered.
Helen's hair stood on end. 'Would you like to know what I see?'

'Yes!' Helen replied without hesitation.

'There is a man, he is not on this earthly plane. He has long blonde hair, curly, and carried a guitar in this life. He has an earring - a cross - and wears leather trousers. But he has no tattoos, funny image for me to receive - I don't know why he is giving me that message - maybe because from his look you would have assumed he would have several tattoos but he has none - some link to his mother. He is not sad, he is happy. A child's presence is around him. He holds a note, a note for you... it says... it says...' But Serena tailed off. 'I cannot see it clearly and I do not want to give you the wrong information. Leave me your email address and I will let you know if it becomes clear. I leave today and am back next week. You are staying here long?'

'Till Friday,' Helen said.

'Well enjoy it, take time to truly be at one with the land, and remember the motto of our company - spend time In The Now.'

'I will, Serena, and thank you. And don't forget to email me.'

'*Mio caro*,' Alessandro said, stopping for the tenth time in an hour to allow Helen to catch up, 'when we return home, you must get fitter, yes?'

Helen puffed and struggled over a boulder as they approached the temple high up on the hillside. She and four others on the expedition had succumbed to several doses of the emergency oxygen but Alessandro had done without. His chest and forehead were glistening, his jacket undone through exertion, but he was hardly out of breath. After the session with Serena, Helen had felt strangely unnerved, even though it had been relatively harmless stuff. The vision of the long haired man played on her mind and Helen had made up her mind if she ever made it up with her mother, to ask her if any of it made any sense.

Now, having told Alessandro about what Serena had said - well, all of it except the bit about reigniting passion - they were enjoying a slightly lighter mood - if she wasn't mistaken, the lift she got from Serena seemed to be catching and the joy was coming back - well, a bit of it.

She drew level with him and took a deep breath - as deep as she could, considering the thin air 12,000 feet above sea level. He offered her a bottle of water. 'Your body is toned,' he said, smacking her bottom playfully, 'but I'm guessing you do not do much to keep it that way, am I correct?'

'You know I am always down the gym, Alessandro. Their coffee shop does a killer cappuccino.'

He laughed and they continued up the roughly hewn pathway, mostly carved into long shallow steps, on their way to the hill-side temple cut into the rock. The rest of the little party was quiet - it had been a hard walk, but a slow one since being dropped off by the jeep - they could see it below - it wasn't too far, really, but in this climate it felt like miles. The guides were careful to make sure everyone was dressed right, drank enough water and were going at the right pace.

'Perhaps we could, er, get a bit of exercise when we get back...' Helen said, playfully patting his bottom in return. 'If you know what I mean.' Ordinarily she would never have insinuated anything of the sort, it's just that it was nice to have this geniality back between them, and the flirty mood seemed to be spurring Helen on.

'Oh, you mean horizontal gymnastics,' he said, surprising Helen with his directness.

'Well, yes.' She laughed. 'That's exactly what I mean! Horizontal Olympics. You could do the upward thrust and I could do the pole vault...' She giggled and he shook his head, laughing at her.

'You are so funny. They are not even gymnastics moves,' he said.

'No but I'm sure we could make up some moves of our own,' she added, stepping a little closer to him and raising her chin towards him. For a moment he looked at her mouth, but then wrenched his gaze away, and took a big step backwards.

'Anyway, I like it when you make jokes. It is good that you are joking,' he said, 'but no more now, this next part of the path is difficult and only 8 inches wide in some places - you heard the guide. It is time to concentrate so you do not break an ankle. It would not be good to be airlifted back to the hospital and to cut short your trip.'

Jokes? Ok, so that didn't work, she thought. Also 'your trip?' Did that imply that he would not go with her if she got hurt and had to return home? Helen quietened down after that, and walked the rest of the way with her shoulders slightly slumped.

They finally reached the top of the trail and there before them was a little cave opening, cut into the solid rock and so low that most of the tall men had to duck, and so did Helen. Once inside, she gasped. Somehow there was a distant gong sound - or maybe it was just the wind. The air was musty - full of centuries old dust. The older guide's voice spoke reverently and echoed slightly in the strange hollow chamber. There was a wealth of ancient art work - it was another of the cave shrines, built for important Lamas to come to meditate and pray - or 'prostrate.' The guide pointed out the wall art. There were magnificent paintings of ancient deities - some were partly-finished black line drawings on crumbling white plaster, with splashes of red paint - the early stages and never completed. Others were eroded but still showed the final, full colour images of gods holding jewels and sitting by caskets. They covered the walls and the ceiling and there were offerings, and messages, and ribbons, and clay domed pots containing remains of the locals' ancestors, scattered all around the edges of the floor and filling every tiny shelf and ledge.

They listened to the guide talking about how the people revered their monks, worshipped at their shrines, and held dear such man-made enclaves - a place to connect with their god, with the universe, with themselves.

'It makes you feel so tiny, in the grand scheme of things, doesn't it,' Alessandro said, as he stood behind Helen, whispering reverently as they gazed on several hundred years of Tibetan history.

'Yes, tiny,' she said. He moved even closer and she felt his energy, rather than his warmth, almost touching her back. A curious feeling began in the pit of her stomach. 'I feel tiny,' she said. And then she realised what the feeling was. 'But then, in many ways, I always have...' she whispered back, and he rested his hand gently on her shoulder. As soon as he did that, Helen surprisingly - suddenly - felt an overwhelming tide of emotion welling up, filling her throat with a choking feeling. Was it the air? She coughed violently to make it go away.

Alessandro turned her to face him, patting her back and holding her shoulder, pulling her near, concern filling his eyes, but the flood of angst just came back even stronger. She felt tears threatening at the backs of her eyes. *Be strong, be strong.*

'What is wrong, *amore mio*?' he asked. Helen held up her hand whilst coughing into the other. 'Here,' he said, unscrewing the water bottle, 'have a drink.' Helen took it, then rubbed her face and tried to take a deep breath. The tightness was still there in her chest, made worse by the lack of oxygen. She held up her hand to him, giving the bottle back and making it clear she was going to go back outside, still coughing.

'Shall I come with you?' he asked, worry etched on his face.

She shook her head and just pointed outside. He nodded. Helen kept her head down as she pushed past the other members of the group, faces all upturned in wonder, and when she reached the entrance once more, she slumped onto the ground next to the younger guide, and gratefully took another dose of oxygen from the bottle he thrust in her face.

'Sit, sit,' he said. Helen straightened her legs and plonked herself down beside him, exhaling sharply then breathing in a long, deep breath of relief, then rubbed her face again. It was colder now, and she did up the zip of the jacket she'd been given to guard against the coolness of the thin air and high altitude. In fact, she shivered. Must have been because they'd stopped climbing and had cooled down a little inside the cave, she thought. The guide was all smiles.

'You had the awe rush?' he asked.

Helen looked at him strangely.

'The Awe Rush - often our visitors step inside the cave shrine and are overcome. They cry and cry because they are overwhelmed by the energy and vibrations of the place. Just like in the Mustang caves, part of Nepal now, but once part of Ancient Tibet - where I worked before. People see how small they are in context of faith - and the universe. It overwhelms them sometimes. And they cry. You too, huh?' His accent was not as strong as some of the other locals and it was tinged with a slight American twang. On the way up, he'd described how he'd gone to study abroad like so many students who then returned to their homeland to work. He clearly adored his heritage and seemed to love that it made world-weary Westerners all emotional. He rubbed her shoulder. 'High five me, you had an Awe Rush,' he said, beaming and nodding. She slapped his raised palm and smiled at him. For a few minutes, they both sat in silence, staring out across flat, barren land, dusty and brown, at cliffs higher than this one, far away in the distance.

'Thank you,' Helen said at last.

'No problem,' he replied. 'Many who come feel the same. They report to me afterwards that the energy inside the cave shrine is like nothing else - it reaches their soul - helps to put things into perspective. Makes clear what is really important.'

Helen just listened, nodding. Sounded about right.

'After, they put right what is wrong, as it makes you feel you must live in harmony. Is that true for you? Is that why you cry?' He was nothing if not blunt.

'Yes, I think so,' Helen said, finding a tissue finally in the depths of her bag and wiping the corners of her eyes. The feeling of overwhelm had dissipated somewhat and she felt cleansed somehow. She looked at the sun, beginning its long descent over the distant horizon, and heard a hum of voices as the party began to re-emerge for the journey back. And suddenly she knew what it was that she had to do - and she had to do it soon.

'Are you recovered now?' Alessandro asked as Helen appeared at the door ready for dinner. She was wearing a beautiful turquoise shift dress which complemented her colouring perfectly, and she'd tied her long blonde tresses up in a top knot, just one or two dangled teasingly over her shoulder and around her face. He didn't say anything, but she could tell by the way his eyes skimmed her body that he liked what he saw.

'Absolutely. Totally recovered. Can't you tell?' she said, throwing her arms up in a 'look at me' pose.

He nodded and smiled. '*You're* better.' He gestured to the door and they left for the restaurant. 'I'm glad you liked the personal meditation - thank you for accompanying me. I told you it was worth it - even though you were tired.'

'I was tired - very tired,' she acknowledged.

'It is good, this place, is it not? To help to discover who you are, and begin to love yourself.' He looked down at her with a twinkle in his eye. 'You're obviously doing very well at that, judging by your mood this evening.'

'Cheeky,' she said, aware of his hand in the small of her back, guiding her as they walked down the corridor to the restaurant. It occurred to Helen that not so long ago, feeling a man pushing her along would have offended her, but now it didn't feel so bad. Actually, it felt quite nice. Actually, it felt VERY nice.

He'd been more tender towards her this evening, after the thing at the cave - caringly helping her get settled for the personal meditation, and had even opened the bedroom door for her for the first time since they got here. Generally it felt like he was being more attentive.

Or maybe it was because she'd become more vulnerable. *Who knows.*

After her little episode up at the cave, she'd certainly felt different. Less...

'Less prickly,' he said, 'it's nice.'

'Prickly? Me?' Helen made a surprised face and opened her mouth pointing at herself with wide eyes in mock horror.

'Yes, you've lost that edge - you arrived with it - at the airport.'

'Did I?'

'You certainly did, *carina*. I saw you striding towards me with that look - the, how do you say it - the 'don't fuck with me' look.'

'Oh!' Helen tried to remember how she'd arrived at the airport then remembered the shoes, the strut. 'What were you expecting?'

'I am not sure, but what I got was not how you had been when we were together at the conference. I found you more unreachable - pushing my hands away from your suitcase. It seemed like if I questioned you, you might bite off my head.'

'God, Alessandro, I'm sorry.' She stopped him, and turned towards him, looking up into his eyes. 'Sincerely, I'm sorry for arriving like a Queen Bitch. But you put me in the guest room and I thought...' she tailed off, watching him searching for how to respond. 'That you were being stand-offish to *me*. To be honest.'

His deep brown eyes with their long dark lashes flashed with something she could not decipher. For a long moment it looked like he was going to kiss her. Then he didn't. 'Come, I am hungry,' he said, without explaining.

The subject didn't come up again all through dinner and Helen was having too relaxing a time to bother to bring it up and spoil the moment. Instead they talked about the sights they'd seen that day, and eventually the topic got back to Helen's psychic session that morning.

'So I've decided,' she said, 'I made my mind up today, up in the caves, to be honest. I've decided as soon as possible, I'm going to phone mum.'

'You mean, after we leave here,' he said. It was a question, even thought it sounded like a statement.

'Er, yes, of course,' she replied before she could stop herself. *What?* Dammit. That wasn't at all what she should have said.

No of course not - tomorrow morning first thing. That's when. But she didn't say it. And somehow, Helen could feel the teensy tiniest bit of prickle begin to re-emerge.

The day's events had exhausted Helen. The trek and the running seemed to do the same to Alessandro because he was asleep when she got into bed, and she remembered nothing after her head hit the pillow. The next morning, he repeated his routine, kissing the top of her head as she lay in bed watching him in his running gear. No sooner had he gone than she snuck out to meet Paul at the office. It was becoming a regular rendezvous and he'd kindly arrived a little early to open up.

'Mum, mum it's me,' Helen said, talking into the office handset. Grace's voice at the other end was sleepy.

'Oh, yes, it's you. It's the middle of the bloody night, Helen, I was just about to go to sleep - I beat Herb at bridge this evening, you should have seen me, I was on fire.' Typical Grace, acting like there's nothing to discuss. It would all be down to Helen. Helen swallowed and cleared her throat.

'Mum, I have to talk to you.'

'Yes, I wondered how long you'd take.'

'What? No, I mean - well, of course I mean that too. But...'

'Yes, what have you got to say?'

She wasn't going to make this easy. 'I've got to say...' *Oh, sod it.* 'I've got to say I was wrong, mum. Completely wrong. And you and Sadie were right and I was totally, utterly wrong.'

'Are you taking the piss?'

'No, of course not, I'm...'

'Are you drunk?'

'No mum, unless you count butter tea - the Tibetan barley wine here is not very nice.'

'Oh, you're in Tibet. Oh, yes, the girls said - you've been doing all that New Age stuff I used to do back in the day. No wonder you're all 'zen'd' out. Makes you want love and peace with the world doesn't it.'

'Er... Yes,' Helen said, making a face down the phone. *This woman never ceases to surprise me.* 'Anyway, I mean it. And I've been trying to be a bit less...'

'Bossy?'

'No, mum, less...'

'Domineering?'

'NO, mum. Less...'

'Controlling,' they both said at once. 'Yes,' said Helen. 'Less controlling.' She wasn't in the habit of having heart to hearts with her mother, not since she was twelve anyway, and she wasn't really going to start now. Not yet. Not whilst she was on borrowed time. Helen glanced at the clock on the wall - ten minutes at most, then she'd better be out of here in case Alessandro came by. Grace was finishing a little speech about how Greta and Phyllis at the club were controlling Herb. 'Mum, I need to ask you something. Something important.'

Two minutes later, she'd outlined Serena's vision.

'So you want to know,' said Grace, slowly, 'if some psychic woman's description of a shaggy haired man in another plane matches any of the guys sharing free love with all of us female spirits in the Utopia commune just before you were born.'

'Yes. *Eouw*, by the way, but yes.'

There was a long silence. And then Grace spoke. 'I can't remember.'

Helen's shoulders slumped and she let out an audible sigh - an exasperated one, ending the anticipation she'd been building up inside since yesterday.

'And before you ask, yes, I'm sure,' her mother said immediately. 'But if I remember anything, I'll get Abi or Georgia to email you. I still don't understand that new tablet thing and Sadie's off gallivanting - getting everything ready for her business trip to Hawaii. She goes soon, you know. She's so excited, and the marketing award will be coming back with her - it's a big shield, maybe even bigger than she is, unless she holds it near her ass, nothing's as big as that. Anyway, I have to go take my HRT before I forget, it's supposed to help your memory - ironic isn't it? So anyway, is there anything else?'

'No mum. Just that...' *in for a penny...* 'I luv ya.' It was the first time Helen had said it so directly in ages, and it felt weird. Good weird, but weird.

There was a little pause on the end of the phone.

'Bye mum.' Another pause.

'Bye sweetie... Look after yourself.' *That will do.*

Maybe this place was going to give me more than I bargained for after all, Helen thought.

She fiddled in her bag looking for coins to leave to pay for the call, but couldn't find any - she'd have to settle up with Paul later. Then she turned to leave the office, a warm fuzzy feeling pervading her belly.

But there, standing in the doorway was Alessandro.

She halted stock still, looking at his face but it was unreadable as usual.

'What have you been doing?' he asked immediately.

Shit. If he saw, and she lied, that meant trouble. If he didn't see, and she told the truth, that meant trouble too. Which was worse?

'Looking for a USB stick.' She said, which was partly true. She had been looking for a USB stick in her bag because the tiny USB stick in the shape of a green sports car was in her purse, which was also where her money was.

'I thought you were going to write up your notes on your laptop? Why do you need a USB stick?'

'I am - I have been - I did. But I need to transfer them onto the office computer here in order to send the files across.'

'Ok, see you back at the suite,' he said. And he was off.

Helen walked back to the room in trepidation. She couldn't for the life of her work out if he'd seen her making a call. Would she get a mouthful from him once inside the bedroom? Would he be angry? Would she turn all prickly again? Was she already part-prickle just by being afraid of being prickly? God this self-discovery stuff was doing her head in.

She opened the door and there, coming out of the bathroom was an Italian god in a towel. A small towel. *Déjà vu.* Her heart responded first, her body next, and all Helen could do was put her head down and march towards the dressing table to unload her things before changing into loose clothing ready for the morning Yoga session.

She smiled at him. He smiled back, then narrowed his eyes. She had to walk past him to get to the dressing area, and he didn't step back, meaning that she had to squeeze by. The aroma of freshly washed hunk invaded her nostrils and she inhaled ever so slightly louder - she couldn't help it - his chest just ten inches away from her face. Her eyes were drawn to his body, and she unconsciously moistened her lips as she explored the look of his tanned skin, the defined chest and the washboard stomach. A drip of water descended between his pecs and she looked at it, then at his face. He was watching her watching him. She reached out a finger to halt the drip's flow, and he caught her hand by the wrist and held it firm.

'Never,' he said, menace in his eyes. 'Lie to me again.'

There was no point explaining, she'd been caught fair and square. He was obviously listening to her call. Alessandro didn't say anything else, the looks said it all, as he stomped about the room getting ready. Then unexpectedly, he sat on the bed.

'What are you waiting for?' she asked.

'You, of course,' he said, surprisingly pleasantly.

'Oh.' They eyed each other up. Was there a catch? 'I'll just, er... get ready then.'

'You do that.'

Then he took his turn to watch her - in fact, he didn't take his eyes off her. At one point, she had to swap her tops and she made a gesture as if to say 'are you going to turn around.' He didn't move, his eyes focussed on her legs. At least, she thought it was her legs. So, brazenly, she whipped off her t-shirt, and stood there before him in her push-you-up bra. She twirled her finger in the air as if to say 'will you turn your head?' but again he didn't move. Just sat looking at her breasts, bulging out the top of the bra. So she turned her back this time, and removed her bra, but as she went to replace it with the vest top, she caught him staring at her breasts in the reflection in the mirror. She covered herself with one arm, grabbed her top, and marched into the bathroom to change, and kicked the door shut tight with her foot, knowing she'd left him with a beam on his face. But once inside she smiled a big, broad smile and enjoyed the feeling of her heart going pitter-pat. She'd missed this.

A few minutes later, with her loose vest top and shorts now in place, and white pumps on her feet, she stood in front of him, ready to leave. But a sneaky smile came over his face. Helen was disconcerted. He was looking her up and down in 'that' way - which he hadn't for the longest time and it took her by surprise.

'What?' she said, finally, urgency in her voice. 'What are you thinking?'

'Helen,' he said, 'you don't want to know.' Then he stood up and walked out the door, leaving her to trot on after him.

'Same time again tomorrow morning, people. Namaste.'

'Namaste,' said the yoga group.

The wonderfully therapeutic hour long class had helped to ease some of the tension Helen was feeling and she stretched and yawned. At last, she was able to breathe a little more deeply again. However, she still planned to take a whiff of oxygen later. She'd been short of breath since the little episode in the bedroom earlier - more because it had been a huge turn on despite her best efforts to ignore it. As the class put their mats away in a rolled up pile at the edge of the room, Paul appeared at the doorway.

'May I ask anyone enrolled on the Tantric Massage class to remain behind please?' he said, and a buzz went round the room, with several of the couples nudging each other in expectation.

When the stragglers had gone, eight people were left standing in front of him. Alessandro was about to walk out the door when Paul stopped him. 'It's best if you both listen - it won't take long,' he said, ushering Alessandro back inside and closing the door.

'Just a little announcement to make - it's all in the brochure in the small print under the heading for this class, but I need to do a reminder. I hope you don't mind.'

Alessandro had joined Helen and he gave her an evil stare. He wasn't expecting to be here, she recalled, having signed him up without him knowing. All she could do was shrug at him.

'Tonight's session will be what we call a closed class, there can be no photography, no recording of any kind,' he was looking straight at Helen, 'and once it has begun, we ask that you remain in the room silently until the end. It is a live demonstration - so we ask that you also remain respectful of what you are going to see. We used to do this on mannequins, but it had nowhere near the sign-up rate.' A titter went round the room and an embarrassed shuffling of feet. 'The course tutors are a couple, and you may well witness fulfilment of the sexual experience - the "happy ending" as some masseurs call it.' Another titter. 'You will not be able to ask questions until the class is over and the lights are no longer dimmed, the candles are out and the tutors are dressed once more. We do this so there is adequate separation. Is that clear and does anyone have any questions now, which I may be able to answer?'

An old grey haired couple raised their hands. 'Will we be able to join in alongside?'

'Not in this session,' Paul replied, shuffling a bit himself as he looked into their seventy year old faces. 'But the good news is that there is a follow on. A special channel on the in-house television system has been enabled - but only for your rooms. It is scheduled to begin playing out a guided tutorial video soon after this evening's class. Then you may put into operation what you have seen with the benefit of a running commentary. The ending, however, will be completely up to you. Plus if the massage just makes you fall asleep, no-one will know or mind.' The old couple laughed the loudest. This guy was real joker. 'Oh, and the tutors have asked me to inform you that anyone wishing to buy the candles and music pack after the class can do so - it may help to complete your own private experience tonight.' He paused, there were no more questions. 'So - Darius and Yokita will await your company in the Lotus room at 8pm. Enjoy your day.'

The other people filed out of the room, saying thank you to Paul as they went, until only Helen and Alessandro were left standing there, looking at each other, saying nothing. Paul went to say goodbye, then changed his mind and just backed out and closed the door behind him.

Alessandro was looking at Helen menacingly.

Then he burst out laughing.

Helen couldn't have been more taken aback, but she laughed too. 'What?' she asked, '*what*?'

'You've signed me up to go watch live porn. I cannot be held responsible for the circumstances. Oh, and Helen,' he said, picking up his water bottle and towel and heading for the door, 'I'd love to see the look on your Boss's face when he reads this article.'

If he reads this article, thought Helen, contemplating the look on The Intern's face instead.

Helen had a lot of writing up to do that afternoon, for the amazing cave shrine TiFFT from yesterday and for her arrival into the beautiful country of Tibet. Once she'd done her very first one, she was down in the office again before she'd remembered to clear it with Alessandro first. And then she remembered she wasn't living in the 18th century and did it anyway.

Whilst she was logging on, though, and inserting the USB stick, she couldn't help acknowledging a strong feeling of guilt. She had, after all, agreed - Helen Parker-Todd was supposed to be living by the rules. But she still had to file this piece - there had been another three emails when she'd last looked, all wanting updates. But nothing from her mum about that vision. Not yet. OK, so Helen agreed a compromise with herself and decided she would just file the pieces, no more emails and definitely no checking Facebook or Twitter to see what her nieces, sister and best pals were doing.

As a result, she typed even faster and got it filed quickly, recruiting Paul to stand on watch. Helen was pleased with the first submission - she'd decided to write it like an ongoing diary and refer back between assignments, linking forward to the next one, giving it a good build up. If there was one thing she'd learned in the year or so she'd been writing these high profile online columns, was that she had a way with words.

Usually.

But, a couple of hours later, she wasn't so sure - in fact, according to *madam* back at the office in New York, that wasn't the case. Before she'd even pinged across the second piece, there was another arrival in her inbox from Cheryl, picking apart her opener and her ending. *Grrrr!* Helen angrily fired back 'tell the Boss to contact me himself,' and signed off. Who did The Intern think she was?

With no-one to talk to about it, she paced the bedroom. Serve her right for sneaking by the office again when Alessandro was at another class. And where was he now? She checked his printed schedule lying on the coffee table - at another class. Helen gulped down a bottle of water and took a couple of doses from the oxygen bottle, picked up her book and tried to get settled. But she couldn't stand it.

The door to the office flung open and Helen burst in, making Paul jump. He didn't speak, just hopped up out of the chair sharpish and swept his hand across it as if to say 'yours.'

Helen opened up her inbox again and there was another one from Cheryl - this time saying the Boss had asked her to dictate a reply since he was busy in investment meetings. It said that the first piece she'd filed was 'evocative, filled with superbly atmospheric prose and punchy emotion.' BUT it needed to 'lose the time specific references in case he wanted to run them out of synch.'

Now that sounded like something the Boss would say. BUT it was only from Cheryl flaming Goodman. How did Helen know she hadn't made it up? The final paragraph was the kicker.

'So do you want to re-edit it or shall I tweak it for you?' the email asked. Helen jabbed at the keyboard, closed down the email without answering and stormed out of the office, leaving Paul standing in the doorway staring in confusion after her.

A little way down the corridor, behind Paul, a lone head poked round the door to the treatment rooms. Alessandro. He furrowed his brow, narrowed his eyes and withdrew silently back into the room before Paul turned round or Helen looked over her shoulder and saw him.

Helen was pounding the treadmill. Her earphones were on loud and with the water bottle in her hand she ran at a steady pace, sweat beads forming on her forehead, chest and back. She hadn't bothered putting on her exercise gear, she'd just gone straight there and her breasts were banging up and down uncomfortably as she jogged up and down. Despite the driving beat of exercise music filling her ears, a constant stream of self-talk was filling her head, as she stared at her own reflection going redder and redder in the big mirrors in front of the bank of treadmills.

'You really must stop bucking the system and do as you're told for once,' she said to herself. 'All you do is get yourself in one pickle after another. Helen thought over her own reaction at the earlier email and tried to be kind. What if it *was* from the Boss, and he'd emailed her direct? Would she have just focussed on the nice comments he made and taken on board the bit about the top and tail? What if the Boss had asked Cheryl to suggest she do the edit for the sake of timing, or speed, or to save Helen doing it? And then Helen recalled Kate's comments about not trusting Cheryl and the whole thing started again.

At least after twenty minutes, she'd pounded the anger away - and at least her changed demeanour could be blamed on a gym session. As she left the gym, she noticed a very dark, Greek-looking guy with long black hair and beefy shoulders doing some stretching moves, standing next to a gorgeous, lithe, olive skinned woman with slightly oriental features who was lost in her downward dog. Helen hadn't noticed them before and with a jolt, remembered what was in store this evening. No recording, no notes - just a whole hour watching a tantric massage tutorial - live. This was one TiFFT she had to get absolutely right, so she'd better be at her sharpest. She headed straight for the snack bar for something she knew would help, and hang the consequences.

Chapter Eight

'Annnnd breeeeathe.'

The lights were down, the candles were lit, the room was filled with a fragrance of neroli and ylang ylang - well known aphrodisiacs, the tutors had explained, and everyone had just joined them in a ten minute meditation accompanied by the magically hypnotic sounds of Tibetan singing bowls - played on a Sony CD player in the corner of the room.

Darius and Yokita were beautiful people - good job, thought Helen - if they'd been like the old couple, it would have ended up a completely different article.

Alessandro inhaled deeply beside her.

'Where were you?' she hissed, quietly, whilst Darius went over to change the CD. He'd come in just in the nick of time, as the meditation was about to begin and the door about to be locked. He'd disappeared straight after dinner, looking perturbed, and said he was going to personal meditation to deal with some personal stuff that had come up during his personal stretch class with his personal trainer - who was a woman, Helen had noted according to the printed schedule. Hmmm. Helen had no idea what that was all about. But it meant she'd escaped any inquisition about what she'd been up to. It was his turn to be prickly. In fact, he was giving off vibes like a porcupine, and she had no idea why, and no chance to ask. Perhaps that's why he'd disappeared.

'We will discuss it later,' he hissed back and then let out a long sigh. Helen followed his gaze and saw that Yokita had emerged from behind a screen in only a g-string, her olive skinned body and pert breasts a vision of perfection. *OK, focus - this is important* Helen told herself and suddenly the tantric session began.

Talk about tantalising.

Darius similarly stripped down to his g string, and surprising to Helen, didn't seem too turned on at that stage. You could have heard a pin drop, as everyone in the room stopped shuffling, stopped whispering and watched avidly as he bent down and picked up some oils, as she lay face down on a huge pile of cushions and a massive blanket in front of him, and he removed her g-string so she was now naked. He warmed the oils in his hands, and began his commentary.

'A Tantric Massage is a tool for preparation of personal growth, spiritual growth, other Tantric practices, intercourse with your partner or self-pleasuring,' Darius said, as he began to rub his oiled hands over Yokita's back and shoulders. 'A true Tantra Practitioner will involve all of your senses working with your chakras, sexual energy, physical, mental, emotional and spiritual bodies.'

As the next hour passed by, Helen found herself watching the most erotic thing she'd ever seen in her life - it was like a choreographed massage ballet, and long before Darius got to the grand finale between Yokita's legs, the most erotic parts were where he and she seemed to melt into one as he entwined his limbs along hers, rested his head on her back between her shoulders and reached out to touch her fingertips, or, once she'd turned over, pulled his hands underneath her lower back so she arched skywards, making the most ecstatic moans she'd ever seen another woman make - live. Sure she'd prepped this trip by watching the 'tantric massage' videos on YouTube, most of which had the prerequisite authentic ending of sprinkling the woman's root chakra with rose petals and leaving her to relax. But nothing had prepared her for the all-engulfing powerful climax she and Alessandro and all of the other open-mouthed attendees witnessed when the stroking, kneading and tantalising touches finally peaked and Yokita's body released the powerful energy like a spring. A collective huge deep letting out of breath could be heard around the room, and slowly, Darius got up and turned on the original music again, which was less sensuous and much more relaxing. People around the room gradually began to share their thoughts with each other, mainly couples, and Helen turned to Alessandro.

'Bloody hell,' was the only thing she could think of saying to him, as he sat there next to her - impenetrable as ever.

'Indeed,' he replied. 'It would be interesting to see how you responded to such treatment.' At that, he turned to face her squarely, and added, 'It's just a shame, then, that you continually prove to me that you are not a woman of your word.' And with that he faced the front and spoke not another word.

'You weren't around, and I had to file my piece,' said Helen, alternately trotting and walking to keep up with him as he strode back to their bedroom suite.

'But you know how I feel about being in the Now,' he muttered back, not slowing down one bit.

'And you know that I have to do my job. It's why I'm here. It's the reason I came.' With that he stopped, leaving her to trot on a bit further until she realised and came trotting back.

'Is it?' he asked, stony faced.

'Yes - well, one of the reasons,' she corrected, realising too late.

'I'm going for a swim. You go back to the room.' He snapped.

But Helen had had enough. 'No,' she said, 'I'M going for a swim - YOU go back to the bedroom.' And she stood there with her hands on her hips, challenging him to walk past her. Which he did.

Soon after, they were both rushing down to be the first in the pool, the silent, deserted waters lying enticingly in the leisure complex of the spa, just the silent hum of the filters and the eerie glow of the underwater lamps filling the air. Alessandro was the first to dive in, shattering the glass-like surface of the half-sized pool, and breaking into a frenetic front crawl. Without stopping, he'd completed one length before Helen had even lowered herself into the water. For the next few minutes, they spoke only when they crossed in the middle of a length. She couldn't keep pace with him so she swam in the opposite direction, their interchanges short, staccato - using scarcely spared breaths in between strokes.

'You made a phone call.'

'I had to talk to my mother.'

'You said it would wait.'

'No *you* said it would wait.'

'You agreed.' And then he was out of earshot. Dammit, thought Helen, I'll have to do better on the next pass. Half a minute later, he was getting closer.

'You were on the computer again.'

'I had to file my article.'

'You didn't let me know first.'

'You'd cleared off with some woman.'

He slowed down a little at that. 'You mean my personal trainer.'

'Whoever. If you'd been *with* me I'd have asked you.'

'You could have found me. Did you even look?'

'I... I looked at your schedule.'

'I trusted you and you let me down.'

'I let you *down*?' Helen asked incredulously, slowing and reversing her direction, so she kept within earshot. 'It's not all about you!' She swam as fast as she could to keep up with him.

'Not all about me? And don't I know that! Since you so plainly told me - the reason why you came to Tibet was your job - not to be with me.' He actually looked a little hurt. Helen felt a pang in her heart, and started treading water. Actually, it could have been a stitch in her side - she hadn't been swimming for quite a while. 'I wanted this to be a new start for you,' he said, stopping too, the mask that usually hid his true feelings beginning to slip a little. 'As I told you during the conference - what if it was time to stop running, to start loving yourself more - what if I was the man to help you do it? This was the key. Open up, be who you truly are - a beautiful person, Helen, without you needing to keep the lid on, to control - everything - the whole time. Why, you even enrolled me on a class I said I didn't want to go on. You just had to have things your way.'

'Well, aren't you glad you came with me to the class?' she said, getting her breath back now they were treading water. In fact, he was still - he must have been standing. She tried to touch the bottom, but her head just ducked under and she spluttered. A crinkle creased in the corner of his eyes. She spat out some water and repeated her question. 'Well, aren't you?'

'Yes, I must say it was... enlightening. I will use those methods with all my future conquests.'

'Oh,' said Helen - the implication of that one sentence hitting her between the eyes. 'Right.' She trod water some more, looking at him, standing there defiantly. A huge knot swelled up in her stomach and she began to get short of breath once more. She struggled a little, ducked under once more and turned as if to head for the side, but she felt a hand grab her. Alessandro drew her to him with an arm around her waist, pulling her back so his stomach was against her spine and his arm on her belly. The skin on skin touch was electric, given all they'd seen tonight. He must have felt it too, as he turned her around to face him. Their faces were now only a few inches apart, she looked at his mouth. Without thinking, she licked her lips, which acted independently of her brain - that was fighting to stay... in control. In control of her pride. And this was exactly what he was talking about, wasn't it.

All at once, she let go of control, let go of the tension she felt in her body, and let go of the resentment she felt towards him. He was right.

'I'm sorry,' she said, and with that, she found her chin rising up of its own accord, lifting her mouth as if waiting for him to kiss her.

He licked his own lips, now, and looked deep into her eyes. Then at her mouth, then all over her face, his look filled with desire. She felt him pull her more tightly against his body, and the pangs of desire began to course through her. Then he drew back, and spoke.

'Come, Helen,' he said, his eyes dark, 'we have an assignment to fulfil.'

Helen had ordered one of the tantra packs with all the candles and aromatherapy oils. They checked, and Darius and Yokita's video was due to start again precisely fifteen minutes after Helen and Alessandro arrived back in their bedroom. Naturally, there was an air of sexual tension so thick, you could have cut it with an ancient Tibetan sword.

He laid out the pillows on the floor.

She laid out the blanket.

He lit the candles.

She mixed the oils.

And then the opening titles of the little video began.

'Alessandro, before we do this, I just wanted to say I...'

'Hush, *carina*,' he replied, putting his finger over her lips. 'No provisos, no conditions, no doubts. This is my gift to you, and your gift to me. We will learn, together. It is just a massage, after all...'

And with that, he undid her bikini top, leaving her breasts to fall exposed before him; he paused, and then signalled for her to turn around and lay flat. Then he gently eased her bikini bottoms down, the touch of his hot fingers making her tingle all the way down from her waist to her hips, to her thighs, to her feet.

She was naked, and about to get a tantric massage from an almost-naked Adonis. Life didn't get much better than this.

But, thought Helen, what if the oil stains the covers… But - what if I start to laugh… she began thinking. Then realised once again that it was her stupid brain stepping in to try to control the uncontrollable. She had to just give herself to him, and allow it to happen. Whatever 'it' was. She would go with the flow and totally, utterly, hand herself over to him.

So she did.

She could hear the sounds of Alessandro rubbing the oil in between his big, hot palms. Then the feeling of exotic deliciousness, as his palms lay flat against her back and shoulders. He rubbed over from one side to the other, then down her spine, then along her arms. She could feel him emulate one of the positions they'd seen earlier, as the feel of his head touched between her shoulder blades, and his hands extended down the length of her arms, then stopped at her fingertips, rubbing his fingers up and down them very gently. Every so often he paused, clearly looking up to the video for guidance, and she'd feel him change his position and begin massaging another area of her body. Every so often he'd stop and the sound of palms rubbing meant he'd replenished the oils, after which the slip of his hands on her skin increased, making it even more slippery, even more erotic.

From her shoulders down her spine to her midriff, he rubbed and gently kneaded and smoothed. Then as she lay still flat on her front, she felt his hands go underneath her body by her waist, just to her belly button, then glide back out, around and over her bottom, down the sides and back up to her waist, skimming her hip bones as he went. It was heaven.

Darius's voice sounded on the TV, and Alessandro faithfully followed every motion. 'A relaxed abdomen allows your breath to extend downward circulating the energy and blood freely through the waist to the groin. Now your lady should take a deep breath.' Helen did so, 'Deeeeep,' said the commentary, 'And now you must continue working on the back, relaxing and opening the neck, shoulders, spine and sacrum. In a moment, watch out for some additional techniques on the sacrum and low back for awakening the Kundalini.'

Oh my god, he's going to awaken my kundalini, thought Helen, and smiled to herself. This was utter bliss.

Pretty soon, Alessandro's hands were back down at her hips, and his fingers began to trace concentric rings across her bottom. With her ass cheeks on show, with a cushion propping them a little higher than she would have normally preferred, Helen felt a powerful pang of longing shoot up her centre. But she couldn't move. She was just transfixed by his touch, by the chanting melody playing from the video, and by the sensuous sound of Alessandro's breathing as he clearly became aroused at this point.

'At this point you may become aroused,' said the voice. 'This is quite natural. There is no shame in feeling the power of intent and the connection of the energies as two bodies become in synch - both in vibration and in heartbeat. You may find you wish to continue to full intercourse at a later stage, but at this point, we urge you to complete the full Tantric massage.'

The image that came into Helen's mind 'at this point' made her groan a little, just a tiny bit, but that was all Alessandro needed as encouragement. Bearing in mind Helen had not been touched since that incredibly passionate weekend during the conference, and now here was Alessandro's skilful touch doing it to her all over again, she couldn't help but picture herself making love with him, astride him, riding him and his enormous... *Helen, you're taking control again. Let go...* she thought. And she did, as his hands took her deeper and deeper into an awareness which was perfectly captured by the commentary from Darius.

'We are working to release the physical and emotional tension, awakening the senses and working on the sexual energy from a place of love and heart. And now we integrate the back of the legs and feet with long full body strokes to build up sexual energy again.'

Alessandro's hands skimmed from her feet to her shoulders, over her buttocks and down again. She felt his hands following the instruction exactly and she wondered, if there'd been a male version, whether she'd have been able to be so self-controlled. She doubted it.

'Next we use light finger-tip stimulation all over the entire back of the body, building sensitivity, energy and awareness while you both use the breathing techniques again.' Alessandro's fingers made like raindrops with a light tapping motion, stimulating Helen's nerve endings and making her writhe a little beneath his touch. She felt him place another cushion underneath her pelvis, raising her ass right up and exposing her wetness to the air. More rubbing of oil down the centre of her spine. More rubbing of oil down the sides of her body. This time, he reached round underneath as he did it, and she felt him touch the sides of her breasts on the way down, then push underneath her rib cage to touch her solar plexus area then run his hands right down the front of her abdomen then skim sideways across her hip bones, and, yes, do it all over again.

The next time, as per the narration, his hands stayed on a constant journey down the sides of her body, past her hips to her thighs. Then he began a series of movements round and round across her buttocks, moving ever inwards to the centre of where her thighs met her bottom. It felt utterly explosive. His thumbs began to protrude as he got nearer, and slowly but surely, his thumbs began pulling back separating her buttock cheeks, exposing her even more, then scooting down the centre of her towards her thighs. With every stroke the touch got closer, closer and closer to her core. And then he rearranged himself into another of the balletic poses, pushing her legs wide apart and she felt his stomach being pushed against her ass, against her wetness, his hands sliding up the sides of her body, and then down again, down her thighs to her knees. And then he changed position again, the cushions under her hips were being propped right up so her bottom was completely in the air.

He knelt between her legs and began small circular motions with his thumbs around her skin right next to her exposed lips, and Helen felt a pulsing begin there, eager for his touch. He kneaded her buttocks, and then circled her lips, kneaded then circled, and then finally, he stopped. She was in a bit of a trance by this state, but found her focus straying to the commentary, unable to match up what was being done to what was being said.

'Finally we do the Yoni Massage,' Darius was saying, 'to finish building the sexual and Kundalini energy until it climaxes into a spiritual release, coursing up through your spine, all of your chakras and filling your entire body with raw and powerful orgasmic energy!'

Helen knew from earlier what the Yoni was, and her heart beat double time. Alessandro was about three inches away from her Yoni, by the feel of his breath. But nothing happened. *What was he planning?* And then, his hands on her upper thighs, he pulled her apart, and her flesh was exposed, waves of coolness from the air touching the wetness, as the feel of his breath got stronger and stronger until she felt his hot tongue touch her buttocks. She had a sharp intake of breath.

'Ohh!' *I don't remember that bit.*

She stayed still as she could, luxuriating in every second of his contact. His lips came closer to hers, and she felt him kiss, then suck, then insert his tongue in between her, she felt him flick her pulsing nub, suck once more... and then nothing.

'And now, turn your lady over...'

Helen felt incredibly exposed as she turned, her breasts pinging to attention almost immediately beneath his scrutiny.

'If you have the tantra premium kit, this is the time to place the blindfold over the eyes and prepare the feathers, leather straps and other textures to use in massage. If not, use more oil and prepare for the next phase.'

'Next time we'll get the upgrade,' Helen said in husky tones, without opening her eyes. Alessandro said nothing, but rubbed more oils between his palms as she lay on her back, pulsing with anticipation.

Then his palms were at either side of her body, and moving down across her collar bone, then from her shoulders, down under her arms and down the sides of her breasts - but not touching them. She worked hard to control her breathing, to keep doing the regular tantric deep breaths which would help 'distribute her sexual energy.' Alessandro's fingers kneaded around her breasts but not on them, in between them but not over them, and then finally scooped underneath them but not across them. Helen moved her hips and licked her lips, then remembered it was only supposed to be massage, so stopped herself forcibly. And then remembered she wasn't supposed to be in control so she let herself go and allowed her body to start writhing again. She arched her back and felt her stomach touch him - he must be kneeling across her. She arched again and felt him move - away, so the next time, he was out of reach. *Tease...*

'And now, watch the techniques we are using here and emulate them yourself, you will find they stimulate the main chakras of the woman's sexual organs.'

And after that, Helen was lost.

Alessandro's hands moved slowly - so, so slowly down her sides, till he reached her hips, then his thumbs came up across her hip bones, and his fingertips scooped underneath her, towards her buttocks. His thumbs then did little round circles down to her groin, but did not go further, before looping downwards and over the tops of her thighs, and repeating it all over. He did this several times and then she felt his palms sliding down, round, underneath her body, into the arch of her back, where he pulled her into a bridge shape, pushing her breasts in the air. He must have been leaning over her to get purchase, as she felt the warmth of his breath on her breasts. Her neck arched too, a huge languorous arch lifting her back off the blanket, until the very crown of her head touched the cushions, just like she'd seen Yokita do earlier. She let out a groan, luxuriating in the stretch. His mouth must have been only inches away, his breath felt so near. Then it was gone, as he lowered her down slowly, allowing her to flatten out once more.

'Now we continue with the light fingertip stimulation on the entire front of the body while you both continue to do Tantric Breathing.'

The fingertips were exotic before, but now they were purely erotic, as Helen felt them dance all around her torso, touching everywhere including her breasts and now her nipples too, which felt taut and erect. His fingertips graced the edges of her pubic area, dancing around her light covering of hair but not touching it, then moving back up the centre of her body, through the middle of her breasts and down over the insides of her arms to her palms, then back again.

Then she felt him pause, maybe watching the video for the next bit, and then he moved down the cushions to sit alongside her legs. His hands were then lubricated with more warm oil and Helen found herself overcome with a wave of relaxation, and his strong palms pushed up the outsides of her legs, and the heels of his hands firmly pressed into the large muscles of her thighs. It was delicious. And such a turn on. She couldn't help but move her thighs and grind her hips slightly, matching his rhythm, as he repeated the motion over again. Then his hands were on the inside of her legs and everything slowed down. He gently rubbed her inner ankles, then her calves, then as his hands went higher she felt him push aside her legs slightly. Then he rubbed around her knees, doing the feathering motion again, before resuming the journey up higher. He stopped half way up her thigh, spread her legs a little wider, and caressed the skin there carefully. She knew that her sex was fully exposed to him at this point, and she felt that it was already fully ready and wet for him. She wondered if that was why he had paused, then felt him adjust his sitting position - he's probably rock hard, she thought. Which made it even more erotic, as he moved his hands more and more slowly up her inner thighs until his little fingers were just touching her lips, repeating this process again and again, stopping only to re-oil his hands until Helen was panting and practically gasping.

Alessandro grunted and gripped her thighs. This time, she flicked open her eyes very briefly to peep at him, magnificent in his nakedness, clearly struggling to retain control - his face was red and his pants were bulging - huge like never before. Helen was unbelievably aroused. But she closed her eyes again. *Go with the flow.*

Alessandro now positioned himself above her body, at her head, with his knees facing her shoulders. He began massaging again, from above her this time, around her neck and chin, and jawline, and collar bone, then on down to her breasts. He circled them several times and then skimmed his fingers over her nipples - she flinched and sucked in a breath.

'Deeeep breeeathing now,' Darius was saying.

She breathed as deeply as she could which made her breasts rise proudly from her ribcage, and she swore she could feel the most delicate of butterfly licks from his tongue on the tips of her nipples. And then she relaxed back down again. She felt him lean down over her, rubbing his hands in long strokes down her stomach then her abdomen, then her hip bones, then her pubic area, then down to her thighs. But because Alessandro was now directly above her, he had to lean over her body as his hands moved down, and she opened her eyes to see a bulging outline straining to be loose of the cotton pants, just inches from her face. She couldn't help herself - she raised her head up and licked it, breathing our hard so he could feel the hotness of her breath through the fabric. He recoiled immediately, kneeled up and began taking deep, deep breaths. The urge to turn and grab him, and straddle him and plunge him into her was absolutely overpowering, but Helen fought it and fought it, battling to keep her eyes closed and to regain her composure. And then before she knew it, Alessandro was back down sitting between her legs.

He harshly pulled her downwards towards him, by her thighs, with a tell-tale grunt that he was finding this as hard as she was. Literally. And then she knew the pinnacle of the Tantric Yoni massage was very close, as he folded one of her thighs back across one of his, and positioned himself kneeling, directly between her open legs.

Helen kept her eyes tightly shut. If she'd have opened them, she feared that would have spurred on a frantic coupling that would have made them fall at the last hurdle. They were so nearly there.

'Nearly there,' she heard Alessandro say, in a gruff tone she hadn't heard before, like he was finding it hard to talk.

And then the narration continued. 'And now we take a breather for a little explanation,' Darius's voice was saying.

'You've got to be kidding me,' she heard Alessandro breathe.

'Time to switch oils, since the one you've been using is not suitable for Yoni. Yoni is a Sanskrit word that translates into *Sacred Space* or *Devine Space* referring to a woman's vagina,' the voice of Darius continued. Meanwhile, Alessandro had reached for the correct oils and was pouring a few drops onto his hands. All the while Darius spoke, Alessandro's fingers were warming it up, looking at the exposed area he was about to massage. After all this time, all this build up, he was about to massage her *there*.

'Now watch this segment,' the voice over said, and they both looked at the screen. 'A Yoni healing massage is a gentle circular massage with my fingers working gradually all around the outside and inside of the Yoni.' A diagram came up on the screen. 'When a numb or sore area is found, light pressure is applied and you breathe deeply until the soreness goes away. This is done until every bit of the Yoni is massaged and cleared of any blockages.

The second Yoni massage is a Yoni Pleasure Massage. This massage is done to stimulate all of the tissue around and in the Yoni to heighten feelings and pleasure. Although blockages are often released during a Yoni Pleasure Massage the purpose is to stimulate circulation and enhance sensitivity through pleasurable massage. A Yoni Pleasure Massage can make intercourse more enjoyable, help achieve orgasm more easily or allow orgasms to be more intense and last longer. For some people it will be longer and more intense than ever experienced before.' Darius finished, and Alessandro and Helen both looked from the screen to each other. Helen swallowed, Alessandro adjusted his still swollen bulge. The shot on the screen switched back to Yokita laying with one leg across Darius's lap, as he sat between her thighs. And then it continued.

'Now, using the different oils for lubrication, gently you must stroke your lady once more from the abdomen down around the Yoni and down the sensitive inner area of the thighs...' And Alessandro obeyed. Helen lay back again and closed her eyes tight shut, thrilling in the complete rapt attention she was receiving from this gorgeous man. Up, around, down, back up again, he stroked her, getting ever nearer to the area she'd been wanting him to reach since they first laid down.

His fingers were skilled, and pretty soon she had a buzzing feeling going on across all of her skin where his hands had touched. And now he was getting nearer. The instruction on the TV faded away until all she could hear was the music, and Alessandro's breathing. It came in little shudders now - he seemed to be having as much trouble getting through this as she did. And then it was time. Time to touch her. He hesitated just a second and then his fingertips were massaging her throbbing lips, running down one side, then the other, making small circular motions. Then moving to the inner lips, making tiny circles. Helen opened her eyes - she couldn't stop herself - and caught his gaze, as he reached her swollen nub, which reached up to him begging to be touched. And then he was touching it and sliding his finger inside her. He'd gone freestyle now, but she didn't care. He did it again, but slower, his eyes had gone black with desire and he inhaled deeply, seeing her buck with pleasure. Then his fingers and thumb were all over her most sensitive areas, following the narrative from the expert, but using an expertise all of his own, and she rose and she rose and she rose. And then she flew over the edge, suspended in mid-air by an all-consuming lightening and only the overpowering waves of pulsing from between her legs could be felt rippling through her, but it kept building and didn't stop - it just kept coming and coming and coming, longer than she'd ever known before. The sensation overwhelmed her to the tip of her head and the soles of her feet, as it rocketed through every chakra, down the insides of her arms to the tips of the fingers, making her palms jangle and her fingers twitch, through every inch of her stomach and abdomen and across every part of her body with a thrilling almost metallic ringing - deafening, intense. Then finally it subsided and the world went black; and this time, unlike almost any time before, she felt as though her mind had disappeared into an abyss which kept sending aftershocks up her root chakra and spine, and down again, gradually subsiding as she juddered over and over again.

She did not know how long it took for her to come to, but when she opened her eyes, Alessandro was smiling.

'So I think you can say - I did good?'

'Oh yes, *yes*, you did good, Alessandro. Bloody hell. But...' she looked down at his groin - still woefully unsatisfied. 'What about you?'

'Helen - *mio caro* - they did not teach us how to massage tantrically the male body.'

'I could make it up as I go along?' Helen said, offering her hand towards him.

'Thank you, but I think I need a cold shower.' And with that he rose and walked to the bathroom.

Helen lay back on the cushions, filled with a mixture of peace, exultation, happiness... and confusion. She felt the most connected she had ever been with herself. But was Alessandro really only a conduit for that to happen? Because somewhere inside, a little niggle was forming, and she thought back to his late arrival at the class, then his attitude afterwards, and in the pool.

And he'd left her without sprinkling the all important rose petals all over her body as a final act of tantric reverence.

She looked at them lying there patiently waiting to fulfil their sacred purpose, then up at the screen where a blissfully contented Yokita was laying peacefully, covered in petals. Helen took a handful, lay back on the blanket and just drizzled a few of the delicate pink shapes absent-mindedly over her belly and in between her naked, oiled breasts.

But as she gradually became grounded, somewhere in the depths of her memory the niggle was beginning to make sense and she started putting two and two together. With her mind working overtime, she rose up furtively and searched for his mobile, and found it in the pocket of his trousers. With a trembling finger, she pressed the button to turn it on, and the little screen lit up. Why was it even on? There was no mobile signal. No signal meant no messages, no nothing. *Of course there was no signal, idiot.* She said to herself and shook her head.

Helen replaced the phone exactly as she found it, and went back to exactly the same place on the cushions - body inert but mind working non-stop.

Sometime later, Alessandro emerged from the bathroom a lot less tense. She could guess what he'd been doing in there for so long. He came and lay back down next to her, smelling fragrant and fresh. His mop of dark brown hair was damp from being towel dried, and a drip ran over her breasts. He idly ran a finger over it to catch the drip and she shivered. Her nipples hardened again immediately.

'Helen,' he said, a little hesitantly. 'Did that experience meet your needs regarding the column you need to write?'

'Erm, yes,' she replied slowly. 'It was… perfect. Thank you.' *Thank you? Idiot.* 'I mean, yes, you performed exactly as expected, oh Tantric master.'

He chuckled. 'The pleasure was all mine.'

'I do feel guilty though,' she said.

'Well can I make a suggestion?' *This was more like it.* But her glee was short lived.

'Yes, darling, of course,' she said, and leant up on her elbow.

'*Carina,*' he said, 'I know you have not been happy during this past year. From what you told me during the conference, maybe it is to do with the stage you are at in your life. I am the same. That is why for people like us, it is vital to take a leap of faith. I left the family business to seek an academic release, but once more I find I am not fulfilled. So I looked around and wished for a sign to come to me and lo and behold you arrived in my life and my bed. I asked you to travel with me on a journey - to step outside your comfort zone as it may help you... get a grip on what is real, get connected once more with what is... what is...'

'...Important? Alessandro? Is that what you think? That I don't have a grip on what is real?'

He hesitated, then nodded. 'Helen - you have to remember what I know of you so far.'

'Which is what,' she asked, shifting away from him slightly, 'that you think I'm shallow?'

'No!' he replied, firmly, taking her hand in his and twisting round to face her. 'No - if I had thought that you were truly shallow, you would not be here with me now, I would not have had the foresight to arrange the visa in advance, I would not have...'

'Hang on a minute,' Helen said. 'Arrange what?'

'The visa...' his face changed as he realised what he had said.

'I thought you said you got it done last minute because you had connections?' He said nothing, just looked at her. 'And now you're saying that you arranged it in advance? What, ten days in advance? How did you know I'd come back to you? We hadn't even spoken again at that stage.'

'It was a precaution,' he said, quickly, 'I was arranging mine, so I arranged yours too - using your passport information I copied down when you stayed with me.' He paused and looked at Helen.

She blinked several times. She didn't know whether to be flattered or furious. He continued. 'I wanted to surprise you. If I had managed to do what I planned...'

'Which was...'

'Courier your tickets and visa to New York and tempt you to meet me in Tibet.'

'Really?' Helen said. He nodded. 'Treat me? Really?'

'Really,' he replied, pushing back a strand of hair from her face.

'You'd have done that for me?' She was touched, despite the subterfuge - and genuinely felt a lump in her throat. Results by any means, then - he truly was a man after her own heart. 'Even though you thought I might be shallow?'

'You called yourself that, I didn't think so. Not then - but afterwards, Helen... *mio caro*... I was not so sure. The days went by and you did not respond to me. We'd been so close - then... nothing.'

Helen looked up at him, realising for once what it was like to be on the receiving end of her running away.

'Your job and your friends in New York were clearly more important - you proved that when I disappeared from your mind. I hoped you would eventually call, as we'd discussed when you said goodbye to me at the airport. You promised you would, you know.'

Helen nodded. 'I know,' she said, in a small voice. 'But you didn't disappear from my mind, completely...'

'But I heard nothing. I was... sad. I'd already requested moving my sabbatical so I could depart sooner, told the family, and prepared my travel information.'

'I'm sorry - my work - my life - it all went wrong,' she said. 'All at once.'

'How could I have known that?' He put a finger under her chin. 'You could have called me, and shared it with me. I would have been there for you.'

'I'm sorry. I...' She paused - a long, ponderous pause. 'I was scared.'

'I could only assume you had moved on from me.'

'That's why you asked someone else?'

'I asked another, as time was running out. She also said yes, then cancelled me,' he said, waving a hand to brush it aside. 'I was beginning to think I would end up travelling alone. And you see, I so desperately hate to travel alone...' There was something poignant about the way he said it, Helen thought. He hesitated, then carried on explaining. 'So I asked my office to make my arrangements, and...'

'Your office?'

'I mean our family office - not my paleo-astronomy department at the university. No, the uni would not help me leave them - they were reluctant to part with me. Unlike you...'

'I couldn't come, then, Alessandro - it was a difficult time for me. Your offer scared the life out of me. Then I argued with my sister and my mum, and then I lost my job.'

'So do you not see - the universe was creating the *perfect* time for you - but you did not understand that. You did not see what I saw - how immersing yourself in another side of the world - of life - may put things in perspective. How valuable this trip would be - and how it may be a turning point for you - for both of us.'

'It kind of already has been,' she muttered. 'I just couldn't commit. I... I didn't trust you.'

'Even after we spoke together so intimately that night, and you shared many things?'

'Even then,' she said, miserably. 'It's part of who I am. My luck with men.'

He was silent for a little while, then he said. 'You remember what I said to you, then?'

Helen racked her brains, which were a little fuzzy now from the massive exertion she'd had earlier. 'You said you would teach me to love myself.'

'Well now you *are* here. So. It means things have changed. Are you prepared to trust me now?'

She nodded, just a little, shy nod. 'Yes,' she said, wondering what was coming. 'I'll try.'

'Well, here is my suggestion,' he said, sitting up and taking a deep breath. 'Do you know of the *Live Like a Local* organisation?'

'What?' she asked, a surprised look on her face.

He sat up and faced her, and Helen found herself responding to his mood change by automatically reaching for her nearby robe to hold across her middle as she sat up opposite him. He continued,

'Tomorrow, I am due to go to a typical Tibetan mountain village where I will live with them for one day and one night.'

'You're what?'

'The charity supports the indigenous populations and it gives people like me the chance to fully understand what it is to be at one with them.'

'Okayyyy,' she said, narrowing one eye and turning her head slightly towards him. 'Go on?'

'I did not enrol you to come, instead I organised a pamper spa day because I thought you would prefer that to basic conditions, being amongst the women who cook and clean for the men. I did not think you would like to live as the indigenous women do. It is a very subservient lifestyle. But...'

Oh oh...

'But?' she asked.

'But now I am thinking it would be the most wonderful experience for you. We could cancel your facial and pedicure and so on and you could come with me down to the village, leaving behind all the trappings of your modern lifestyle and joining in with the ancient traditions and methods of home-life. It would be a challenge - assuming you could last the day.' He was teasing now.

'Are you challenging me? You think I can't do it?'

'Can you?' he goaded, and the crinkle in his eyes was back. 'I must tell you, that I am honestly not sure whether you can. Or whether you will run. There is an opt out point at the end of the first evening, you see, for any westerner who fails to see the value of it as part of their spiritual journey. The guide comes to collect anyone wishing to leave - and they leave with love - no-one is forced to stay. Only your own sense of adventure would keep you there - if you dare.'

Helen looked at him, and thought about it. Her immediate reaction was *'hell no'* - she was already feeling the stirrings of angst in the pit of her stomach. She didn't think she could. Which was probably exactly why she should go. What a challenge. Could she do it? Plus it'd prove to Alessandro that she really wanted to show him another side to her, a softer, non-controlling, go-with-the-flow side - that's what he wanted after all, right - to see if one existed? And it would be another feather in her TiFFT cap - Martha blinking Crowne wouldn't have anything like *this* in her line up, that's for sure. She smiled.

Alessandro was sitting up expectantly, and when he saw her face change, a genuinely joyous air of playfulness came over him. 'You'll come?'

'I'll come,' said Helen. And he jumped up, held a hand out so she got up too, and lifted her off her feet, swinging her round.

'You'll come! I will make arrangements in the morning,' he said, putting her down and grabbing a bottle of water to drink. 'What a night.'

'Indeed,' she said, taking the rest of the bottle from him when he offered it to her, and finishing it. She went and sat on the bed, thoughtful. He came and joined her. He turned towards her and for the first time in a long time, he kissed her. Only a short kiss, but a full kiss, tender and deep. They lay back on the bed for some time, not talking, just soaking up the tide-change tonight had brought.

Helen relived the last few hours, mentally editing the article she'd be writing up tomorrow - just describing the experience of taking the Tantric Sensuality class (not the bit afterwards...) and trying to decide upon the level of 'nitty gritty' to include for Mr Adams. She decided on quite a lot - he'd asked for it after all.

She still felt very calm, sated.

She stretched a little, then looked over to the little side table and her computer, sitting waiting for her to get the feature filed before they left tomorrow, and she noticed sitting next to it, the small green racing car on a key ring, which housed her USB stick. Her body was still ringing with her earth shattering tantric climax. *Almost the only time she'd ever experienced one like it...*

And then it struck her when the other time was. And who it was with.

Jason.

Her heart sank a little, and her brain started playing around with a memory hidden deep inside her, trying to shove it back into the past. Twenty years or so later, and he still played on her mind. Twenty years later and until tonight, no-one else had managed to make her feel that way. Was it because she was settled? Comfortable - as with Alessandro? Married? Had being married made a difference to feeling secure and able to relax, like tantra had made her? Hell, that would solve a lot of marriage problems right there if all Relate advised was to sign up for a subscription to Darius and Yokita. That'd be a good punch-line for the TiFFT piece too. Help save your marriage with a massage.

But the annoying little wasp of a memory was still buzzing around in her head. Yours failed, it was saying - yours failed.

Marriages did that, didn't they? She was a statistic - she was one in two - nearly.

After all, 43% of women live alone, the smug newscaster with a ring on her finger had recently pronounced. And Helen certainly had no examples of anything other than failure. Nearly everyone around her was single or divorced or unhappily married or playing away. And anyway - it hadn't been all her fault - had it? If she hadn't run, would they ever have managed to work it all out? *No of course not.* Ancient history was ancient history. Although he had been incredibly good in bed...

Then she did that falling thing and jogged her whole body and realised she was nodding off. So she moved, and stirred Alessandro out of his stupor. She brought him back to the present with a kiss on his forehead then she pulled back the bed covers. The clearing up would have to wait till tomorrow. Helen yawned and stretched and when she opened her eyes he was already getting in bed. There was so much more that she wanted to ask him, but he was yawning too now, and leaning over to turn out the light.

She snuggled down beside him in the crisp cool bed sheets and cuddled close, and Helen realised that this was the intimacy that they hadn't had here, before tonight. She'd missed this in her life. Truly missed it. And in so many ways, this time was very much like her first time. He even looked a bit like Jason. Perhaps that was part of it. So much like the first time. She hoped this wouldn't be the last time.

'It will be fun tomorrow - I'll make sure it's fun,' said Helen, sleepily.

'Yes, even getting there will be an experience,' Alessandro said. Helen waited for him to say why. 'It's so remote, you have to go up the mountain in a cable car...'

Oh.

Ohhhhh shit.

Chapter Nine

Shit shit shit. Helen was saying to herself the next morning at breakfast, as she stared into space and idly stirred her Jasmine green-tea-in-a-bowl. Alessandro was looking at her strangely.

Shit. Cable car. Shit.

She wouldn't be able to keep her stultifying heights thing a secret for much longer. But what would he think then? He already thought she was shallow. She'd made him sad and let him down and now he'd challenged her to join him on something that was obviously really important to him so she couldn't possible start thinking of backing out. And all because of a cable car. A very high up cable car.

If she told him, then cancelled, it would ruin everything. It would be over. After what had happened the last time he'd asked her to go on a trip with him, she simply couldn't let him down again now - however much she fancied a pedicure.

So for the rest of the morning, in the run up to them leaving, Helen duly finished her piece on tantric massage (completely omitting the 'part two' back in the bedroom but including as much 'nitty gritty' as she could get away with) and dutifully got Alessandro's 'permission' to go email it to New York from the office.

Paul was there as usual, and helped her get set up. This time she even managed to nearly complete the login without needing his help. She started fiddling around, then an email notification popped up. She nearly jumped for joy when she saw who it was from - her sister.

Sadie.

Helen had promised not to do anything other than file the report then go get ready to depart on the trip to the village. But she couldn't ignore Sadie's email, could she? Within twenty seconds and a couple of clicks, she had her answer.

'Helen,' it read, *'I'm leaving now for Hawaii and I'll be out of touch for a little while. Just wanted to touch base and hope you'll get this, although Georgia told me that you 'wouldn't be communicado any time soon' and Abi said you're up a mountain somewhere. Just be careful you don't go too near the edge. *joking*.*

Anyway, mum's finally stopped slating you - she's been acting really weird lately, the last time I went round there she'd been turning out old packing cases and negatives and the mess was awful. So she's been at mine a bit more. I'm so lucky she'll be looking after the place when I'm gone - and the two renegades - well, three if you include Crystal at the shop. Or more like Crystal will be keeping an eye on mum.

Am very, very nervous about it. But so glad the prize money will help keep the shop going for a little while longer. It felt so good letting Crystal pay all those bills.

I'm all prepared - I've just put the finishing touches to the presentation for the award ceremony and it's as geeky as ever. And the finance advisor - a guy called Simon - has been super and helped no end with the business plan. I'm beginning to feel a bit like a proper business woman! I keep trying on a wig I bought to see what I'd look like with blonde hair too - it's very different - every time I look in the mirror, all I see is you! Well, apart from the ass - that's definitely mine. But the shoes and the suit... they're yours. Not really. Well, YES really, but don't worry, I'll keep them safe. Anyway, I know we won't speak for some time, so I better go. Take care of you, and whatever you get up to in the next few months, however it changes you, remember I'll always love you. And if I'm not in touch, it means I'm having fun.

Sadie.'

Helen was quiet on the way to the cable car. Her heart was in her mouth for more reasons than one, and she just prayed that what was about to appear round the next bend was a particular type of carriage. She'd seen two pictures of the cable cars in use in the nearby mountains, and one was a death trap, like an open chair ski lift. And in the other - well, at least she might stand a chance of surviving the journey without cacking her pants. Or deafening the whole carriage as soon as the contraption started to move.

As the van drew near to the bottom of the cable car building, Helen finally opened her eyes at Alessandro's bidding, and looked up. 'Oh, thank God!' she exhaled heavily, her shoulders coming down abruptly, making the old grey haired lady next to her jump. Helen didn't look round, just said sorry. Alessandro just looked at Helen curiously and gestured her to get out of the van once they'd parked.

Getting into the enclosed cable car was easy - there was a fully enclosed platform so it was just like getting into a lift. Inside, it was like a little bubble, a tiny version of a tube train, and if she imagined she was on one of those and closed her eyes… She got on, and waited, heart pounding thirteen to the dozen. Final thing - if she was lucky, when the doors closed, they'd be a tight fit with absolutely no gaps to see below, and everything would be fine…

From the moment it pulled away with a mechanical hum, and swung very slightly before moving quite fast upwards, Helen held her breath but left her stomach behind. At least it seemed like that. Alessandro kept having to whack her on the back to remind her to breathe. Finally, at the other end, as the cable car coasted into position in a bay identical to the one they'd alighted from, Helen took her head away from Alessandro's chest as he patted her on the arm. She saw him shrug to the couple opposite - he was apologising for her, again. Then she stepped out of the car. No-one was bringing much luggage - it was only for one day and the idea was to do *literally* everything like a local. She'd got permission to take pictures, most people did, so she'd brought her camera as well, but was instructed to keep it low profile and act like the locals. Otherwise, only obvious things like medicines were allowed, and a toothbrush if you really felt the need. Helen did, Alessandro didn't.

She also hoped she wouldn't feel the need to go home that night. But she had a quiet word with the younger guide just in case, whilst being painfully aware of it falling into the category of 'running away again...' and also that it could potentially add to a smaller, dust-covered category called 'Helen ruins everything.'

The little party then travelled on the backs of donkeys in a convoy that lasted nearly an hour, so that by the time they arrived, Helen's bottom was well and truly battered. Better than walking however. Especially considering how thin the air was. They were all asked if they needed to rest every so often, as the oxygen was only for emergencies this trip, but everyone - including Helen, and definitely Alessandro - was eager to get to their destination. In fact, his donkey happened to find its way to the front of the group most of the time, whilst Helen's stayed near the back.

As they got nearer, the older guide gave them the run-down of where they were about to arrive. He spoke with slightly more pronounced consonants and elongated vowels, like he'd said it a million times, and each time a little bit like Manual from Fawlty Towers.

'Kunlun is a tiny villaaage specialising in hannnd-rolled Tibetan incense stickks and the occasional elaborrrate heirloom Ralo carpet. Many of its original inhabitannts lived for many months of the year in a nomadic lifestyle further north, herding yak on the grassy plains,' he said, took a breath and paused to wait for someone who was blowing their nose - this was obviously his big moment. 'But for the benefit of foreign visitors, they recreated a little experience of it nearer the village. It was the perfect place for our *'live like a local'* spiritual experience. Kunlun is selected because it is close enough to access from the deluxe spa areas and tourist packed hotels, but far enough to feel remote. We will be there in about fifteen minutes. Now anyone want travelll siick piiill?'

After the speech, Alessandro dropped back to check Helen was OK - quite considerate of him, she thought. Quite - it was only once or twice. Then she heard Alessandro talking with the older guide about the altitude of the village, and how sick some visitors became, especially with the work load they were going to be given. She could have done without listening to that. Once he'd trotted up the front again, she managed to sneak several sprays of oxygen from the emergency cans whilst no-one was looking to help herself get through this. She didn't care that the young guide caught her once - she'd bribe him if need be, she needed that oxygen.

Well, she could start obeying the rules once she was in the village, right? She knew it was important to Alessandro, and she had promised. But could she stick to that promise?

The guides said they were all going to help with dinner that night, to clean up, sleep as the locals do - on mats and under quilts and skins - then help make fuel for the village, churn butter and help make lunch the next day. The men's duties were completely separate from the women's. Women were definitely treated differently from the men in this *'live like a local'* experience. Hearing that made Helen surreptitiously reach for another lung-full from the oxygen can.

When they finally rode into the little village, they were instantly surrounded by the village children, most of whom were wearing traditional dress. It was quite cold up at this altitude, and they wore quilted, embroidered jackets with woolly polo necks underneath, and a skirt-like garment below. Helen looked around and spied a mother, curtly dragging one child in a football shirt out of sight into a hut. He emerged a few minutes later in the usual garb and ran to carry on kicking the ball around with the others.

Within half an hour the greetings were completed, and the visitors were given traditional outer jackets to put on, and invited into one of the mud-brick houses with colourful blankets on the walls and decorated wooden chests containing possessions. They were about to be told about the traditional drink, butter tea. Helen found herself being scooched along the bench with all the women, several feet away from Alessandro who had been put with the men.

And so it begins, she thought.

A different guide - a permanent village interpreter called Samdhup was embracing Alessandro like a long lost friend, followed by a bit of whispering. *Hmmmm.* Then he stood up, did his introduction spiel then started to explain what was going to happen. 'Before work a Tibetan will typically enjoy this butter tea -

so will you. Then work will begin. For tonight, that is chopping firewood for the men and preparing dinner for the women. Now who is first to taste our traditional tea?' It was thick and looked gruesome, but Helen was quite hungry.

And she'd had worse things in her mouth.

'It is butter from the yak, so is very high in calories - needed for hard labour in fields - men are pastoral, and do heavy work. Women get up early before the men, and spend the day making home. You will make home for your man, tonight, in shared house. Then the women will rise early to do the chores before the men get up.'

Helen could swear Samdhup was looking straight at her when he said it. She felt a kick in her diaphragm and forced herself to breathe deeply.

'Now, I will show you how to make butter tea. It has been stewed for many hours to get the flavour. Gentlemen will you help me?'

'Don't you ever use tea bags?' asked Helen. It was out of her mouth before she could stop it. The guide's eyes flashed, and he glanced at Alessandro, who raised an eyebrow.

'No - only the leaves,' Samdhup said. They are cooked for a long time by the women - village women have already made it for tonight's tasting. But since you are interested, tomorrow you can make next batch by yourself.' That shut her up.

He then went on to explain the tea making process which was basically to stew the tea for ages, then add yak butter and salt then churn till it's the consistency of thin stew or thick oil. As Samdhup waved his arm around at the men they churned a little more energetically and smiled and nodded. Helen felt curiously proud of 'her' man as he churned. One Tibetan woman seemed to be particularly enjoying watching Alessandro, nudging her friends and pointing and Helen felt a tinge of jealousy. *Don't be ridiculous,* she told herself. Another slightly taller Tibetan woman, standing on her own away from the group, thrust up her chin and exclaimed some sort of rebuke, it looked like. Then the ringleader of the group said something back, pointing at the tall one, and the whole group laughed. The taller one just looked disgusted at them and looked away.

Once the tea was churned, the guide stopped the men, the whole group applauded, and gestured for them to sit down, where they were handed a decorative ceramic bowl each as a cup. The women then had to get up and each pour the tea into their man's cup, then into their own. The couples who were just women took it in turns to pour for each other.

Helen sipped it and surprised herself with how palatable it was - that is, if you like something that tasted like tea that had been made with a full fat version of thick goats milk and a dose of the ocean. Once she'd sipped it, she placed the cup down and it was immediately filled to the top by the guide's little old right hand man.

'Er, actually, I don't...'

'Do not insult Yongten - it is tradition - the cup is never drained or it is bad hospitality,' said Samdhup - is always refilled - until it's time to leave.'

Yongten beamed at her showing his tombstone, yellowed teeth and a leathery face etched with deep lines and years of character. Then Samdhup explained that Yongten's name apparently meant 'virtuous life,' and that most of the Tibetan names were unisex.

Helen picked up the tea again and looked at it. A glistening layer was accumulating on the top. It was steaming, but not actually too hot to drink. She made a face. The old grey woman - the one from the tantric class - was sitting by Helen and leaned over to whisper. 'If you don't like it, dear, my fiancé will have it - it's supposed to make a man more virile I've heard!' The old grey man beside her was gulping down his cup eagerly.

Helen just smiled, cringed, and moved very slightly further away from her on the bench. The lady kept talking to Helen though, as if they were kindred spirits - having been through a 'shared tantric experience.' Helen was pleased they'd only shared the observation element. Good job it wasn't the actual... Eurgh. She shuddered at the thought and listened to the woman discussing the way Tibetan trips made her feel rejuvenated. A little boy came up behind them - a football t-shirt logo was just about visible beneath his embroidered jacket.

'More? Madam?' he said. Helen pulled back, surprised at what she'd heard. An elder villager came up and clipped him round the ear, gabbled some angry Tibetan words and stood there whilst the boy just topped it up in silence.

'He's not supposed to spoil your "local" experience,' said Samdhup the guide coming up behind Helen and rubbing the boy's hair. Then he uttered something with an edge to his voice, that must have meant 'run along' as the boy vamoosed. 'By the way,' Samdhup said, to the group, 'Normally a pastoral Tibetan would drink up to 40 cups a day for nourishment in the cold weather. But if you cannot do that, if you cannot even act one fortieth like a local, and you do not like it, just don't drink anymore, so it is not topped up - then when time to leave - then you must drain it all as respect, but at least you have avoided the top up. There you are - *Hashtag* Insider secret! Haha!'

Did he just say 'hashtag?' Samdhup was obviously pleased with himself at how he'd surprised them all and was laughing out loud at the group's faces.

Helen glanced at Alessandro who was stifling a grin. That just made it worse and Helen got a fit of the giggles. She felt a degree of connection then, as Alessandro's eyes met hers and a warm glow went down her body. Or maybe it was butter tea.

Then it was time to separate. The men went out to chop firewood and the women began preparing the spicy mutton stew with potatoes. Helen could guess what her job would be.

A million potatoes and forty minutes later, she and three other women in the group were so slow, several of the children in the village were assigned to help them out, and they cut through the pile with gusto. There was something calming in the mindless simplicity of the task - the repetition, the little thrill of fulfilment when each new, clean potato was finished and thrown into one of the big pots of water being brought slowly to the boil over yak-dung open fires. The growing element of camaraderie. At least it was warm next to the fire. And her mind was free to drift...

And drift it did - back to last night, and the blissful oblivion she had felt after the session with Alessandro in the bedroom. Revisiting that feeling made her relaxed, and very happy and content all over again. So much so, that Helen started to hum, then to sing. A couple of the other women hummed along with the chorus, a catchy pop tune from a few years ago. But it was when the youngsters began picking up the tune that the trouble started.

Sometime later, Alessandro walked into the hut, where Helen had been isolated, whisked away from the potato gang. She had been sitting quietly, waiting on her own. Her heart leapt when he walked in, but she forced it down again when she saw he had a 'here we go again' face on. He stood for a second, then came and sat wordlessly beside her.

'You made me a promise, and you decide to break it? Helen, *cara*, do you have any idea how hurtful that is?'

Well that wrong-footed her. She was expecting him to be angry and have a go at her. In fact a dressing down would have been much more preferable to this.

He caught his lip in his teeth and looked at her ponderously. 'And you know how inappropriate it is, on our 'live like a local' trip, to start teaching western pop lyrics to the villagers?'

'Well, it just happened, I didn't do it deliberately, they just copied me.'

'You're supposed to learn from *them,* not the other way around. Living like a local is not teaching village children about *all the single ladies* "putting a ring on it."'

Alessandro was angry but Helen always felt like laughing when she was told off. And it was quite funny, when he said it like that. The giggles welled up inside and she forced them down with everything her life was worth. He continued, unabated. 'The village elder is not too happy with you. He asks if you would like to leave.' Alessandro said, clearly a little exasperated, and still glowing with sweat from the exertion of wood-chopping.

'Is he telling me or asking me?' she said her face suddenly stony.

'He's asking, at the moment, *carina*. Which is a polite way of saying *fit in or ship out*. But it is really important, is it not, to blend in? To live by their rules? That's why we are here?' He looked at her with a pained expression which clearly showed his frustration with her. She felt the connection of last night slipping away further and further out of reach, but she couldn't help it. It was just who she was. Decision time.

Well maybe it's not who I SHOULD be? Could I do it, just for him? she thought.

'Remember - you have to live like a local, obey the rules, no exceptions - that's why we're here - agreed? You act like a Tibetan woman, I act like a Tibetan man. You're making a promise - to me - promise?'

'I'll try harder,' she said. 'Really I will. I want to stay - after all, it's not every day you get to make yak-dung-patties.'

The next morning, after a sleepless night on a rock-hard bed underneath warm animal skins that smelled of goat, and a woman and her husband and two young children stirring and snoring and farting all in the same mud-hut as Alessandro and Helen, she was beginning to wish she'd said yes to going home. She wandered outside in need of a pee. At least they'd set up a latrine - although a hole in the ground in a make shift tent wasn't the best thing to greet you when you're feeling slightly queasy from altitude sickness. It was just before dawn, and the women had woken all the female visitors to go start the cleaning and the breakfast and the tea. Helen managed to aim true, crouching, then got back out again from the smelly midden as fast as she could.

She looked around her, at the mists still evident across the plains, and breathed in deeply of the cool damp, dawn air. Then felt another wave of nausea as a waft of the latrine filled her nose.

Eurgh. Surreptitiously she glanced side to side, then turned her back and pulled out the mini can of oxygen from her jacket, which she'd bribed the young guide to give her. But as she looked up from inhaling it, she saw two almond shaped dark brown eyes looking at her from an extremely inquisitive young face. It was the boy again, standing there tossing a football up and down in his hand. He cocked his head to one side, then held out his hand.

Oh dear god no, she thought, but he opened his mouth to shout something to the nearby hut, so she put her fingers over her lips to say 'shhhh,' and allowed him to take a spray of purified medical grade compressed oxygen. He inhaled awkwardly, not fully understanding what it was, and coughed loudly. She tried to help him stop coughing, and smacked his back a little too hard, and he jogged forwards somewhat, just as his mother - the tall woman from last night - emerged from the hut. Furious, she marched over to Helen and snatched the oxygen from her. The woman unusually had blue eyes, like Helen. Then before Helen could do anything, the woman clipped the boy over the back of the head and ordered him away. Beckoning Helen, the woman looked around her and Helen had no choice but to trot along behind her into her hut.

Once inside, the woman looked at Helen and pointed to the can. Helen just shrugged. Then amazingly, the woman held the can mouthpiece to her face, took the most enormous breath, held it, opened her eyes, smiled at Helen, exhaled loudly and said 'Ahhh, that better. Thank you, lady.'

Helen couldn't have been more surprised. She looked towards the door and the woman just put her fingers to her mouth. Three children came into the room and she said something and then they nodded and trekked outside. 'They look out for me.' She had a strong accent, slightly different from what Helen had heard so far. The can was handed back and she gestured Helen to sit down. She offered her some tea, but Helen put up her hand - that's all she needed, another dose of goats cream and the sea, this time in the morning. But the woman insisted, and Helen was relieved to see it just black. And had a tea bag in it.

'I lived in Lhasa, many people drink milk tea, not butter tea. Tea bags - less mess - good, huh? Good western invention! Western ways are good.' Helen sipped the hot, black liquid gratefully. The woman topped up the pretty bowl then did the same to her own and started to drink it.

'Fantastic,' said Helen - it was just what she needed. Then she felt really guilty. 'But Tibetan ways are wonderful too - you're so lucky to be here, without the pressures of the outside world.' The woman was nodding, so Helen kept going. 'Keeping up with appearances is hard. So is the rat race. Sometimes I hate the rat race,' Helen said, realising it was true. 'If I was truly a local here, I think I would embrace the old ways as you do - it's such a simple way of living.'

The woman was still nodding, then paused. Helen wasn't sure if the gracious Tibetan had quite understood what on earth she was talking about. She said something in Tibetan, then got up and opened the front of a huge decorated wooden cupboard, so the long doors swung back. There inside was a wind-up radio, and a little generator with an ancient mobile phone. 'Too simple,' she said, 'Somba wants to watch the soccer - like his friends - live in next village - they have generator and small satellite dish and television. We only have radio. He drive me mad. It cost so much money - we never have enough.'

Oh.

My.

God.

'Plus ça change, plus ça même chose...' said Helen.

'Oui,' said the woman.

Whilst the rest of the women toiled outside, Helen and the woman, who introduced herself as Rinchen - meaning treasure, or precious - sat and put the world to rights over black tea and Tsampa bread, made from barley dough. She'd lived in the big city until she'd married a former client who had inherited a farm - and had moved here with him. Her English was good, and she also spoke four other Chinese dialects as well as German and French. She was the stand-by translator if Samdhup wasn't available.

The children trooped back in, hungry, the youngest jumping up into his mum's lap. Two girls and the little boy were handed some Tsampa. The soccer boy was the biggest of the four, he was still outside.

'What are their names?' Helen asked. Rinchen pointed at them, one at a time. They were called Rinzen - the holder of intelligence, Rabten - steadfast and faithful, and Sonam, the fortunate one. Helen smiled at all of them sweetly and they smiled shyly back, barley bread in their teeth.

'And what of your oldest boy?'

'He is called Somba.'

'And what does that mean?' asked Helen waiting for the most impressive answer of all.

'Socks,' she said.

Helen made a face as if she hadn't understood. 'Socks?!'

'It was cold that winter,' said Rinchen, 'I thought it funny.'

Helen laughed and felt a natural affinity to this woman, thousands of miles and hundreds of worlds apart, there was still a natural instinct that made us human.

Just then, Helen heard her name being called and with the sun almost up, she stood up to go. 'Thank you so much, you've made my day.' She turned to go then stopped in the doorway. 'Would you like anything for the children? I don't have much but I can maybe...'

'Email me?' said Rinchen. 'In case my boy want to talk about world things - maybe come study one day. Maybe ask your advice for job - he want to... what he say - bend it like Beckham?'

'Er, my email? Sure - give me yours too.'

The woman took out a pencil and a scrappy piece of torn off envelope, scribbled on it and thrust it in Helen's hands. 'Do not tell the elders,' she said. 'They already think of me bad - I am too... disobedient.'

Helen smiled at the irony and looked at the note. Then she read it aloud. 'Rinchenwarrior1976@yahoo.co.uk.'

'Yes,' said the woman, 'best tariff.'

Helen emerged from the hut and a small group of Tibetan women including the taller one who had taken a fancy to Alessandro were waiting outside. They gave Helen daggers, started jeering and gesticulating ten to the dozen, and she slipped away to go help make dung patties. *Oh joy.*

Her new best mate Rinchen was nowhere to be seen for the rest of the morning, and Helen suffered her tasks in a world of her own. Her mind was racing, deciding how to write up this amazing experience for her TiFFT column.

She was eager to get back and file it, and make sure things were settling down with The Intern. She had a growing suspicion that Kate was spot on about Cheryl, about minding her back. She decided to double check that Mr Adams was getting the right info through. Yes, she'd do it as soon as they got back that night.

After the dung cake session, the patties were laid out to dry alongside the walls of the houses nearby, and Helen was put on tea duty. Stirring a slow boiling pot for an hour wasn't exactly her idea of fun, but it allowed her to more or less plot out the TiFFT article in her head. She took a few photos with her digital camera and did a few arty ones of the fire and the boiling pot. She also did some longer range ones of the huts with their colourful ribbons, one of the prayer wheels outside a shrine and several of the people in the distant fields, using her zoom. Then she took some close ups of the buildings around her without even getting up off her chair. In fact, with the powerful zoom, she could almost see right into some of the huts themselves. Then a half-dressed figure with no bottoms on walked by the camera lens and she snapped her camera shut. *Ooops.*

More stirring. More waiting. More contemplating her navel. Actually maybe she should contemplate her navel - she could do a 'getting a piercing TiFFT,' or maybe she'd give that one to Cheryl. Along with getting a tattoo.

Which reminded her of the psychic's vision. So she pondered who on earth it might represent, with its long blond hair and weird description.

Then more stirring, more waiting, more thinking.

Getting bored now, Helen thought, and wondered if the tea was nearly done. She looked around but every woman who passed by seemed for some reason to be avoiding her gaze, until a very tiny, very old Tibetan lady walked slowly by carrying some bowls. Helen made a motion like eating, pointing to her mouth, and got given one of the cup-bowls. But when Helen tried to dip it into the boiling tea, she accidentally splashed herself, recoiled, and dropped the cup in the pot. Before her very eyes, the Tibetan woman reached her fingers speedily into the roiling bubbles and retrieved the cup. Helen just gawped. She grabbed the woman's hand, looking at the front and back. It was hot, but not scalded. Then the woman took Helen's hand and tried to force it into the water. Before Helen could stop her, Helen's fingers had dipped below the surface. A blood-curdling scream came gushing out of Helen's mouth, but stopped midway - as she realised it wasn't boiling at all. It was very hot, but not boiling - not in her normal sense of boiling anyway.

'Oh my GOD!' she said, dipping her fingers in briefly again. Rinchen had appeared because of the scream, and ushered a growing group of women away from Helen. Helen pointed, and showed the old woman picking bits of scum off the surface of the pot with her bare hands.

'We high up,' she said. 'Water boil at lower temperature. Even lower up Everest.'

Schoolgirl physics came rushing back to her. Of course. They were so high, the air was thin and water acted differently. The actual temperature it began to boil was much lower. *Well!* This was the best TiFFT picture of all, she thought, and got the Tibetan woman to let Helen take a photo of her with her hands very briefly in the boiling tea in the pot, smiling away at the camera.

'HELEN!' came a voice across the compound. And when she turned, Alessandro, the guide, the village elder and several of the menfolk as well as the nasty Tibetan bitchy woman, were all watching her with faces like thunder.

Oh shit. She thought.

Oh shit was right. The rest of the day she'd been banished to one of the huts, in solitary, sharing it with three goats and four Tibetan Mastiffs. She was well and truly in the dog house. And she'd had the most almighty dressing down from Alessandro.

When he'd found out - from the Tibetan slapper no doubt - what Helen had been doing in Rinchen's hut, and then he'd looked at Helen's camera and seen half naked pictures of one of the elder's wives inside her hut, regardless of whether '*it was an accident, honest,*' he'd been less than impressed and demanded the complete truth. The slip of paper with the email address on was the last straw, and he didn't talk to her any more that day. *You broke your promise to me - you promised. You broke it...*

Even on the way home, in the cable car when he allowed her to bury her head in his chest again, he didn't really speak to her. In the bedroom once they got back and thankfully out of the day-old sticky clothes, once they'd showered and changed, he only replied in monosyllables. And for over an hour whilst he laid on the bed checking his phone - only the fitness app (she did ask) - whilst she finished her next TiFFT article, he uttered no more than a dozen or so words.

And none of them were *Cara, Carina* or *Tesoro mio.*

Helen felt a bit wretched but was ashamed to admit that she was also a little bit exalted to have discovered that living like a local was not that different - even 11000 feet up a mountain in Tibet. And she had some damn fine photos to prove it. If she used them. So many lovely little First Time experiences in one place. All for her latest piece. She couldn't wait to file it, and didn't even mind when Alessandro said he would accompany her to the office to get it done.

Fine if he wants to check up on me, she thought, *I'm not even doing anything wrong.* Totally ignoring, as usual, the long list of 'wrongs' from the past 24 hours. From the past few *weeks*, if truth be known. But then, *that's what I do,* thought Helen. She felt like she was being accompanied to the headmaster's office by the head prefect.

Alessandro disappeared into the inner office to talk privately with Paul, leaving Helen to send her email to TransGlobe Inc. this time she made sure she sent one copy to Cheryl, then another to Janice asking her to ensure it got to the Boss. It gave her the opportunity to sneakily check her inbox and as soon as she'd done so, she wished she hadn't.

'Dear Helen,' Cheryl had written. *'Since you haven't been available for the past day or so, I went to see The Boss (isn't it nice how everyone calls him that - I think we should write it in capitals, like The Fuhrer or The Master, don't you?) He has allowed me to make some tweaks to your first piece so it reads as a stand-alone. He was really quite receptive when I made the suggestions - and it's all got his approval. (Attached.) He says if you get the rest of the articles written 'ship shape as requested by me' (his words) - like, done properly, then it'll only be this first article that gets published with my name as editor added to the by-line on the Try it For the First Time Club home page blog. I hope you won't mind? It'll look good on my CV so thanks in advance. When can we expect your next piece? I'm just working on the tantric one now - it may have to be censored a little bit though, don't you think? Hope you're having fun with hunky Alessandro - when you're finished with him do send him my way. Best wishes, Cheryl.'*

Helen nearly exploded.

Alessandro came running back into the office to see Helen picking up the broken pottery vase of bright yellow peonies and mopping up the water with her cardigan.

'It, er, broke.'

She almost couldn't contain it any longer - she just wanted to rant to him about Cheryl and her 'bloody cheek,' but it would fall on ears so deaf, it would be like talking to someone floating in outer space.

'What the hell happened?'

She daren't say *I threw it at the wall*. So Helen, red faced and suffocating with rage, burst into tears and slunk into a nearby chair, gibbering. For nearly half an hour. Alessandro, far from comforting her, had disappeared back into the other room and closed the door.

When he came out, she'd got through several tissues from the Tibetan secretary sitting in the next office, and had drunk three cups of jasmine tea, and was feeling depleted and flat. She looked up at him with a 'go on then, shout at me,' face, but he just walked over and stood her up with a hand on her elbow and started walking her back to the room. He was carrying a new-looking folder and when the door was closed, he sat on the bed and handed it to her.

'What is it,' she sniffed, gulping a little bit. *Oh god,* she thought, *I'm doing that 'after-a-good-cry' hiccupping that some women do. Oh god, I'm 'some women.'*

He didn't answer at first, just placed it in her lap, but she just sat there looking from it to him and back again.

'Open it and see - I did it for you.'

Curious now, she pulled out a revised travel plan.

'Helen,' he said a minute later, then took a deep breath and continued. 'We both know this is not working. It would not work to come back with me, even for a few days. So I have rearranged your travel to take you straight back home.'

'But the cost...'

'No cost. I'd treated you to an... upgrade,' he paused. 'You wanted one did you not?' He smiled and she caught the subtle reference to a more comprehensive tantric pack and a promise that would never be kept. 'To a Club Class flight - and they can be rearranged anytime without paying any extra.'

Helen blinked. A lot. 'Another surprise. You are kind.'

'You don't have to stay with me any longer. You need to be you, not someone I want you to be.' He paused, poignantly, and there was just a little moment as their eyes met. 'Tonight I will move to another room and tomorrow lunchtime when we were due to fly back to Tuscany, you will go to New York and I...' he coughed slightly then continued, '…I will be staying on here. There is much I wanted to get done, but have not been able to, because of … distractions.' Helen just listened to him, watching the amazing mouth move, the perfect chest rise and fall and the deft hands gesticulate, one index finger picking continuously at the cuticle of his thumb. He continued, 'I know in the grand scheme of things, everything is exactly how it is supposed to be - but so is our desire to change it. And after what has happened - in the village - and here - it needs to be changed.'

Helen waited for the tears to start flowing again, but strangely enough, they just didn't come. She touched base with her heart, then her soul, then her eyes, but nothing except relief could be found and the realisation washed over her. She looked him in the eye. 'I'm sorry Alessandro. Truly sorry,' she said, and he gave the tiniest nod. 'At least I kept you on your toes. Are you very disappointed with me?' She said it, but she wasn't at all sure she really wanted to hear the reply.

'Oh, *carina*,' he said. 'I am disappointed with myself. Not you. Well, not just you. I believe - I rushed you - you are the most wonderful woman, in so many ways - so unlike any that have gone before in my life. And that is why I wanted to pursue you - to help to enlighten you. But a person cannot enlighten another - they can only become enlightened by themselves. It is your journey, not mine. And I cannot control you any more than you can control me in this amazing life we live.'

He looked at her with such empathy, such honesty and such love that she now finally felt a tear prickle at the corner of her eye. She reached out a hand and touched the side of his face, his gorgeous face with its huge brown eyes and defined cheek bones, and its olive skin against her hand and the ring she always wore. *The ring.* And suddenly she was transported back to exactly the same situation, the same feeling, and almost the same sight, many years before.

It disconcerted her and she felt a rush of emotion. When she reached over to kiss him, he did not pull away. Instead, he kissed her passionately back, with all the power and lack of restraint she had not felt previously. The Tibetan secretary walked in, stopped in her tracks, and walked back out again, shutting the door quietly behind her.

Alessandro finally finished the kiss, rested his head against Helen's forehead and sighed.

'What?' she asked him.

'I was just thinking of what might have been. If you just need more time, you must let me know. If you feel you are ready to come with me on a journey of transformation, you must come back to me and try again, promise, *Tesoro Mio*?'

'I promise,' she said, and nibbled around his ear, then his neck then his jawline and they ended up in another clinch. When they parted, Alessandro reached down and adjusted his crotch slightly. 'Ahem,' he said, 'the message has not yet reached my trousers.' Then he looked at Helen knowingly. She looked back, equally as knowingly.   'I tell you what,' he said, 'Let's have dinner together one last time tonight. As friends?'

'Of course,' said Helen, the corner of her mouth quirking up in amusement. 'As friends.'

All through the meal, it was like the first time they met. The electricity was overpowering, overflowing, and carried them on a wave of desire right the way through a light dinner then a delicious layered creamy dessert, which they shared - messily. Helen sucked some of the juicy cream top layer off Alessandro's finger, after he'd removed a blob she'd dropped on her chin. Then she did it again, spilling a droplet of cream from her spoon onto her décolleté. He looked her in the eye, then lifted his finger over to her chest, very near to her rounded bosom, half exposed in the pretty black dress, and then sucked it off his own finger. The intent was clear.

The bedroom door burst open and it was all they could both do not to rip the clothes from each other's bodies. The room had been made up, and they jumped back onto fresh bed sheets and devoured each other's mouths, chins, necks, shoulders, chests, stomachs, thighs, and finally took it in turns to devour each other, Helen at pains to make sure Alessandro finally experienced her version of Tantric massage. Using her mouth, her tongue and her hands, she brought him almost to the point of no return, over and over, until he could stand it no longer, and finally he threw her on her back and thrust into her. He nearly couldn't stop himself to use protection, and after several more strokes, he quickly sheathed himself. Then a tempest was unleashed and he set about furiously taking out all his frustrations, all his anxieties and all his sexual energy on giving her the seeing-to of a lifetime. It lasted an hour, before she finally threw him off and cried 'no more.' The condom had split slightly, she noticed, as he rolled it off, but only at the top. He looked at her, concerned, and she examined it, then told him not to worry.

They both took a long languorous shower, touching each other's bodies as if they knew it was the last time, and tenderly caressing and kissing each other till midnight. Then Alessandro gathered his things, left her with a butterfly kiss on the cheek, and told her he was going back to the village first thing, to take care of some unfinished business there. He would get in touch as soon as he was home, and he hoped she'd enjoy the luxury of the 'upgrade' he had taken care of for her on the flight home. He said 'upgrade' with a wink, then closed the door and was gone.

Helen lay in bed thinking for a long time afterwards, pondering his words. Not about whether she'd ever go back to him if she found it was finally time for her transformation. But about his use of the word 'home.' He'd meant New York. But was it?

Where the hell was home, now, exactly?

Hard one. Different job, different town, different man… But there was a constant.

Sadie. The girls. And begrudgingly, her mum.

The nearest answer was Surrey, and looking at the time, Helen suddenly found herself wide awake and with a burning desire to check her emails to see if there was anything from her mother or to be precise, from the nieces on behalf of her mother. Helen had a feeling there was. Every so often, she got this feeling and it was usually correct. Most of the time it was about Sadie - they were close after all - even though they were only half-sisters, no blood sisters could ever be closer. That's why she always knew Sadie was ok - and why they'd always had this thing about 'if you don't hear from me, I'm having fun.'

But this time the feeling Helen had was about Grace.

Maybe her mum had managed to locate something for Helen - something about who was her dad - which of the 'many men' could possibly match Serena's vision? She should wait. But waiting till morning would be murder when she was so full of emotion.

Helen suddenly had an idea. She knew the code, she knew where Paul kept the key, and the time difference might be about right? And more importantly, there was no more Alessandro to *tut tut* every time she went off piste...

Half an hour later she'd crept back down and booted up the office computer. But soon after, what she saw there made her wish she hadn't.

The quiet of the office after midnight held a particular type of calm. It was Helen's time of night - the time she came alive. Blamed it on the days of clubbing then just kind of got stuck. But now it meant she was laser focussed as she scanned through the email inbox, looking for anything from her family.

There wouldn't be anything from sister Sadie - not whilst she was away in Hawaii, Helen knew that. But maybe one of the nieces? Maybe something had been located in the depths of an old album, a battered suitcase, a stuck drawer in the loft room. Or maybe her mum had just had a lucid moment - it did happen now and then - and memories of Helen's real father may yet materialise.

'Spam, spam, groupon, freecycle, Viagra - must adjust my spam filter...' Helen muttered to herself as the sounds of night filtered through the windows of the office - and the loud tick of the clock on the wall kept time with the tapping on her keyboard.

'Ooo.'

There was an email from Janice, the Boss's PA.

'Helen, info dump for you - stand by.

First, I have sent your piece direct to Boss's personal email account - and copies of your tantra one too in case he didn't see it yet. It did go into his work account, I take care of that, but he's been busy entertaining investors - aka playing golf.

Second - the Godiva Briber. I was surprised to hear you've given the go ahead to Cheryl to edit for you - very generous of you, considering her background. I'm sending you another copy of the schedule of assignments which Cheryl has summarised for the Boss and the marketing team - you're packing a lot in, good for you. I couldn't do half of what's on that list. Anyway, it needs to be signed off by you - soon as possible - so we can reach the relevant sponsors and advertisers before Martha Crowne's team do. The Boss's sources say she's following a very similar schedule just in a different order - well I guess you used her list as a basis huh? I have to ask you though - have you asked Cheryl to book herself on some of the simpler TiFFT's? And write them up as if she's you with her as editor? At least that's what she's been saying at the water cooler. Check the list and adjust it double sharpish, if not. Not sure what's going on with that girl.

Finally, you're creating quite a buzz over here, I can tell you. I'm not sure how, but your tantra thing is currently doing the rounds on the internal email. The IT department have tried to call it back, but it was too late. But if it gets you noticed, then what the heck, right, sweet pea?

Tell you what, reply to me on this email address - it's my own personal one, I don't want to alert any company IT audits with the word 'tantric' - and tell me what REALLY happened after that massage class with the delicious Italian, would you? I need something exciting - there's nothing on TV tonight - 'tee hee.' (Or what does Cheryl say? 'LOL?') Can't wait to see you. You're not due in till next week are you? After a few days back in Tuscany doing something with a sword according to the schedule - you can imagine my first thoughts when I read that! Anyway, Kate's back around then, so let's have a massive catch up. Best. J.'

WHAT?

As soon as Helen flew into JFK she'd be straight on the bloody phone to arrange a meeting with Cheryl goddam Goodman to tear her a new one. 'Permission' to edit? And a quick flick through the list of assignments had Helen's heart doing somersaults. All the ones she'd researched herself were there all right - duly confirmed and scheduled in. Then, right at the bottom of the list, were three she'd never seen before - a whole week of daring stunts, at one of the daredevil festivals - the one she'd asked Cheryl to tentatively look into, in Hawaii in just over five months' time. With C.G. in brackets next to them. *Gaaah! What the hell do I do now?*

Helen wanted to thump something but she'd learned her lesson earlier on. She stood up and stretched, to alleviate the tension, bending over double to stretch her back, and saw the stains on the carpet from the broken vase earlier on. The poor battered peonies were temporarily rehoused in a cut off plastic water bottle by the cooler. Perhaps an ice cold drink of water, would cool her down. She thought for a while, drinking several of the small cups, and started to feel the knot in her chest unwind as soon as she made up her mind what to do.

She drank another cup of water, scrunched up the cup and went back to the computer. First she bashed out a reply to Janice, telling her exactly what she thought had happened - Janice could at least be her eyes and ears in the office. And secondly she Helen sent an official email, copying in everybody including the Boss, and Cheryl, and the marketing team, telling them how glad she was to be accepting the many assignments, *including the ones in Hawaii* and she would get back to them in the next day or so with the final schedule, which would come direct from her. She thought for a moment, then added that for the time being, they should also only accept communications from this, her personal email account, since the one she'd been using had been compromised. She pressed *send* with a flourish and instantly felt better. Helen only had a hunch, but she knew there were some devious people out there, who thought nothing of hacking into other people's accounts. The cheek of it. Not everyone was honest like Alessandro.

Thoughts of their earlier encounter filled her with a hot fire, and she wondered where he was. Using the password she knew by now from all that logging on, she searched the office computer amongst Paul's documents, typing in the word Alessandro and 'reservations.' She'd find out exactly where he was. Maybe if he was in a nearby room on the complex tonight, she could go and surprise him one final time - *that* would work the tension out of her body. And that last session with him was unbelievable, after all.

Helen's nipples twitched against the silky surface of her little chemise which she'd pulled on for the sake of the journey to the office. Plus the spa dressing gown of course - it wasn't that warm in this office. But it wasn't that cold either. In fact, Helen was now feeling quite hot.

Soon she found what she was looking for - a note of Alessandro's new booking. Now she just had to find his new room number and...

But something else appeared on the screen which made Helen stop dead. She went cold, and couldn't believe what she was reading. She held onto the arms of the chair and started taking long, slow breaths to calm herself down. There must be some mistake. Surely...

Well that changes everything, she thought, suddenly coming over all composed.

Yes, it actually changes everything.

With this new turn of events, she knew exactly what to do - and where to go - next. And it wasn't back to Tuscany with him, nor somewhere *he* wanted to send her. *Would she have time?* Looking at her schedule of assignments she might just be able to squeeze it in. It would take a major rearrange, but considering the time differences around the world, Helen felt confident that after a couple of hours making phone calls, it would all be done.

Helen looked at herself in the pitch black of the windows, at her reflection, still a bit crabby and puffy eyed from her crying session earlier and made herself sit up straight. She felt a resolute determination in her gut and a banging realisation in her heart.

This was one scary situation when Helen Parker-Todd would most definitely *not* be running away. She picked up the phone and began to take charge of her life again. After all, it was what she did best. The clock ticked on...

Over in New York, meanwhile, another person was working through their lunch break. The computer screen, facing the wall so no-one could see, displayed a number of emails, some of them very similar to the list Helen was just looking at in Tibet. An email popped up - the one Helen had just sent. Fingers tapped at the keyboard, the cursor scanned down the message and a big sigh escaped the lips of the person doing the tapping. Then an unhappy grunt. The cursor pointed at the box 'new email,' and a blank template popped up. And there at the top, it said 'FROM: HELEN PARKER-TODD....' and the tapping began again, only this time it was louder and much, much faster.

Chapter Ten.

Helen was not surprised to find out the next morning that Alessandro was not there to see her off, nor to accompany her back to the airport. It was a long journey and she filled it with snoozing, reminiscing and planning what western 'stuff' to send to Rinchen and 'Socks.' And she rather hoped that Alessandro would be there in the village when it all arrived. Although she had a feeling he wouldn't be going back there at all.

At the airport, she checked in, deposited her designer suitcases, and was about to go through passport control when she looked up at the arrivals board. She made a face, then instead of heading for the Club Class lounge and ordering a zillion cocktails in cool air conditioned luxury, she doubled back on herself and went to the arrivals gate. A stream of people were coming through the gate and she wondered if her hunch was correct. And then she saw her driver - the same one who had brought her from the spa - standing with a name board. Helen smiled to herself and didn't need to see anything else. It was family she needed now, more than anything. Even if it meant breaking the habits of a lifetime.

Many long hours of airport lounges and flights later, Helen was back in her mum's lounge listening to her talk about one of her old flames - with the emphasis on *old*.

'I really didn't know him very well, none of us did,' said Grace handing Helen a couple of old, faded polaroids and a grainy group shot. 'It was so long ago, darling. And you know how the memory goes when you get older…'

'Actually mum, not yet I don't, no.'

'Fibber. Ha ha! Oops - oo, hang on, just got to go for a tinkle. That gets worse as you get older too - well you must know how…'

'NO! Mum, I don't. Not yet - I haven't had babies like you and Sadie have - my undercarriage isn't so weather-beaten,' she said.

'You sure? Have you seen it lately?'

Helen spluttered into her tea. 'Just go - hurry up, I've got an appointment this afternoon.' Nothing changes here, she thought.

'Talk amongst yourselves, ha-ha!' trilled Grace, leaving Helen on her own with the doyleys and the collectable china wall plates with pictures of gypsy caravans and meadows.

Helen had arrived back late yesterday after many long hours travelling - with no fuss at all, she'd changed the Club Class ticket Alessandro had booked her - they'd been more than happy to send her to the UK instead of New York. After all, that talk of 'home' made her pine a little. Plus she'd arranged a packed couple of days here. She had to snap herself out of it, stop pining for men, and get ahead of the game with her column. Yes! That's my girl, she told herself as she got up and looked in the ornate mirror hanging with a chain from the lounge wall above the brick fireplace. Helen looked at the old photos on display around the room - her and Sadie when they were little - with five years apart, there was always a gap in height. Helen was filled with protective feelings towards that little girl in the photo - ones that had started long ago and had never gone away. Even now. Then there were several of Sadie and her father and Grace too, but not a single one of Helen with the three of them. Sadie's dad George looked happy in those photos. Maybe if Helen had given him a chance...

She heard her mother singing in the toilet - she always did that when she had company, even if it was Helen - although apparently she didn't feel the need to do it when it was Sadie in the house. Helen looked at her watch - she hoped it was just the one chorus of Bohemian Rhapsody this time, rather than the whole song. *Please let her come back soon.* If she didn't, exhausted Helen would be snoring and dribbling on the sofa. Fiddling in her pocket, she produced the print-out of her itinerary - she'd been busy, and it was about to get busier.

With the help of - thank you God – in-flight Wi–Fi, Helen had used her time wisely and - running on adrenalin - she'd set up five more TiFFTs that were crucially not like anything else on the original Martha Crowne list and emailed them across to the office.

She was very pleased with her efforts, including some last minute ones. From appearing on stage in a musical via an old college friend, to riding an elephant in Thailand courtesy of Damian Grant, she was pulling in every favour, exploiting every resource in her contacts, and using every trick in her repertoire. That way she could hopefully soon confirm those all-important last minute bookings which would turn the tide of approval from The Boss back in her direction. Instead of Cheryl's.

With time on her hands, Helen reinforced this vision - as Serena had told her she should - by scribbling over and over in a notebook, her visualisations for her future - the spa retreat had taught her the value of being positive if nothing else. Plus she felt strangely more at ease in her body since the whole Tantric massage release. Weird. She scanned the list and read selected phrases.

'Dreams - to build MY Try it for the First Time club into the most visited online blog of its kind before the six month deadline...Win the bonus... Write the book of the blog for Damian /new publishing venture... And...' She was about to write 'meet up again with Alessandro and who knows what?' But she thought she'd stick with the things she could control.

Arrrgh!

The C word. *Control.*

One day, if Helen reached the stage in her life, in her career, in herself, where she could finally relinquish the thing she coveted most, being in control, well maybe then she'd go see Alessandro. She added 'And who knows what might happen with a certain man coming back into my life...' and left it at that.

One day, maybe before the dreaded Daredevil festival in Hawaii, with its parachuting and paragliding and para-god-knows-what-else, she'd reach the *aha* moment where she could let go. Let go of the one thing that might stop her from achieving those goals - by bottling out, losing face, getting beaten by her arch rival and losing her job. And bonus. And everything.

But there was no doubt that the things that scared her most were some of the best TiFFTs on that list. Ones that The Intern would have no problem with, damn her. And considering how simpering she'd been to the Boss, he'd also have no problem letting her do it. He'd probably get a *year*'s worth of Godiva for that.

Helen knew she had to stay one step ahead - it was crucial in the coming months - because there was more than one person snapping at her heels, ready to fill her shoes. And Helen was very protective about her shoes.

'No-one filling *my* shoes except me... Boss happy with me...' she wrote.

There! Nothing wrong with a bit of positivity.

Talking of the Boss, she'd had a curious out of office message from him, and she couldn't remember what she'd emailed him. Whatever it was she'd better remember and try to send it again from her personal email account. But at least it meant she had breathing space - according to his out of office message, he was not back at work till next week either. Thank heaven for The US Open and corporate hospitality - he'd no doubt be supping his fill of champagne and canapés.

Helen on the other hand, had to put up with a cup of tea and a hob-nob.

Grace's lounge was that of a typical sixty-five year olds with the prerequisite dried flowers, Tiffany lamps, and so on, plus an oversized bowling bag in one corner of the room. In the other corner, was an old stuffed badger which Helen remembered telling Sadie stories about when they were young. Apparently it had belonged to Grace's grandfather. Looked like her grandfather too. Maybe it *was* her grandfather, thought Helen, idly, and realised she was probably a bit more jet lagged than she'd thought. She looked at the floor, still littered with Grace's clear out, and the packing boxes and dusty old paperwork and files went a bit blurry. Helen blinked hard.

'All Sadie's father's, that lot,' Grace said, walking back in fastening her stretch jeans. 'George was a stickler for accounts - drove me mad - he'd brought the lot with him when he came to live with us. Do you remember when he first moved in darling?' she said, then went off on one of her reminiscences that always left Helen with that gaping chasm of loneliness she always felt when stories of 'the three of them' meant Grace, George and Sadie rather than Grace, Helen and Sadie. She interrupted her.

'Mum - the photos? The blond guy? Which one is he then?'

'You know it's a long shot, don't you? Even thinking that the psychic woman could know who your father was? It was wild back then - it could have been any of them. The one most like the description is the one in the middle at the back. He was much older than us girls. You can't really tell from this photo, but that blond hair had quite a bit of grey in the temples. It's feasible he could have kicked the bucket by now, I suppose.'

In the middle of the grainy group shot, a proud long haired blondish hippy guy stood *peacocking* amongst his harem of attractive females. His arms were draped over two of them, another two sat at his feet, and several other men and women appeared either side of him, men bare-chested with long hippy hair, women in either bikinis and sarongs or kaftans.

'Wow - motley crew!' quipped Helen, 'That you with a bikini or is that you with the kaftan?'

'Bikini, sweetie of course,' Grace said, snorting a little in disgust. Only the pregnant ones wore kaftans.'

'So what was his name?'

'The thing is, darling, I can't tell. It's not clear enough,' she said picking up the magnifying glass again. 'There were two of them very similar. It was either Zoodle or Pyewacket and I can't recall that photo being taken - you lost whole weekends back then. Hmmm, Zoodle or Pyewacket...'

'I thought they were Kate Bush's cats?' Helen laughed. 'Maybe her mother was at the same commune as you lot.'

'Anyway, that's a picture of one of them, and they both looked quite similar. One or the other. That's who the sidekick woman might mean. Either Zoodle or Pyewacket. Now we just have to figure out which.'

'Not Zen, then?' asked Helen.

'No, Zen was after that.'

'Or Ziggy?'

'No he wasn't around till after Sadie came along.'

'Or Earthman?'

'Now you're being silly - you're trying to have a dig aren't you? No, not Earthman - you know that was much later - he lived with the three of us in his caravan one summer, remember? Let me think now.' She lifted her spectacles off her nose and rapped them against her palm. 'No, of all the men I shagged who could have been your father...don't make that face Helen, those were the days of free love, everybody did it with everybody, it wasn't only me... Of all the men, it's definitely between those two - they're the only ones that fit that description from that fortune teller woman. What did she say again?'

Helen took out her notes whilst giving a theatrical mock-shudder. She flicked through a few pages. On her way she passed the page where she'd written down what she'd seen on the office computer on that last night at the spa, and a big 'ouch' kicked her in the stomach. She flicked forwards.

'Ah, here we go. "Not on this earthly plane... long blonde hair, curly... played guitar... a cross earring... leather trousers. Definitely no tattoos - which was something to do with his mother. A child's presence is around him..." Plus she said something about a note, but she hasn't had anything else on that yet.'

'Did she say anything else?'

'Yes. Serena also told me, mum, that you and I have a prickly relationship because we're alike and I inherited my worst traits from you.'

Helen's mum raised one eyebrow and appraised Helen, looking her up and down a couple of times. 'Take a look at this face,' Grace said, indicating herself, 'is it bovvered?'

Helen burst out laughing and the two women settled down with the magnifying glass to look at the others in the group. Grace went through pointing a few out. '*He* was totally bald - all over... *she* only ate chick peas, no-one wanted to share her caravan... those two on the end were the real junkies - they had an annual competition to see how many joints they could sell at Glastonbury...'

'Mum! You really were a rebel, weren't you?!'

Grace made a V-peace sign with her fingers and nodded her head lazily. 'Love and peace, man,' she said then pretended to puff on a make believe joint between her fingers.

'Did you all smoke weed back then? It's a wonder any of the men could even get it up, let alone father a child. It's supposed to dampen their ardour, if you know what I mean.'

'Ahh, that explains quite a lot,' she said. 'Which brings me back to Zoodle. Or was it Pyewacket. I wish this photo was clearer. It's amazing how seeing old pictures brings back memories.' She was holding a magnifying glass over the man in the middle once more.

Helen peered over. 'Mum - is that a tattoo on his arm?'

'Either that or a South Western Indian's Shamanic armband incorporating locks of hair from everyone he slept with,' she said, making a face. Helen made a worse one. Grace carried on. 'Or it might be a tattoo - of some feathers.'

'Really? Ok, so obvious question, but - Mum - if you can't remember, can you be sure you definitely had a thing with him?'

'Yes, of course, he was head of the commune, we all did, but...'

'But what?'

Instead of replying, Grace just held up her pinkie finger and waggled it, then made it collapse. She shrugged. 'All that weed,' she said.

Helen was unabashed. 'But - bear with me on this - sounds like it could have been him as much as any of them if you were all off your nut much of the time. Oh well. At least this might help build me a short list... Mum!' exclaimed Helen suddenly. Her mother jumped a little and looked up. 'In all this time, in all these years - we've never even had a *long list*. It's closer than I've ever been to knowing who my dad was. Even if he's dead at least I'll have somewhere to start my research - maybe find some relatives.' Grace made a 'big deal' shrug. Helen exhaled. 'I know it's never mattered to you.'

'It never mattered to *you*, darling. Or so you used to declare whenever Sadie went on about George. Why dredge it all up now? I thought you didn't do ancient history? Same as I don't?'

'Well, partly for my column and, Mum, because of Serena. Whatever you may think about her, some of the stuff she said was pretty accurate - like my green sports car - green. That's unusual, right? And she mentioned Alessandro...'

Grace interrupted by rolling his name on her tongue, 'Alesssannnndrrro,' she said, theatrically. 'Was *he*...?' and she wiggled her little finger again. 'I do hope not - you need a man, honey. It'll close up again if it doesn't see some action soon.'

Helen talked over her. '...And what's more, Serena basically said that my intuition was strong, and I've got a feeling about her vision...' Grace scrunched her face up and picked up her cup and saw it was empty. Helen went on, 'I told you what I saw, right - when I held her bracelet?'

'Yes, yes. Tell you what, if you're *sidekick* too, what do you see when you hold this?'

Grace picked up a small embroidered bag from the pile and delicately pulled out a little plectrum. It was old, scratched and faded. 'It was Zoodle's. Or it could have been Pyewacket's...'

Helen held it in her hand. She knew her mother was taking it all with a pinch of salt, but *was* there something in the feelings she'd been getting? In the depths of her mind, she'd suspected Serena was making things up for effect, to tie in with Helen's visions of the key and the cruise ship and the seven year old in front of the class. But what if she hadn't? Helen was hardly confident in her own abilities, but what the hell. She closed her eyes.

A sound of wailing began from somewhere close by, and Helen opened one eye to see her mother sitting there with her eyes half closed, arms out to the side, swaying and making the noise through an open mouth. 'Is there anybody theeeeeere?' Grace said, then opened one eye and laughed. Helen cocked her head deprecatingly on one side. Grace made a move to get up. 'Tell you what, darling, I'm going to make a cup of tea. Sadie leaving me in charge of the shop at least means I can pinch her tea bags - what'll you have? I've got extra-caffeinated ones - zinnng!' She made a crazy face and then stood, patted Helen on the shoulder and went out to the kitchen. 'Ask the spirits if they want a cuppa,' she chorused on her way out.

Helen focussed on the plectrum. It felt smooth, apart from scratches on one side. She held it up to the light. Then she closed her eyes and concentrated. By the time Grace came back in with two mugs of hot, weird-smelling tea, Helen was sitting looking very pleased with herself indeed. 'I've got something, mum,' Helen said. 'If this was definitely what he played his guitar with, his name was definitely Zoodle.'

'What? How did you know that? Did it come through to you from the other side?'

'Yes,' said Helen, 'the other side of the plectrum. Look.' And she held it up to the light where the etched-in outline of a scratched Z could clearly be seen.

'Well if it was definitely Zoodle that's easier.'

'Why?' Helen asked, sipping the hot tea and burning her mouth.

'Because Zoodle's real name was Gordon McDingleberry. Says it on that leaving card over there. If it had been Pyewacket you'd have been looking for a John Brown.'

Grace handed her a faded seventies style greetings card full of signatures and messages and real names in brackets so they could all stay in touch. Helen perused it. It said 'To George and Grace, and the bump. Love and peace, man.' Then Helen turned the photo over. It said 'me with Weasel, Stoat and chicks, Shyanne Class of 72.' It also had a photographer's stamp. And a scribbled-on reference number with a dash in the middle. 'Have you tried tracing the photographer, mum?'

'Darling,' Grace said, tucking into a hob nob cookie, 'I haven't even tried tracing my best friend Alice - sitting next to me at his feet in that pic. Bikini's, see? If I was going to trace anyone it would be her.'

'Silly question to ask you if you remember *her* surname?' Helen said, taking one of the crumbly treats.

'Easy - Springs,' laughed Grace. Helen just rolled her eyes and her head jerked upwards. 'No, really,' Grace went on, 'that was her name. Alice Springs. I only just thought about it when I saw all these pictures again - after all these years. But of course she might be married - or buried. Married or buried, ha-ha! Mind you...'

'... don't tell me, for some it means the same thing?' said Helen, anticipating her mother's usual low opinion about the state of wedded bliss. The fact that Grace's only experience had been fairly enjoyable - even if it was more a case of convenience than mad passionate soul-mate love - was irrelevant. She now saw it as her duty to advise people to go back to the 'old ways' - living in sin. Having seen both her girls through disastrous marriages, she wasn't shifting.

'You got it, cookie boy,' she said to her eldest. 'Maybe I should try searching George's ring binders for contact info - he kept lots from that time - people he'd sold weed to - in case it came and bit him in the bum and he needed to blackmail them later.'

Helen hadn't taken that much notice of her step-dad back in the day, but he just went up in her estimation. Not about the drugs, but about the back-up plan. 'Bit of a wheeler dealer, was he?' Helen asked.

'Oh yes, he supplied the Shyanne once a week. He did all sorts, did Sadie's dad. That's why I'm not surprised how she can turn her hand to virtually anything. So proud of her, he would have been.' She paused, thinking. 'Hey, maybe the next time you speak to that Serena, you can ask her to see if she can detect George sitting on a rock somewhere playing a tune with his mouth organ, smoking his ganja, and Bossing everyone about.'

'Will do mum,' laughed Helen.

Helen had a busy couple of days, having packed out her UK schedule. Now she sat on Sadie's bed looking round at her sister's life in microcosm - pictures of her daughters, of Helen and Sadie, one of Grace and George, and a plethora of make-up and toiletries covering her dressing table, along with brushes covered in Sadie's dark hair. Another way they were different, thought Helen. But not for much longer. She made a mental note to see if she could get Abi to send a pic of their mum's newly blonde locks once she got them done. She'd be blonde and curly - like the guy in the vision - like the guy in the photo - like Helen's if it had curl.

Helen finished checking out the photographer on the back of the photo, but nothing online matched up. Then she set about rearranging her schedule to make it fit her own purposes, rather than Cheryl Goodman's. Helen sat looking at the list of dates she was copying across, having covered it with arrows to rearrange them so they fit in with her intended flights for the next few weeks. It was going to be busy - almost as busy as Sadie with her gallivanting. But if anyone could do it, the Parker sisters could.

The last thing Helen did was reply to an email from Alessandro, just a simple 'hope you're well.' Her heart had skipped a beat when she saw his email in her inbox. But she had something very important to ask him before she allowed herself to think much more about him, and she needed to do it face to face. So for now, she'd ordered herself to place all thoughts of him on the back burner, where they ticked over quietly out of harm's way. She packed up the laptop and her things, and went downstairs to see her nieces, who were back from school, playing computer games on an X–box.

'So where are you going next, Auntie Helen?' Abi asked, handing the controller to her sister. She knew the gist of what Helen was up to, as the two kept in touch quite frequently online. 'Nana said you're off to India soon to ride on elephants.'

'Thailand, but not just yet - yes, an old friend of mine is arranging the elephants for me - that'll be great fun.'

'Do you have to wear a riding hat, like my friend Cosita?' asked Georgia.

'Er, I don't think so. Does *she* ride elephants?'

'No, ha-ha - silly Auntie - she's got a pony - called Grommit.'

'Oh, right. No, no helmets - at least I don't think so - it's all very *ad hoc*.' Both girls looked quizzically at Helen. 'It means they make it up as they go along.'

'Is that what you'll do when you're on the stage? In that Happy Day musical?'

'You'll find out tomorrow night,' she said, ruffling her youngest niece's hair.

Abi the older one was pondering, creasing her brow deeply above big green eyes and playing with one of her brunette locks - the image of her mother - Helen recalled Sadie doing exactly the same at her age. 'Auntie Helen...'

'Yes Abi?'

'You know mum's gone to Hawaii, and now Nana says you're going there too. It's like, it's like...'

'What sweetheart?'

She took a breath. 'It's like everyone's going somewhere really nice and I'm not even sure that I'm allowed to go with all my friends on the school trip to China. Now that dad's... you know.'

'Skint,' chipped in Georgia, then thwacked a button on her games controller. 'Hah! I beat you at Boyband2.0!'

'But I whoop your ass at Boyband1.0, and you know it.' Abi sniped, making a *'ner ner'* face that looked every ounce of her 14 years and reminded Helen how young they still were. At least they'd had a dad for most of their life, even if he did turn out to be a useless dickwad. Helen, on the other hand, didn't even know who hers was... yet.

'Tell you what, if I make it through to the final,' she said, 'I'll invite you both to come and watch me in Hawaii, how about that? Ever seen someone plummet into the sea from 5000 feet?'

Their faces were a picture and she laughed, so they laughed too, relieved she was joking.

But, thought Helen, *if the same thing happens again as happened last time, I won't be laughing then...*

The next day Helen was up bright and early - she had a long train ride. She'd had a very nice catch-up with her nieces and had a surreptitious peek at those of her belongings being stored at Sadie's. She was on her way to one of two TiFFT's for today - and this one might provide some answers no-one else would have ever dreamed of.

Chapter Eleven

Helen arrived at the head office for 'GeneticBase UK' - an imposing building with lush gardens and a marble entrance. She'd heard a lot about it, researched it on the train, and hoped she was going to get her assignment filed before Martha Crowne did her version in the US. It was becoming quite a race - and the latest feedback from TransGlobe Inc - via Janice - had worried Helen. Yes, she had started off with Martha's original list as a basis, but how come Martha's team were apparently *coincidentall*y booking her on a Yoga retreat? At least she couldn't post any of them until her three months' gardening leave was up. Thank God for a head start, thought Helen gratefully.

She'd made sure her latest pieces were ready to go and emailed The Intern in no uncertain terms, NOT to edit or change any of her documents, dates or assignments. This next month of TiFFTs would be crucial to set the tone and help decide whether Helen would eventually stay ahead in the online stakes. But with the marketing power behind the upcoming ParlourGames Channel launch, you never know.

Janice had also casually thrown in, with much amusement in her voice, that the 'Tantric massage class' document had now started to go viral amongst students at a particular campus in New York, with the headline 'Tantric porno - got to watch!' Helen shook her head and smiled - she bet it was the full unabridged version too. *Any publicity is good publicity* Janice had said.

This next feature couldn't be further removed from that one, and lacked a certain amount of 'nitty gritty' - but all Helen could think was it served the Boss right for making her keep it - just to deny Martha's gang the sponsorship deal. Tracing your ancestors isn't the jazziest topic but it was a huge trend and if one of the ancestry sites was willing to pay, well who was she to argue. Having done the research on it, she now actually found herself looking forward to it immensely. Partly because she'd warmed to the whole tracing our ancestors thing. And partly because you did it with your feet firmly on the ground.

She stepped onto a marble step, pushed a button on the big entrance door, and almost immediately, a fresh faced, smartly dressed receptionist buzzed her in. After being supplied with the prerequisite visitor's pass, she was met by a distinguished looking grey haired man in a white lab coat, not unlike a mad professor.

'Ahh, Miss Parker - welcome. Doctor Hannover. We spoke on the phone.' He shook her hand vigorously. 'I'm so glad you were able to come in person - it makes such a change from dealing with swabs and test-tubes with people's names on all day. Come this way,' he said, in a fuddy-duddy, public school accent, and led her through the security gate. A swift tour of the facility followed and then they went to his laboratory where Helen began to get excited about the idea of knowing what part of humanity she was descended from. This place could trace your genetic material and even find out what part of the world your ancestors evolved in - Helen was fascinated, even if it wasn't doing much for 'sexying' up the column.

They sat down either side of the desk in his office - a glass-walled corner of the clean white lab filled with microscopes, glass tubing, computers and intense-looking students who'd hardly looked up as they'd passed by. At least his office was a bit more lived-in, but still far tidier than she'd expected a mad professor to have. Niceties over, she pressed 'record' on her hand held device.

'So what made you think of choosing this as one of your - em, what did you call it? Try it firsts?' he asked.

'Try it For the First Time club,' Helen replied, thinking she'd better not say the real reason - that she'd been forced to.

'You see I'm a bit of a nomad,' she said quickly, thinking how true that was, given what had happened in Tibet and virtually everywhere else in her life - full of temporary abodes.

'Ahh - we were all nomads, once,' he said. 'The descent of humans began in Africa but spread across the Middle East and up to Europe then to Asia and the rest of the world - we nearly all came from that small clutch of Homo Sapiens around 60,000 years ago.' Helen looked up, a quizzical look on her face. 'Yes, it's true,' he said. 'People find it hard to believe but it has been proven with DNA testing across all the continents - people outside of Africa - all people - came from a nucleus of a few thousand who crossed out of Africa.'

'Really?'

'Really. They spread around the world, their genes mutating a tiny amount every generation, and diversifying into the races we see today around the world. Some of them encountered Neanderthals across Europe, some met another species existing at the same time in Siberia, called Denisovans - after the Denisova cave in which the recently identified remains were originally found. And possibly there were other ancient beings we still have yet to discover - whose DNA may lie hidden amidst the thousands of man-like bones in our museums, mixed up with human beings - the likes of you and I.'

Helen smiled sweetly, and suspected he was dumbing it down a little just for her - sometimes it didn't pay to be blonde.

'And all of them came originally from *Homo Heidelbergensis* around half a million years ago?' she said, beaming innocently at him. He opened his eyes a little wider. *Hah, Google in ya face.*

'Er... yes, that is correct. And within Africa itself,' he continued, encouraged, 'the indigenous peoples who never left, continued their descendancy, and they have a completely different mix of genes to most of the rest of the world.'

'Because they never interbred,' Helen asked.

'Well, not as much as the rest of us mongrels,' he laughed, and the crinkles in the corners of his eyes spread way past his glasses almost to his hairline. 'I'm joking, but of course as this chart shows,' he turned to a big illustration on the wall behind him in the clean white lab, 'most of modern humanity is also around 2% Neanderthal.'

'Some of us more than others,' quipped Helen, but the joke was lost on him as, absorbed in his theme and with a seemingly enthusiastic new student before him, he told her all about the spread of humans around the globe.

'So,' he said, 'now all it takes is for you to spit in this tube and we can begin the testing process. I'll go get the required forms.'

After taking a bit longer than she thought it would to deposit enough spittle in the tiny tube, and passing the sealed container back to Doctor Hannover, he said, 'there you go - we can give you an idea of the geographical areas from which your ancestral line originated, usually in percentages. Your heritage, all from this little tube. Isn't technology amazing?' Helen nodded in agreement. 'We'll contact you as soon as it's available,' he said.

'Thank you - it's been enlightening,' she replied, standing up to go.

'Helen,' he said, with an interesting intonation to his voice. 'I see you haven't asked about the Y-chromosome test.'

'No I don't think so? What's that? And don't restrict yourself to layman's terms.'

He took her at her word, and went into great depth about how they did the tests, and she immediately yearned for layman. *Thank goodness for the recorder.* She could always google-translate later.

'So basically,' he finished, 'Men who have had their Y Chromosome tested can look at an international online database and possibly confirm or deny legitimate familial connections. For instance, solicitors use it sometimes to check inheritance claims. But if you're interested in...' he looked at her face a little warily – *oh-oh,* thought Helen, *I must be going glazed again.* She refocused her eyes and he seemed to regroup. 'If you're interested in all that family tree... ah, *stuff*... you might like it. We tie our results in with the world's most powerful online DNA genealogy project - an online scientific community if you like, all double-checking their family trees.'

'Ok?' Helen said, waiting for more info.

'Tell you what - as it's so new, I can offer you an exclusive - it'll create quite a buzz if you're the first to feature it.' Helen wasn't so sure it would, but he'd got her attention.

'So what do I need to do to get that done as well?'

'Just get me a sample from one of the men in your family - like your father?' he said. Helen shook her head. 'Brother?' she shook it again apologetically. 'Son?'

'Nope. Sorry.'

'Oh well, never mind. You can always come back to us later if you find someone you can use. That means we will just do your maternal DNA - that's where the test tube of spittle comes in - we can use yours to find out your mother's line, because all of us carry our mother's DNA signature within our cells...'

And if Serena the psychic is right, I carry a hell of a lot of it in mine, thought Helen. Then she decided to get a bit of the person out of him.

'Have you had it done?' she asked.

He puffed up a little. 'Why of course! Very interesting mixture - even more so with these latest methods of testing - didn't even know I had any Scandinavian in me at all! Bit of a Viking on the quiet, my wife said! Ha-ha!'

'Well I look forward to finding out mine,' Helen said quickly, getting off the subject of Vikings. 'Just the maternal side then.'

'No Y chromosome test for you, ok,' he said, putting crosses in some boxes on the form.

Dammit.

'Any chance of that changing?'

'Probably not. I'll keep you informed. Let's hope the results come out ok?' Helen was frustrated, thinking of Martha Crowne with her big family, smugly going along to do her test in the US with the complete set of spit samples - bet she'd be able to provide a father, a brother *and* a son.

Helen had none.

'Oh and are there any case stories you can tell me about which I can use in my article?' asked Helen, considering she wasn't going to 'find' a male relative any time soon.

'Well I tested a man recently,' he said, as he leaned towards her slightly and raised his eyebrows conspiratorially, 'let's call him Bob - Jamaican on his father's side. Well, I expected an African connection - due to the trans-Atlantic slave trade via the Caribbean of course. And yes, he has a marker that's in 96% of people from Central West Africa.' He beamed, obviously responding to Helen's big ingenuous smile, glad because she didn't have to take notes, it would all be on the recorder. 'What's more amazing is what we saw when we looked at others on the database. That's when it gets really exciting, as you can see who else you're related to - albeit via a distant ancestor. We found that certain sequences of his DNA matched up perfectly with a man from Zanzibar, Tanzania, and another from the Democratic Republic of Congo, who also had their DNA tested recently.'

An interesting thought occurred to her. 'Can you trace paternity?'

'Well, we're allied to a DNA paternity testing arm, but that's a different process. Why, my dear, do you have a sample of DNA from a *potential* father which you'd like us to test?'

'No. it doesn't matter. But the genealogy one sounds great. Please.'

'No problem - I will have our team take care of it for you. It's been a pleasure meeting you.'

'Likewise,' said Helen, and spent the rest of the journey back to the train station with her head in the clouds wondering what they'd find. If she couldn't know her father, if Serena's vision came to nothing, at least she might find some long lost cousins somewhere down the line...

'Nana - there she is!' hissed Georgia, sitting in the stalls at the big theatre production of Happy Day - the Musical and elbowing both Grace and Abi who were sitting either side of her. Helen could see her excitement from her vantage point standing in the wings. Once again her heart was pounding, as she was about to take a walk-on role in a musical adaptation of a popular eighties TV series, doing a tour of the country and looking for extra publicity where they could find it by offering a small cameo. Including a local radio, TV or some other personality in every performance was a perfect solution for them.

The idea for this one had come from Grace, whose team mate at the bowls club - the one who had her eyes on Herb - had waxed lyrical about her niece being 'the announcer' in the Woking production, and how 'only a few special people ever get to do something like that'. The marketing guy had been delighted to hear from Helen and a few calls later, he'd happily moved some guest appearances around in return for a mention on TransGlobe Inc's online worldwide platform. It might help their chances of setting up tours in other countries, plus, he thought he recognised Helen's name. Which was a bit of a worry until he said he spent all day looking at online blogs, forums and news sites, so she figured he must have found a mention of the tantra thing doing the rounds on one of the student forums.

It was a rush to get back from the DNA place, and she'd written up most of the article for that one on the train home, leaving a lot of the technical stuff in the research appendix - just in case Mr Adams was inexplicably found that 'nitty gritty.'

Then she got ready for her stage debut, whilst absent-mindedly dreaming about magically finding a bit of the curly haired man's DNA in Grace's old dust covered files and taking it to Dr Hannover's lab to prove paternity.

Then she had to learn her lines for her walk-on part. The girls helped, both testing her over and over on the hour-long car journey there, with Grace driving and chipping in every so often. Then they had a sing song and arrived in good time for Helen to go off for a rehearsal. By the time Helen stepped out on the stage, the three faces sitting in the audience were all mouthing the lines along with her.

She was in a 1950's dirndl skirt cinched in at her non-baby-thickened waist and she'd had her makeup done backstage, and had big red lips, and her hair pinned and curled into a big pony tail. She was proudly able to provide her own shoes - kitten heels - and a yellow cardigan draped over her shoulders. She looked every inch a fifties chick, and felt it too - she loved this stylish era. Around her neck, she wore some of her mum's pearls - Grace had complained loudly about it, but she was secretly chuffed to bits knowing she could show off at bowls this weekend about her oldest being 'on the stage, you know, sweetie.'

The auditorium went quiet as Helen strutted comically over to the huge stand up microphone - she was playing a local celebrity announcing the annual fete - and, with her tongue fuzzy and dry in her mouth, she said her lines in a kitsch American accent. She could hardly hear her own words, and what was worse, there was an echo to every syllable, which meant she talked a lot more slowly. The words came out in slow motion, and she hoped *they* could hear her because *she* certainly couldn't. Then a huge laugh from the audience and titters from the fellow actors on the stage proved they could. But what she'd said that was so funny, she had no idea whatsoever.

'Hahahaa!' Georgia and Abi laughed as they played the YouTube clip someone had loaded, over and over again the next morning before they left for school. Helen had tried not to look, but sadly on the back of the massage feature, her name was quietly trending on the internet and as soon as 'someone' picked up the on-stage boo-boo on YouTube, it went viral amongst the New York students again, then started to spread, taking her tantra article with it, until it really took off.

'You've got 120,000 hits,' said a delighted Abi, who was planning to show off at school that her auntie was the next YouTube star. Georgia just sat there - laughing, but still slightly bemused.

'But why is saying "prick of the show" funny?' she asked.

'Come on, dad's here with our lift, I'll tell you on the way to school,' Abi said. At her words, Helen pricked up her ears, and then jumped out of her chair towards the door.

'Don't forget to go upstairs and kiss Nana goodbye.' She grabbed a packet out of her bag and ran outside to catch the girls' smarmy father who was sitting waiting in a convertible Golf. He looked shocked, and for a fleeting moment looked like he might take off. Then he composed himself.

'Helennnn - sweetie pie. How ARE you. Grace tells me you're peddling porn on the internet now,' he smarmed.

'Not quite, but you better stop looking at it all the time anyway - in case you learn something,' she said at his pathetic attempt at a dig. Typical exchange between them - *nothing changes there then*, she thought.

'See this car?' he said in return. Helen nodded, confused. 'Giselle's. She's 27. Don't need porn. Nuff said?'

Helen rolled her eyes and ignored him. 'Listen,' she said, brandishing the packet with the little tube in. 'I'm doing an article about DNA and I don't have any Y chromosomes...'

'Oh I wouldn't say that.'

'...you're the nearest I've got to a male relative right now - even if only for Abi and Georgia - so will you spit in this?'

He looked dumbfounded. 'DNA?' he asked. 'Like with paternity testing?'

'Er... yes but that's their sister-company, it's not directly connec...'

'Not a chance,' he replied, cutting her off. 'No, no, no.'

'But - why won't you do it for the girls? To find out which part of Europe or Asia they came from?'

He gave her a look along the lines of 'you're out of your tiny mind' as the girls hopped into the car with their bags.

'Cool new car Dad,' exclaimed Georgia, playing with the buttons on the dashboard.

'Leave it alone, Giselle will kill me,' he said, and turned back to Helen. *'New girlfriend,'* he mouthed smugly. *'Another one?'* Helen mouthed back. He 'humphed' and made sure seatbelts were done up, then revved the engine. Helen tried another tactic.

'It would mean a lot to them,' she said, jerking her head towards the girls, 'and you might find proof you're not as closely related to the ape as everyone thinks you are. Look - I needed a man to do this test, but you'll do. You're still Sadie's first husband and the girls' father. And the nearest I've got to a male relative. I just thought you might...'

'Look Helen, I'm sorry you don't have any men in your life *whatsoever* - but that's not my fault. And the DNA thing? It's not my bag, capiche?'

Helen shuddered. What Sadie ever saw in him God only knew.

'Isn't Jason still your next of kin? You've got as much chance of *me* doing it as him, your first victim, I mean husband. Any news on how poor Jason is nowadays?' he asked. 'After you terrified him and he ran off to the jungle never to be seen again. Tell you what, you find him and get *him* to do it first, and then I'll do it too? Deal? Girls, say goodbye to Auntie Helen.'

'Goodbye Auntie Helen,' said Georgia.

Sitting in the back seat behind Stuart, Abi just smiled apologetically at Helen and made a big 'L for loser' sign with her fingers at him. 'Bye. See you in a couple of months. Love you,' Abi replied.

Helen smiled back, and they were gone. She was left standing there with thoughts of Jason Todd in her head. And then Alessandro. And then Jason Todd again... And then... *Oh dear.*

Helen walked back inside, up the winding front path past pretty early summer blooms with a vague buzz of honey bees in the air with a yearning for flapjacks then remembered they'd eaten them all already, and Sadie wasn't due back till next week.

She looked at her watch - she had a flight to catch. The Boss had called a crunch meeting, and this one was very likely to be a tad uncomfortable - and not just for Helen.

Just then a voice came squealing from inside the house. 'Heleeeeen!'

Helen bounded up the stairs to Sadie's room where Grace was in repose. 'You're awake then. How was the night with Miss Kick-a-lot?'

'OK. I just kicked her back,' the older lady said, sitting there for all the world looking like some Hollywood movie star in her negligee with feathers round the collar, china cup and saucer in her hand with her pinkie finger extended as she sipped it. She had an old laptop on the bed beside her.

'Good job I know you're joking. Right, what did you call for? I haven't got long before my taxi comes to take me to the airport and...'

'Yes, yes. OK so as you know I was looking for Alice online - Abi helped me. You'll never guess who got back to me on Friends Reunited?'

'Where? I didn't think there were many people on that site anymore.'

'Ah well, the Silver Surfers have taken over since the youngsters like you and Sadie went over to Facebook and Twitter. Phyllis showed me. Well Alice popped up! Look!' Grace pointed to a message on the screen.' Helen was distracted by a knock at the door.

'That's really nice mum, but you'll have to tell me all about it once I'm back in New York.' She leaned over, kissed her mum goodbye and disappeared out the door. But she popped her head straight back round again when she heard her mother say, 'She thinks she knows what happened to Gordon McDingleberry.'

'You're not still mooning over the Italian stallion are you?' asked Kate, pushing a big round oatmeal cookie towards Helen who was sitting in the coffee shop in New York with her chair pushed back, her head resting on her arms on the table in front of her. Her black coffee was so far untouched.

'No. Although another nice massage would be absolutely perfect right now.' She hadn't slept much on the plane and she'd dreamed of Zoodle, Alessandro and elephants gate-crashing a 1950's summer picnic intermingled with being back at school and being told off for jumping off the annexe roof to try to beat the boys' jumps. *Weird*. 'A nice, long sensuous massage. Mmmm.'

'Well, not *right* now, huh? Especially if it was that "upgrade" massage you were telling me about last night!' Kate laughed.

Helen giggled and lifted her head. Ouch. She put it back down again fast.

After the comforting few days back in the UK things had started catching up with her. And a few 'first night back in town' drinks in O'Reilly's bar last night hadn't helped - topped up by Brad the barman, who listened eagerly to all the gossip from her trips and was super-excited about the next one, when Helen would hook up with Damian Grant who was on holiday in Thailand.

But her brain hurt, and right now she needed a long hot soak in a bath - not a public ear bashing in the board-room in an hour's time.

'Here, does this help?' asked Kate, pressing her thumbs into the knotted muscles around Helen's shoulders and neck.

'Yessss - that's - oo right there,' Helen groaned, making two be-suited, be-spectacled businessmen turn round mid-sentence with interest. 'If you learned that from that latest date of yours, he's a keeper,' said Helen. But behind Helen's back, Kate pretended to the men that she was really enjoying rubbing Helen's shoulders, and the men looked away again, nudging each other. 'Is he?' asked Helen.

'Maybe,' Kate said, joining her at the table, 'Five date rule, so we'll see. Anyway, you'd better slow things down a little - you've been so crazy this past fortnight - your shoulders felt hard as iron. And not in a good way. Too much time in the air - the Boss is working you too hard - you should give him a piece of your mind.'

'Yeah, like that's going to happen,' said Helen, sitting up with half her hair still over her face. She blew it all away and reached for the cookie. 'I missed Sadie's home-baking - the cupboards were bare.'

'That's because Sadie was away being a big girl, collecting her award for being a genius. What you really missed was not hearing a blow by blow of what's happening in Hawaii. Just remember what you said about not contacting her and leaving her be - *it was time*.'

'I know, I know,' Helen said, dunking the biscuit and losing half of it in the big mug of coffee. As she fished it out with her fingers again, Kate went and got her some napkins. *Eurgh* clumsy. It wasn't just jet lag, this time. It was definitely something else.

The hectic schedule of assignments, the angst she felt when she remembered what she'd seen on the spa computer the night before she left Tibet. The lack of contact with Sadie... none of them helped her feeling of disquiet. But there was still something else. And now that Helen's curiosity about being psychic had been piqued by Serena and that reading, every time Helen got a little feeling, a little niggle in her belly, she tried to hone down what she thought it was.

And then she realised. At least she realised one of the things that were niggling her. And as soon as she thought of it, her heart sank again.

The list.

A long list of her top secret ingenious, innovative suggestions for the next few months had been secretly leaked to the competition. Mr Adams' insider said so, so it must be true. Which of them would they copy? If any. And who was responsible? Helen had a good idea. She had a big confrontation to contend with this afternoon - straight after the board meeting. She put her head back down in her hands.

'Oh look, there's Alessandro,' said Kate, coming back. Helen's head shot up. 'Made you look! Ha-ha!' teased Kate.

'No you didn't, I was just checking where my coffee was...' they both knew she was lying. 'As if he'd turn up here.'

'Cheer up - maybe he'll come looking for you again. He emailed to ask how you are, didn't he?'

'Just a courtesy, I'm sure,' Helen replied, resting her cheek on the back of her hand and flicking some crumbs off the table. 'He'll be with someone else by now, someone less controlling,' she said, then inhaled deeply and let out a big sigh.

'Like I said, mooning over the Italian stallion,' Kate said, and tucked into a Panini dripping with melted mozzarella. The two guys were still watching so she picked it up and licked at the drips of stringy cheese provocatively. Helen nudged her to stop being gross. 'I'm just playing around, Helen - maybe you should too. I can fix you up with a date - I've got quite a system going now.'

'No,' Helen said. 'No dates.'

'Well how about some mindless sex then? I could probably fix that for you too!'

'Maybe,' said Helen, to shut her up. She didn't want her best pal to think she'd completely lost her old feistiness and spark. And after all, Helen had been a bit of a player in the past.

But in reality, Helen hadn't stopped reliving those nights in Tibet. And thinking of Alessandro. But if they weren't compatible, they weren't compatible, and that was that. Wasn't it? And sure, she fantasised about meeting him again - and that upgrade kit.

But men were kind of off-the-agenda for now. She thought of Sadie again and felt a pang of missing her sister - Sadie was currently on a man-ban too. Maybe Helen should be. After all, she had more urgent matters to attend to.

The Boss was on the warpath. And whilst her short diversion to the UK had achieved some fabulous TiFFT articles, plus what she'd achieved so far had set 'Helen Parker' and 'TransGlobe Inc' trending online, he still wasn't satisfied. And neither was the key investor.

As the board room full of concerned faces found out later that afternoon, everyone had to buck their ideas up - even Kate and Kieran, who were blue-eyed boy and girl most of the time. The DNA piece hadn't excited him, he was impatient to hear the results and told her to cut much of the explanation and get some more case stories. And neither had the other pieces she'd filed so far, including a simulated parachute jump in an indoor wind tunnel - he said he'd only publish it, if it clearly stated it was training for a real one. Helen gulped and nodded and felt that familiar feeling of dread well up inside her. Only the fish pedicure, where you sit in a beauty salon with your feet in a tank and tiny fish nibble the dead skin around your heels and cuticles, had hit the spot - the video of Helen screaming with laughter, unable to stop, had once again set the online student community buzzing and demand for the pedicures around their campus had gone up ten-fold, as had comments from the students on her blog pieces. But it wasn't enough - because of a new update from the Martha Crowne camp.

'And I'll share it with you, in private, Parker - you'll see why when I tell you - stay back afterwards, OK?' Everyone turned to look at Helen with pity on their faces and she felt the bottom fall out of her stomach. Just like at school. *Oh-oh.*

Then the Boss turned his attention to two other columnists and their recent 'efforts at being witty.' Even The Intern didn't escape this lambasting session - Mr Adams squarely blamed her for the 'lost' memo that had found its way into the ParlourGames Channel's hands. It had been left in a public place, according to the Boss's inside source.

'It wasn't me, I'm sure I didn't even print it out,' she'd protested but he'd ripped her off a strip or two in front of the whole conference room. Cheryl had spent the rest of the meeting, quivering, face cherry-red, sitting like a wallflower in the corner of the room, and Helen almost felt sorry for her. Maybe Helen would postpone her intended dressing down session until tomorrow. *Maybe.*

Then everyone was filing out and Helen wished they'd slow down, postponing the agonizing moment when he'd give her the 'news.' But the wait was short-lived. He gestured for her to sit down on the slightly lower chair again, and fiddled around with a few buttons on his phone. Then he spoke.

'What do you know of the Bunn-Sinclair Leisure Group sponsorship deal?' he asked her outright with no preamble.

'The what?' Helen replied.

'We lost it. What do you know of the deal?' he said.

'Again, the what?' she answered. He visibly relaxed and reached into his desk to get his E–cigarette.

'Martha Crowne's lot have stolen the deal from us - for the spa piece.'

'Shit,' said Helen.

'Very eloquent and lady-like, but yes, *shit* just about sums it up. The investor's not happy. I'd sold the deal myself and suddenly it's gone and they won't take my calls. Anthony Adams is not a happy bunny,' he said, blowing vapours in the air angrily.

'Isn't there anything we can do?' asked Helen, shifting in her chair. 'Isn't she tied to some sort of fine print, isn't...'

'No, she's not. If I'd known what would happen, I'd have re-written her goddam severance contract myself instead of leaving it up to some brainless numbnuts newbie in Human Resources to make sure her employment house arrest was watertight.'

Ah, he means her gardening leave.

'Anyway,' he continued, 'however she got it, she got your list. But that's not all,' and he proceeded to tell Helen about something disturbing - something very disturbing indeed - before excusing her and telling her to shut the door tightly as she left the room.

As soon as Helen had banged the door shut, he punched a button on the side of his phone. 'Did you get all that?'

'Yes,' the tinny voice sounded. 'You still think she's not the one?'

'I'm positive - I'd bet the farm and all the cattle that she's not the one. I'm putting my neck on the line here,' Mr Adams said to the voice.

'Well as long as you're sure - because if you're wrong - your neck might well be what's at stake.' And the voice was abruptly replaced by a hollow silence and Mr Adams threw his E-cigarette against the wall and it shattered into tiny pieces and hit the floor, just about the time Helen was knocking on Kieran's office door.

'Let me guess, let me guess!' said Kate, 'It's not what I think it is, is it?!' Her face looked like she was going to heave.

'Exactly! I just hope there aren't going to be photos,' said Helen, unsure whether to laugh or throw up. 'The insider reckons Martha's been so miffed with me getting all this attention whilst she's lying low, that she's raised her head above the parapet...'

'Stuck her craw on the line... Let me guess the rest,' said an excited Kate.

'No - you'll never guess what's happened.' Helen proceeded to tell Kate about the Martha Crowne shock of the century. Namely that this erstwhile middle aged grandmother had suddenly had a complete turn up for the books and that, to get ahead in the viewership stakes when the time came, she was intending to do some very weird assignments.

Risqué, according to Mr Adams's insider source at ParlourGames Channel. She'd even started dropping enormous hints and telling all her Twitter followers that her new column wouldn't be for the faint hearted. The topics that had been mentioned implied some very unusual TiFFTs indeed. Including 'that' one.

'We need a solution,' said Helen miserably, 'otherwise her buzz will outweigh my buzz and then where will we be?'

'Buzz–t?' offered Kate. 'Busst? See? No? Suit yourself...' At that moment right on cue, the door opened and in walked Kieran. 'Although, I bet given half an hour and a strong coffee or several, Mister Ideas here will come up with a solution you never would have thought of.' And he did.

Three weeks later, Helen was riding high on the YouTube search, and had been courted by several local radio and TV stations for her fifteen minutes of fame.

A short heart-felt, simple piece to camera was at the bottom of it, and Mr Adams had been overjoyed at the immediate viral spread and this time, not just amongst the students. It showed Helen facing the camera in the most flattering lighting possible, in a come to bed voice, talking about her recent mishaps, introducing what they were for and wanting suggestions for TiFFTs she could do that were 'edgy,' and 'daring.' The Boss had allowed a competition for the best one. They'd come flooding in in their droves. Some in the form of simple links to other short videos showing bareback riding, swimming with sharks, all sorts of beach sports and the like. And some mundane predictable ones, followed by a genuinely intriguing one from a person who posted under the name 'NExUS X.'

'Hand yourself over to the wild side,' it said, followed by a link to a site which simply said 'NExUS X - striving for Xcellence' and a short sound-only clip on the home page which sounded like someone was being hunted, then laughing then heavy breathing then screaming, then text on the screen which looked like a disclaimer.

'This you got to do,' Kate said, beginning to phone the number immediately.

'Oi! It could be some nutter!' Helen protested. 'Let me think about it.'

'Hello, Kate Campbell calling on behalf of Ms Helen Parker - it's about your email...'

The following afternoon, Helen was on another plane, having told Mr Adams only the bare minimum - just in case this was a hoax. Their credentials as a business had checked out though - service industry - wealthy clients the world over - testimonials which said everything and nothing all at once. *Curiouser and curiouser,* Kate had said. She got hyper-excited about it after the in-depth phone call, declaring that the guy on the phone sounded kosher and dispatching Helen forthwith.

As the jet rose higher and higher into the sky, Helen felt an uncanny jingling in her stomach and wondered what on earth it could mean. But if she'd known, in that moment, maybe she wouldn't have gone walking into one of the biggest confrontations of her life.

Chapter Twelve

To say Helen was intrigued was the understatement of the year. She was met at the airport at the other end and whisked away immediately by a corporal in a camouflaged jeep who showed her a copy of the email Kate had sent - it matched her own one.

So far so good.

She was told there may be a delay in the pick up at the next point because there had been an alert in the area and the whole division had gone to Code Red.

'You mean, real Code Red?' she said, flippantly, filing one finger nail as they drove along a bumpy track that got even more dusty. 'Or just pretend, for this exercise? I know we're on some kind of training mission - this is NExUS isn't it? You google it and it comes up with a Director of Operations, codename Frankincense. It's all quite a jolly jape, as they used to say in the RAF, isn't it?'

The corporal didn't reply, just fixed her with a look of thunder in the rear view mirror. For the rest of the journey her bravado gradually suffered a battering as she heard distant sounds that unsettled her. Gunfire? Explosions? Must just be a training exercise.

'Just a training exercise?' she smiled, disarmingly. But he just shook his head. Even he was looking worried now.

Helen had heard of the pockets of insurgents and terrorists who made their way living amongst locals and acting like them too. A cell could be activated at any time. Maybe this wasn't make believe, maybe this was really happening.

After another short time bumping up and down - so high now, her breasts lifted and settled over each bump, much to the corporal's amusement, if the look of his face in the mirror was anything to go by.

Then suddenly the road ended in a wide clearing and people were walking around - all dressed the same way the Corporal was, all military looking - and male. No children or other women come to that.

 A uniformed person helped her out of the truck and into a tent. There, her belongings were excavated as if she was carrying a bomb herself, in amongst her high pink shoes, her face cream and her various electronic devices.

Shortly after, they'd kitted her out with a rucksack, and sensible shoes had replaced the pumps. She'd cherry picked the things she'd need, and replaced them with other more practical clothing and footwear and head gear, as well as an array of tools, rope, knives, string, containers, and matches. By the time she'd been dropped at the rendezvous point, in the middle of a clearing an hour into the forest, she was hot, wearing just a white cotton vest, no bra, a camouflage jacket tied around her waist, a pair of combat trousers (into which she'd squeezed her lip salve and her tea tree antiseptic stick, her camera and her mobile - just in case of emergencies) and a comfortable pair of walking boots with thick sweltering socks. She sat on the single log right in the middle of the clearing and had a strong feeling of being watched.

'Please take good care of my shoes,' she called pathetically after the truck as it pulled away and the sounds of the engine faded into the distance, replaced by the sounds and the smells of the forest. After a few minutes, Helen could no longer pick up the odour of engine oil and exhaust, instead inhaling the freshest pine-tinged air and smell of the undergrowth. After an hour she'd become aware of her own body smells, thinking it's a good job she smothered herself in deodorant that morning. But after three hours, she was beginning to get worried.

It was comfortable here in the forest, but there was no mobile signal (naturally - stupid idea to bring the mobile phone.) And for the very first time as her watch hit three and a half hours since she was dropped off, she actually wondered if she might die, right here in the forest in deepest Colorado.

'What the hell am I getting myself involved with?' she said to the trees around the clearing.

Then one of the trees spoke. 'Well that depends how long you last, doesn't it. Many can't take it, and they turn back before they even reach basecamp,' said a voice from behind a massive pine tree.

A camouflage jacket moved and suddenly Helen could see two eyes looking out at her from a blackened face. Then the wash of bush and foliage took on the outline of a man. Helen thought she was imagining things - she'd been sitting there so long. But a second later, a burly soldier materialised in front of her, with a name badge on his pocket saying 'Rains.'

'Sergeant Rob Rains reporting on duty ma'am. Come this way if you please,' he said, and without even asking, he picked up her rucksack as if it was a feather and disappeared back the way he'd come. She trotted to keep up, ducking branches that flicked back into her face and freeing her hair from leaves and twigs and before she realised it, he had stepped aside and stopped, and she ran straight into a massive chest in a combat jacket. She looked up and up and into the deepest brown eyes she had seen for a long, long while.

'Major James Segal meet Ms Helen Parker.'

'Ms?' he said, a dark brown eyebrow lifting quizzically over the most gorgeous dark brown eyes with long black lashes. His face flashed a look of surprise and then it was gone, recovered instantly. He reminded her so much of... She opened her mouth, but nothing came out. Those eyes. *Of course.* A picture of Alessandro niggled at the back of her mind.

His face was tanned - almost leathery, from being outdoors for many years, she imagined. But the eyes crinkled into a massive smile and perfect white teeth peeped out from in between a giant grin. The guy was a man-mountain. With huge arms and a barrel chest. She almost forgot the question. He looked around him at all the other military types who were gathering in curiosity, a crowd starting to form. He glared at them, and then glared at her, at them again, then jerking his head towards them all he barked,

'Back to work!' and the group immediately dissipated. 'So it's Ms Parker?'

'Yes, *Ms* that's right.' His question mark meant 'why' but she didn't feel the need to explain. 'Parker-Todd. Actually.'

'Parker-Todd?' he asked, pronouncing it as if he hadn't heard it right.

'Yes, it's double-barrelled - I kept my married name.'

'You kept your married name. After what?'

'Our divorce - what do you think?' Helen replied, and the officer flashed a look around him at his subordinates. *Oops, obviously doesn't like back chat,* Helen thought, and went on 'observation' mode before she said something she shouldn't.

'So you kept the name, just tagged on like an afterthought?' he asked. There was an air of superiority in his voice that made Helen's hackles rise - *so it was going to be like this, was it?* 'What happened to the poor guy's opinion?' he asked with a sneer.

Helen sneered right back. 'The husband didn't have any say in it - we didn't last long. But I liked the name so I kept it. I certainly don't have to go into it now. I'm here to write a column. I'M the one asking questions.'

'Not on my soil. Here, you'll do as you're told.' And he leaned a bit closer towards her. 'Like a good girl.' Then he slapped her bottom.

Helen couldn't believe it. The couple of guys nearby chuckled. 'OK, enough, *Major.*' I'll deal with you later. 'Now, let's bring this to a close shall we? Is it time for you to take me to your commanding officer? You're a Major, so I guess it'd be a General or some such, ruling the roost here in this...' she gestured around at the tents and the piles of logs and food cans, '...*camp?*'

'Nope, there's only one Boss,' said Rains, 'and you're looking at him.' Major James Segal stood up even taller at that point and must have been at least 6'3". He towered over Helen, and glowered down at her, his nostrils flaring dangerously. Rains took a step closer. *Oh shit. Better play along.* She swallowed. *OK, let's play it another way,* and held out her hand to shake his.

'I do, er, apologise. Let's start again.'

'You... *apologise?*' he said, incredulously, his face contorted with disbelief. 'So you turn up here, larger than life, look down your nose at our camp, and at me, and think a Major is too lowly to be in charge of affairs. Then you think mere *words* will make it all better again?'

'Words can work - the right ones,' she said. 'Not that you seem to be in the mood for any of them.'

'Well let me tell you, *Ms Parker-TODD,*' he spat the last syllable out, 'you either show some respect or you ship your sorry little *ass* straight back out the way you *came!*' His face had come over all dark and menacing as he leaned down towards her. 'Now *which* is it to be?' He glanced over at Rains, who stood up straighter.

For a split second Helen wanted to run. But then she remembered she didn't do that anymore. She pulled herself up to her full height - as high as she could muster, pushed her shoulders back, which meant her breasts stuck out proudly, so she rounded her shoulders again to make them 'stand down,' then she spoke.

'Major, James, did you say...'

'Major Segal to you, whilst you're here with this unit.'

'OK - Major Segal - or whatever you want me to call me - if I've offended you, I'm truly sorry.' Then she found herself looking into eyes that were predicting a certain reaction from her, because of who she was, what she looked like, and what had already happened between them - the menacing look darting from her to Rains and back again. Her voice softened. 'You see - I can be sorry - truly sorry, if we started off on the wrong foot. I knew what that was like, once, for someone to look at me and assume stuff. Make me feel like I was nobody - nothing. And it's not fair that I did it to you. So I apologise unreservedly. For that bit. But,' she said, and then her voice became less vulnerable again. 'The rest of the offence belongs to you, I did not create it, you did. So that either makes us equal, and you can apologize too. Or else you can take me straight back where you found me.'

Major Segal looked a bit confused and pursed his mouth, moving it, thinking. Another man in the same uniform as Rains came up and stood waiting nearby, demanding the Major's attention. 'Apology accepted. No more talk, it's time to bunk down. Good night, MS Parker-Todd,' he said, and gave instructions for this new guy to take Helen to a small cabin set some way from the main camp, for the night. It had basic facilities - and at least it wasn't a tent. She settled down after scolding herself for the way she came across in front of him - she hated it when he made her feel weak. She resolved to act exactly as he needed her to - and be strong - as strong as him if need be. And he did look pretty strong... She lapsed into dreamland wondering what on earth the morning would bring.

Helen woke up to an eerie silence. She forgot where she was for a moment, then with a jolt, remembered. The first face flashing into her sleepy mind had dark eyes, long lashes, defined cheekbones, and tanned skin. She'd dreamed of an Italian, of course, but the British Major was the one here controlling her fate - for the time being. If Alessandro were here, what would he do now? Would he look after her? Did she even need looking after... But in the dream she'd just had she'd given uppity, so-called *Major James Segal* a piece of her mind amidst some sort of thunder storm - and she'd awoken feeling just in the mood for a confrontation. She got ready and stomped out of the cabin, slamming the door behind her.

But as soon as she stepped back onto the clearing where the camp should have been, the feistiness vanished. Helen slapped her hand to her mouth and gasped. All around she saw nothing of the camp she'd seen last night - instead there was a war zone.

Signs of a fight - burning embers - cinders where tents once were. A singed jacket here, a smouldering piece of equipment there, and no-one. No-one. And no voices or sounds of life. But there was some blood.

Suddenly before she had time to assess, a man with a gash on his face came running out of the bushes next to her and she jumped.

'What the fuck?!' she cried, 'What's going on? What happened to you, Rains?'

'Insurgents,' he said, 'No time, come quickly,' and he grabbed her hand and began pulling her back into the forest, barely even allowing her time to grab her rucksack.

'If this is… some sort of … trick…' she started to say, in between jumping logs and ducking under branches, 'then…'

He turned, aggressively, pointing to a deep gauge in his cheek, still matted with blood and tissue and oozing. 'Does this look like a trick?' Helen was shocked. It didn't. It was either an elaborate Hollywood makeup job, or it was real. She didn't want to contemplate the latter.

She followed him as best she could, and didn't say another word, getting caught a couple of times as her rucksack straps snagged on sharp foliage.

'Leave it, just drop it,' Rains shouted, pulling ahead and having to keep stopping to come free her.

'No!' she exclaimed, but stopped short of telling him why. She couldn't leave it behind, not yet.

They continued on, her heart pounding more and more with her rising heartbeat - a mixture of fear and exertion. Then, just as they reached a sun-dappled opening, as the hot sunshine hit her skin, and she paused to take a breath, she felt herself being lifted from behind, out of nowhere, and suddenly everything went black.

Three or four hours later, Helen was still blindfolded sitting on what she assumed was a flat log, smelling once again the odours of the forest, and hearing nothing but wildlife. Nothing. She was confused now - three or four hours - again - was that part of some sort of initiation? If this was all a game? Some sort of breaking your spirit process? Well it wouldn't work - whoever they were. But then - Rains's face - that gash...

In need of movement in her cramped limbs, she stood up, carefully. With both hands and feet tied - wrists and ankles sore now, having struggled to break free from the harsh ropes that smelled of hessian, or, well, rope - she tried to jump a couple of steps, if only to banish the cramps that threatened. Then she felt herself start to topple, and had no choice but to drop to her knees before landing on her side. She rolled awkwardly onto her back, and sat there for another long time waiting. And waiting. In the end, she made a decision. It HAD to be an exercise - it HAD to be fake. And Helen Parker-Todd didn't do what was expected of her - ever.

And she began singing - softly at first, including a whistle - about always looking on the bright side of life.

'De-do. De–do, de–do, de–doo.'

Then when nothing happened, she sang it louder. Then by round six, it was so loud, she was practically shouting.

'What the hell are you doing?' said a voice. It was Rains - at least she thought it was. And she felt him undoing her hands and feet and help her get up. 'Come with me, and this time leave that bloody rucksack.'

Not bloody likely, she thought, and grabbed the rucksack as soon as she'd pulled off the blindfold.

'Leave it! They've put a homing device in it - now hurry! Unless you want to be target practice.' And he indicated towards her chest. She looked down and saw that there was a big red spot painted right between her breasts. She felt a wave of shock rattle through her, and looked up at him and opened her mouth to speak. If he was acting, he was very good, and that gash on his cheek had started to ooze a little bit more from bending down to help her. Suddenly the certainty that this was all fake was on shaky ground. He grunted angrily. 'We've got to make a rendezvous, crazy woman. Come on!'

She looked at the bag in her hand, made a mental calculation and then hid it behind her back, running after Rains as he disappeared into the greenery. He seemed to not know which way he was going, this time, kept looking at something in his hand, and Helen could only follow blindly on, panting and getting hotter and hotter as the sun got higher and higher. They waded through a stinking swamp, up to the knees, splashes of stink whipping up into her face from his boots. Helen recoiled and tried to wipe them off whilst attempting not to fall over. *Huh, okay for some - he's all right, running in the front, he's not getting splashed with shi...*

And then it all went very weird. Rains fell, but didn't stop himself. He went down. Right down. Face down, in the fetid mud.

And a new puddle of blood was coming from his head - but this time, he didn't get up.

Helen screamed, long and loud, and then looked around her, terrified. Shit, shit, SHIT. This was no make believe. She went cold when she saw what was in front of her.

Two steps further and a group of soldiers in black uniforms with guns in their hands and complete head masks materialised out of nowhere in front of her, and she nearly fainted. Pretty soon, she was wishing she had.

Helen was on her own once more, shivering with fear, and with the sharp cold of the water being sprayed from a hand pump - she came to her senses and looked at the men who were hosing her down. The soldiers were all smaller, and wiry, with scars all over their arms and necks. One of them only had one hand. Her heart was going like wildfire as they took turns in spraying her - seemingly for their own benefit more than to get the stink off, as the hose kept making its way from her mud-covered calves up to her vest top, wetting it thoroughly, much to their amusement. Then thank god she was left to dry in the sun before being shoved along a pathway and lowered into a pit with a wickerwork layer over the top of it. There was only a blanket on top of a crude camp bed, and the floor was covered in dried leaves and branches, with sparse amenities including a bowl and a jug of water. They threw her rucksack in after her, but it was minus the tools or anything useful. She tried to find any kind of tracking device in it, but to no avail.

So, overcome with fatigue, and with her body utterly exhausted from being flooded with the adrenalin of terror, Helen laid down on the makeshift bed. But sleep was the last thing on her mind. Visions of Rains body face-down in the mud, and the oozing puddle of blood, kept filling her mind every time she got anywhere near to sleeping.

She was in completely uncharted territory - a TiFFT with a capital T, in bold, underlined. Her mind drifted to the battles she'd been fighting all her life, trying to buck the system, go against the grain, overcome resistance to even small matters. And she laughed at herself for being so het up about such minutiae.

Small when compared to seeing a man die before your eyes.

She found herself thinking of home - a warm bed, and a nice bath and the reassuring calm that comes from knowing you're safe. Even if your work mates do annoy you and your rivals are stealing your ideas, what did it matter?

What did men matter too? Men - like Rains - poor Rains. The shock wore off and she began to sob silently to herself somewhere in the wee small hours. Then finally she slept. But not for long.

Helen woke with a start - there was a noise up above her. It was still dark, and she was cold and the roof above her was being opened up and suddenly there were people there, making a scuffling noise. She got up and cowered in a corner, finding herself shaking. A huge shape fell down into the pit with her, making her jump, but she stifled her scream.

'It's OK, it's me, it's Major Segal,' he said. *Oh My God.*

Helen was overwhelmingly relieved, and allowed him to reach out a hand to her to help her up. *Sod being independent,* she thought, and realised how pleased she was to see him. Even if he had insisted on introducing himself as 'Major Segal.' With the gap in the makeshift roof allowing some light from the moon, Helen noticed a bloody bandage on his arm and an even bigger one on his thigh, a big dark patch showing in the middle of both. She looked up at him and when saw the look in his eyes, she couldn't help it, she just rushed over and hugged him and wouldn't let go. He pulled her away roughly - she wasn't expecting that - and pointed out a camera high up on one of the walls, crudely mounted on a wooden frame, with a little antenna pointing up from the top of it.

'Are you ok?' he whispered. She started to talk but he put his finger on her lips. 'Shhh. Surveillance area.'

'Where are we? What is this?'

'Don't talk - seriously - don't talk. *At all.*' The menacing tone was back.

Helen's shivering resumed at that point, more violently than before. He gestured over to the bed, and she laid down on it, still shaking. Then he pointed to himself and then at the space behind her and she nodded, so he laid down behind her and she felt the welcome rush of warmth from his big, hot body.

This was weird. And definitely a first. But it felt good. She eventually warmed up and found herself smiling ever so slightly, thinking of the write up for THIS little expedition on her TiFFT column when she got back.

If she got back.

'Will we get back?' she whispered. But his only reaction was to touch her hair and pull it back from her face. It reminded her of a very long time ago when a certain person used to do that as they lay talking in bed. About a future filled with hopes and plans. When there was a future to be filled. And then it vanished. And then she slept.

Embarrassingly enough, when Helen woke, she found she had turned over and was facing him, in a safe, warm cocoon of entangled legs and his big muscular bicep under her neck. She felt the pulse in his body and the big chest rise and fall with the deep breaths of slumber. With her heart beating ever so slightly, she thought about the feelings filling her body, and realised she'd awoken from a delicious dream about having sex - with this man. And sadly for Helen, in those surreal moments in between waking and sleeping, her all-important 'censor' button was turned to *off*.

She felt a little pang fill her abdomen, and her first impulse was to reach out and touch him. She knew she was playing with fire, but, Helen being Helen, she didn't stop. Gently, she ran her fingers down his injured arm, around the bandage, and down to his hand, which was lying across her hip. She spread her fingers over his, and felt his hand respond, by parting the fingers and allowing hers to insert between his. Then he closed them tightly around hers, and she felt a warm rush inside her belly.

Then he opened his palm flat, released her hand and moved, palm-down, ever so slowly, further down over her hip towards her butt - and when he got there, he squeezed.

Is he awake? she wondered, or in a stupor? Whatever it was, it was a huge turn-on, with the terror of the situation temporarily banished from being in charge of her consciousness. Instead, something far more primeval was taking place. Helen felt herself push down on his hand as it gripped her ass.

'If I can't talk, at least I can do this,' she whispered and reached over and kissed his chest, which was level with her face. The slightly salty taste touched her lips, and he stirred. He pulled her towards him, and dipped his head down to the place where her neck met her shoulders, and gently, so gently, kissed her there. It was so sensitive there, she felt herself shudder with desire, and in this rarified atmosphere and with the thrill of the dream-state residue lingering in her psyche, she would have let him take her there and then.

But any pangs of longing were roughly chased away as suddenly above them, there was more noise. She didn't know whether to be annoyed or relieved. They both came-to swiftly, separating and listening.

In the early morning light, shadows crossed the leaf-roof of the pit, some running, some scuffling, and then shouting. He woke up fully, made a face as if to say *what the hell were we doing,* and flinched away from her immediately.

More noise, and then the full strength of her terror returned, with the sound of gunfire. And this time it was close.

But no-one came near.

More noise, more gunfire, shouts, cries of pain - further off this time. And the unmistakeable sound of an approaching helicopter in the distance.

'Come. Now - with me,' he said, brooking no refusal, 'let's see if I can lift you up to the edge.' He was so tall, he could reach above the wicker roof, and lifted Helen up by the ass with both hands, then balanced carefully so she could get her soles into his hands, leaning forwards to steady herself by grabbing the ties holding the roof in place. Helen pulled herself up slowly, tentatively peeping out from under the raised roof hatch.

'Keep your head down!' he declared, and this time, she wasn't affronted by his bossiness, she just complied.

After a minute of observation, she whispered down at him. 'I think they're all over the other side,' she said, rising to the challenge. I can hoist myself up if you push just a little more...'

'If you get out, run and don't stop - don't come back for me. Head for the sound of the helicopter, OK?' and with one last hard push, she was high enough to pull herself out of the pit and run.

But once she'd run to the safety of the trees once more, with the helicopter hovering some way off, she looked back. Helen found herself overcome with a sense of loyalty, and instead of running away, she ran straight back to the pit.

She looked around for something - anything to throw in to help the burly, gruff Major climb out. Her heart was pounding like it had never pounded before, and with the tidal wave of adrenalin rushing through her body, she found herself laser focussed and able to function in a way she hadn't experienced before. Using that focus, she located a length of strong cable emerging from the ground near a tower that was topped by a rusty satellite dish, and threw the end down the pit. It was tugged really hard - he must be seeing if it would hold.

It did. *Thank god.* Helen felt enormous relief wash over her, when a minute later, Major Segal was standing beside her, rubbing his injured arm and looking around, searching for something. He held out a hand for her to stay there and duck down, and he ran off towards the other side of the area. Helen took one look down in the pit, tugged on the cable once more, and when it held, she abseiled down into the pit, and was back at the top, rucksack on her back this time, by the time Major Segal appeared with two more men, both injured, one of them quite seriously from the way he was limping.

Then the race was on.

They could hear the gunfire coming from the direction of the helicopter and with the utter panic filling her body, she could only follow them on, blindly, on autopilot, dodging when they dodged, ducking when they ducked, and hiding when they hid.

They skirted right around the source of the gunfire, until they were as close as they could get to the area where the helicopter was hovering. And then - tragedy - there came an almighty bang and the helicopter took off fast, turning and accelerating away as another loud bang deafened Helen and the three men.

Her heartbeat in her chest was almost louder than the sound of Major Segal's whisper, as he encouraged them all into even deeper hiding. A moment later, a little way off, a group of men in black ran back through the forest back towards their camp. As soon as they'd gone, Major Segal motioned to go, and they all ran as fast as they could behind him.

When they stopped she almost kept going, and if she had, it would have been straight over a sheer drop. The Major grabbed her waistband and she swung round, away from the edge and ended up flat against his chest, her breasts pushing against him. He jumped back, as if he'd been stung, and looked skywards. The helicopter was now poised some way in the distance across the other side of a gully. The men looked around them - for some way down? Or some way round? Or some way... across.

Helen stopped, petrified. She then pushed herself back against a tree trunk and followed their gaze. There, a few hundred yards away, was an aerial walkway - a rickety old bridge made of rope and planks, the kind you see in those old movies, when you knew - just knew - it would break in two when you got half way across it.

'I can't!' She said.

'You must!' the Major hissed. 'Come on!' He grabbed her hand and tried to pull her away from the tree. Helen swallowed, and felt her heart drop through her stomach, and her tongue go numb.

Then suddenly, with a shout in some sort of Asian language, a figure emerged in front of them holding a gun. It was one of the enemy - in black - and before Helen knew it, the three guys had overpowered him and thrown him over the side.

She couldn't believe what she'd just seen, but there was no time to see what had happened to the guy - and no way she would look over the side anyway. Not a chance. So she gave in and allowed herself to be pulled away from the tree, following the others as they forged ahead, aiming for the bridge. But she had that funny feeling again in her bones. She got slower and slower behind them.

'I can't do that,' she said finally, pointing at the bridge. 'We'll die - it's not safe - I just know it.'

'This isn't the time to get the jitters, lady,' said one of the two men, with a slight Ozzie twinge. 'If this is part of what we have to do, we have to do it. I'm game.' He looked at the second guy who nodded vehemently with crazy eyes. 'This is no time for running away.'

'Trust me. I'm not running away, I just know,' she cried. 'I can't.'

'Well you can stay here then, if you...'

'Wait!' shouted Major Segal, and she saw he was looking intently behind her. The other way, back up along the ravine, and several hundred yards behind them, there was a sudden flash of light. It lit up a small area, a long way below them, and a whooshing sound could be heard in the air. Then a big *bang* and a huge tree, down further from Helen, shook like crazy. Then another whoosh, and another bang.

'I know what that is,' said one of the men.

'They've done it!' cried Major Segal, and he set off at a pace towards the shaking tree. As they got nearer, Helen could see there was a strong cable being winched up via some sort of mechanism held in place at the top with a giant harpoon style anchor, embedded in the tree. Suddenly she knew what was happening.

A zip wire.

Noooo!

But she found herself running along with them towards it, despite her fears. Only... she realised with a jolt that something was different - this time she knew it was OK - *this* she could do. Because she *had* to.

Very soon she found out there wasn't any choice. The men secured the zip wire, released the loops they'd need to hold on to, and tested it by tugging as hard as they could.

First one man went, tying himself on tightly and in an instant he was gone. Seconds later, he landed at the bottom, instantly surrounded by others who appeared out of nowhere.

'I'll go last,' said the Major, after the second man had gone. 'Can you do it? Can you trust destiny?' He looked at Helen and for a moment a flash of a distant memory crossed her mind, and she narrowed her eyes briefly, but then it was gone.

'If it's meant to be, it'll happen,' she replied. Behind them there came a shout, and more gunfire from deep within the forest.

'Hurry,' she said, 'there's no time to lose,' well aware that she would absolutely be writing those words in her article as soon as she got home. *Home.*

Because she *would* get home, and that meant this had to work. It had to. And once her body knew that, she found herself filling up with the self-control she needed to overcome her fear - and for that moment at least, in these circumstances, she was able to picture herself arriving safely at the bottom.

Then, more gunfire, and with a few brief words of instruction, she was over the edge and away.

With more gunfire ringing in her ears, she felt the wind whizzing past her, as she hung on to the strap for dear life and thanked the lord she was strong enough not to fall. Nor to let go. For all of that few seconds it took to reach the bottom, her mind was focussed solely on holding on, and imagining the moment when she... and then it was here, and she found herself being grabbed by hands and cushioned from impact and... safe.

But James wasn't.

Somewhere up above, there was an explosion and then as if in slow motion, the zip wire went loose, and fell to the floor, hitting the ground like a dead snake, from one end to the other, with a dull thwack.

Even the winching up into the helicopter could not distract Helen from the desolation she was feeling - if he truly was captured - or worse - the men seeming to feel the same, and none really spoke much to her, save to say thanks on the helicopter flight for dabbing their little cuts and scratches with the tea tree stick she produced from her combats, thankfully unharmed by stinky swamp or prickly bush. Even her little rucksack - battered and flaccid - seemed sad. The only saving grace was that when she checked, her smuggled camera pen was still inside it, and seemed to be intact. She got some surreptitious shots, just in case she ever got back to civilisation with her life still intact and her column awaiting.

The journey was coming to an end. Safely inside, with the door locked, Helen sat staring at the back of the chair in front of her and under her breath, started singing nursery rhymes to distract herself, as she slowly began noticing the smells of the cabin, the sounds of the men's banter and the familiar sensation that, once again, she was trying desperately hard not to look out of the window, at the drop below.

Soon afterwards, she felt the drop in altitude and the buzz of men preparing to disembark. The helicopter landed, and came to a juddering halt, as the door was flung open, and rotors still revolving but slowly coming to a halt, the vehicle spewed out its human cargo, who ran, back-slapping each other, towards the familiar sight of their own base - now fully manned again and buzzing with life. No-one seemed to be as distraught as Helen about what had happened to the Major. Perhaps they lost people all the time. Unless...

Helen waited till last, to get out of the helicopter and accompanied by one of the men, she made her way towards the camp. As she got closer, she noticed them all gathering round in a circle. *This is weird.*

Suddenly they burst into a big cheer and a massive round of applause, and Helen burst into tears.

Rob Rains appeared out of a tent, perfectly well, and everyone began throwing off their various 'war wounds' and bandages.

'You bastard!' she said, hugging Rob. But the true target of her emotions was visible over his shoulder, inside a tent, being attended by a medic. She finished a quick chat with Rob, then slowly walked into the tent.

There, large as life, already washed and changed, was Major James Segal. He looked up at her and a huge smile crinkled the corner of his eyes.

'Hello, spitfire,' he said. And Helen felt an arrow of emotion course through her veins. 'Go and wash and brush up, and I'll see you for some chow a little later.' And this time, she didn't argue. As she left the tent, he added, 'unless you fancy being on the other team in the baseball match we're about to play. The men reckon you're a good bloke, so they might let you join in...'

After a wash and brush up Helen enjoyed a makeshift baseball match, the 'black team' including all the masked insurgents, who turned out to be just locals who were particularly small and good at accents, versus the 'outsiders' as the NExUS squad were always called. She found herself thoroughly enjoying it, lining up with the smaller guys and pitching a mean strike or two. She thanked her stars she was so good at rounders in her Surrey school. And it was great to release the tension of the whole NExUS experience. The end of the match came when Helen slid into a base and ripped her combats completely, rolling over and over with Major Segal who was trying to get her out, but fortunately didn't get dust in her lip balm.

They allowed Helen to take some group shots, and enjoyed being 'interviewed' as soon as they gave her back her belongings and she could take notes. Major Segal even allowed her to take a couple of photos with just him. It made her smile. They sat together, some way away from the group - Helen thought it made a nice backdrop to her two-way selfie.

'You have to blank out some of the faces, please, if you're going to publish them,' he said, 'but then I guess you've read the contract through thoroughly.'

'I know the terms, nothing will be published that gives the game away completely.'

'Part of the deal,' he said, nodding contentedly. 'What happens at NExUS stays at NExUS.'

'Oh really.' She was issuing him with a challenge, but he had a challenge of his own.

'Sure - apart from what you take away in here,' he said, gently tapping her head, 'in here,' he said, tapping his finger on her stomach, 'and in here,' he said, putting his palm across her chest, flat against her breasts, over her heart. He looked deep into her eyes and she held his gaze, noting the bright sparkle of desire she saw in them. 'What's in here will remain,' he said. She reached for his hand and held it there, warm against her body. A burning heat began rising up from the pit of her stomach, stirring her senses and making her move slightly against his hand. Then he stopped and removed it.

'Come walk with me,' he said.

'I was going to ask you...' she began saying, as they made their way down a winding pathway through overhanging vines.

'Not yet,' he replied, so they just walked on. The afternoon was cooling into evening and she was grateful for the relief of a gentle breeze - it had been hot all day and the air had been quite still -

apart from when it was full of gunfire, explosions and grown men play-acting Call of Duty.

She picked her way around big rocks and trotted a little to keep up with his giant strides. What a once in a lifetime experience this had been - so had he. She wondered where he was leading her and whether this would be part of the forbidden topics list. But whatever she ended up writing, it'd all make a damn good Try it For The first Time piece, and her head was bursting with all the things she was planning to say. And there was one particular subject making her so uptight, if she didn't blurt it out soon, she swore she would explode.

He led the way down to a secluded pond where a table with towels and a screen were laid out - a regular facility, it seemed. There was a little waterfall on one side coming from a man-made overhang, just high enough for him to stand underneath it, and he stripped down to his shorts and allowed the crystal clear waters to trickle all over his chest.

'Come join me,' he said. It was more of a command than a question, but Helen wasn't arguing. Not now. Not this time. Not like so many times before.

'So,' she said, 'what happens in the forest waterfall, stays in the forest waterfall?'

He nodded, and beckoned her to him.

'Including that Major James Segal is not your real name?'

'Especially that. But for now - just for now - let's not talk. Let's just feel.' Then he opened his hand, and put it back on her chest, just above the neckline of her fresh white vest top. 'What do you feel, Helen?' he asked, as she placed her hand over his.

'Curiosity. Overpowering curiosity. Relief. And regret,' she said, 'for so many things I should have done, and didn't. And so many things I shouldn't have done... and did.'

'Oh I don't know,' he said, with a smile breaking the tension, 'I think you did pretty damn well on our challenge myself.'

'Like you said, I'm a good bloke.'

'Yes, but not literally,' he said, his voice becoming huskier, 'or I wouldn't be able to do this,' and he leant down and gently kissed her on the lips. The waterfall above their heads trickled water down over their faces, giving the moment heightened sensuality. She felt like destiny was lending a hand once more, and was willing to give herself over to the moment. Almost. She felt the warm mouth exploring hers, his tongue tenderly flicking across her lips and teasing inside them, and she responded, making him moan a tiny tiny bit. Then she moved his hand lower down, to her breast. He inhaled deeply, and deepened the kiss. His hand was closing around her full breast and she was running her hands over his muscular arms, and down to his smaller wait. Such a big guy, such a strong guy. But whose guy?

Then he stopped and rested his nose lightly on hers. He seemed to be making up his mind about something.

'Oh, Helen Todd,' he said, 'that feels so good. But we can't - there are people - they wouldn't like it.' His hand withdrew and he walked out of the water, grabbing a towel before disappearing behind a screen to get fully dried then dressed again. Helen joined him a minute later, but as soon as she walked behind the screen to get undressed, voices signalled they were no longer alone and he left. 'See you after dinner. Go have a drink with the lads, I have to go make some calls. Short jeep ride to locate a signal,' was his parting shot, making a phone shape with his hand and then waving to the two guys who had come to shower. And for the first time, Helen noticed the look of a slightly whiter patch on his wedding ring finger - or was it a trick of the light - she couldn't be sure.

After a hearty dinner, she found out more about the NExUS project from the other men, who were sharing a bottle of Jack Daniels and taking turns to regale her with some of their more exotic adventures. She made them promise that one day, they'd take her on the pirate one, and thought that when the girls were older, they could come on the desert island one.

'Oh, no, you don't want to be taking youngsters on the Excalibur Expedition,' teased Rob Rains, and the other guy laughed.

'Why?' asked Helen, noticing how much younger than her Rob was, much younger than she'd first thought, when he was covered in camouflage makeup deep in the forest. What he told her made for some curious reactions, and she made a note to revisit The Excalibur Experiment at some stage in the future, when she was feeling in the mood for a bit of sexual bravado. That certainly wasn't now. ***

The grand finale was the Unveiling of the Truths. This was the bit the guys all liked best - especially the ones who were only temporary recruits. After Rob had made sure everyone had signed their Non-Disclosure Agreements, and handed all the NDA's to one of the medic guys, the Unveiling began. They each took it in turns, and announced their names and their real jobs, some as funny as 'garbologist' meaning bin man, and others including lawyer, teacher and builder. Then Rob Rains - a mechanic by day but mostly working full time for NExUS, stood up and said, 'And of course a big hand for our leader and the co-founder of NExUS X - Major James Segal. Better known as ...' he paused for a bit of drama and some of the men did a drum roll with their fingers on the tables. Helen held her breath and her heart skipped a beat. She'd known this right from that very first moment, but had had to play along.

***(The Excalibur Expedition – for future release.)

'...Jason Todd. Major Jason Todd.'

Jason Todd. Helen's Jason. Helen's first love - the one which had never left her mind, never been bettered, had lived as an exalted memory never to be touched. And now here he was in front of her helping her create what she hoped would be ratings winning writing.

His eyes met Helen's and she raised a glass in his direction.

After all these years.

Helen was glad to know where he'd ended up - ironically having literally 'scared him off into the jungle,' as Sadie's ex, Stuart, had so eloquently put it. Jason was patted on the back and interrupted, all the way back to her table, where he joined her for a brief drink, but surrounded by people, they said nothing of what was on their minds.

Later that night, Helen was in her bed listening out for any signs of footsteps approaching her little properly insulated cabin, with all amenities - even a TV for God's sake. This one had been hidden, naturally, set away from the others. Eventually she gave up waiting and the hypnotic sounds of night time in the forest transported her to dream land.

The Major came just before dawn and looked in on Helen to see if she was ok. She felt her heart leap when she heard him, amidst dozing, in and out of sleep. She was on her own on a wide bunk, completely tired out and beckoned him in. He smiled when he saw her greeting, and he sat down beside her.

'Can we finally talk now?' she said, 'No cameras or surveillance anywhere?'

'There never were, it's just a bit of drama. But it wouldn't do to spoil the project for the others.'

'What the other staff?'

'Mainly for the other fee-paying customers - none of whom you will ever find out about, and all of whom were involved in this extravaganza. It's quite a spectacular, a - what would Mr Williams have said in year 13 - a "veritable feat of logistics"' He laughed, and Helen did too, feeling a flood of warmth warming up her chest, and transporting her back to a bygone era in her memory file, one that had cobwebs on. It was nice.

'Well you do it very well - should have been an actor.' She replied. 'You looked genuinely surprised,' she said, 'when you saw me arrive.'

'I didn't know it was you coming, you have to believe that,' he said, earnestly, his dark brown eyes burning into hers with an intensity that took her breath away - just like the old days - just like the first time round. 'It was the lads. They called you the one that got away.'

'You talked about me?'

'Sure - followed your career in the news, online, from time to time,' he said. Her heart leapt. 'Just like anyone does with old flames - you know, curiosity. But all of this - it wasn't my idea.'

'I - I do believe it - of course I believe it,' she replied. He'd been nothing if not honest, their whole life together. If only she could have said the same of herself. She looked at his hands fiddling with a toggle on his jacket - big strong hands - capable of amazing things.

'One of the lads got sent your YouTube appeal for unusual activities and they joked, saying you should come do a NExUS project. Took bets on how you'd cope. I said I knew what you would do.'

'What?'

'Exactly what you did do - I told them you're a good bloke.'

Helen smiled - there it was again, and he explained that is was a big compliment in the military world and it was no reflection on her womanhood. She glowed a little.

'They took it on themselves to make the rest happen, without me knowing. They know that I...' He paused but changed tack. 'I'm glad they did. It's been great to see you again. Knowing how busy you are. I'm glad we got the chance to have a catch up.'

That sounds like it's got an air of finality, thought Helen, deciding to tread very, very carefully around what was coming, but she knew it had to be said. *It was time.*

'That's what happens when you trust destiny,' she said. It had been one of their catch phrases - when they were young and just starting out and full of hopes and dreams.

'It's a great operation you've got here - you could really make some serious money - like you always wanted to,' she said, tinged with nostalgia at the words that took her back a million lifetimes ago - a thousand versions of herself, ago.

'What makes you think that I haven't,' he said, and for the first time since they'd met back at basecamp, the old Jason was back - the look of menace was completely gone and he poked her in the ribs - hard.

'Owww - you bastard - I told you not to do that!'

'When, in about 1994? Water under the bridge,' he said, and did it again. The laughter died away and the mood became slightly more sombre. They got up and went out to sit side by side on the threshold to the cabin, breathing in the rarefied dewy air as the dawn started to break on the distant horizon, and the bird song began in earnest, welcoming in another brand new day. It was going to be a good day, Helen could tell.

For more reasons than one.

The level of peace flooding through her veins was incredible, and Helen felt her whole diaphragm let go. She nodded as he gestured whether to start up the campfire outside the cabin and watched him as he collected more sticks and got it going. He was still as adorable.

She sighed a deep sigh and relaxed completely. Maybe it was just being around Jason again - like slipping on a pair of old shoes. Or maybe it was everything she'd been through, and survived intact. Like she'd had a physical clear out. And she was about to have a mental one too.

'So - what about you then, we'd better have "the Chat" before they put your blindfold on again and fly you back to your life,' he said. 'Give me the potted version.'

'I'm glad you said that,' Helen replied, 'the unexpurgated version would have blown your mind.'

'Oh, you don't know how many times my mind's been blown already - it's used to it by now. I don't think anything can surprise me again after what I've seen in my time.'

'What - what have you seen?' she asked, sidestepping the question about herself. He told her of his time with the real military - of battle zones and prisoners of war and interrogations and kidnappings and hostages and releases and rescues and dawn raids and medals and honours and a thousand heroic things that left Helen stunned. Everything sounded like it should belong in a computer game, only in his world, when the men went down, they stayed down. There was more, but it was the top secret stuff - which had led on to more top secret stuff - hence the NDA's - several years of NExUS events involving A list celebrities, the richest men in the world, top politicians or top military for training.

'None of which you can talk about,' he finished, 'or ...'

'Or you'll have to kill me?' she teased, still taken aback.

'Something like that, spitfire' he said, using the pet name from their youth.

'Maybe it's worth the risk...' she said, looking at him slyly out of the corner of one eye. A flash of something crossed his face. Uncertainty? Of *her*?

'Of course, everything I've just said could be completely made up - fantasy - the fabricated background of one Major James Segal.

Perhaps I'm just reciting his profile and as much a part of this whole carefully crafted NExUS event, as your TiFFT is.' He laughed and she joined him.

'And what of Major James Segal?' she asked, raising her eyebrow, pronouncing the names staccato.

'Steven Segal, clearly,' he replied.

'Naturally, I remember, you were obsessed,' she said. At college he'd been first in line to watch all the latest action movies and had a substantial video collection during their brief marriage. 'And James?'

'And the name James is in case one of the team forgets - we always choose names that sound like our own real ones. In moments of pressure when someone's about to crack, that's when it gets intense and slips of the tongue happen.'

'And is there...' she said, catching herself as the words came tumbling out, but she had to ask. 'And is there a Mrs - Segal?'

'A fake wife? No.'

'And what about a real one? Did you get married again?' Helen asked, swallowing hard. 'Or am I still the only one you ever loved?' She was teasing him, but in a flash she realised she was only teasing herself. And now she really didn't want to know. The feelings threatened to overwhelm her, taking her suddenly and by complete surprise, and she glanced up at him from beneath her long eyelashes, the mascara completely gone now after two days in the wild without a mirror or makeup bag. But she didn't care. The emotions filling her body were almost the same with him as that last time she saw him. Coupled with the same longing too - a deep, aching longing to be in his arms and to have him stroke her hair the way he used to when she was his wife and...

'Yes,' he said.

Oh. OH NO she thought. But what she said was, 'Oh.' And then, 'Cool.' Though it very definitely was anything but.

Her heart was racing as she knew the next question she must ask. If she could put it off, hold this one moment in time and capture it, make it last forever, throw herself into his arms and have him never let her go, she would. But instead, if she asked the next question she knew that moment would be shattered. But still she said them - words she thought she'd never be asking. Not of him.

'And what about children?' Her voice was small and she'd shrunk back into the shadows from the firelight, so he could hardly see her face. Somehow, deep down, she knew what the answer would be.

He didn't respond immediately, just dug in his BDU's for his wallet, and took out a faded picture of himself and two boys. He showed it to Helen. She took it, fighting to stop her hand shaking. 'They're older now, that was about five years ago but it was such a lovely shot. I took it - we were out camping together - just me and the boys. Their mum was back at home making a lovely dinner for when we got back.'

So many questions filled her head, so many answers she needed to hear, but so many ways of avoiding them. She really did not want to know - about their mother. Because, when she looked at those eyes, the boys deep brown eyes, they were the same as Jason's. And her heart melted in that moment and she felt the unleashing of floodgates she'd bricked up for years. Years of wondering if they'd ever gone on to have children, would they have looked like those two lovely teenage boys. About what might have been, had she'd stayed - if she'd not run away as soon as she found out she - she... But this was the new Helen, wasn't it? The new honest Helen. If she could do it with sister Sadie, she could do it with an ex-husband who she hadn't seen for nearly twenty years and probably after today, wouldn't see for another twenty. This would be a TiFFT for sure. She took a deep breath.

'Jason - I'm so glad you had kids. Really. I know we talked about it when we were together and we split up before we ever really had the chance to know what would have happened. In some ways I wish I could turn back the clock - and have done every year since we said goodbye...'

'Since *you* said goodbye...' the edge in his voice was unmistakeable. Helen faltered, but knew she had to finish now she'd started.

'We never had the chance to find out whether it was a boy or a girl, right? That's what I told you, the day we, the day I...'

'Aborted our child.' He said. The warmth had gone and the menace was back. Coldness. She couldn't blame him.

She swallowed, and tears threatened behind her eyes, hot and burning and burrowing into her sensibilities and making her knees go weak. Thank goodness she was sitting, thank goodness there was a warm fire.

'I was 21. At college. Setting an example for Sadie on how to be successful - her dad had gone, I was the role model. Then I found out that...'

'You mean you knew what it was after all?'

'Well it was a little boy. He was so tiny. Barely even a human being. They showed him to me - lifeless - he'd already gone, you see.'

'What?'

'He'd already died. In the womb.'

'Helen, what are you saying?'

'I'm saying - they all would have died. They did tests, when they weren't sure about the damage on my womb. It was me - my accident when I was a teenager - and - Jason - I can't carry to full term. They told me it wouldn't live anyway, it had some sort of genetic problem, that it would never have, never have... the chance to live. And it would happen again - with me - it's me, I'm faulty - always have been. I can't be a proper wife and mother and I never was to you. That's why I changed afterwards. I couldn't tell you - because you were a good man - and I knew you'd give up everything you'd always wanted to stick with me. And I couldn't face the pity.' It had come out in a rush and she took a breath - a deep one. She needed it. 'And all because of my accident.'

'That wasn't your fault,' his face was confused.

'It was - you know what happened. You know how I get. It...' she felt a convulsing sob building up but she swallowed it. 'I... ruined it all, back then, in that one moment - and I never knew it.'

His face was stony.

If she didn't keep talking, she'd melt into a gibbering mess. 'I knew how important having your own children was for you - after all our discussions. And I couldn't deny you that. And I couldn't stand by and watch you have a baby with a surrogate or adopt or anything second best to what you had wanted your whole life. So I ran. That's why I ran. And I've been running ever since - from every man who starts talking about family and settling down and kids.'

He was silent. Then so was she. She needed to breathe slowly and focus her attention on her solar plexus, *in, out, in, out.* She thought back to the tantra breathing and found an inner strength. She felt in her pocket for an object she'd carried with her ever since Tibet. She breathed, she focussed and she was back in control. Just.

The crackle of the fire and the morning dawn chorus of birdsong high above the camp were the only signs that her wish for an eternally still moment in time hadn't been granted. It almost could have been - now she was back with him, reliving those moments. All of them. She could tell where *his* mind was - back there, in the hospital, on the day he'd come barging in demanding to see her and pushed his way through, shaking with rage and incomprehension. And all she could say was 'I had to - career first, babies second.' And he never forgot and he never forgave. And that's where it had ended in her mind, and she knew she had to let him go. She felt herself begin to shake, partly because of the sheer exhaustion of the intense experience of the past couple of days, and partly because of the massive burden that had been lifted from her shoulders. One she'd been carrying around all her adult life, and one which would no longer keep her awake at night, wondering what might have been. If she was still Mrs Helen Todd.

'But,' he said, 'you didn't even give me the choice - to be with you after that. You took that decision for me. Ever the controlling one,' he said. And as she tried desperately to stop her body shaking - with cold, with fear, with dread, with relief, with shock at his reaction, who knew - he got up, placed one hand on her shoulder, and walked away.

Chapter Thirteen

The *Forest Warfare* TiFFT was an online hit - once again - taking Helen's ratings higher. But the bad news came fast on its back. Well, bad news for some - amazing news for others.

The first part of Helen's bad day was when she was hauled into another meeting with the Boss, this time to hear the actual investor's dulcet tones over the conference call saying he was pleased with her latest TiFFT and could he have the contact info of the organiser as it's something he'd like to take his high-net-worth individuals to. They met three times a year to go golfing on glaciers and the like, so he'd much appreciate her help, he said. The Boss had sat there, wide-eyed, monitoring the conversation. He nodded at her vigorously, and she replied.

'Sure,' she'd said, as she took out the contact details she and Rob Rains had swapped as he dropped her back at the airport. The Boss snatched them and read them out to the man listening at the other end of the conference call.

Rob had taken her to her flight, naturally - it wasn't as though Jason would be in touch with her any time soon - or ever.

She felt like she was betraying him, with the amount of detail she'd put in the piece, but more because of the feelings she'd included, feelings about this dashing Bourne-like character who'd wooed her in the woods. She really hadn't meant to write it that way, but they'd all come tumbling out anyway - like therapy.

And now she'd calmed down again, it was too late - there it was up on her blog for all the world to see - like some saddo singleton who was pouring her heart out online. Jason had even allowed some photos too - that didn't show his face, and she'd given him a pseudonym. Ironic - a fake name for a fake name. She'd called him GT - as in MGBGT - the little green sports car he'd bought her.

The memory of which had led to a pathetic little self-indulgent session in her pal Kate's garage, sitting in that very car, now completely dilapidated and smelling of old boots. Just being inside it, remembering how things were, back in the day, with Helen always in the driving seat - what a metaphor for her life *that* had become – it had conjured up enough emotion for ten articles.

Strangely enough, it seemed to have worked - now not only were the students leaving their comments - their mums were also posting reassurances about finding a man and learning to love yourself instead. It made Helen smile. And made Kate jump for joy, declaring that they would be the perfect market for her dating thing, when she finalised it. But she was having a few problems with Kieran at the moment and wasn't opening up like she normally did. So Helen had dealt with her feelings of being alone, by herself. And when she'd heard Sadie's news, well...

Whilst she waited for the Boss and the investor to finish their chat, her mind drifted to the last couple of TiFFT's - and the next one. And thoughts of Alessandro.

Was he a better man? So similar facially to Jason, but so, so different in how he'd treated her. He'd cared about Helen - enough to want to help her change for the better. 'So controlling,' were Jason's parting words.

As Helen watched the Boss disappear in another cloud of vapour from his E-cigarette - puffing like mad and going a little red-faced, listening to the investor talk - she had a dawning realisation.

With everything she'd felt in the forest - in a life or death situation - at least she'd thought it was - things had taken on a new meaning. Since she'd got back, the anger inside her had quelled. And whilst she still couldn't go too near the observation tower at the top of the building, she truly felt different.

Maybe it was time to change - for good, she was thinking, maybe *it's time…* when the question came again loud and clear through the conference call, and she realised Mr Adams was glaring at her to reply.

'I'm sorry - what? Bad telephone line,' she fibbed, and shrugged at Mr A.

'I said - have ParlourGames Channel made you an offer to go join them?'

Helen was stunned. She hesitated. 'What? No, no they haven't. What makes you think…'

'Well your hesitation, for one,' said the voice. 'You see, the investor group is a very small world. At this level there are not that many of us. We have quite competitive natures and there is one adversary of mine - an adversary many of my counterparts would love to see quashed, if truth be known - who wants to not only beat us hollow with his new ParlourGames Channel ratings, but he also wants to leave us floundering. When we first discussed initiating these ventures, into online platforms like yours, we wagered a bet. And I don't want him to win this bet, do you understand!?' His voice had risen very slightly and he was hardly pausing for breath.

'Sure, but you don't have to worry, because no-one's approached me.' *Not yet anyway,* thought Helen. 'Any tips on who to look out for just in case?' she asked, 'better to be forewarned.'

'So you can go and contact him yourself?'

'I wouldn't do that!' Helen said.

'She *wouldn't* do that,' added Mr Adams, leaning up towards the phone, then glancing at Helen and sitting himself back down again, coughing slightly.

'Hmm, well, we'll see - and remember we have spies in their camp too! He wouldn't contact you himself - his assistants maybe. Just look out for anything with the name Tremain in it.'

'Tremain?' repeated Helen.

'Yes, he's just finalised a venture in the health food industry which was a compromise, and has got his appetite back with a vengeance. He wants this badly and our source tells us he'll stop at nothing to win.'

Then Mr Adams spoke up. 'If you hear anything from any of them - from ParlourGames - tell me immediately, Parker. From *anyone,* OK?'

'Sure,' said Helen. 'I don't suppose they'll contact me. Is there anything else?' she asked. She had some urgent work to do, then an urgent call to make, based on an urgent email she'd received late last night.

'Just one more thing,' said the voice, 'my daughter - thank you for being gracious to my daughter. She's not the brightest spark in the box.' Helen winced slightly at this man's description of his daughter. 'It's been a bit of a battle, I can tell you - daughters - who'd have them!' He laughed loud, and the Boss - who had some of his own to contend with - laughed louder. The two men traded banter about the vagaries of their female offspring.

Helen didn't laugh. *Who would have daughters?* She would. Well, she would have had them once upon a time - with Jason. Who now knew the truth about their break up and would never speak to her again. But neither would she speak to him, she reminded herself.

Before Helen could ask if that was it, the voice on the phone added one more thing. 'And Ms Parker, there's a mole in our camp. If you can help to find him - or her - you'll get a bonus. Big. Huge. Tell her, Anthony,'

Mr Adams nodded, 'Bigger than you'd imagine, and coming out of *his* pocket,' he said, vehemently making the point loudly into the telephone. And then it was over.

'Dare I ask,' Helen said, as she stood at the door, 'is the daughter…'

'Cheryl. Yes.'

'The Godiva Briber…' Helen muttered.

'The what?'

'Nothing. But what did I do that was kind? Not yet give her the telling off she deserved for trying to elbow in on my articles?' In truth, it was only luck that Helen hadn't torn into Cheryl as soon as she got back from the Forest TiFFT, warning her what would happen if she stepped out of line one more time. Helen had come back in a no-nonsense, all-guns-blazing (so to speak) mood, determined to get her own house in order, starting with The Intern. Now she'd have to watch her step with Cheryl. This might throw a spanner in the works.

'I hear you allowed her to get an editing credit on one of your pieces,' the Boss said, 'it's that - he thinks that'll make it easier to sell her in the future.'

'To *sell* her?'

'Her CV - wants her to rise through the ranks - be successful like her older brother. Bit of an uphill battle by all accounts. But she's thick-skinned that one - thicker than most. But she's a good kid - so far,' there was an emphasis on the 'so far.' 'Can't say the same for the boyfriend she bats her eyes at - keeps giving him chocolates. Damn CNN jockeys. Damn college kids. Caught him in here with her not long ago - "showing him the view" she said she was. WHAT view, I wanted to know, in a closed office after hours...' He looked over the top of his specs at Helen, and she could swear there was a slight twinkle in his eye. 'Didn't ask her though. Not with Geoffrey Goodman as a father.'

Helen nodded and got up to go. 'Yeah, guess we all have to watch our step - you as well.'

'Powerful man, that one, Parker - you don't cross men like that. Don't ever beat him at golf either,' he added, and this time the twinkle was definitely there. 'Oh and before you go, take this.' He was pulling a sheet of paper off the printer near his desk. 'It's Martha Crowne's latest schedule from my insider - and you'll never believe what she's planning. You better start pulling some serious cats out of DNA bags - performing elephants, or naked wing-walking, come to that... Don't make that face, I'm joshing with you, Parker. Ignore the notes on the bottom - that's just an idea I'm working on to help you out. We need all the help we can get with that grand finale in Hawaii 'cos if all this doesn't work out, you can wave goodbye to your ratings win, your bonus and a happy Mr Adams. And Mr Adams will be waving goodbye to this view.'

Helen walked over and took the paper. The twinkle in his eye had gone completely and instead, his whole face was going a darker shade of beetroot than ever before.

'Helen,' she halted, and her eyes opened wider - she'd never heard him call her that. 'There's a mole - we gotta find the mole. I never had a mole - never had so much at stake. Find her - or him - whatever it takes - and you got a column for life. Hell, I'll even take Ki-Ka back off your old column and give it back to you - turns out she gets away with chatting to people on the TV, but she's illiterate as hell - keeps getting trolls posting vile comments about her articles. And can't book her own guests for toffee. Godiva covered toffee. Want one? Last box,' he said, and he took it out of the drawer almost lovingly and thrust it in her hands, as if saying goodbye to an era.

Helen didn't have the heart to refuse, and anyway, the mood she was in, she felt like ice cream, or cookies, or - yes, these would do, and she knew exactly where to eat them at lunchtime.

For Helen, the bad day got worse, when she sat in the coffee shop nearby, chomping on the candies and reading through the new smuggled schedule from ParlourGames. *Oh good God.* Was Martha Crowne serious? The notes from the Boss on the bottom were almost illegible, and Helen was going to ignore them as instructed, when she noticed one of two key words and her heart began to pump a little faster. If this was his idea, it was brilliant. But it would put Helen right back in the very place she was trying to escape.

She wished Kate was there to sound off about it, about men, about life.

Then if it were possible, it got 'worser' - a word used by Cheryl in her latest email - when Helen finally heard the rest of Sadie's news from home.

It had been a while and only the scantest gossip had escaped her daughters' lips as their mother had made them promise to let Sadie herself speak to Helen and tell her the 'massive news'. Helen was bursting with curiosity - but when Sadie did this, it was usually for a reason, and often meant that whatever Sadie was up to, it impacted on Helen. And more often than not, it wasn't in a good way.

After many weeks without seeing it, her beloved sister's face appeared on the Skype app Helen was connecting to, balancing her tablet on her knee, in the corner of the coffee shop. Tilting the device, she plugged her earphones in. It was as good a Wi-Fi signal as she was going to get for this important call - the first proper catch up they'd had in what felt like a lifetime.

The *brrr* noise sounded, then a click, and after a few seconds Sadie's face finally popped up on the screen. There was a relief in her voice and the initial greetings were warm and made Helen glow. But she was filled with trepidation.

'So, when are you coming home?' Sadie said, face glowing and tanned and looking better than she'd ever looked in her life.

Massive news - could it be...?

She'd followed up the Hawaii trip with another short one to Monaco. Then to Hawaii again, that much Helen knew. But the precious space they'd needed to give each other had been heeded, and radio silence kept, more or less, give or take a short text or a brief email here and there.

Like with bloody Alessandro, thought Helen.

Even Abi and Georgia were keeping shtum as well, and not even Grace had let on - this was weird, and there was definitely something going on. Something big.

'Sadie, just spit it out. What is it?'

'I'm sorry to have to do this to you, 'cos I know it will kill you, but I just can't tell you over Skype,' she said.

So Helen tried to guess. 'The shop is safe? You got a deal? Someone bought it? You got more money from the bank? You like being blonde? Georgia passed her Geography? Stuart's paying for Abi's China trip? Mum's finally tracked down Gordon McDingleberry...? Errrrr... Rumplestiltskin?'

Sadie had been shaking her head and laughing more at each suggestion. 'It's German not Geography, no Stuart's still skint - ha-ha - and who the hell's Gordon McDingleberry? And God help him if mum's on his trail! Why's she after him anyway?'

'Ask her - it's complicated - and tell her to hurry up and find him, I have to file my DNA piece soon, before Martha Crowne hits the airwaves and at the moment it needs help! This could be the twist. But come on, sis, not even a hint?'

'Not even a hint!' she said. 'But it's good news - for me - for the kids. It means big changes though...'

Oh-oh.

'...and you might find it's a bit different the next time you come to stay. But I need to finalise a few things - it's all happened so fast. It hasn't really sunk in...'

'What?!'

'Good news - for us anyway. For us all. Well, nearly all of us, depending upon your point of view...'

Helen had a sinking feeling. She ended the call knowing big changes meant MASSIVE changes, and the little rumbling, stirring feeling deep down in her stomach seemed to agree with her.

Or maybe she was just hungry.

She got up to go fetch another drink - this time a Sadie-style super thick hot chocolate with *extra stroodles* - a.k.a. chocolate shavings, she told the bemused student behind the counter, who started nudging his colleague when Helen went to pay. He gave her the change, and then red-faced, brandished a napkin and a pen asked for an autograph.

'For my mom,' he said, 'she reads your column and really wants to find a man too - she's about your age. She might be in soon - she'd be maxed out if she saw you! Oh and this one for my roommate at college - he's a big hit with the girls now because of your piece on...' he lowered his voice, 'tantric - you know what. Tells them all he was taught it by a Cougar!'

Now I'm a Cougar. Great.

Helen took her drink and decided to have it back at her desk. Maybe she could catch Kate before the end of the day - even on the phone? She desperately needed to talk to a kindred spirit.

She made her way back to the front of the coffee shop, past buggies and bags and half-finished bagels, and as she reached for the door she looked back. She'd very nearly missed them. They'd tucked themselves away right in the corner of the store, in a booth for two set back into the wall, just a single bench seat.

Her back was to Helen and his was facing. Helen could see he was a huge hunk of a quarter-back type of guy - massive shoulders and a distinctive broad face, perfect for a CNN jock - which was what he must be, as the girl he was gazing adoringly at was Cheryl. Just at that moment, he took her face in his hands and kissed her tenderly - and Helen's shoulders drooped. The Intern was getting a right good seeing to, even if Helen wasn't.

Get a room, thought Helen, and as they once more embraced in a passionate clinch, she turned tail and left in a huff. If seeing Cheryl Goodman with a hot boyfriend was enough to make Helen feel down, things were really bad.

The rest of the afternoon didn't get much better.

Helen finished her work on another couple of TiFFTs that were overdue, and decided - what the hell - to add some personal pay offs at the bottom of each. She was just in the mood and talked about her feelings and how she was looking forward to her next trip immensely as at least it was *on the other side of the bloody world.* In the second one, she even put in about not knowing who her father was, seeding the way for the DNA piece - *when it finally came* - and then, what the hell, she gave it a grand finale, with a pay-off paragraph about being single and feeling crap when she saw other couples together.

Jeez, it's me that really needs a good seeing to, she thought, *that's what the old me would have told me.*

But the old Helen was having a sabbatical.

A bit like Alessandro was, she thought. It's all right for him - off on his travel-break from life, with god knows who. She'd almost rung him to ask him the burning question that had been bugging her since leaving Tibet. But as usual she bottled out, and sat idly circling her finger around one of the chocolates from Mr Adams last box and reminisced.

Alessandro.

Pound, pound, her heart leapt into action, predictable as ever.

Dammit.

And in a sudden impulse of bravery, she'd typed the email and sent it before she could stop herself. He wouldn't reply, she knew he wouldn't reply - he hadn't been in touch for some time now, but what the heck. At least she'd now made an effort, even if he'd dropped off the face of the earth.

Or the roof of the world. If he was even still there.

And if he *was* still there, who could she ask? Well, a certain psychic may know - especially if she was back at the spa. And maybe even if she wasn't - being psychic and all that... Helen chuckled at herself.

At least Serena would respond even if he didn't - she'd already been in touch to say thanks for the mention in the spa piece - she'd had a few bookings out of it. So, possibly in return, Serena could find out some news of the hot Italian last seen gracing one of the most luxurious spas in Tibet with his delectable presence. Perhaps she may even be able to surreptitiously find out why he hadn't been in touch. And whilst she was at it, maybe Serena also had some more inklings about the man in her vision - and that note...

She looked at her watch, as the words 'email sent' popped up on the screen - although if she came back with bad news it would probably just about round off one of the worst days ever, Helen thought. Maybe there might even be a reply from Serena before close, who knows - depends on what hours she's keeping over there at the moment. *If she was that good, maybe I wouldn't even have to send the email, she'd just know that I was trying to contact her,* Helen thought with a smile.

'You've got mail.'

The noise pinged and the reply was so immediate it made Helen jump. And she couldn't believe her eyes. Serena's reply.

'Darling,

I woke to go pee and was checking on a singing bowl on e-Bay and lo and behold, an email from you, dear one. So, how lovely to hear from you.

I can't believe it - I'd only been thinking of you today. You see - I did a little meditation to tidy up some unfinished visions, a bit like when you make yourself use up the scraps from the refrigerator, you know? And some lovely stuff came through. Including about you. I have a little more to tell you about that note and the man carrying the guitar. First to reply to you - no, your lovely chap hasn't been seen here in weeks, sorry to tell, but I will put the feelers out - psychically on the unified field, and also on the earth plane - via Facebook mostly.

Anyway, the vision. There was a small triangular object and the note said 'I will be your serpent' - or it could have been 'servant,' I'm not sure. Going back to bed now. It's a full moon tomorrow and I'm off to do some man-manifesting with the Wikken group in the evening - you should try it sometime. Best wishes and cosmic hugs, Serena.'

There was no-one to tell. No-one to vent to. Even Janice was off today - so there'd be no gossip from her camp. The Boss was out golfing again and a male clerk Helen had never seen before was sat at Janice's desk. Then, as Helen watched him typing away furiously, Ki-Ka came by and annoyingly, blew him a kiss. And bugger me, if the guy didn't blow her a kiss right back.

Is nowhere safe? Helen thought? Anyone else want to rub it in?

What a day - can it get any worse?

And then she remembered what a worse day *really* looked like - to the kids in Tibet without food, begging in the streets of Lhasa, and the military types living in combat zones - flashbacks began and Helen could taste the dust of the forest and the smell of explosives in the air - it had been terrifying enough and hers wasn't even a real combat zone. So *quit the pity party*, she told herself, looking into the mirror in the restroom, washing her hands with cold water to try to make herself feel better.

What would Sadie say? Try to feel positive. Happiness is a decision. No, a - what was it now...?

'Happiness is a choice,' Helen said to her reflection. And felt in her bag for her lucky charm - that's how she'd come to think of it. Yes, that was definitely a nice feeling.

'Now, what would make me feel even better?' she asked herself out loud.

'Ben and Jerry's - two litres of cookie dough - that's what I had last night,' came a voice from behind the cubicle door. 'Mind you, perhaps that's why I've spent half the day in here!'

And out came Ki-Ka.

'Oh, it's you,' she said, adjusting her clothing and going over to wash her hands. 'You got men trouble too huh? Happens to the best of us,' she said, flicking the water from her hands vigorously all over the place, some of which went on Helen. 'And to some of the worst.'

She said the last bit whilst looking pointedly at Helen, who guessed she would have been quirking one of her eyebrows, *if she'd been able to move them,* thought Helen, watching her immobile face attempt a furrowed brow. All that happened was that the top of Ki-Ka's nose, right next to her inner eyes, wrinkled, and the tell-tale diagonal lines going downwards away from her eyes, became more pronounced.

'I take it you're trying to do this,' said Helen and narrowed her eyes towards Ki-Ka, screwing up her face in all sorts of positions, 'or this... or this... or even this...' None of which Ki-Ka could do, and she knew it. So she just flounced out of the ladies room, bashing straight into the couple of Executive Assistants who were coming in to touch up their already perfect lipstick for the gazillionth time that day.

Let me outta here...

Helen filed her articles and told the web team they were to go live online as soon as possible - with no Janice here, she sent them herself and bypassed Cheryl - whose hands were obviously tied up with other more 'pressing' matters. And anyway, Helen had since found out that The Intern had lately seemed far less bothered about working really hard and proving herself, and had begun taking longer and longer lunches with lover boy. After all, everyone had begun treating her differently now they knew that her father was indeed the new investor in TransGlobe Inc... *Funny that.*

The Boss had returned and hauled her in for another pow-wow so that just before home time, Helen was sat finishing the job she'd been putting off - researching the ghastly, scary, heart-palpitatingly terrifying list of extreme events for the Daredevil festival, most from a great height. Annoyingly her issue with heights was had returned. She blamed being back here in her normal routine, her body recreating 'normal,' and then she wondered what on earth 'normal' actually was. *One thing you've never been, is normal,* she told herself. Or was it Jason who had told her that once? Well most of the Daredevil list was not normal. It was just plain weird - for instance, the people who jumped off a cliff into the sea, just to get kicks. Helen shuddered.

The worst of it was, the Boss had had an idea, and following another afternoon on the golf course with an old colleague who ran a top TV chat show, he wanted it actioned.

'You don't have to do it, but it would be great publicity,' he'd said, then he'd uttered those immortal words, *play around with it and come back to me, will you,* which really meant, 'just do it'. And without spilling the beans about her fears, she had no choice but to go along with his 'stupendous new innovation' - an appearance on television. But no ordinary appearance.

Helen would be interviewed, about her column, and her pieces that had been making news and trending on the internet lately - including the Tantra, plus the on-stage 'prick of the day' boo boo, and now the 'pour your heart out' extended-length James Bond-esque Forest TiFFT. Despite her protests, apparently she was now newsworthy enough to merit going on there as a guest.

Then Anthony Adams' genius twists came in - the first was that her very appearance on the show, would mean Helen would be creating another significant first - everyone wanted to be on TV, said the Boss, and this is how they can get the blow by blow account of what it's really like in the subsequent TiFFT article. And the second twist - one that the Boss took great delight in confirming to her - was that he and his golf pal had decided to run some sort of competition - details to be decided nearer the time, but might involve the winner choosing an event for her to do.

So now her damn column was going to be controlled by the viewers of a TV chat show - the only consolation being the way the Boss had described the programme - he'd said it was 'proper mainstream, not just internet and cable like Ki-Ka's' - that had lifted Helen's spirits. Anyway, the guest spot was being arranged for a show happening soon - a pretty high profile slot in a few weeks' time.

You can bet your life I know which they'll choose, she thought, scanning the list which included cliff jumping, parascending, parachute jumping, fire-walking, telegraph-pole-leap and... *ooer*. The last one had made her need several cups of water from the water cooler. It helped but it wasn't great. It was at moments like this, she really yearned for some oxygen in a can.

There was that feeling in her tummy again. Or was it abject terror? Maybe she shouldn't have had that thick hot chocolate at lunchtime, even if it did remind her of being in Sadie's kitchen in the old days. Or maybe it was just the thought of being up so high, and so near the edge...

Suddenly an idea struck her - perhaps she could try to recapture that Forest feeling - when she'd gone down a zip wire and up in a helicopter without a second thought - all due to the extreme life or death circumstances. When it came to the crunch she'd done it, and if she'd done it once, she surely could do it again.

Well, if she needed any help preparing for them, she knew just the person to advise - and immediately dug out Rob Rains' contact info. The NExUS guy might know exactly what to do. Some sort of practise - somehow? Just having him there at the festival for moral support would be great - she could always offer to pay him, like a proper business arrangement. Or even better, maybe he'd dress up as her, and do it instead of her - now there's an idea! She smiled at the thought of it.

Then she finished the day by making one final purchase online that made her feel a lot better still - a little gift for Rinchen and one for Socks and his siblings. And a quick confirmation email to let her know it was on its way via the Spa.

Job done.

Amazing how many loose ends you can tie up when you haven't got a best friend around to distract you, nor anyone else to talk to in the office. Helen sat in her office chair and span herself round a few times, garnering a couple of glances from the Exec Ass's again, but she didn't care. Not the mood she was in. And now she really needed to unwind.

There was no point waiting for Kate - she'd most definitely had some sort of spat with Kieran. If Kate wouldn't even come down to the bar after work, to debate the day's events, and tease Brad the barman, things must be bad. She had to go help with an evening event at her daughter's vintage clothes store, apparently, and had disappeared by the time Helen popped into her office on the way to *cocktails-o'clock* at O'Reilly's. Kieran was still sitting bashing away at his keyboard, with a face like thunder, and the mood he was in, Helen didn't even bother to say hello.

At least there'd be one place she could find sanctity - and a lovely big Manhattan in an ice cool glass, to boot. She took the rest of the chocolates, plus the list of Martha's upcoming events, just to make sure she'd really read them correctly and to rack her brains for something to beat them. Soon she'd set herself up at the bar, ready to have a banter with the delectable Brad.

As usual, he didn't disappoint.

'She's having her *what* pierced?' he said, screaming like a girl, and calling his fellow bartender over. The noise was making quite a scene within the early evening bar crowd.

'Shhh!' said Helen, 'it's supposed to be confidential!'

'Yuh-huh, and you've got this list *how*?' Brad said, scoffing, and making a gesture like he was patting the air down. '*Oh.Emm.Gee* girlfriend,' he squealed. 'Is she really doing this? But she's ancient - she's got to be at least fifty? The next one's even more *gross!*'

A new guy Helen hadn't seen before slunk up alongside Brad behind the bar and joined in, saying to Helen, 'You know, like, er, that Tantra thing you did? Yeah, well it's like, been set to a soundtrack and made into a music video on Youtube now, it's trending big-time - nearly a million hits now, it's huge,' he said. He was thin, all in black, with face piercings and dyed black hair, and Brad introduced his new bartender, Wayne. Wayne sniffed a bit, and added, 'Perhaps she's trying to, like, "out-gross" you.'

'Sounds like she'll succeed - especially if there are pictures,' laughed Helen, 'and anyway don't be cheeky - Darius and Yokita weren't gross in that video. And fifty is not old.'

'No, darling of course it's not,' said early-thirties Brad, patting her hand. 'And I've seen that tantra video and I can tell you they're not gross at all. In fact, just to check, I had to watch it five times. Hell, that female body was steamy - off the scale! I nearly turned!' He laughed, then so did Wayne. A group of suits who had just come in were signalling, so Brad ushered Wayne away to serve them. Then Brad leaned in to Helen and lowered his voice.

'I think Martha Crowne could learn a thing or two from tantra diva and her man.'

'I know, and it was all done in the best *possible* taste,' Helen added taking back her list and shaking her head at it. 'Whereas this...' She flicked her fingers at the sheet of paper.

'Yes well we don't all have your class, your elegance, your sophistication... by the way, Helen, you've got olive in your teeth.' Helen started to pick at her teeth and he shook his head. 'Just teasing.'

'Well at least Darius and Yokita are doing well out of it,' she said.

'Are you kidding me? You're a little star-maker! Your darling tantric twosome have been signed up to launch a new series of *how-to* marriage-saver videos! They announced it to Ki-Ka on her latest recording - she was in here boasting as usual after the show.'

'She booked them on her show!?' exclaimed Helen, nearly knocking over her glass.

'You spot them, she interviews them - it's a beautiful harmony don't you think? You should ask for commission!'

Helen sighed and shook her head.

Brad continued. 'Whoopsy, not best friends, are we, you and Madame-de-la-Botox?'

Helen just looked at him from under her eyelashes and made a face that said *what do you think.*

'Well if it makes you feel any better - Nathan, that guy she stole from me? Who she recommended for your Mr Adams' accounts team?' Helen nodded, and he went on, 'Well he dumped her. An accounts clerk - dumped pregnant Ki-Ka!' He laughed comically, and Helen had to smile.

'She went off to pay homage to the white powder train, as far as my new boy over there tells me,' Brad said, pointing at the black haired youth who was ever so slowly pouring drinks for the after work crowd. 'What do you think of Wayne?'

'He seems very - laid back,' said Helen.

'Hmm. I'm not sure about him yet. He's Nathan's roommate. Nathan felt so guilty leaving me in the lurch that he went and found me a new bartender to take his place. And trained him up for free. He's a good boy, Nathan. Especially now he's dumped Miss High and Mighty. Drama, drama, drama!'

'Wow, it's all change here as well then,' Helen said, being aware of a growing feeling of being left out of the loop. Again.

'Well, no good making that little pouty face, honey - you'd be in the know if you hadn't been gallivanting around the forest with some squaddie - a damned hunky one, according to those amaaazing photos on your TiFFT column. Huuuuge *Gluteus maximus*, am I right?'

'It wasn't like that - we didn't actually gallivant,' she said, remembering the moments with the stranger she used to call husband. 'Not really.'

'Well that's *not* how your article makes it seem. People want to know, honey, it's like a reality show instalment! They keep asking me if you're coming in here - and not only students. A proper little celeb you're becoming,' Brad said, and patted her arm adoringly, and cocking his head towards Wayne who was clumsily pointing out Helen to two of his customers - they all looked away as soon as she glanced across.

'Well if any hunky men - available ones - come asking about me, just take their numbers. I could do with a good...' she stopped herself from saying 'seeing to.' 'Er, a good night out.'

'What about Nathan - he's single again now - he knows how to treat a lady. Rather than a queen.'

'You're the one that likes toy-boys, not me,' she laughed. 'Did he really dump Ki-Ka?' said Helen, and Brad nodded, whilst pouring a little drink for them both.

'No wonder Ben and Jerry got a bashing yesterday,' she pondered. 'Well, wonders never cease - proves it's not only the women using the casting couch.'

'Honey,' said Brad, fixing her with a knowing gaze, 'if you only knew...'

Just then a whole load of office staff arrived and Brad gave Helen a wink, thrust another cocktail her way and went to serve, leaving her sitting alone. She began studying the new Martha list once more. Shock tactics, gawp value, voyeuristic - it was gross. But with a sinking feeling, Helen also had an inkling it was brilliant.

How they think they'll get away with these images, God knows, she thought. But then she furrowed her brow. Come to think of it, the most popular posts she'd done of late had gone against expectations. Perhaps Martha's new list really could hit the mark - become a zeitgeist and not only catch Helen up, but pull ahead as well, as people at the water coolers all over the USA said to each other 'Have you seen that old bird on TV who does that weird thing with hosepipe.' Helen sighed a long sigh, and swigged her drink. *Troubled times.*

'Penny for them?' came a voice - a female voice. It was none other than Cheryl.

Well if that isn't the perfect end to an imperfect day...

She plonked herself on the stool next to Helen without asking. 'You weren't in the office when I got back from an afternoon of doing errands for Mr A. Thought I might find you in here.'

'I was in the coffee shop at lunchtime,' Helen said, dispensing with niceties. 'But I don't suppose you saw me, with that jock's tongue down your neck.' Helen looked at her sternly then laughed. 'I'm teasing you!'

Cheryl's shocked face flooded with relief.

'Don't worry,' said Helen, 'your secret's safe with me. Daddy doesn't know, right?' *Spot on.* Cheryl blushed.

'No,' said Cheryl, sitting up on the stool and looking concerned. 'And daddy would kill me if he found out. His first wife left him for a sports star, so he wouldn't be too happy if he caught me with C.J.'

'C.J. - funny how they all have names like that,' Helen said. 'C.J. what?'

'Nothing,' said Cheryl, cagily, 'just C.J.' She shifted a little on her stool and started looking in her bag. 'I'm dehydrated, need a long, cool drink of something good. Thirsty work, today.'

'I'll bet it was,' said Helen, 'don't worry, my treat.' Helen signalled and Wayne came across and gave Cheryl the once over, then took her order and shuffled away to get her a gin and pink lemonade which she downed practically in one.

'Ahh, that's better, thank you,' she said, and visibly relaxed back into the chair.

'Daddy says you're all set to earn big bucks if you hit your targets,' she said suddenly, and the bluntness made Helen nearly choke on her cocktail. 'Now that you know - about him, I mean - there's no point beating around the water cooler bush is there?'

'No, I guess not. Must be nice having a fairy god-father who can wave a wand and you get what you like.' Helen couldn't help it.

'Sometimes,' Cheryl said, 'but most of the time, I think that it must be nicer having free reign to make your own way - like you do,' she said. Helen's eyes widened and she narrowed them a little. Cheryl continued, 'You're doing so well, making this column your own - making your mark on the company. It must feel good, Helen.' Cheryl swivelled to face her with an honesty in her eyes that made Helen look twice. 'And no-one did it but you. Not your father or your mother or an older brother...' *Or an older sister,* thought Helen, suddenly feeling sorry for Sadie. '...you. And if you make a mistake, it's *your* mistake, no-one else's. What *does* it feel like to be a self-made woman?' Her look was one of utter admiration and Helen was taken aback. 'I've always wondered.'

Helen wasn't sure how to answer. She'd never really thought of it like that before. 'I didn't have a choice - didn't know my dad...' Helen found herself stumbling a little, looking at the big blue eyes staring at her in adulation. 'Actually - it feels quite good,' she admitted, 'but I'd have swapped it anytime to have a father who was around, to influence me, to just, be there, you know?'

'Yes,' said Cheryl, her voice taking on a hollow tone, 'more than you know. But what's worse - not to have one at all? Or to have one who's not really there, even when he's *there*... You know what I mean?'

There was a moment between the two women. Helen looked down and realised the Martha Crowne schedule was still on the table and Cheryl was looking at it. She caught Helen's worried look. 'Don't worry,' she said, with a little sad laugh, 'my father tells me everything.'

So she's seen it, thought Helen.

They spoke for a little while longer - having a proper chat, for the first time ever, like two mates after work - about life. Cheryl's ears pricked up when they got on to the topic of the TiFFT's schedule and the TV Chat show and Hawaii. But Helen had had enough for one day. And what a day it had been. Anyway, one little chat didn't make The Intern suddenly become The Confidante.

'If I manage to hit my targets and get the bonus - god willing - I can maybe go write a book about it for a friend of mine, his name is...'

'Damian Grant,' interrupted Cheryl.

'But how did you...'

'Talking of whom,' Brad said, appearing like a homing pigeon at the name of his crush. 'When do you get to ride on elephants with my favourite businessman?'

'You're riding elephants? Oh yes! That's soon isn't it!' said Cheryl, picking up her bag as if it was time for her to leave.

'In less than a week with a bit of luck,' said Helen, thinking it couldn't come soon enough.

Chapter Fourteen

'So where are you now?' asked Kate in a very dodgy Skype call a few days later. 'Are you at the train station or what?'

'Internet café in Chiang Mai,' Helen said, shouting a bit. 'Stiff as a board - that sleeper train was 14 hours - did me in! But Mr Adams said he wanted nitty gritty so this one's going to be one of those bucket list journeys - you know, warts and all. Just waiting to be picked up then I'm going off to the elephant thing.'

The line went a bit fuzzy - Kate's signal was hampered by being somewhere ridiculous underground, doing her next Real Grown Ups Guide shoot with Kieran. And Helen's was hampered by being in Thailand, amidst what seemed like a thousand other people all trying to use the same Wi–Fi signal. There were lots of internet cafés but far fewer with a good enough signal for Skype. The air was humid and musty, spicy food mixed with spicy geeks, the café was busy and Helen thought she was going to melt. She wafted her camisole top and the guy next to her looked over his specs and peered down her top. She made a face at him and turned away. 'You're certainly keeping it pacy. You didn't want to be there for when Sadie got back from Hawaii? You're not still fighting are you?'

'No - she spoke to me, I spoke to her, we had a nice chat.'

'Well why didn't you detour? Especially with her news about... '

The signal went again then, and Helen thought they'd have to end the call soon, having established that Kate and Kieran had cleared the air, although she still wouldn't let on exactly what had happened. Helen tried to guess. Hmmm... But what was that about Sadie? And her news? What did Kate know that Helen didn't?

'... investor, what a turn up for the books!' she was saying as the signal returned, but a very heavy set man was now hovering directly over Helen, looking at his watch - her time must be very nearly up.

'What? What? I didn't catch that - I didn't... Email me it!' she said, as the call died for good.

She was rattled now, for sure. Helen's mood had been a bit iffy since the 'day of hell' last week, and nothing much had changed that. She'd had to go straight off to fulfil another few of the original commitments on her TiFFTs list inherited from Martha Bloody Crowne, as she now called her - all of which were 'Boring as F**k' as Kate had called them - a couple of times.

And all of which were now done, filed and would probably remain un-posted for a long while - unless a 'fill-in TiFFT emergency' cropped up, ie, never. The Boss was pacing up and down the last time Helen had seen him, almost invisible behind vapour, indicating he was getting an ear bashing from the Father of The Intern, which Helen had irreverently dubbed Geoffrey Goodman. But she did feel for Mr Adams - he'd staked his job - his career - on his gamble that spicing up the Transglobe Inc output would pay off - it had to.

His biggest bug bear was 'that DNA thing' as he now called it - with a big banner payment in the offing - as soon as she could only 'sexy it up a bit.' The lab had come back with the standard results, which were quite interesting but nothing to set the world on fire, and Helen had stopped reading when the first paragraph needed a translator to understand it - is was all 'haplotypes' and 'haplogroups' and H markers - and anyway she needed the Y

Chromosome bit - that only a male could provide. She'd examine it soon - and work out how to spin it, she'd been too busy driving racing cars, learning how to clay pigeon shoot, doing a dive to a wreck and - most enjoyable of all, swimming with dolphins. Well, dolphin - the others must have had a day off. And other less interesting than those, but all on the bucket list of Try if For the First Time events.

And she certainly hadn't run it by Cheryl, who since that sharing heart to heart last week had been acting a little bit cagey around Helen, who couldn't for the life of her, work out why. Helen tried to guess.

Was it because her father - Geoffrey Goodman the Secret Investor - had told his daughter something about his plans for Helen?

Was Cheryl keeping her distance because things were getting serious with the CNN jock - because they were - Helen knew they were. The water cooler drums - and Janice - spoke of nothing else. But why would that make her keep her distance?

Was it because she'd felt overwhelmed when they'd talked about fathers? Helen, having never had one and wanting one; Cheryl having a domineering one she found TOO helpful sometimes?

Who knew? Anyway, Helen's gut instinct about Cheryl now matched the warnings from Janice and Kate, to 'watch that one.' So she did.

When she was there. And when Helen was there.

They'd become a bit 'ships in the night.'

Helen went back outside - it was a bit less hot out here, being so late, but at least it wasn't so muggy. She looked at her watch. She went back to the place she'd stored her designer luggage and waited for her lift. She couldn't wait to see Damian again - he was an old friend with whom she could relax. And you couldn't make old friends, she thought. Only new ones.

Old and new.

Jason.

And Alessandro.

Both had been on her mind - a lot.

The long train journey had made it inevitable. Yes she was feeling lonely, missing someone in her life to fill that gap - someone to care for. She'd always had someone to care for, and to care for her - sometimes a couple at once. And she was - naturally - always the one who left in the end. *Job to job, man to man...*

Jason had been playing on her mind mainly because the more she thought about him being married, and kissing her under the waterfall, the more irritated she got. So much for him being honest with her all her life. Bloody men.

Then she thought of Alessandro who'd been completely up front with who he was, and what he wanted from her - but she hadn't been able to give it. Then. But maybe now she could. Maybe now, after the Forest experience and the dawning realisation of what was really important, maybe she could see her way to valuing a man who wanted to ... be the man.

Ah, who was she kidding? He still hadn't contacted her anyway so it was purely academic. She sat down on her hard suitcase. At least she was nearly there now. And she was glad she'd done it, but she wouldn't go on another fourteen hour train ride anytime soon. In the end, she'd got on her own nerves, keep thinking the worst. Bad habit.

By around five hours into the train journey, she'd begun to worry about Alessandro and kept going over and over again in her mind, the conversations they'd had about her promises. And the spectacular way in which she'd broken them. After going round and round in circles in her head, her silly little mind wound up taking her step by step through the tantric massage. She missed him, she missed his hands. And his smile. But most of all, she just hoped he was ok.

She took a deep breath, and felt for her lucky charm in her bag once more. She'd nearly panicked on the train when she couldn't find it, and then realised it had dropped through a little hole in the bottom pocket of the rucksack and into the lining. She retrieved it, and felt a little reassured, even if not a lot. This was one thing she couldn't lose. Not now.

Helen looked around her - she stood there head and shoulders above many of the people - women and men - in the bustling city, some smart and suited, others in as few clothes as possible, mainly vest and shorts. They were mixed in with every type of tourist you could imagine. She started to compose the piece she'd be writing, and took in all the sights and sounds - and smells. The usual array of market stalls and street vendors were there, and she'd half expected to see the ones who followed you trying to sell you an old mobile phone case for a defunct model, or one of a thousand bracelets shown off by extending one arm and following you down the street till you bought one or gave them some money just to go away, but there were surprisingly few. Rather, there were conventional looking business-like vendors, in charge of efficient stalls and stoves and assistants. Heck, there was even a Tesco. A Tesco Lotus maybe, but there were hundreds of them over here.

Earlier on she'd gone to stretch her legs and found the night market. It was heaving - travel guides she'd looked at when doing her research had listed it as one of the big must-sees if you're going to Chiang Mai - and she had to say, she was impressed with the freshness of the huge, whole crabs and lobsters, the mounds of fresh fruit and vegetables and stalls selling every type of Thai food you could wish for. Helen had chosen omelettes in banana leaf, bypassing the raw hearts and livers sold in the same way they were selling peppers and spring rolls. It was ridiculously cheap - you could get a three course meal for just over a dollar, she discovered. And if she had to stay, a good room with a ceiling fan for twelve dollars. Maybe not round here though - some of the smells were a little nauseating, she had to admit - or maybe it was the omelette she'd eaten.

Helen had continued on her little solo sight-seeing tour. It might be late, but it was still very warm so she'd meandered a little way down Thanon Kon Durn (Walking Street Market) which was only 'walking street' technically every Sunday when it closed to cars and filled up with purveyors of everything from giant artworks on canvas to carvings, jewellery and racks and racks of clothes. She was warned by one of the locals to avoid the red light district as with her blond hair and long, bare legs, they might see her as competition and try to shoo her away. Apparently for many of the 'women of the night,' the opening of the Pretty Woman movie was a 'how-to' guide.

Helen had circled back and found herself in the internet café, where she'd made the call.

Her bum was numb from sitting on hard cases, and she stood up and dusted her shorts down, when someone tapped her on the arm.

'Hello missus, need a lift?'

'Damian! What a rubbish English accent - twenty years of trying and you and Kate are still crap at it!'

'Come on, air conditioned car awaits Madame this way,' he said, trying again and doing it even worse.

They talked non-stop on the drive back to the hotel he'd booked her in - one with air conditioning - *just for tonight,* she'd insisted - and by the time she was showered, unpacked and changed into a fresh cotton dress and sandals, she was feeling a whole lot better. A big hug had made the world of difference.

Damian had been particularly perturbed by the whole 'mole' thing. He too played golf with Anthony Adams and the other investors sometimes - they were all part of that circuit - and he made some guesses as to who it was.

'Yes I thought the mole was Cheryl, too - but her father is the investor.'

'Geoff Goodman - of course - tricky character,' Damian said, putting one foot on the wicker armchairs they were sitting in, outside the bar area of the hotel. His beige shorts were pressed and almost pristine, and his vest was whiter than white. The chest underneath it was not. He tanned easily and whilst he wasn't a big guy, he oozed style. Helen was pleased to be sitting there with him, and quite happy when people mistook them for a couple. Although he'd taken to disappearing for most of the year recently, when they were younger, he'd been her 'plus-one' on more than one swanky occasion, and played the role perfectly. Even when it came down to it, they fancied the same men. 'I think I recall him talking about his son - bursting with pride about him he was, at a venture capital meeting once. But I don't know anything about his daughter.'

'Neither does he,' observed Helen wryly.

And Helen was struck, in the stillness of the Thai night, that she probably had more in common with Cheryl Goodman, The Intern than she thought.

Damian sadly only had tonight to spend with Helen - partly due to his schedule and partly due to hers. 'You squeezed our overlap,' he teased her, 'and if anyone is good at squeezing my overlap, it's you.'

'Or your damned brother,' Helen added. Damian's brother, Helen's ex-Boss, was the reason Helen had changed careers. But she hated to talk about him - the two brothers couldn't be more different. 'I guess he's the elephant in the room,' she said, and they laughed, and got on straight away to talking about Helen's big TiFFT the next day.

She woke early and went down to the internet room to check her emails. The half-finished sentence from Kate yesterday had played on her mind all night, and her dreams had once again been full of the endless possibilities for the other half. In the end, there was the email. And it wasn't anything Helen was expecting.

'Dear Helen,' Kate had written, *'just a quickie to finish what I was saying - I think your final words were to send an email about it? Well I just wanted to say congrats to your sister - I can't believe she's only just met the guy and she's getting married...'*

Helen blinked in surprise and felt her tongue go numb and her limbs go cold. What?

She read it again. Oh my God. Oh my GOD. OH. MY. GOD.

Coupled with the rest of the news, that Martha Crowne had gone ahead and got 'that' piercing, and had leaked news of it onto the internet, but also it hadn't been a joke that she was going to do a videoed colonic irrigation - bringing a new meaning to talking shit, Helen's day could not be lifted. Even her old pal Damian, with all his attempts at his usual gay humour which normally made Helen roll about laughing - or ROFL as her nieces said - couldn't lift her spirits. In the end as he said goodbye near the elephant venue, he gave her a good talking to.

'Helen Parker-Todd - you have precisely thirty minutes before you get on that elephant to snap yourself out of this stupor. Because elephants know - and they don't forget. And neither do I. So cheer up on command now, otherwise if you get bucked by the elephant - I said *"bucked"* - my last memory of your beautiful face will be of it looking like it's been Ki-Ka'd in *Kah–Kah*.' That made her smile a bit, and she bid him goodbye with a heavy heart.

Her mind wasn't really on it, not at first, but as she began the journey, she became so fascinated by the majestic creatures that she lost herself in their majesty, their awesomeness.

Helen had the best time, and because the nieces had been looking forward to this for so long, she got back and immediately wrote them an email to tell them what it was like.

Dear Abi and Georgia,

It was surreal being on a red dirt road, next to a river in the middle of the jungle with a group of local guys that spoke broken

English (but a lot better than my Thai I might add) with them all wearing the latest sports gear! There must be a FootLocker in the middle of the jungle I don't know about! The ground was sooo dry that a little cloud of dust surrounded my every foot step, with grass that was so coarse you could hear it crunching under your feet. It reminded me of Honey I Shrunk the Kids - remember we watched that film when you both had chicken pox at the same time? Well anyway it was because of the giant blades of jagged grass.

As we descended the bank to approach the river, that's when I saw them. There must have been at least 5 elephants, some were bathing in the water, others on the bank and one kneeled down peacefully about 10 meters from us. I'd never been this close to an elephant, their size was epic, but I wasn't scared of him and he wasn't scared of me. I approached him alongside the trainer, and I say trainer with the loosest of terms because he was just a man with a hook on the end of a stick! As I looked back over at the elephants in the water I saw all the little local boys that had run down the hill with me, they couldn't have been older than 12 - like you, Georgia - all jumping from the back of one elephant to another! This was the craziest jungle gym I'd ever seen. It was all a game, the elephants were like toadstools to them that they would jump across to escape their friends. It was surreal.

Now we've seen elephants at a zoo, right? Behind bars or big walls? So to see them with children draped over their backs in a river was completely new, like an eastern zoo. The trainer said something to my elephant and tapped his leg with a stick, the beast slowly rose and put his knee out and the trainer pushed me towards him and gestured to me, "up". Being a city girl, and having not ridden that many elephants in my time, I looked back at him begging to know how in God's name I was meant to swing my leg over an elephant! Let me tell you now, girls, and for future reference for when you go on your gap years (and insist your mother lets you have one, so you can do things like go to Thailand and ride elephants) - there's no lady-like way to get on top of an elephant! I reached over to his spine to try and pull myself up. His skin was so rough with deep wrinkles throughout, you could lose a hand in it. I pulled my stomach against his ribs and tried to pull myself up and swing my leg around. He was so patient he didn't move an inch, or make a sounds. It was me doing all the huffing and puffing! I finally got sat up straight and tried to compose myself after looking like "Cousin It" (from the Addams Family - the one with all the hair over its face), I then realised how high I was and the elephant hadn't even stood up yet! His skin was warm with hair sprouting out from his back as thick as wool! Before I knew it we were off, and a dust cloud appeared around us and I was back in Spain on the Bucking Bronco! There was nothing to hold on to so I gripped his back so tightly with my legs and reached around his neck like a baby sloth. As I said, nothing lady like, it's not like the movies when you glide onto its back and gracefully walk into the water, I was a hot mess! Once everyone was up on their elephant the trainer shouted and one by one they all started plodding toward the river bank. They were silent giants and they swayed from side to side floating toward the water on a cloud of red dust. The elephants must have been hot 'cos as soon as they got to the water they were spraying everyone with water from their trunks! It was official playtime! One second you were up, and the next they would dunk you under as they rolled themselves around to cool down. It was so funny, you really had no clue when they would go down. You'd get that feeling like on a roller coast when it drops and your stomach goes. I remember the heat coming off the elephant once in the cool river, with my feet just dangling on the surface. The water was warm, but it almost felt cold compared to the elephant. It was mid-morning and it was just starting to get really hot, so I quite enjoyed a trunk spray to cool off. The young boys were still jumping from elephant to elephant when it was time to *come in. The older guy called them all and the young boys would sit on top of the elephants head and using the hook that looked like the toe claw from Jurassic park, they would dig the elephant behind the left or right ear to signal which direction they wanted him to go. The holes were so deeply ingrained it was quite disturbing. It was then I realised actually, these elephants are no different to any I've seen in a zoo, they are no freer, it's just a different kind of prison.'*

Helen sat back in her hotel room once more and looked at what she'd written, then pressed send, before she added anything about Sadie's news. No - if Sadie wanted to tell her herself, tell her she would. Little did Helen know that the rest of the news from Sadie's camp would be so life-changing. She had no clue at all.

And little did the nieces know the rest of Helen's news. Because there was one important detail she'd left out of the tale. As Helen prepared to check out of her hotel, en route for home, a day later than expected, she felt herself beaming. Sadie wasn't the only one with secrets.

Chapter Fifteen

Helen gave the taxi driver the address, and settled in the back of the cab, her luggage firmly stored in the boot. He was the funniest cab driver, who sang and banged his hands on the steering wheel whilst dodging his Buddha prayer beads that crashed together and swung around the mirror. If someone had told Helen yesterday morning how her world would have changed by today, she would have told them to keep taking the crazy pills. But not only had her 'man ban' sister come back from a short trip to Hawaii engaged, according to Kate and details 'TBC,' but Helen had had the most amazing experience of her life, on so many levels, and it all began on the back of an elephant.

The email to the nieces had been accurate, right up until the final bit where the older guy called the younger lads in and stopped them jumping from one to the next. That was when Helen found herself on an elephant that was turning and heading in the opposite direction from where it was supposed to go, following the shallow river. The young boys were skipping along the bank laughing and pointing and shouting. Were they following it? Or was it following them.

She looked over her shoulder, but the older guy didn't seem overly worried at their disappearance. So she wouldn't be either - the huge animal must know where it was going and would come back eventually. And anyway - she was getting a bit of a longer ride so she wasn't going to complain too much.

The slow ponderous movement of the limbs and sinews and muscles and bones beneath her continued, and Helen began to relax and enjoy it. She'd played up the height for the girls' sake - it wasn't a height that bothered Helen - only much higher heights bothered Helen - that's when her height thing kicked in, and she found herself wanting to... *stop it!* She focussed her mind on the almost hypnotic movement of the creature beneath her, and found herself relying once again on the tantric breathing to calm her down - the techniques she'd experienced in Tibet, what seemed like a hundred years ago, with a gorgeous Italian. A man who gave her heart pangs every time she thought of him. A man who was there when she had her very first 'Awe Rush' - and her second, and third, come to that. A handsome man called...

'Alessandro!'

What? Helen looked up, and there on the bank was someone shouting towards another even bigger elephant further down the river. She must have been hearing things. The boys were still there, shouting again and pointing, only this time they were pointing towards the other elephant, one that didn't have a bare back rider on it, it had a sort of a bench seat and a more regal brightly coloured embroidered cloth thrown over its back. And there astride it, sitting upright and proud, was... no it couldn't be. But it was.

As the elephant got nearer and nearer, there in the 'driving seat' in just a skimpy vest top, and shorts, showing off muscles that were somehow even more defined and tanned than she remembered, was Alessandro. Her Alessandro. *Or was he?*

The other regal elephant approached and it seemed as though Helen's one knew it, and they slowed to an amiable closeness, and began spraying water around once again. Alessandro smiled.

'Hello, Helen,' he said.

'I... don't know which question to ask you first,' she said, beaming right back at him.

'Well I'm guessing one of them can be answered by my saying I read your last email to me saying where you were going next. Then I tracked your Damian Grant down when I read that you were coming here. He helped arrange a more suitable... ahh, shall we say "overlap"?'

'Yes, we can say that,' she said, pushing a strand of her hair back out of her eyes, into her top knot, and still holding on to the elephant's neck for dear life. 'Question two?'

'Can be answered by my saying that I opened this email this time because I had been following your TiFFTs, and...'

'You read my columns?'

'... I did. And was especially alarmed at my feelings of jealousy when reading about your time in the forest with - what did you call him in your online column? 'GT.' I'm guessing that was Jason Todd, yes?'

She just nodded. Knowing everything she'd told him it about herself, it probably wasn't hard to read between the lines.

'So I figured you may have got back with him. That was until I read the next one, where you mentioned being single was not a nice thing and you wished for your soul mate to come along. I think the words you used were - *to show up in your life*?'

Again, still gripping on for dear life, Helen just nodded, entranced.

'And soon afterwards, I got your email. So I decided to go with my gut, and not my head. To overrule what my logic was telling me to do, and to track down the only one who - so far - has, how do you say, "got away."'

'So far, you say?'

'So far,' he repeated and the corner of his mouth quirked.

'Well, you found me,' she said. 'Well done.'

'I wanted to surprise you.' He was still sitting calmly and serenely on top of the bench which meant he could hold on more easily. There was room for two. Helen eyed up the seat behind him and then her own 'vehicle.'

'You certainly did that,' she said, 'I still feel like I'm dreaming. Is it really you? Here? Now? I didn't know what had happened to you - I was beginning to worry.'

'I know. Rinchen told me. I was spending some time with the monks up in the mountains - some valuable time, *Carissima*, away from modern technologies - apart from my fitness app,' he conceded and laughed at himself. *Blimey, self-deprecating? This was new.* 'She says to say thank you for the gifts that came via the spa with your note to her - you are very kind, even though some of the gifts are not necessarily the best choices - her four children have been crazy from eating sweets and making the whole village despair,' he said and laughed again. 'You can imagine how funny, no?'

Helen could indeed imagine. And she was so glad he could too.

The elephant man had finally caught up with them and had waded into the river to take control of the elephant once again. Helen looked at the creature bending down as it was bidden, obeying the commands by habit. And she wondered how things stood between her and Alessandro now. Maybe she was about to find out. The man gestured for Helen to dismount onto its knee, the water was very shallow indeed and she would hardly get wet. She thanked him kindly and did as she was told.

Alessandro, however, stayed firmly put. What, was he going to make her walk back to the bank alongside him?

'*Tesoro mio*,' he said, 'I have room for one more up here on the executive club class elephant. Would you care for an upgrade?'

The next morning, for a change, Helen was up first. It was a combination of the heat and the sound of the river rushing by that woke her. She had joined Alessandro in his accommodation, and been totally amazed that it was not some five or even four - or even three - star hotel, but some kind of a shanty hotel that was literally floating on a river. Damian had offered to help him book a better place, but Alessandro was determined to live like a local and in particular, to live like the little elephant herders lived, in similar huts nearby.

Last night, they'd begun with a little talking, and talking had turned into hugging and then suddenly before Helen knew it, she was on her back being given, finally, a proper seeing to. She laughed, thinking of that description, and wondered if Cheryl's CNN jock was as skilled as Alessandro. But only briefly - she knew he wouldn't be, even though he'd been very handsome. Nothing like Alessandro - her Alessandro. Dark skin, dark hair, dark eyes. Prominent cheekbones - that would be her type forever more, she thought. But would he?

They'd fallen asleep to the sound of the river but the mid-morning sun was up now and it was stifling. She stumbled over to the sliding wooden door that led out to the decking, and started to wriggle it back until it was as wide as possible, to let out the fog of heat that had filled the room during the night especially after their love making. As the door came up, the room instantly filled with light, and Helen stepped out onto the decking.

Underfoot, about eighteen inches down, the river was rushing along in between the bamboo poles. Helen looked up and the sight took her breath away.

'Alessandro!' she called, hearing him stir, 'I think we're in paradise.' He came out to join her, and stood behind her, his arms around her middle.

'It's a sight I'll never forget, *mio caro*,' he whispered in a throaty morning voice. 'We step out of the dark hot room into what I can only imagine paradise would be like.'

Helen couldn't help but agree. She considered how she would describe it on her column. As though the saturation of her eyes was set to maximum - the green was the greenest she'd ever seen, the crystal clear river that seemed so dank in the night was a vivid, sparkling blue, the rough wooden planks under her toes a contrasting brown, and in the sky was the brightest yellow sun she'd ever seen.

'It is most strange,' he said. 'I feel as though I am fully aware of everything around me at one moment. I can see everything, hear everything...'

'... feel everything - I know what you mean, exactly,' said Helen. 'Let's try to remember this moment forever.' The sticky atmosphere of the room had disappeared and in its place a cool breeze was bouncing off the water and dancing with the sunlight that shone around the terrace like their own private disco.

'You know what this feeling is, don't you,' she said, softly. 'An *Awe Rush*...'

He beamed at her and hugged her tighter to him with a shared memory of an amazing moment in Tibet. 'Come, let us go eat,' he said, taking her hand, a while later, 'and then you and I really must talk.'

Still sated from their session the night before, Helen stretched languorously as she finished a fruit platter at the local café. Alessandro was just sitting watching her. There was something new in his eyes and she was keen to work it out.

'So, *mio caro*,' she said, and his eyes flashed at the use of his mother tongue. 'What is it? What is it that truly brought you all the way out here to find me? It can't just have been to surprise me, can it?'

'Helen, you know I was determined to change you,' he said, 'well I see how wrong that was, now. No-one is on this planet to live their life by another's rules. We must be who we need to be, in this plane. And I needed to tell you I was wrong. To your face, so you know that I mean it.'

Helen waited for some more, but he just sipped his water and looked out at the river. 'Well, thank you, Alessandro. I appreciate that.' Then he turned to look at her, expectantly. 'And, I,' she began, 'er...'

'You do not have to say it, that you are sorry you broke your promises to me in Tibet - and therefore forcing me to take the decision to change your flight so you did not stay with me any longer,' *ouch!* 'For you did not know the reasons why. Why those promises were so dear.'

'And will you tell me now?' she asked, moving her hand across the table towards his. She held her breath as he hesitated, but then slid his other hand over hers.

'It was my family,' he said. 'No, before you say it, not my brother and my parents. My...wife. And my child.'

'Oh,' said Helen, trying to maintain a steady voice, *oh shit*. 'Oh?'

'I lost them - both - at once. The child was still born and my wife died soon afterwards. I loved them both very much,' he said, and there was the most heart-breaking anguish in his voice.

'Oh, I'm so sorry, Alessandro.'

He swallowed slightly and continued. 'It was not her fault, not exactly, but she broke a promise and I swore not to get involved with anyone ever again who did the same. And yet I was scared to be alone. I always had girlfriends - women - around me, with me - helping take my mind off the memory. But if they broke a promise, I had to leave.'

'Like I did,' Helen said, and felt the utopian atmosphere begin an inexorable slide away from her. He nodded. The look in his eyes was full of blame. 'But I couldn't be that person.'

'Then you shouldn't have promised me,' he explained, a slight quaver in his voice but still soft, controlled. Controlled, like he wanted her to be all the time. 'You should have been honest and up front about who you are. Then no hearts would have been broken.'

The implication hung heavy in the air. Helen had broken his heart. But what about her heart? Time to ask.

'And what of the woman you invited to the spa when I first turned you down?' Helen asked, before she could stop herself. 'Did she break one too? When she backed out of her promise to accompany you - to be your distraction from your past?'

He looked up at her, a little surprised, and reached for his glass of water from the café table, but continued. 'Exactly one such as her.'

'Joanna,' Helen added. 'She was called Joanna, wasn't she.' It was a statement, not a question.

'Yes, but how did you...'

'I saw your reservation - that night you changed rooms - I found it on the computer after you'd left me. There were two names, not just yours.' She felt her pulse racing, this was it. He narrowed his eyes at her. 'And that's not all, so don't bother denying it. At the airport, my driver was meeting someone else after he dropped me off - I saw him, and the name card he'd been given - I assumed by you. It said "Joanna, *Carissima*." I knew, back then, Alessandro. That made leaving easier. You made it easier - being so eager to be in control of me, of who I am. And knowing you had my replacement lined up ready to take my place.' She was about to say 'one out, one in,' but stopped herself just in time, given the sensitivity of the moment. 'I figured you would be with her, once I'd gone,' she said, more tactfully.

'I was,' he said, 'but not in the same room.'

This was news to Helen, and her face told him so.

'I stayed in her room that night, but it was before she arrived. She had texted to say she was going to suddenly turn up. She'd changed her mind, and expected me to fit in with her plans. I intended to put her right, to say this cannot happen, and I planned to go straight to the village to get out of her way until I was ready to see her. On my terms, not hers. Remember I told you I was going back to the village?' Helen begrudgingly nodded. He seemed totally believable. 'Joanna texted to check I was still at the spa and not off on 'one of my jaunts' I think she called it. She is German, and very blunt.'

'So you weren't sharing with her after all? After me? Not at all? Not doing the classes and sharing the... upgrades?'

'No - no sharing, no upgrades,' he said, looking serious. 'And no more broken promises - from either of you. As it happens, she found out soon afterwards from the staff there that I had been there with another. She accused me of cheating on her and left on the next flight home. I was so angry - because it was she who had ended things with me, just before you emailed me from New York. In fact, I was so angry - with both of you - I had to disappear for a while.'

Helen looked at him for a long time and wasn't sure what to say. Eventually she said the only thing she could say, given the circumstances.

'Alessandro - I'm so sorry. I was wrong - you were, and I was too. Can you forgive me?'

'Forgiveness is divine, that is why I came to see you,' he said, and Helen breathed a little sigh of relief, 'and I am glad that is now cleared up.' Again Helen nodded and felt her shoulders relax. 'But,' he added, 'now that I know what you assumed about me - that I would go from one woman to the next so easily, I don't know that I can forget.''

Oh. But - well, you'd done that going from her to me. How is that different?'

'That is very different. And it was not overnight - like, one out, one in? You seemed to think I was capable of doing that however. It seems, *Tesoro mio,* that we do not know each other as well as we think, you and I.'

Helen felt a trickle of dread begin at the nape of her neck and start filtering through her expectations of a future with this man.

'We are two different people, after all. Not, as I thought, one heart and one soul reunited. I believed we were, *mio caro,* and that if I could only help you to let go of the need to be so in control in every aspect of your life - maybe we could be one. Would you have liked that, Helen?'

She looked into his eyes and found herself hesitating at the question. And she knew deep down what the answer was. 'Yes,' she thought. *Yes I would.* But what she said was 'In another life. I can't be with you, knowing that one day, I might let you down again with another broken promise. Or hurt you if it all became too much, and I had to run. Because that's who I am,' she said, tears in her eyes, 'and that's what I do.'

Alessandro straightened up somewhat. 'I owed you an apology - in person - that's why I came and found you. And I'm glad I did. You're a wonderful woman, Helen Parker-Todd.' He smiled, a new level of understanding in his eyes.

'And will you please accept mine - for promises broken and moments lost?'

'I will,' he said, and tenderly raised her hand to his lips and kissed her fingers.

'So where does that leave us?' Helen asked.

'It leaves us with another day in this paradise, and nothing ahead of us apart from finding as many first experiences as we can, before you fly back tonight, and I continue my sabbatical. Deal?' he said, and smiled and squeezed her other hand which was rested on the white tablecloth on the café table. 'Oh,' he said, realising she was holding something. She opened her palm.

'You still have it,' he exclaimed, taking it from her and examining it closely. 'Thank goodness! I forgot about it in the heat of the moment.' He looked at it closely, and then at Helen, searching her eyes. 'It has been in my family for generations,' he said, hopefully, but still placing it back in her palm.

The little burnished brass shape, the one he'd given her right at the start of this journey, the one with the two little cymbals and the tiny fragment of red enamelling left on the front, had been her lucky charm. Thinking it would always return her to him, if it was meant to be. 'It's - your brooch. It's been nice to look after it - temporarily,' she said and rubbed it with her fingers. 'You want it back now, right? It needs to go with you, on the next part of the journey. To find the one you'll give it to forever?' Helen held it out to him, with the feeling that she was handing over a symbol of fate.

He looked thoughtful. 'You are a unique woman,' he said, 'and one day a unique man will sweep you off your feet - one that appreciates you for who you are, and knows that you are the best that you can be - you are not broken and you don't need fixing.'

If only he knew, thought Helen. And then he took it from her with thanks. Only then did she allow the tears to flow.

Chapter Sixteen

'She's on, mum - she's onnnn!' called Georgia to Sadie as she and a crewman in a white uniform managed to finally get the 40" screen in the cinema room to play ball - Helen's first ever TV appearance was due to begin at any minute.

'Great,' said Sadie, appearing at the door wearing a sarong over her voluptuous curves. 'I'll just go get the others down off the deck.'

'I'll go, I'll go,' Georgia cried, scooting past her mother eagerly. 'I'll tell Abi it's time - time to leave those sailors alone. Ha-ha!'

'It's not Abi you'll have to tell,' Sadie muttered under her breath, and looked up to the deck. Silhouetted against the bright sunshine stood Grace, happily throwing her head back laughing. In her fifties-style cossie, a big sunhat and a matching sarong tied at the waist, and a big cocktail glass, complete with little umbrella, in her hand, she shamelessly flirted with the Captain of the ship. Sadie watched her youngest bound up the steps, tell her Nana something and then rush off in search of big sis.

No-one was going to miss Helen's big moment thanks to clever online availability the on-board IT team had managed to hook up. And somewhere in the Pacific Ocean, the massive boat powered on across the waves towards a date with destiny in Hawaii - if Helen could carry it off.

'And we're live in five, four, three...' the floor manager said, his fingers counting the two and the one in silence.

Helen sat with a fixed grin on her face, dying with nerves inside, about to appear on her very first local TV interview. The chat show host patted her hand as the opening titles and music played, and the audience clapped loud and long, delighted to finally be seeing internet sensation, Helen Parker, in person. She was here to talk about her column Try it For the First Time Club, the introduction explained and the story everyone wanted to know about - what was happening on the man front now?

The host was a blonde in a suit, called Catherine, gracious and quaffed, and she was busy with a recap for the benefit of those who hadn't read Helen's ongoing saga on TransGlobe dot com. It had heated up since she last saw Alessandro weeks ago. Kate's succession of suggestions had made for some hilarious columns as each week Helen wrote about a new First date - it was subtitled 'Try HIM for the First Time Club.' The following was massive, but so had been the attempts by the Martha Crowne team, now launched, with their ever more gross TiFFTs.

The TV host then ended the introduction by inviting anyone who wanted to talk to her - live in the studio - to call in.

'And the most exciting part of the night, ladies and gentlemen, you - yes, you, my Friday Night Chat audience - get to vote on which three daredevil stunts Helen gets to do at the upcoming festival in Hawaii. And there's a twist in the tail - so don't miss it at the end of the interview.'

What? She thought, *what twist? No-one said anything about a twist.*

'But first, why don't you tell us why you're dressed as a cavewoman and the exciting news about who you're related to!'

Helen sat in a Raquel Welch–esque outfit, only '20,000 Years BC,' which Kate's daughter Lucy had helped to provide for the photo shoot for the long-awaited DNA column two weeks ago. Although not technically vintage clothing, Lucy fashioned it out of some tattered old fur coats her mum had found in a relative's attic, and it worked, as did the DNA piece - finally.

'Well as those who have been reading Try it For The First Time club on TransGlobe dot com will know…'

In a crowded office on a 26th floor, a certain Boss and a corpulent middle aged investor jumped from their chairs and shouted 'One!' - they had bet her a bonus for every time she could get the name of the site mentioned live on air.

'Hah - I knew she wouldn't let me down,' said Mr Adams, high fiving Cheryl Goodman then Kate then Kieran. Ki-Ka merely shook her head in disgust, already devastated at being overshadowed by Helen, and she stomped off in the direction of the drinks.

Helen was continuing. '…my intrepid investigations into my maternal DNA led me to the headquarters of GeneticBase UK. Three weeks ago they got in touch with me and as you'll have read in the article, Dr Hannover the guy in charge there, told me some very interesting news,' she said. *But nowhere near as interesting as the news I DIDN'T print,* she thought. *About my father.* That was one piece of news she was saving for when she met up with Sadie and co, after the event in Hawaii.

She went on to describe the testing process, briefly - she'd been warned against too much jargon by the producer before the show - and that they'd finally traced her maternal H marker.

'It revealed that I can be traced to...' she paused, for effect. You could have heard a pin drop. '... a woman living in the Dordogne region of France 20,000 years ago. Hence the outfit. It's very exciting as nearly half of all Europeans are descended from her.'

'Really?' the host asked, fascinated. 'From one woman?'

'Yes - from her haplogroup as it's called.'

'Ahem, geek alert! Nearly half, imagine that,' said the host. 'And as a result, if you look at this diagram,' a big family tree type graphic appeared on full screen which stretched 1000 generations back. 'What are we seeing here Helen - our superstar Brit from abroad?'

'Well, with current testing, you can *guestimate* that about half of Europe is distantly related to everyone else. Like the Royal Family - for instance, the new baby Prince George - there's a 50% likelihood he's my 1000th cousin, 1000 times removed!'

'Gahhh! Now you know I'm allergic to statistics! So anyway - Helen Parker here, could be the future King of England's 1000th cousin!' The audience gasped, and clapped, and the noise covered up Helen trying to add the '1000 times removed bit.' She just smiled and bowed her head a few times. Then funny pictures came up of Helen related to all sorts of other famous people, from celebrities to presidents to a Hobbit. Then they briefly showed a chart giving the other regions of the world Helen's ancestors came from. It showed 68% from Europe West, including Germany, France, Northern Italy and so on. Then 9% from Ireland, 9% from Great Britain and 5% Scandinavia. The rest were minor percentages. Then the final graphic had the punchline - a slither of the chart came up as joke 2% Neanderthal.'

'It's official, lady,' said the host, to the audience, 'your husband really is part cave man!' The audience laughed and there were shots of women nudging their men, including close ups of a couple of hairy thick set guys who laughed in embarrassment and looked daggers at their wives for making them come.

'And talking of husbands, Helen,' the host said, her voice full of telly-sympathy, 'what's the latest about a man? Any news?'

'Afraid you'll have to read the columns for more on that, Catherine.'

'Well at least let's discuss this latest no-hoper - I mean, girls, poor Helen - fancy turning up to her date in a dirty shirt and plaque-ridden teeth!'

The discussions were comical and back in the offices of Anthony Adams, the mood was jolly everywhere, as an IT nerd on a laptop in the corner announced that subscribers for the TiFFT column leapt at every mention of the website address. And somewhere in the Pacific, two nieces, a mum and a sister - and a certain husband to be - were laughing at Helen's descriptions of her latest dates.

'So tell me, Helen,' the host was saying as the segment was coming to a close, 'in an ideal world, who would be your perfect man?' The audience laughter subsided as they waited for her reply. Half of the New York online community had really taken her to heart. But the other half were fascinated by Martha Crowne and her antics. It was neck and neck so far and the leaking of secrets was reaching epic scale on both sides. And still the mole and the insider had yet to be found.

'Anyway Friday Chat audience, it's time for the vote - and the twist...'

Helen sat up in her armchair, wondering what on earth was going on. *What twist? I don't know about a twist?*

'Now Helen here doesn't know about this twist,' Catherine the host said. *Shit.* 'But it might be a crucial part of your vote - will you be kind to poor Helen, knowing her well-publicized fear of heights? Or will you be naughty - and choose the three she'd hate most?! This is the list, and you vote by texting the number on your screen.' A short list of a dozen activities appeared and a text number below it. Each person could vote for one, and the three with the highest would be what she had to do. Helen was feeling very uncomfortable indeed, and a very, very strong niggling feeling was beginning to grumble away in the pit of her stomach. She didn't like this, she didn't like this at all.

'But before you vote, let me tell you a story. A little birdie tells me that our Helen, the columnist we know and love, has a very specific kind of phobia. You see, she has been plagued all her life by something recently dubbed *High Place Phenomenon*...' Helen gripped the arms of her chair and felt herself go cold. No-one knew this - no-one. Unless the mole had been into her private documents. Helen had been trying to compose a letter to Alessandro, to tell him all about it, and why she couldn't have kids, and she was indeed broken, and... *who had seen it?* Surely only someone with access to her emails? The host went on, as did Helen's palpitations. 'Now sufferers of this High Place Phenomenon report that they not only hate heights, they have something extra to contend with. You see, they don't fear they will FALL, they fear they will JUMP! And yes, it's really a thing - google it if you like!'

I

Will

Personally

Kill

That Mole…

'So Helen, how did it happen?'

Helen was like a rabbit in headlights, and mumbled her way through an explanation about the trip up the Eiffel Tower with her step-dad, mum and Sadie - he'd been bossing her about so she rebelled and threatened to jump, and he'd said 'go on then, do it.' Then when she'd got close to the edge, she was overtaken by a strong urge to actually do it - she'd nearly jumped - his reaction had made her want to do it more, and after that it got worse and worse through the years until she couldn't trust herself to walk near ledges unless she was fully enclosed, finding any kind of air travel an excruciating nightmare.

'And now Helen's climax to this year's season of TiFFTs will take place at the Daredevil festival in Hawaii! Ladies and Gentlemen - place your vote - what will it be…?' the host said. A sound effect a whirring, some clicking noises, and then a countdown sting filled the air. 'We'll be back with the results after this - and then, our roving reporter will be out and about finding out your reactions to seeing a real life colonic irrigation on your TV. '

A week later, the whole of New York knew exactly what the result would be. The audience had been split - some wanting to spare her the challenges with heights, and others choosing them deliberately, specifically because of her problem.

'Of course, it might have been a double bluff,' said Kate, 'some may have also chosen this first one because they knew you like to jump over the edge of things - maybe they thought it was easier?'

'Ten minutes till first jumpers are called,' came a voice from the door of the backstage area where both girls were sat - a makeshift tented affair in humid Hawaii. The Daredevil Festival was in full swing, and Helen was here for her grand finale. And still Martha Crowne was hot on her heels with her carnival of gross. It was still anybody's bet. Helen was in pieces, and Kate had come along for moral support. It didn't help that Helen was being dragged off to be interviewed every five minutes. It seemed everyone wanted a piece of her at the moment - except one person - the one she missed most.

Helen couldn't wait to get outside, although she didn't know how she'd feel when the moment came to jump, attempting the first of the three TiFFTs chosen by the TV show. Thankfully, since Sadie and the two girls and mother Grace couldn't all fit backstage, they were watching elsewhere. Helen was nervous enough as it was, facing her triple whammy of firsts, all way out of her comfort zone, and still filled her with dread - her hands were clammy and she kept feeling the dull, gnawing grumblings of panic rising up in her diaphragm. Kate prattled on about nothing, keeping Helen's mind off the events to come, then went off to get them some more water. That's when Helen's mind went into overdrive.

The first of the TiFFTs was jumping off a trampoline - but not just any trampoline, one strategically placed right next to a cliff next to the ocean. This was a sport, a ridiculous, pointless, adrenalin-junkie's sport, and for the very first time, Helen would have to be one of them. She shook her head, wondering if she'd ever have done it if the TV audience hadn't forced her hand. Probably not - but as soon as the news was out, her hits had sky-rocketed, so maybe she should kiss the mole instead of wanting to throttle whoever it was.

She couldn't practise, of course, given the nature of a TiFFT - but Helen being Helen, she didn't let it lie that easily. With a few calls, she'd got as near as dammit to a hurriedly arranged mock-up in a desert, courtesy of NExUS - although it was Rob, not Jason, who had helped her. Jason had been nowhere to be seen.

Jason.

She did as she always did, now, when fleeting thoughts of her ex-husband popped into her mind - she found herself thinking back to the waterfall, and dappled sunlight and a big broad chest and a kiss. Then the big brown eyes and long lashes came to the fore, and suddenly it was Tibet and a certain tantric massage which occupied her mind. Helen shook herself and snapped out of it.

She closed her eyes and used the tantric breathing method which was always so helpful nowadays, as she mentally prepared to do the first of the events, walking through in her mind everything Rob Rains had told her about what to expect. But this time, it would be the real thing, with a long drop and a big splash at the end of it, and all of it witnessed by cameras and journalists from all over the world, many from New York.

Look on the bright side...

Well, at least she'd got out of wing-walking - this season anyway. That truly would have been the last thing she ever did.

Kate came back, having helped herself to a massive apple from the hospitality bar, walking across the lemon-scented, clean, air-conditioned behind-the-scenes waiting area and offered a bite to Helen, who was so nervous she didn't even reply, just shook her head.

'Penny, for 'em, *guv'nor?*' Kate said, and Helen rolled her eyes at the still-rubbish attempt at an English accent.

'I don't know if this first one will be easier?' she said to Kate. 'I might bounce wrong and hit the cliffs - anything. They're all sadists. It still freaks me out - that so many people voted to see me jump!'

'Excuse me, Ms Parker, there's yet another reporter would like to be added to your interview list,' asked a red-faced young girl in shorts and a black t-shirt with a skull on it, appearing round the door with a clipboard. 'Is it OK to squeeze him in?'

'Yes, whatever,' Helen said curtly. She was getting nervous and that meant getting ratty.

'Hey, *Mrs Snappyson*, don't take it out on the volunteers! Would you prefer *no-one* wanted to interview you?'

'Yes if it meant they'd stop talking about HPP.'

Helen and her *High Place Phenomenon* had become quite big news in her adopted home town of New York and the reporters were out in force. Her followers were now so addicted to her shenanigans - especially since she began sharing far more personal insights about her life - that she'd earned a nightly slot on their home page, with an update of her progress.

'So can I tell you my gossip now?' Kate asked. In an effort to take her pal's mind off things, Kate told Helen of the latest news from the water cooler - passed on by Cheryl, of all people, earlier that afternoon.

'Yes, that's what I said, Ki-Ka called in '*sick,*' blaming morning sickness from her bump - a suspiciously inconspicuous bump, given how many months pregnant she's supposed to be,' Kate said, her eyes gleaming. Helen just listened. 'But she's more likely to be laying low, given that - get this - she's been discovered getting her fancy men to hack into company emails. Including - guess who?'

Helen's focus sharpened. 'Who?' She remembered some suspicious looking emails a while back.

'Only Nathan the accounts guy!' Kate now relished having Helen's full attention, and filled her in with the rest. Nathan had been instantly sacked, despite his protestations that she'd put him up to it. Another young guy was being investigated too.

Nathan had gone straight back to cry on Brad the barman's shoulder, who'd been delighted, and taken him back on in an instant, then immediately sacked him again when he revealed he'd hacked into *Helen's* emails in order to help Ki-Ka. Nathan had also circulated several private company documents to his room-mate Wayne, according to Wayne, who was in full-on confession mode to escape being similarly given the chop. So that explained the emails trending at the nearby college campus, but still no clue as to the mole.

And there was more, Kate explained, shoving a half-bitten apple at Helen, insisting she take at least a little bite. Because Ki-Ka's slot had been filled with extra coverage about Helen, it was making Martha Crowne livid. Therefore she'd resorted to even more extreme posts of her own in an attempt to steal readers, viewers and website hits from Helen. But this wasn't going down too well with certain people high-up in her company.

The Insider had told the Boss that the investors at Martha's ParlourGames Channel were getting more and more fidgety, due to the graphic nature of her reports.

'They might even be considering clipping her wings, restricting her to online-only,' said Kate, reaching the end of her gossip-update. 'She's very close to crossing the line of what's acceptable - what with her ever more gross topics - but her figures are still huge. So the jury is still out on who's most popular out of both of you. But if it's you - and it might be - think of that bonus, HellsBells!'

Helen nodded thoughtfully.

'But...'

'But what?' Helen said, 'What's *but*? I wondered what took you so long - what did that researcher with the clipboard say?'

'*Well!*' Kate was positively glowing. 'There's a rumour going round that Martha Crowne is planning something massive here - to compete with your challenges - the New York people are betting that she'll somehow or other trump your appearance here - like, turn up at the Daredevil festival - or someone from her camp will.'

'Competing?'

'Or spying! Or...'

'Or what, you've got a weird look on your face,' Helen said to Kate.

'Or spoiling your chances if they get close enough.'

'She wouldn't!' Helen said.

'Who knows - maybe she's run out of shock-tactics, so she's looking for another way to retain audience share - or lose out to you, when the grand tally is taken next week.'

'The question is how much more unsavoury can she get with these topics?' said Helen.

'The answer is, I'll try and find out, and if I do, I'll let you know - and meanwhile, just watch your back.'

'Helen Parker?' came the announcement, and Kate squeezed her hand. 'You'll be outstanding!' she said, and Helen was gone.

Could she steel her nerves, execute her first Extreme TiFFT and be back here again in about fifteen minutes? That's the scene she visualized, over and over as she queued up, waited for the announcement and saw the short run-up in front of her open up, feeling a thousand onlookers' eyes and dozens of camera lenses on her. Then in the blink of an eye, she was back - soaking wet and in need of a shower.

'One down, two to go,' she said to Kate, who took her quivering friend's hand and led her towards the changing rooms.

All over the internet, the reports immediately began to go viral - Helen TiFFT Parker - the girl with the fear of jumping - running as though her life depended upon it, screaming 'Geronimo' towards the edge of a cliff in Hawaii. She ran past hundreds of cheering people, and using a giant trampoline to get even higher, leapt straight off the cliff and plunged into the roiling waves far below. When interviewed on TV straight afterwards draped in a towel, she said she'd like to thank NExUS for their help in preparing her for a High Place Phenomenon of a different kind.

Her relief was short-lived - the fire-walk was next.

The second event chosen by the TV show was just plain terrifying - fifteen feet of red hot TiFFT and no mistake. Rob Rains had attempted to galvanize Helen, telling her that a fire-walk was awesome - as a metaphor for life - *'I did that so I can do anything.'* But no-one in NExUS had done one - or had any experience of one whatsoever.

But happily for Helen, no-one was allowed to do it without full preparation - an intense couple of hours of almost trance-like self-hypnosis, and visualisations so powerful, they carried the physical body into a new realm, where human skin could actually walk on hot coals and not get burned. Most of the time. Would Helen be one of the ones who failed? She needed a different kind of support now, and when she saw who was leading the fire-walk team, suddenly her heart leapt.

The coals weren't just fiery, they were throbbing. Or perhaps Helen was. The fire-walk was getting closer - just a few rows of chanting people in front of her. It gave her palpitations. Smoking, glowing, smouldering - and very, very daunting. Oh and rather hot.

So much for this Try it For the First Time lark.

She could feel the vibration throughout her body - the rhythmic drum, beating in time with the chanting crowd - urging them on, nearer and nearer, to the point of no return. Every now and then the embers flared, accompanied by a scream, and the tell-tale *'tssssst!'* sound.

How the hell did I get myself into this? Thought Helen, as she broke out in a sweat. She could feel the heat, smell the smouldering coals and the perspiring bodies either side of her. Pretty soon they would block her escape. It was now or never.

Focus, she said to herself, *cool moss, cool moss, cool moss...*

Only twenty four hours before, she'd been throwing herself off a cliff and tomorrow would be the biggest challenge of all.

If her sister Sadie could see her, she'd be proud. If her mother Grace could see her, she'd freak. She'd roll her eyes, and tut, as usual. Not that it mattered - Helen and her mum were currently just healing after a rift - giving each other space was part of their thing. And spurring each other on was part of her and Sadie's thing. *Thank god for sisters*, thought Helen.

And thank god for... the guy on the stage... What was he to her, now, anyway, after everything that had happened in the last six months? And now he was standing there, banging a drum.

Cool moss, cool moss! Chanted the crowd at the front.

Shit, shit, she told herself frantically, realising that she was now just two rows away. She tried to hold back but an over-excited woman behind her pushed forwards a little too hard, and Helen ricocheted into the tall guy in front. She flung her hands into the middle of his back. He turned, eyes blazing, and Helen gasped. He was young, and very handsome... and she knew that face from somewhere.

'Sorry!' Helen shouted, above the pounding drums, jabbing a thumb over her shoulder. 'Eager crowd!'

'I can't hear you,' said the entrancing face, 'but next time, give it a little rub whilst you're there!'

'I'm sorry?' she cried.

He smiled and pointed over his shoulder at his back. 'Joking,' he added, 'I meant give my shoulders a rub - they ache from karate chopping all those planks earlier on! What else are you doing, whilst you're here?' he said.

If it hadn't been a complete impossibility to back out now, Helen would have made herself scarce as fast as she could. 'Cos that's what she always did - well, nearly always - when a gorgeous stranger made a pass at her. She didn't trust handsome men - not any more. Not after all the recent experiences on her friend's dating experiment. Heck, Helen had even talked about them on TV, so it wasn't a matter of being brave. But still he smiled, and still she was wary.

'Run, run a mile, don't get involved,' the little voice inside her head usually said. But maybe he wasn't making a pass - after all, this request for a back rub was not out of place in this new community of happy-clappy people - with their frequent massages, hugs and instant familiarity amongst strangers. So Helen just smiled and played along - she'd come too far to back out now - so she reached up and rubbed his shoulders a little.

They were rock solid. And not in a good way.

'Jesus, they're hard as granite,' she shouted, leaning into his ear from behind as she pushed into knots the size of golf balls. She felt him laugh. Smelt his fresh male body scent. She rubbed harder and felt him relax into it - rolling his shoulders against her touch, almost in time to the all-engulfing pounding of the drums. And then she remembered where she knew him from. *Oh god.* She stepped away and looked round her, frantically.

And then it was his turn at the front.

And then she caught the scowl on the face of the man banging the drum.

And then she realised with a jolt that the outstretched arms of the Fire Crew and the maniacally grinning faces lining the fire-walk were all beckoning *her, come on Helen* - she was next. And he'd distracted her and her trance was broken, and every bone in her body began rebelling, screaming *'run'*...

Her knees went weak and the air went thin. This was going to be interesting.

'And was it?' asked the reporter, later, 'interesting I mean? Or was it scary, devastatingly frightening, absolutely terrifying - you know, all the words we usually roll out at these events?'

Helen was utterly exhausted - the fire walk having taken out of her every spare ounce of energy - it had left her with a euphoric feeling, which quickly passed when she felt the tiny blister on one of her heels, and realised she'd actually walked down a fifteen foot fire-walk on 550 degree Celsius hot coals and lived to tell the tale. Plus, she'd survived being nearly sabotaged by a very charming man just before the big moment, until a big brown pair of eyes, gazing down at her from a podium, had focussed her again, enough to get through it, and to do one of the most amazing things she'd ever done in her whole life.

Talking about it now brought some of the euphoria back, and she shrugged at questions about how she thought it was possible, brushing aside uppity comments about *thermal effusivity* and the *Leidenfrost Effect* and when the final reporter asked her the final question - about how it made her feel, she couldn't help it.

'Fucking brilliant,' she beamed. Needless to say, there was another viral video on Youtube shortly afterwards.

She was then led away from the cameras and news crews, to the one-on-one interview booth area, and was met by Kate, who patted her on the back for making 'that snotty journalist speechless at long last.'

'Helen - your final interview is in booth 3,' said the researcher with the clipboard and skull t-shirt, 'come this way.' And she was off. Helen and Kate trotted to keep up. Everything seemed totally surreal, even down to the unusual blue of the Hawaiian sky, and Helen had that 'forest-feeling' once more - as though she was in a waking dream.

It was made even *more* weird by the excited conversation Kate was trying to have with her. 'I *found out!*' she was hissing, as they walked faster than normal to keep up with the researcher.

'What?'

'I found out - Martha Crowne's trump card.'

'Don't tell me her next report will be even more voyeuristic than the last one?' Helen said, getting out of breath, with all the nervous energy and walking. 'It's not possible, surely?' But Kate nodded. Helen needed all her focus to just walk. 'Tell me when we stop,' she begged, and Kate nodded an 'ok.'

As they power-walked along, Helen remembered the Boss's reaction to the most recent Martha Crowne sensation. Helen had enjoyed telling Kate about that one.

'The Boss couldn't believe his eyes!' Helen had said, recapping it later, for Kate's benefit, using all his gestures as well as an attempt at Anthony Adams' strong New York accent.

'*Parkerrrr*!' Mr Adams had shouted. The yell had come right across the crowded 26th floor of TransGlobe Inc, - so loud it would have reached the 30th. The Boss had been watching a local news report in his office, and Helen and her TiFFT column were due to be the lead story. But that yell meant he was not happy, not happy at all.

'What, Boss?' Helen had said, clip-clopping in her high heels into his office carrying her tablet ready for action.

'Look at this... this... travesty!' he had said, and there on the big TV screen was a close up of a length of tube with a viewing panel in it, with suspicious looking dark shapes floating by in some sort of liquid.

'Oh God, is that what I think it is?' Helen had asked.

'Yes! Martha Crowne's turds! How can they shunt our section down in favour of this? Darren at K97 News told me - *promised me* that they were definitely going to lead with your latest TiFFT - and instead, there are turds from someone's guts floating across my screen! Whatever next?!' he had declared.

And now, Kate had found out *exactly* what was next.

They drew to a halt outside Booth 3 and the researcher asked them to wait whilst she went off to get the reporter who was to interview Helen.

'Go on then, tell me now,' she said to Kate, both getting their breath back. At least the backstage area was air conditioned and cooler than the 30 degree temperature outside.

'OK - well - the students are going crazy for it - they can't wait to see the pictures she's promised. Martha Crowne is trending like wildfire,' said Kate in between breaths.

Helen shook her head slowly, totally bemused. 'Go on...'

'I think the fascination is that it's being done on a woman of her age,' added Kate. 'And the fact that she's promised a warts-and-all video of the procedure.'

'The what?!' exclaimed Helen, glaring at Kate. And Kate looked around them, just as a group of good looking athletic types walked by. She lowered her voice and whispered into Helen's ear. Helen's eyes shot open.

'Oh... my... god,' Helen said.

'Actually, I'd quite like to see it myself,' Kate added, 'you know, like, to find out which bits they cut off, *down there* - you know?'

'Traitor,' said Helen. 'Actually, so would I. Damn the woman!'

'The words *final cut* will never be the same again...' Kate left Helen with that thought as the researcher came back. Clipboard/skull girl ushered Helen into the booth, saying the interviewer would be along any moment and that she was only to give him five minutes as the booth was needed straight afterwards. 'He's from some weekly glossy called "Fate and Destiny,"' she said, 'oh and he's totally a hunk.'

He was also totally late, Helen thought, after waiting there for a couple of minutes. Her mind began reminiscing, reliving and revelling in her triumph of flesh over fire. She examined the 'fire kisses' as the Fire Crew called the little blisters on her foot, amazed they hadn't burned more. In fact, her feet felt fine. It was her heart that was in trouble - it began doing somersaults as soon as she saw who the next reporter was.

'Hello Jason.'

'Helen.'

'Since when did you get involved with glossy women's magazines?' she said, forcing herself to sit down and be cool, as a man-mountain eased himself through the curtain into the little one-on-one area. He smelled fantastic, and her body began its usual reactions whenever he was near.

'I haven't got long,' he said, ignoring the question and sitting himself down slowly onto the canvas director's chair opposite Helen. His legs were almost touching hers. He picked up the glass of water which had been put out for him on a glass side table and drained it, as she watched him, speechless. He paused, then spoke. 'Obviously Rob told me you were here. Thought this persona would work - it's part of another NExUS - but I can't say more or I'd have...'

'...to kill you,' Helen joined in the last bit and he smiled. She grinned.

'Plus this is the quickest way to get you on your own without going through hoops - or giving off the wrong impression as to why I'm here.' He hesitated, narrowing his eyes - as if to ascertain whether she understood his meaning. Helen wasn't sure she did, and raised an eyebrow. 'Mind you,' he added, adjusting his seat, 'I don't appreciate having to hug twenty people every time I queue up to use the bathroom.'

Helen laughed. 'Happy clappy people, what can I say.' He smiled back at her and she feasted her eyes upon the sight in front of her - so different from last time. He had the same old crinkle in the corners of his eyes and he was wearing smart jeans and a purple polo neck top which showed off his big biceps and well-defined pecs. In fact, this whole vision of *normal* was doing weird things to the pit of her stomach. It was strange seeing him now, outside of her head - of her memories - of the dream-like forest context. When they were last together, events were so surreal, so like putting on old shoes, that she'd accepted the situation instantly. If the dust had settled, the encounter would have opened up old scars and buried memories from a distant time in her life. But if the context had made it ok to be around him for one reason - it wouldn't be permanent.

But this time, right now, it was different - he looked normal - almost. As normal as a six foot three inch hulk could look, whilst shifting in a seat which barely held him.

'I've been thinking,' he went on, 'and here's the thing. What was said, last time we met. I wasn't happy about it. I couldn't get it off my mind afterwards. There are some things you needed to know - about me. That I should have told you, but I was angry...'

And then came the bombshell.

'I divorced the boys' mother.'

Helen just stared. 'Recently?' she said, agog.

'Six months ago.'

'So you were single in the forest, too?'

'We both were,' he nodded.

She opened her mouth to say something but changed her mind. There was indeed no ring on his finger, and whatever mark had been there had faded since they were last together *under the waterfall...* 'But why didn't you just tell me?' she asked, reaching across and touching his knee.

'You'd already made up your mind,' he replied. And the look on his face said everything she needed to know. '...*hadn't* you.'

She removed her hand, and an old feeling from many years ago began to resurface. If Helen *had* listened, waited, given him a chance - before jumping to conclusions - would it have made any difference to her reaction in that moment? Deep in a forest, under a waterfall? Twenty years ago? ...Ever?

'Helen - I liked seeing you again. I have something to ask you - and I want you to take some time to think about it,' he said, looking deeply into her eyes. She swallowed.

And when she heard what it was, she knew what her reply would be immediately - she didn't need any time to think about it at all...

But before she could tell him it, he was gone.

She shook herself back to the present, and followed. Outside, she looked around for him but all she could see were the two people lined up waiting to use the private interview booth. One was a tall, good-looking man with his back to Helen. She recognised that back. It conjured up the aroma of burning coals and pounding drums. As she walked by him, Helen could almost see his name on the pass he was wearing. Then she realised it wasn't his name she could see on the pass.

Walking back outside, the bright light suddenly hit her and so did a realisation. She could see the words she'd be writing in her blog about this moment...

There are many reasons why we change our minds about people - even a tiny titbit of information may be capable of producing the most devastating turn-around. And this was one of those moments...

But what should she do about it? And would the universe play ball and allow it to happen? So much was changing - in everyone's lives - perhaps it was time to take a leap of faith.

Literally.

The final challenge in Helen's Try it For the First Time finale was the one she'd been fearing the most - the parachute drop.

At least it was a tandem one - thank god, or she most definitely would have died. Helen being Helen, her High Place Phenomenon would probably have meant not opening her own chute on the way down either. So thank god there was going to be some professional 'chute-puller' strapped to her back like a papoose. Or maybe *she* would be the papoose. Who cared, as long as someone else was there to be the grown-up. A Real Grown-Up, like on Kate's internet channel. *Would Helen ever be one?* If there was ever a time to bow to authority, this was it. Apart from one little trick up her sleeve...

Kate gave her a pep talk, Rob Rains' text was galvanising, and Helen was all set. She walked into the arena with the rest of the small group due to go up next, and listened to the safety video. They would be climbing in the little ten-seater plane for 20 to 30 minutes, in a spiral up to about 10,000 feet. The plane would be noisy - hand gestures only, so they learned a few. Procedures for the release of the chutes, including the reserve chute, emergency processes, and finally the outfit they could wear - unlike most other places in the world, said the instructor, you could choose a traditional jump suit, or if you preferred you could sky dive in just a t-shirt and shorts - well, this *was* Hawaii. Just make sure you choose proper footwear, he said. But Helen had other ideas - if she was going to make this her last TiFFT, it was going to be a good one. And she had to beat Martha Crowne.

Kauai Island looked smaller and smaller as they rose, and Helen tried to stay mostly in the middle of the plane and just not look down. Well at least that was an improvement on screaming the house down like she usually did.

She thought of the person to be tied to her back - he already had on his goggles and head gear - the full McCoy. He looked a sneaky bit like Rob Rains but that wouldn't be possible - not here on Hawaii. There was very little talking by this stage, and soon the time came to buckle up, and the guy who was about to strap himself to her back shuffled over, nearer and nearer - until they were kind of like spooning in bed. Then the next time she looked up, Helen was sitting in her shorts on the edge of the open plane door, staring into oblivion. Empty nothingness stretched out before her. The ground was a very, very, VERY long way off. In fact, this was the highest open high place she had ever been in in her life. If ever there was a time for Helen to just let go and jump, this would be it.

But, strangely, because she knew she could, she suddenly didn't want to.

And then she really didn't want to.

And then she really, *really* didn't want to, and began struggling to get away from the edge, which was a bit like trying to escape being tied to a giant armchair in a straitjacket and with your legs dangling over the edge of nothingness. Helen could feel the panic rising up in her chest and a scream building in her throat, and her intended TiFFT of taking something sneaky with her for the landing was beginning to get away from her. The item was hidden - stupidly, she thought now, and the thought it might fall out just made her even worse. She gestured around but no-one could hear her attempting to explain - but no-one could understand her frantic gesticulations meaning 'I have shoes up my top' at 10,000 feet...

Then it was their turn and they were freefalling - it felt like forever but was probably only about 30 seconds, going at 120 mph, before serenity kicked in, and a 5–7 minute parachute ride began, twirling round, slowly, going down, down... and now Helen really got the picture as to why people get addicted and keep coming back for more. It felt like she was falling and then it felt like she was in the windiest wind tunnel, staying afloat like a bird, the ground getting bigger and bigger. Helen wanted the wisps of cloud to feel like marshmallow but instead it felt like tiny pin pricks of ice, gone as soon as they'd appeared. Then down draughts caught her chute, and blew them towards the beach instead of the soft landing area.

Whilst her instructor was pulling one way then the other, Helen had surreptitiously whipped out her pink high heeled shoes and was holding them down near her thigh. He was completely oblivious as he turned and pulled and yanked on the cords, guiding the parachute nearer to the landing zone. Helen tried to look back and up, and checked the instructor couldn't see the shoes, but hundreds of spectators could - and so could her TiFFT photographer too!

With the ground coming up at them fast, she tried - and failed - to put her highest heels on - much to the instructor's disbelief when she felt him stiffen and nudge her. She could reach her shoes, or she could reach her feet but she couldn't reach both at once. So the photographer's shot on a long lens from the ground became a picture of her in the chute, dangling a pair of shoes to her side. She tried to ignore the seething venom emanating from the man tied to her back.

And now for the landing which would hopefully get her some serious coverage. As they were only a few hundred feet from the ground, she managed to get one shoe on one foot, and was struggling with the other one when the instructor knocked it out of her hand and it spiralled to the floor a hundred feet below.

But she didn't have time to object, he was shouting in her ears to get ready to land, which happened seconds later, but sadly not quite in the way Helen had planned.

As she and her instructor glided down onto the beach, planning a gentle 'step off the kerb' type landing, the instructor shouted at her some more, but Helen barely heard him, too bothered about losing her grip on one of the shoes.

So the landing they actually got was a hefty, awkward slap onto the ground, followed by Helen catching her foot on something and falling face down on the sand, taking the guy strapped to her flat on his face too - laying on her back.

It took them a full minute to disentangle, all caught on countless cameras and smartphones. Needless to say, it didn't take long before there were a dozen different YouTube clips of her 'hilarious beach landing FAIL'

But it was over.

She'd survived.

A sudden calm overcame her as she realised what she'd just managed to do - despite the comedy ending. She didn't intend on going back up high again anytime soon, but Helen had a strangely comforting feeling that if she did, she'd be able to sit tight instead of rushing for the edge and launching herself over.

Now if she could just use that metaphor for her awful love life, then everything would be perfect.

And there was one man in particular whom she had an appointment to see.

Chapter Seventeen

The Nomad was out at sea - but not too far out. There in the distance was a launch, coming at speed towards the yacht. The huge vessel was about to welcome on new arrivals, and from the sound of the girls' shouting, Sadie knew exactly who it was. And she couldn't wait to see her - it had been too long.

But the big question was - would she have asked anyone else to join them for dinner later tonight? The text earlier had implied there might be a companion. Had she sorted things out with Alessandro, Sadie wondered.

As the launch got nearer and Helen saw Sadie waving from the deck - the high, high up deck - Helen felt a little nervous. It wasn't every day you got to meet your future brother-in-law for the first time, on a 124 foot long Superyacht. One that Sadie now had as a holiday home. Her little sis had always fantasised about staying for a week or so on such a vessel as this - and now she would have a husband who owned one and presumably she could stay as often as she liked. How times had changed. Six months, all in six months.

Having chatted at depth and realised the amazing love story her sister had experienced, Helen was pleased for her now. Maybe it was partly because of what she'd been told in the last 24 hours. In fact, Helen fleetingly imagined what it could be like - if, just say... you know, like, supposing for one second... that - by some miracle – it all worked out, then... maybe, *just maybe*, her own *'man-ban'* could also be about to end.

Then the sisters would both have the most amazing partners with whom to share their hot chocolate and stroodles. Helen looked down into her hand at the little object she'd been given and felt happier than she'd ever done. The demons were well and truly at rest and at last, high places were no more 'phenomenal.'

Now there just remained one more thing to tell Sadie - and it promised to be the biggest surprise of them all.

'Hi, I'm Mac,' said a handsome Daniel Craig-esque rugged looking man with the most worldly-wise air about him. That's what you call being comfortable in your own skin, Helen thought and liked him immediately. He welcomed his new sister-in-law-to-be onto his huge Ferretti Custom Line 124 and showed her around proudly, allowing Abi and Georgia to take Helen to the quarters she would sleep in. Once they'd finished jumping all over her with glee, she unpacked. To Helen, seeing them all here was a bit too surreal to take in at first, and the most incredible part of it was all still to come.

It would be a full house tonight, and Captain Wiltshire explained to Helen in a quiet moment, that he was very proud of Mac - at seeing the transformation in his old buddy. His long-time pal, playboy billionaire and a former loner had shunned permanent relationships for many years, and now Mac looked happier than the Captain had ever seen him. No-one deserved it more than Mac, he explained, telling Helen - when she probed - that Mac had been a Barnardo's boy and hadn't had any close family for many years. Well, now he appeared to be taking to it naturally - good job, the Captain said, considering Sadie's latest news. *More news?* thought Helen, *I wonder if her news is as surprising as mine...*

Then Helen tracked down her nieces, who were getting ready for dinner in their cabin. The kids were over the moon about this new arrangement, as this investor guy called Mac was 'loaded' according to Georgia. Helen told her not to use that term when she visited America unless it was describing someone like Nana's friend Greta down the bowls club.

Abi, on the other hand, had told Helen that 'mum's new man seems really cool,' which was no mean feat given how cynical Abi was by nature. He'd promised her that her place on the school trip to China was no longer in doubt, and, she told her Auntie Helen proudly, he'd accepted her offer to work some of the debt off, helping out. She just seemed to be growing up so fast - walking around the boat chatting to the crew. Helen narrowed her eyes as she watched Abi. *If I'm not mistaken, she's flirting...* Helen made a mental note to go interrogate Mac later - *I mean, 'have a chat with him'* she thought.

As for Nana, well Grace finally deigned to come say hello and join Helen in the girls' room. She had some news of her own. Not only had she tracked down Gordon McDingleberry, who was now 85 and living with his sister in Penge, but she'd also gone along, with her pal Alice Springs and Sadie, to pay him a personal visit, *for old times' sake.* Whilst they were there, they had got him to painstakingly put a sample of spittle into the little tube. Sadie said it had taken him a good ten minutes to do it, 'about three times as long as it had taken me when I went to drop it off at the lab and decided to have mine done too,' added Sadie.

That explains a lot, thought Helen. But it wasn't quite time to spill the beans. Not just yet.

Out on deck, in the Hawaiian heat, it was *cocktails-o'clock* - again, and the girls demanded to know every minute detail about

Helen's recent experiences, during which Georgia kept up a running commentary of how many hundreds of thousands of hits the Youtube clips were still getting, versus 'Martha Crowne's Operation on her Lady's Bits' which was also charting highly.

'So who are you bringing this evening?' asked Sadie, seeing another launch approaching across the water towards the yacht sometime later.

'You'll love him,' Helen replied, 'It's my old friend from college - Damian Grant.'

'Damian as in the brother of your old Boss? The boss who...?'

'Yes,' interrupted Helen, 'he's been looking after me for a long while and he's always wanted to have a look round one of these. Would Mac be able to take him round the yacht so I can have a chat to you and mum - there's something I want to tell you.'

'Funny you should say that,' said Sadie...

'Oh my GOD, Sadie, that's amazing news,' exclaimed Helen when they were all freshly washed and changed and standing on the deck of the luxurious, barely rocking vessel as it skimmed over calm Hawaiian waters. The news was not unexpected... Sadie was not only getting married, but there would be another little niece or nephew for Helen to spoil in a few months' time. 'No wonder you look glowing!' she said to Sadie, who patted her tummy proudly.

'The girls are thrilled - now,' Sadie said, smiling, 'especially once they'd heard the story about Mac's younger brother - but I'll tell you about it later 'cos I recognise that look on your face. You look about fit to burst.'

'Well I am a bit,' Helen said. Ah, her sister knew her well. 'Anyway, let's hope the latest addition's going to be a boy - then at least we can get his DNA tested!' Helen joked.

'Well is that what you had to tell me? Did they help you track down relatives? Did they tell you who your father is after all these years of not knowing him?'

'Yes and yes - well kind of,' explained Helen. Sadie was all ears, and Grace walked over to join them as they sat down together in the shade. The sun was setting on the horizon now, the air was getting cooler and the movement of the yacht was reassuring, gently rolling as a breeze began to pick up, comforting. Helen took a deep breath.

'You see, when you dropped off your test and asked Dr Hannover to do the same for yours as for mine, it meant he also got a profile of your DNA on their computer and asked it to throw out any matches. So that when Gordon McDingleberry's DNA was added at the same time, it spewed out a list of results. And there was a match.'

'What do you mean? How can there be a match between me and him?'

'Not between you and him. And not between me and him either,' Helen explained. 'He's 99.9% certain not to be my dad - or yours.'

'But we know who mine is - it's George. Isn't it mum?'

'Well, yes. Well, I assume so. I would have to say I'm 97.85% confident about it,' Grace replied, and the other two made a face at each other. 'OK, I made that number up,' she said, ending their confusion. But he's definitely her dad, isn't he? You can see the likeness in the distinguished brow and the green eyes.' A flicker of nostalgia passed over Grace's expression.

'Well, I can say with certainty that there's absolutely no doubt...' Helen said, slowly and clearly '...that George is indeed Sadie's father. Yes, Sadie is without doubt his daughter.'

Both her sister and her mum breathed out. She saw the tension leave their faces. 'But,' she added. Then Helen took a deep breath, and the others held theirs. Then she dropped the bombshell.

'So am I.'

Sadie nearly fell over. Grace just looked a bit put out. 'Really darling?' said Grace. 'I didn't remember having a romp with George back then, not when you were being made. He only ever came to the commune with the weekly supplies of weed once in a blue moon.'

'Blue moon, full moon, whatever made his swimmers stronger than the other guys you had sex with the month I was conceived, it worked. And you may not remember George - you said you didn't remember much of that period, the one in the photo right? Well look down here.' Helen produced her tablet from her bag, and tapped until a photo came up - it was a copy of the one from Shyanne class of 1972. She tapped and enlarged it, and there on the photo, right at the end, was a weasely looking bare-chested man called...

'Weasel!' exclaimed Grace.

'Which one? That bare chested guy on the end in front of a load of leaves? That one?' asked Sadie.

'Well now you say that, this brings back some memories and a half!' Grace said. 'They weren't just any old leaves. Poor George.'

'That's dad? When he was younger? A... drug dealer?' said Sadie, looking a bit white.

'No wonder you didn't want to marry him straight away,' Helen quipped. 'I guess he looked a lot better after five years away travelling.'

'Well, not exactly...' said their mother. 'I didn't think I'd ever tell you but... he wasn't so much away travelling as - away in prison. That's why I didn't marry him - and no-one knew where he was, including me. He held you once, Sadie, then I only ever had one note from him after that until lo and behold, he turned up years later, he'd gone straight, sorted himself out, and wanted to marry me. I always assumed he'd vanished because his mother didn't like me - she was very strict. But... both of you?...'

'Wow,' said Helen, putting her arm round Sadie and hugging her, 'sisters, eh? Bloody hell.'

Grace watched them thoughtfully from a distance. Were her eyes a little teary? Or maybe it was Helen's eyes.

'All those years wondering about your father, Hells - and he was right here under your nose,' Sadie said. 'All the things he could have done in your life in those ten years. If you'd known.'

Grace was getting a little sentimental at that point, so she mumbled something and disappeared.

'Oh I don't know,' Helen said, sniffing a tiny bit, 'I think the *George Effect* did quite enough as it was. Bless him.'

And they both had a little cry together remembering the troublesome man who'd never known how to deal with the elder daughter. And somewhere inside her, the deep release she'd begun to feel after Tibet suddenly returned again, and Helen felt a calm she'd never, ever known before. Now there was one more thing left to sort out.

Chapter Eighteen

A week after the Hawaii festival, Helen looked in her bank account and saw a balance which made her think they'd got the decimal place wrong, or one too many zeroes.

And soon after, Mr Adams confirmed it - she'd beaten Martha Crowne's figures hollow, and won him and his investor the bet, and they were cock a hoop. Helen could now finally sit back and relax a bit after six of the most stressful months of her life. And it was time to tie up a few loose ends. Helen hated loose ends.

With Sadie settled now, and a big enough bank balance to take a bit of a break, Helen set about tying them all up.

First on the list - to arrange for the column to be continued by Cheryl Goodman - but not before Helen had an interesting meeting with her - by the water cooler of course.

'Thank you so much for offering me the chance to do some TiFFTs whilst you're away writing your book. It's for Damian Grant, isn't it,' she said.

'That's OK. And - all right, I'll take the bait - how DO you know my pal Damian Grant?' Helen was perplexed - this wasn't the first time Cheryl had mentioned his name.

'Dad knows him - investors all know each other, don't they. I met him at a function once. He... offered me a little side-line. You won't change your mind if I tell you, will you? Only, you told me I should strike out for independence and, and make sure I follow my dream, and...' she looked worried again, like Helen was going to expose her secret. Or bite her. Helen nodded as if to say 'go on.' Cheryl took a deep breath. 'He - he paid me to be a spy, to keep

him informed and make sure things were ok here - ok with you.'
There was a pause. Cheryl swallowed.

'You? A spy? Never,' Helen said sarcastically, but smiling. *So Damian really did have spies everywhere.* And he wasn't the only one. 'And let me guess - did it give you a taste for subterfuge? For going undercover and reporting back?'

'I don't know *what* you mean, and I couldn't possibly comment,' Cheryl said, looking furtively up and down the corridor.

'Don't think I don't know,' said Helen, lowering her voice and leaning in towards her. 'I knew when I bumped into your boyfriend - literally - at the fire-walk - he's the handsome CNN jock, right? I knew I knew him from somewhere. Well, his pass gave it away - when I got near enough to see what it said.'

Cheryl just looked up at her innocently, waiting.

'ParlourGames Channel - Martha Crowne Reports.' Helen said, but Cheryl said nothing. 'Your boyfriend is the Mole. Isn't he?'

'You mean getting secrets from me to tell to Martha Crowne's lot? You think I'd do that to try to get one up on my own father?'

'Wouldn't you?'

Cheryl shook her head and stuttered before merely shrugging. Helen continued. 'To pay him back for being so dismissive of you? Or to stop him winning his bet with that Tremain guy - the investor he dislikes, who took some equity in ParlourGames?' Now Cheryl just raised an eyebrow. Helen took that as a 'yes'. She went on, 'But it didn't work, did it? Your father still won.'

'He still won,' Cheryl said, her eyes flashing, 'but it was with my help, not my hindrance,' she said triumphantly.

'I don't understand,' said Helen.

Cheryl slowly reached to fill up another cup of water and stopped talking for a little while as two executive assistants sashayed by, giving her big beaming smiles and giving Helen dirty looks.

'You said you think my boyfriend was the mole - giving away our secrets. Well it wasn't him,' she said. 'It was me.' She looked triumphant - no one had guessed. They all thought it was the jock and that Cheryl was just a pawn. But there was more. 'I leaked our schedules and gave them little tip offs.'

'*You* did? It was you?'

'But only little ones. And what it meant was - whilst I was inside their building, I got payback - I became the Insider for our lovely Mr Adams.'

'Bloody hell,' said Helen.

'Well, he's the only Boss who's ever treated me like I matter. He's a good guy, that one. And so are you,' Cheryl said, and reached up suddenly, and hugged Helen, then scampered off to go research some of her very own, very first Try it for the First Time Club events.

'I'm a good guy - ha-ha. Or a good bloke,' Helen said, and the corner of her mouth quirked upwards.

Because it was time for Helen to take a break - and head for a venue where a warm welcome - and a warm bed - awaited. Here on Hawaii. She had a decision to make, and finally, she knew exactly where she belonged. She looked at her watch. *It was time.*

After a couple of hours riding in a jeep, Helen got out at the top of a mountainside with far reaching views and looked at the big sign above her head - it was a roundish symbol. In the distance, the wind whistled, a bit like chimes, and if she didn't know any better, she'd have sworn it was Tibetan singing bowls - but it couldn't be, could it? Not in Hawaii, surely. She took a photo of the symbol, got back in the car, and headed down a long roadway towards a brand new spa retreat - Rinchen had told her about it - it was the perfect place to unwind after everything that had happened. The spa would offer many different treatments, including a psychic awareness course, the chance to live like a local and the top attraction - tantric massage courses with a certain now famous couple.

But Helen didn't need any more courses, she knew precisely how to do it, as she'd had one of the best teachers in the world to learn from.

A beautiful little cabin lay set back into the greenery and surrounded by peace. Before anything else happened, she had a meeting to go to, right here, right now, in there.

The nearer she got, the clearer the sound of the singing bowls and when she pushed open the door to the cabin, she saw the source - a big, broad shouldered guy with tanned skin, dark brown eyes and thick lashes, practising yoga moves in a room filled with fragrant candles and trickling fountains. When he saw her he stopped, smiled the biggest smile ever and walked across to take her in his arms.

'Hello Helen,' he said.

'Hello Alessandro,' Helen replied.

'You came. Rinchen told me she wanted to surprise me - but she couldn't keep it a secret.'

'When I heard about this new place up here - in Hawaii - I had a suspicion - my instincts were shouting from the rooftops - especially with you being in town. You were awesome at the fire-walk - banging that drum - I nearly jumped on you, up on that podium.'

'We will offer them here eventually - it will be a unique - ah, *selling point* - is that right? Rinchen and Socks may visit too - the boy has ambitions. Fuelled by a certain westerner,' he said, playing with one of her blonde locks of hair. 'Rinchen admires you greatly, but believes you need a little pointing in the right direction, apparently.'

'I thought she was up to something, booking me in here. But I did suspect. So how could I not come check it out. Come check you out.'

He smiled. And without another word, he kissed her passionately. Their embrace went on for a long time, but it was slow, languorous... tantric...

'Things have... ah... changed somewhat, since I last saw you,' she said, finally finding her voice. 'I've got six months off to write a book, get some rest, spend some time with someone I care for.'

'Looks like we've got a lot to talk about. Dinner tonight?' he beamed.

'If you let me choose the wine?' she said, grinning cheekily.

'Deal,' he said. 'You can fill me in on the latest with your family - I hear there is much to tell.'

'I will,' Helen said, idly stroking his shoulder and neck, as he hadn't yet let her go.

Then a cloud flickered across his face. 'And what of your... what of - Jason?'

'My ex-husband wants me to go into business with him - he said there could be room for a female adventure specialist in his company. But it would involve lots of travel and lots of play-acting. And probably quite a lot of getting down and dirty.'

'And what did you tell him?' Alessandro asked, a vulnerable note in his voice as he waited for her reply.

'I told him I'm taking a break right now. It's time.'

He kissed her once again, and then held out his hand to her and gestured towards the bedroom. A warm glow filled her body, her heart and her soul, and she accepted his hand gladly.

'Just one thing,' she asked. 'What does the symbol stand for?' and she held up the photo she'd taken of the Tibetan logo over the entrance.

'It's Tibetan and it means - Awe Rush.'

'Of course it does,' Helen said and smiled.

THE END.

©flintproductions 2014

More exciting fiction from Debbie Flint, on Amazon:

Hawaiian Affair (Steamy version or PG) book 2 in the trilogy and the story of Sadie, Helen's sister.

Read how Sadie came to be on a yacht and how she meets playboy billionaire Mac.

Feisty single mum and would-be businesswoman Sadie Turner needs an investor - and fast. Nothing can stand in her way. With a life-changing deal on the table, success is finally within reach, but she only has thirty days to sign the contract, so the race is on.

Mac is a playboy billionaire with an appetite for extreme sports and supermodels. But he never mixes business with pleasure. So where does curvy Sadie fit in? From the most incredible board room showdown, via passionate nights on board a luxury yacht in Monaco and in magical Hawaii, their exciting adventure takes them half way round the world. But can they seal the deal, and stay out of love?

Available on Amazon, in either PG or STEAMY (adult content) options.

Search Hawaiian Affair by Debbie Flint

(Amazon.co.uk or search amazon.com.)

Hawaiian Escape (Steamy version of PG) book 1 in the trilogy - introducing both Sadie and Helen and their family.

Feisty singleton and former international jet-setter Helen Parker's life is in crisis, and so is her sister Sadie's. Now Helen has to learn to manifest her own destiny instead of fixing everyone else's. Rookie businesswoman Sadie Turner needs help - but is marketing whizz Damian Hugh her knight in shining armour or her nemesis? With time running out for Sadie, Helen faces the biggest choice of her life so far - to find an escape that could solve everything for one of them - or ruin it all for both. New man, new career, new era. But for whom?

A nail-biting challenge in Tuscany and a dramatic trip to New York lead up to the journey of a lifetime. But there will be no going back once the winner is announced.

ALSO ON AMAZON –

'Diary of a Wannabe Shopping Channel Presenter' - Bridget Jones meets Alan Partridge meets Eddie Murphy in Holy Man the movie in this humorous romp, written in journal style.

'When Dreams Return' - a spooky short story with a twist.

'*Valentine's Surprise*' - a gentle romance to warm your heart, a short story for a rainy day - it's never too late to find your Sir Lancelot.

'*Till the Fat Lady Slims*' - a semi-autobiographical account of how listening to your body's own signals can transform your relationship with food, and how Debbie used Freedom Eating to break free from Food Prison and lose 35lb. Update Sept. 2014. *And Debbie's next intriguing romance novels.*

UPDATES

For the latest updates on Debbie Flint's work, a free steamy download, and news of sequels, prequels, and more romance, visit www.debbieflint.com to sign up for the regular newsletter alerts - be the first to find out about brand new titles.

Twitter - @debbieflint

Or www.facebook.com/DebbieFlintQVCUK

For steamy romance, visit @TabithaDevlin who is the erotica-writing alter-ego of the author, specialising in more raunchy titles.

9625288R00204

Printed in Great Britain
by Amazon.co.uk, Ltd.,
Marston Gate.